ISOLATED FROM THE REMAINING EMPIRE, FLAVIUS QUIRINIUS, A PROVINCIAL ROMAN NOBLE, RAISES AN ARMY AGAINST MARAUDING SAXONS.

The time and place: Britain from 440 to 491 AD, cut off from the Western Roman Empire as its provinces slump into Germanic kingdoms and Italy is reduced to an Eastern Roman vice-regency. This is the period whose events were transmuted into the Welsh legends of the Mabinogion, and into other accounts both fictional and factual, but this book takes a late Roman view of these clashing cultures that made a new world.

Several battles are recounted to mark the rise of Flavius Quirinius, a provincial Roman noble, among them a mucky action against bandits, his first victory against Saxons raiding from the south, a foray to the ghostly and abandoned Hadrian's Wall, where he meets Scottish raiders, and a fight with marauding Saxons along a highway. The peak of Quirinius' career, however, is a large Battle of Badon, at which he decisively defeats a Saxon army.

"A subtle and compelling evocation of post-Roman Britain, and the historical origins of the Arthurian myths. The sense of landscape and nature, and the lives of people living at the perilous edge of history, fighting for a future amid the ruins of their vanishing Roman past, is impressively dramatic and vividly conveyed."—**Ian Ross, author of several historical novels**

"Deeply researched and well-written, this adventure into a time both little known and very seminal to our own is a pleasure to read. Hildinger is at home in this world. I hope to see more of his fiction."—**Cecelia Holland, author of numerous historical novels**

D1120564

Excerpt

"Hmm!" Ater said, frowning, his chin in his hand. "Your correction is hard, Quirinius, very hard." His secretary and attendants laughed obediently, joined by many those in the Council chamber.

"It's nothing to the correction, Eugenius, that you deserve and that, one may hope, you will soon get."

Ater shifted his bulk in his creaking chair and turned to look at Quirinius for the first time full in the face. He narrowed his eyes, like a short-sighted man, or one who looks for something important in the distance.

He's worried, Quirinius thought with some satisfaction. He looked about at the other councillors, whose attention was now about equally divided between the two men. None of them were smiling.

"Let me be entirely clear." Quirinius paused to strain the attention of the councillors, Bishop Marinus, and the three or four kinglets whose attendance made ruling the western hill country easier. And then abruptly he sat up and leaned forward. "I formally accuse the Senator and Clarissimus Eugenius Ater of murder. I lay an indictment here against him for the murder of Senator Marcus Quirinius Claudianus."

There was a silence of the sort that comes when no one moves at all. A long pause, and then Quirinius watched Eugenius Ater stiffen in his chair and flush pink beneath his face powder. He gained control of himself in a moment, however, and forced a short barking laugh. He then looked around at the assembled councillors. "Forgive my laughter, Gentlemen. It was not meant to encourage this young man in his tasteless humor. It was merely the product of surprise. But, before this tasteless joke is pressed further, I might suggest," and here he looked about the room carefully, scanning every face, "that any reasonable man would fear to make such an accusation. Or to support it."

QUIRINIUS: BRITANNIA'S LAST ROMAN

Erik Hildinger

Moonshine Cove Publishing, LLC
Abbeville, South Carolina U.S.A.
First Moonshine Cove Edition November
2021

ISBN: 9781952439209

Library of Congress LCCN: 2021921620

About the Author

Erik Hildinger is the author of two history books: *Warriors of the Steppe* and *Swords Against the Senate* (both published by Hachette). He is the translator of the  *Historia Mongalorum Quos Nos Tartaros Appellamus, The History of the Mongols Whom We Call the Tartars. Quirinius: Britannia's Last Roman* is his first historical novel.

erikhildinger.com

Principal Characters

Flavius Quirinius Claudianus: a provincial Roman noble, nicknamed "Ursus," "Ursinus," or "The Bear."

Marcus Quirinius Claudianus: *Flavius Quirinius' father, known as "The Senator"*

Albinius Maximianus: a provincial Roman noble, Quirinius' father-in-law

Albinia Maximiana: Maximianus' daughter and Quirinius' wife, sometimes known as Ganufara

The Uortigern: a provincial Roman noble

Ambrosius Aurelianus: a provincial Roman noble and military commander

Eugenius Ater: a provincial Roman noble, and enemy of Quirinius

Nonianus Bassus: a provincial Roman noble, head of the Provincial Council

Pulcheria: an abbess

Caelia: Quirinius' mistress, later an abbess

Valerianus: a bishop

Canidius: Quirinius' captain, second-in-command

Moderatus: Maximianus' nephew

Pennomorix: a British chieftain and ally of Moderatus

Trifun: a British chieftain near The Wall

Ambiorus: another captain of Quirinius, later in the story

Uithyl: a peasant

Sequanius: a bailiff of Quirinius

Aelle: a Saxon king

Durotorix: a Druid

Map of Britannia in the late Fifth Century A.D.

(Drawn by Martha Jacques)

Quirinius: Britannia's Last Roman

One: The Monastery, November 491 AD

The monastery stood on a wooded hill, a half-dozen low buildings shambling across its crown, a rounded turf wall encircling the whole. The buildings were of wattle and daub and thatch, like the old temples from before the Romans, and their muted colors blended into the earth around them and with the browning autumn trees. Around the hill and below the wall was a wide, shallow ring of dull gray water; the ring might have been cut from some corner of the pewter sky and slipped around the hill as a protection. A weathered-grey wooden bridge of split logs on mossy pilings crossed the water and joined the monastery to the world. Black-boled trees rattling with brown leaves spread in copses on the land about the monastery, and rooks perched in them fluttering their wings in the autumn air. Sometimes they cocked their heads toward the east wind like an old man trying to recall a name, as they waited for the setting of the sun, invisible behind low, grey clouds. In the meeting house of the monastery upon the hill, serious matters were to be settled, the fates of men, high and low, the disposition of estates.

Bishop Valerianus sat in the abbot's chair, grave as a ruler on his throne, which, in a way, he was. A pair of young priests flanked him, bland-faced and blank-eyed as icons. The abbot, whom he displaced, stood to the bishop's left—an anxious frowning little man hardly bigger than a boy, who wrung his hands together, almost imperceptibly, beneath the gaping sleeves of his black habit. A Briton chief stood nearby, not much taller than the abbot, but bald, skull-faced and expressionless.

Further to either side of the bishop a dozen of his soldiers stood casually behind their round shields, right hands resting on the rims. This blend of two spheres, the ecclesiastical and the military, would signal his power to the Saxon, no doubt of it at all. Bishop Valerianus looked to either side of him, and then nodded to a monk standing by the door to the outside. The monk, intent on the bishop's slightest gesture, opened the door and stepped back. The Saxon (or was he a Jute? No matter) strode in with two of his followers, a creeping little Briton, grey haired and stooped with a wine-marked cheek, who trod at his heel like a dog. The Saxon was typical of his kind, swaggering, strapping and bold, so bold, in fact, that as he advanced and took in the room, its furniture and frescoes—all of it unfamiliar—he showed no unease or curiosity. Instead, he glanced casually about with a nod or two as though approving of something he had casually acquired. He rested his right hand absently on the huge knife sheathed horizontally at the front of his belt, the symbol of his people and an indication that, though he was dressed for the occasion in a fine tunic and Roman trousers fitted into low boots, he was an outsider with no need to truckle to his hosts.

Bishop Valerianus was impressed at the man's stature—he was nearly as big as the old Bear, and the bland arrogance with which he carried himself was much the same. He was younger, though—between thirty and forty like the bishop himself. Without looking to see whether he was obeyed, the Saxon signaled with his left hand, and the little Briton stepped forward on the instant, casting a shy glance toward his master. The chief said nothing, simply looked slowly from left to right, assessing the bishop's entourage before meeting his eyes again. In the silence, the little Briton turned and bent nearly double in obeisance to the prelate, who gave him no more attention than did the Saxon chief.

After a few moments of silence, the chief uttered a sentence or two in his incomprehensible language, the little Briton glancing sidewise at his master, considering every word. The little Briton—it was now clear that he was an interpreter—began to speak.

"Nobilissme Episcope, dixit rex, magister meus, propter proelium est factum, nunc tempus est quam pacem sit et terras dare rege..." The bishop was jarred by the Latin; it irritated him that this little

man, whose speech showed that he was from civilized parts, had chosen to serve a barbarian.

"Speak British." His tone was sharp.

"Of course, Your Eminence," the little man said, sliding into the vernacular. He gathered his thoughts and then continued. "My lord the king says..."

But what was said was unimportant, for this meeting was mere theater—the terms between the parties had long been fixed. This was denouement, the occasion for a handful of ceremonial statements after which the chief would retire, eager to see his new estates. When he was gone, Bishop Valerianus rose from the chair and went to stand by a window, whose shutter he swung out on its hinge. He turned to find the little, wraithlike Pennomorix at his elbow, his calvic face staring up at him.

"I don't like this," the Briton chief said with his usual, direct simplicity.

"You liked it well enough half a year ago. And now it's done."

"That man is now twenty miles closer to my holdings."

"And you are now a king. And never to be troubled by the old Bear again. I confer the title and congratulate you." He turned away from the ugly little man and signalled to the monk by the door. "Call the soldier in." He turned back to the window once more and took in the sky as though its aspect were an augury of the success of his plans. He pulled his shawl more snugly around his shoulders, taking care to do it properly so that it draped well. He turned back when he heard sound of boots. Who was this man? It hardly mattered which of the old Bear's soldiers it was, now that it was evident that Ambiorus, the captain, would not cooperate, had in fact drifted off somewhere. Well, Valerianus would make of this soldier whatever he needed.

He turned to see the man standing before him, young and florid in his fatigue, his ginger hair standing every which way, stiffened with dry sweat. Valerianus noted stray burrs and mats of wet horsehair in his drab trousers. He smelled of sweat, his own and that of his horse.

His coat of grey iron scales hung shapelessly because his sword and belt had been taken from him. He held his helmet before him in both hands, as though to protect himself.

"Your name?" Bishop Valerianus took a careful tone, mildly imperious but with a suggestion of sympathy. He looked the man over critically; the soldier was uneasy in the presence of the bishop, but he was old enough to be put in command. His unease proved he would comply. Good so far.

"Brigantius, Your Eminence." He bowed slightly, perhaps in fear, perhaps in actual respect. Either would do.

"You realize that I did all I could to head off this unfortunate situation, Brigantius?" He pitched his voice so that it was only a half a question, and he watched the soldier to see how he took it. The man seemed doubtful and looked away from the bishop when he tried to fix him with his eyes. The fellow couldn't look right at him—a good sign. "Of course, he was a hard man..." He let his voice trail off thus inviting the soldier to finish the thought, to agree with it. The soldier scowled a moment and, finally, nodded. "And a man who might have recognized your talents had he given you the attention you deserved." The man frowned as though not quite in agreement, but, finally, nodded again.

Good. He was coming around. "Yes, he could be hard," the bishop said again. "He was proud." The bishop shook his head, as though in sadness. "Pride goes before a fall."

Brigantius stood mutely, looking down at his feet, rubbing his rough, unshaven chin.

"And, so, it would be good for you to remember that this whole business could have been settled more..." He hesitated until the soldier looked up at him. "More happily."

The soldier grunted, trying to seem noncomittal, but at the same time he nodded.

"I'm glad you see it that way. Few men in your situation could." The soldier smiled and looked down, shy. Good. He could be usefully flattered. "You were with him a long time, weren't you? Seven or eight years?" It was a guess.

The soldier nodded, startled.

"I find things out, when they are important. So, now, all that time and there was always another captain ahead of you."

"Ambiorus."

The bishop shook his head as though disappointed. "Ambiorus. Well, no one knows where he has gone. Yes, the old Bear missed his chance with you, I would say. But now things are different."

The soldier looked at Valerianus questioningly, too polite to ask what he meant. He tried absently to hook a thumb into his missing sword belt and then let his hand drop to his side, uneasy in his vulnerability. He still clutched his helmet with this other hand. He glanced for the merest second at the bishop's soldiers, who watched him in open contempt. He rocked on his feet nervously.

"Whatever strains there once were among the great men of the province, they are resolved. Now is the time for change, and change brings opportunity."

"Yes, Your Eminence?" The soldier's voice showed mild, polite hope.

"The Bear is gone, but his widow still needs a man to command his soldiers. Of course, you see where I am going." The bishop dropped his voice as though to make a confidence. "She needs a captain, a man of experience, yes, but a man who will be loyal."

The soldier seemed surprised, but said nothing, merely looked from the bishop to the expressionless Pennomorix and back.

"In short, I wish you to serve the widow as you've served the master." He waited a moment and then said, "You will do it?" It was not really a question.

The soldier had flinched at the word "widow," but he didn't object to it.

"I never doubted it." The bishop's smile grew a bit broader, and he could see his expression was having the happy effect of baffling the soldier, of making of any residual distrust a sort of useless skill

13

like tying cherry stems into knots with the tongue. "Things will be different from now on, and a man has to consider his future. Go back to the large estate. I will give you a letter of authority. That, coupled with the widow's influence, will settle everything. Many of the men will have returned—they have nowhere to go—and you will be their captain."

The soldier nodded, his eyes widening at his luck.

"Good!" the bishop said and then let his wan smile fade. "But always remember to whom you owe this sudden advancement and recall that when a man falls, he falls far more quickly than he can rise. If rise he may."

It was time to dismiss him and let him influence the others.

"Yes, Your Eminence."

Bishop Valerianus raised his hand; the audience was over. He watched in silence as the soldier left the room and, when the door had closed, he went back to the open window and looked out.

"All the same I don't like this," Pennomorix repeated.

The bishop turned back to him. "I could have carved that Saxon's estate from your holdings instead of from the Bear's. In a single day your opponent has been removed and your power doubled."

"Moderatus is gone. This has been messy."

"You miss your ally? You're a fool. You have a freer hand than you ever had. Just be careful how you use it." He turned back to the window and put his face into the fresh air.

Pennomorix relapsed into his accustomed silence.

Two: The Monastery, October 491 AD

Flavius Quirinius Claudianus settled himself in the abbot's chair, which creaked at his weight, for he was a big man and powerful, even now, in his fifties. Quirinius put his feet on the footrest, leaned back and looked about the room, at the rush mats of the wattle-and-daub walls showing ghostly here and there through the failing whitewash, and at the roof-beams above pocked with adze-marks, and above them, the underside of the thatched roof, the floor of rammed earth, brown verging on black.

"A hall like this would be an outbuilding on my estates," he said to no one in particular. Ambiorus, his captain, stood watching him intently, as did the diminutive abbot, the latter unsure whether to reply. "I don't deride the builder—it's the best that can be done these days."

"Yes, Dominē," the captain said, to show that he paid attention.

"One can't expect bricks. One can't expect roof tiles. Not anymore." He rubbed his face with both hands and looked at his captain. "Sit down, Ambiorus. Night is coming, and it will be a long wait for the others, particularly for Moderatus and Pennomorix." The captain took a seat on one of the benches that stood along the walls, his sword jutting out beside his straightened legs. "You too," Quirinius added, waving at the abbot, but not looking at him. The little man sat across the room from the captain and, joining his hands beneath the sleeves of his black habit, he regarded Quirinius indirectly, though with care. The man was, after all, not merely a commander, he was a *clarissimus,* a senator, and Count of the Britains. All addressed him with deference. And he had been for years the terror of the Saxons. He made others uneasy too.

Yes, he was worth observing even if close observation carried risks (who could say what his excellency might do if angered?). A tall man and broad in the clothes of a soldier, but richer and finer than those of the usual biscuit-eater--fine white trousers and tunic, and a heavy cloak, like a dalmatic, with purple roundels at the shoulders to show his estate. Although his close-trimmed beard was gray and his hair thinning, he was yet a man who dominated rooms, situations, other men. Clearly. The abbot glanced surreptitiously about the room, to the Count's camp chair, sitting in a corner with his scale-armor coat draped over the arms, his silvered, steel helmet resting atop the coat, upturned and with the cheek-plates and neck-guard folded neatly on their leathers into the bowl. His sheathed sword leaned up against the wall, his red-and blue-splashed shield next to it.

"Host him until our arrival," the bishop had ordered. He had given no further instructions, but they would have been superfluous. Where Quirinius went, things were done his way. Upon first reading the bishop's note the abbot had been uncertain how to receive the Count, and when he was informed peremptorily by one of Quirinius' soldiers, he prepared to stand on his office to demand a few minor concessions to his dignity, but, in the end, there was no resenting Quirinius' take-over of the monastery, of his arrogating the meeting-house for his headquarters, of his quartering the men within the walls. The man had presence.

The abbot was curious about what had drawn Quirinius west from his estates. The bishop had not seen fit to tell him. Well, he would wait and watch and listen.

Quirinius rested his hands on the chair arms and looked down, reminiscing. Then he looked up at his captain and said, "Ambiorus, you've been with me a good long while."

"Yes, Dominē." He straightened up, ready to receive a command.

"I'm getting old," Quirinius said, rather off the point. "It makes one think."

"Yes, Dominē."

"This setting," he waved a hand vaguely. "It might make a man think."

16

"Indeed."

The little abbot, swinging his feet like a child as he sat, almost commented, but then held himself back.

"Let me tell you some things. My father knew some of them. Canidius knew others. They are both long gone. I admit to being lonely at times."

"Domina Albinia?" Ambiorus said.

"She cannot understand things; for her the world is mere illusion."

"Yes, Dominē." Ambiorus nodded meaningfully at the abbot. Quirinius waved his hand dismissively. "Let him stay," he said, as though the little man were not there to hear.

Quirinius continued. "No one understands another unless he knows every bit of that man's story. Maybe not even then." He trailed off; he lost the thread, found it again. Or was it just a trick to draw the listener in? "And so, like an old man trying to fix some detail that seems important—you know what I mean—they hesitate: 'Was it last winter or the one before?'—and the story sags and stops like a cart with a broken axle. My grandfather used to do it all the time. I'd nearly go mad when he began a story—anyone who knew him could see it coming—but my father would just nod and encourage the old man. When I was young, I thought my father was weak, you see. Now I realize that it was largely patience, which he had in abundance. So, we'd listen to some halting, pointless story we'd heard a dozen times. Sometimes it varied and that was worse. Who know where the truth was then? But I suppose it didn't really matter; my grandfather had grown up in quieter times long ago and nothing really happened in his stories.

"It was maybe forty years ago or so, and Aetius was the Master of Soldiers in Gaul. The last but one, I believe. You can figure it out for yourself. I must have been about twelve, and we had all gone to Corinium Dobunnorum, my grandfather, my father and I. Rarely had I been to a city, and it seemed fabulous. You see, I was too young to see that many of the doors were unpainted, and that grass grew in the alleys.

"My grandfather and my father had come to the city for one of the ineffective meetings that the senators and the little kings knew so well how to conduct. It was about the Huns over in Gaul, and everyone was exercised about them, though of course we were safe enough in those days, what with the Saxons still fighting for us and the Channel to keep the Huns away. But what I remember was the news that a troop of soldiers was coming down from the Wall."

The abbot stopped swinging his legs. "Soldiers from the Wall? As late as that?" Ambiorus told him to be quiet.

"That was just it. Of course, we nobles and estate-holders all had guards or toughs of our own, but we thought the last of the Imperial soldiers had been pulled out forty years before. As it turned out, there were maybe a hundred and fifty men maintaining themselves in a fort in some godforsaken district that we'd lost track of. They'd probably been terrorizing the Picts and selling protection to the chiefs up that way for half a century.

"You can imagine how welcome the news was that they were coming. The senators and landlords thought here was a troop we could pay and station somewhere handy. They were cavalry, you see, and could strike anywhere. But they wouldn't take the offer. 'We're going to Gaul,' they said. 'We're going to join the Patrician.'

"No one could believe that Aetius had known where to find them, but I suppose they were listed on some document in Ravenna. But why would they go over to him? How was facing the Huns more attractive than fighting Picts? The Huns were unbeatable, they were half ape, they ate the breasts of virgins, kept pet lions and so on. No truth in the stories, and yet you had to feel there was something behind it all. But these soldiers were going all the same because they had faith in Aetius the Patrician. More than the Emperor did, who finally killed him. They had faith in him because he'd lived among the Huns and know how to beat them, that's what they said. And they were right, as it turned out. Yes, these soldiers were going because they had faith in Aetius, a general of the Empire. It still stood in those days, remember.

"And they wanted to 'go home,' back into the Empire. I don't suppose there was a man among them that hadn't been born in the cold shadow of the Wall. It was the idea that moved them, you see. That was the great thing of it, the Idea. They were Romans. They called themselves the *Ala III Contariorum Sarmatorum,* the Third Wing of Sarmatian Lancers, and they may have been Sarmatians a century or two before, but they all looked like Picts to me, swarthy little men, but without the tattooing, and they spoke camp Latin and were Christians."

"All Christians are Romans," the abbot said, trying to add something to the story. Quirinius ignored him.

"The Uortigern offered them money and land to settle on along the southeast coast, but they wouldn't be stopped."

"You saw the old Uortigern?" the abbot asked

Quirinius looked at him for the first time. "I did. He was stooped and had a white eye. He dressed like a senator, but in his heart, he was a clan chief, as anyone can tell from the crude British title he'd adopted. What is more, he'd married a Saxon girl to keep those people in hand. My grandfather despised him; he said he had never read anything.

"The troops passed by in the late morning about two hundred yards from the city wall—near the east gate, I remember. The other gates had been bricked up even by then. The soldiers took the paved road that leads south and away from town. I remember them as they passed the tombs of the great families that stood on either side of the way as they do in Rome. There were still statues then—bleached white, of course, and grainy from the weather. One of them was a general with his arm raised, and another was a man bundled in a huge toga as though he looked for a storm. The statues are all gone now of course, shivered into fragments and cooked down to lime to mortar up the uncut stones of cowsheds.

19

"I was standing in the shadow of the gate with my grandfather and father, and we watched them pass by. We had a handful of our own soldiers, as I said, and they made a big place for us to stand in the crowd. I could see everything.

"Their captain rode in the van with the standard-bearer. The standard itself was polished up to reflect the summer sun—a dragonhead with a gaping mouth and a scarlet silk tail that floated and curved in the wind. Each troop had a purple drape on a crossbar with a winged victory or gold crown embroidered on it. And the men wore their armor even though they were far from the Wall. I was young, and so I thought then that it was natural for soldiers to look splendid, that anyone with fine armor would wear it, say, to write letters in, or to fry a fish. I can see now that they were armored because they were uneasy. Likely the Uortigern had threatened them while trying to convince them to stay. As before with the Saxons, he had mishandled the situation—the man was, of course, criminally inept. The soldiers were showing us their strength.

"Now the Uortigern had a dozen Saxons with him, but they were nothing compared to the Romans. The plates of their helmets shone like ice in the light, and their eyes glimmered behind the nose-pieces. You couldn't tell the color of their eyes, just that they glimmered, the way it happens when you look at a distant star and guess at its color. The officers had red horsehair brushes on their helmets and gold chasing. The dark-grey scales of the soldier's armored coats glistened with oil, but the officers' armor was tinned and flashing, their helmets were pranked with blue and red glass gems and gold chasing; they looked unreal, like a finer sort of men, maybe from the Age of Heroes. Across their saddlebows balanced lances with sharp bright heads. No man looked aside, and they moved without much noise, even on their big sorrel horses. I dreamt of them after that, and even in dreams I couldn't improve on them.

"It took a while for them to pass. There were a hundred and fifty or so of them, and they'd brought their wives and children and belongings behind them on wagons. One of the last had a mishap; a felloe split, the wheel collapsed and suddenly the spokes pulled out from the hub like fingers from a glove. The captain rode back, saw there was no time to repair it, and ordered everything shifted, so then the column moved on and left the wagon behind. When the soldiers had gone, the crowd took the wagon to pieces--they worried the very nails out of it.

"The Uortigern was bitter about their going because he couldn't put those soldiers to use, and he worried about what might happen along their part of the Wall. Three days before he hadn't known they existed; now he felt like he'd lost his right hand.

"Anyway, he sent a troop of Saxons up where he thought the soldiers had come from to watch the Wall in their place. Their captain married a Pict chieftain's daughter, everyone said so, anyway, and tried to make a kingdom. What do you do with such people?

"But, in those days, I was young and couldn't see what my grandfather and father could see. For me it was a display of magnificence, as when lightning strikes a hill—and good because it was magnificent. The men parading on their ochre horses in such order through the thickets of square-cut tombstones with their sharp lettering—I was learning to read then and the idea that I could hear the words of men dead and gone and far away wouldn't leave me—it was chilling. And then the city with its long streets meeting as square as a good argument. The cobblestones, the fountains still decorated with statuary just because it was lovely. People speaking Latin—even common people—the sort who spoke mostly British out at the estates, and not well either. It struck me then that all this was Roman. Order, beauty, strength, and good walls to keep out the world when that was needed. I knew I was seeing something important even if I couldn't winkle out all the corollaries. I dreamt of that troop many times when I was young. When I slept, I could see them in the watches of the night, commanding and Roman.

"When the crowd went to the broken wagon and dickered among themselves for the parts, I turned away because such pettiness spoiled things. I wanted to keep the picture of those horsemen in their fine bright helmets right behind my eyes. I wanted to see the silvered dragon standard with its red tail lashing unpolluted by even a glance at the broken wagon. But, of course, reality intrudes. Two men with beards, one was bald, I remember. Triviality breaks through. Two men with beards were shoving each other over who would get what. Meanwhile a boy with fox's eyes knocked out the linchpins with the hilt of a knife and crept away with them during the argument.

"I heard laughter and saw the Uortigern's men point the boy out to each other. The Uortigern snapped at them to shut up, but they were slow to obey. He repeated himself in Saxon so they couldn't deny they'd understood. You see, things were getting bad already."

Quirinius was stopped in his narrative by a knocking at the door. "Enter," he shouted. The door swung open and a soldier came in, his hair damp and half standing up, his helmet under his arm. The little abbot looked at him, but the soldier looked only at Quirinius.

"Brigantius," Quirinius said. He took pride in knowing his men's names.

"Yes, Dominē."

Quirinius put an elbow on the chair-arm and rested his chin on his hand. "Well now, where are the Saxons?" The abbot, startled, looked over at the soldier; his pulse rose as he grasped the situation for the first time. There were Saxons about, and there was to be a fight. He glanced over to the open window as though he were close enough to see down to the wall about the monastery. Was it high enough? Did the Count have enough men? The soldier said, "Four and a half miles to the east. Bivouacked in a large wood. They are in no particular order."

Quirinius narrowed his eyes. "In a wood, you say."

"But with a handful of carts set across the paths into the forest. I left Modestus and two scouts to watch them. One of them will come as soon as the Saxons show any signs of stirring."

"Where is this wood exactly?"

"Two miles south of Diviacum." Quirinius frowned, trying to place the obscure settlement. The soldier added, "Near an empty villa." Quirinius tried to recall whose it must have been. Fabricius Rutilianus'? Perhaps. He recalled him as a landholder, neither great nor small. But he could not think where the estate was. No matter; he could fix the location the next day, after the others arrived.

"How many?"

"Not many, Dominē. Of course, it's always difficult to tell—men in a crowd are hard to count—"

"How many!" Quirinius struck the table to emphasize the question.

The soldier looked down for a moment and pursed his mouth. The abbot turned from Quirinius to the soldier, eager for the answer. The world and these rough matters should have had little to do with him, yet Saxons—well, they were unsettling. And so close.

"Only two hundred that I could count." Quirinius looked at the man silently for a few moments.

"You're certain?"

"Yes, Dominē." There was a pause. "And five or six poor horses for the chiefs."

Quirinius turned to Ambiorus, musing. "Too many for a raid, too few for a battle. There must be another band somewhere."

Ambiorus nodded.

"You have been out for what? Two days? Watching and riding?"

The soldier nodded again.

"Then go eat something and rest." The man bowed and slipped out without a word, only the dry iron hinges of the door cheeping softly.

Quirinius turned back to the Ambiorus. "This other band. Now where must they be lurking?"

"Ask the abbot, Dominē. He's been here a good long while."

Anticipating the question, the abbot said, "Count Quirinius, I cannot say." He shrugged to show indicate his helplessness. "I am from the west, from across the Sabrina. This is not truly my country. Others know it better."

"You have been abbot here a good long while?" Quirinius asked.

The abbot hesitated. "Seven years."

"Eight," Quirinius said. "Bishop Valerianus installed you eight years ago. Should a man with such a poor memory have such responsibilities?" He looked at Ambiorus, who dutifully laughed.

The abbot reddened. "You men are in the world. Things are different for you."

Quirinius waved dismissively at the little man. "We'll have supper now. Soup, bread, bacon, cheese. And the best you have of it."

"No stinting," Ambiorus added. The abbot stood up and looked about as though noticing for the first time that he had none of the brothers to attend him and that he was being ordered about like a servant. He suppressed a sigh. After all, this was Quirinius, not some petty border chieftain to whom he might teach manners. He bowed the slightest bit and hurried to the door. "We shall do what we can," he said in defense of his dignity. His heart raced a bit as he said it.

"And some wine," Quirinius said. The abbot at once looked doubtful. "We don't drink wine here, Dominē. A little beer now— that we could manage."

"You don't take communion?" Quirinius asked dryly. He winked at Ambiorus, who smiled. The abbot nodded helplessly.

"Don't concern yourself about sacrilege, Abbot. You haven't seen it. I have and I've dealt with it."

"Yes, there is wine, Dominē Quirinius." The little man hesitated. When he next spoke, he meant what he said—he did not mean to reprehend the count, although he knew that it would sound that way, for he had not the rhetoric nor the tone to express his concern. But he sighed and spoke anyway. "Dominus Quirinius, may I say that I trouble myself more with the dangers invoked by pride than by any, ah, suggestion of minor sacrilege." The abbot looked down as he spoke, as though expecting a blow. He stayed so for several moments, and then timidly looked up at Quirinius, who watched him from across the room with a mixture, apparently, of humor and contempt.

"Do you want to hear about sacrilege, Abbot? I'll tell you an interesting story." He rose from his seat, advanced on the abbot and pulled him to the open window by his habit. He pointed out to the east. In the gloom he could see a soft smudge of smoke, possibly from the Saxon camp. He tried to think where it must be, what the land was like around it. Well, it was nothing to worry about. He would know soon enough. He looked down at the little abbot. "It happened over that way. About thirty miles from here."

From below came the slow clatter of hoofs over timber. A rider was crossing the bridge to the island. Quirinius let go the abbot's robe and turned to his captain.

"See if it's Fabianus." He suddenly felt uneasy and thought back to what the other scout had told him. Quite strange that Moderatus should send such a panicky notice to him about a Saxon incursion, and color it so strongly, when it amounted only to two hundred men and half a dozen nags. It wasn't like the man to be poorly informed, he'd give him that. And quite strange that Saxons should come in such a number. Thirty good horsemen, his of course—there were no others near as good—were all that should be needed. Thirty horsemen to watch and dog them and kill a forager here and there in front of his comrades, and that would have done it. But here he was with a hundred of his men; just think of the expense if not the trouble, and Moderatus saying he'd bring sixty horsemen and Pennomorix fifty footsoldiers. And he would, too—Pennomorix always did as Moderatus told him. And Valerianus the bishop would bring a troop too, mostly the young Bassus' men. The Bassi were the bishop's chief support, though, if Quirinius judged rightly, he would bring a few of his own to prop up his dignity. So many men. Odd, or odd now. Fifteen years ago, it had been harder to get his allies to fight with him than it had been to fight the Saxons themselves.

As Ambiorus left, Quirinius heard the whining door hinges and the scuffle of the abbot's feet as he slid away into the shadows that covered the floor like pools, one in each corner. He felt oddly vulnerable with the abbot at his back, could see the fellow in his mind's eye, dunked in shadow, his black robe invisible, only his white face showing, floating in the air in the dark. He shook his head. *I'm getting old, tired.*

He didn't turn around; he didn't want to speak anymore. He spoke all the time to people about the Idea, and too many of them listened out of respect or maybe fear—perhaps the same thing—and thought about other things to pass the time. Albinia especially. She thought about the next life and talked about it in detail as though she'd just returned.

Instead, he tried to imagine where it was that the Saxons camped, and he decided that it probably was near the old estate the Rutiliani had held for a century until Fabricius Rutilianus and his family had crossed to Armorica during the troubles thirty years before. The villa was a largish house of no particular character. He recalled it because the Quirinii had held land along that way when he was young. They still did, nominally.

Quirinius turned back as a flock of monks flapped in through the door with a huge board, trestles, and a pair of long settles. When they had set up the table and arranged the settles on each side, he ordered them to bring lamps. One of the monks bobbed like a cork to show he'd heard and backed into Ambiorus in the doorway. The lieutenant had brought in the horseman Quirinius had heard crossing the bridge below.

"Where have you been?"

"All around, Dominē. When we learned that Brigantius had found Saxons near Diviacum, we split our troop and went north and south along the road that leads to Glevum."

"And you found?"

"No Saxons. The peasants say the only ones are at Diviacum, and we didn't see any sign that the roads had been travelled much lately."

"How far did you go?"

"We went eight miles north to Cairmacsen; the others went south about as far." Quirinius dismissed the man and waved Ambiorus to the bench on his right side and looked impatiently at the door. Presently another little troop of monks entered bearing a tureen of soup, a platter of black bread, a pitcher of wine, three wooden bowls and a set of fine glass beakers. Quirinius took up one of them and turned it in his hand, looking at the honey-yellow color of it in the light of the lamps now distributed here and there in the room and hanging from a chain in the ceiling. "Surprisingly fine work, Ambiorus." He looked pointedly about the room. "I'm surprised to find they drink from glasses here at all, let alone ones so fine." He extended it to Ambiorus, who filled the glass and then his own. A monk who had stayed behind served soup and then disappeared. The captain tore a loaf apart and gave his master a portion. Quirinius turned the chunk of bread around in his hands. He drank some wine. He watched Ambiorus eat. The abbot cleared his throat from a corner. Quirinius ignored him.

"Why haven't they found the other Saxons?"

Ambiorus looked up from his bowl. "Maybe there aren't any others, Dominē."

"You don't doubt the scouts?"

Ambiorus shook his head. "They're good boys; they're careful. The Saxons move on foot and slowly, so, even if there are more of them somewhere, we know they're too far away to join this band we've found for at least two days." Quirinius nodded but felt unsettled. They were good boys, the scouts, but good boys can make mistakes. There must be other Saxons somewhere about slipping west, sliding among trees most likely, and picking their way through ravines at night to join their friends. But where?

"Moderatus has gotten us to muster half the country when we could have dogged these Saxons for a week and sent them home starving and a lot fewer."

Ambiorus ate diligently and then said, "Maybe he's scared that they're back. Even two hundred is more than we've seen in fifteen years. More than since Mons Badonicus."

Quirinius considered it. True enough, they usually caught Saxons by the dozen, occasionally by the score. But often it was only a large family with children and cattle coming to squat. Then the landlord might let them stay if he hadn't enough peasants. And, in Quirinius' opinion, that was worst of all. But two hundred Saxons this time; this was somehow different. Was the game changing? He shifted uncomfortably in the chair and then rose and went to the door. He motioned to the pair of soldiers posted outside and leaned forward with one hand on the doorjamb and looked back over his shoulder at Ambiorus. "We have Urbicius here. And Marcianius."

"Good fellows," Ambiorus said. "Marcianus has got good eyes. Urbicius might be a bit more persistent, but he's steady."

"Shall we send them scouting?"

Ambiorus frowned, doubting that it was necessary, but he sensed that Quirinius wanted more scouting. "Very good, Dominē. However, I might send them with Drustans and Civilis." Quirinius turned back to the men.

"You heard that?"

They nodded.

"And take two more men as well. I want you to head straight south from here ten miles, then head east and north in a loop and return by way of Diviacum, where the Saxons are. If you see any other parties, then two of you return; the other three stay with them. Each time the Saxons move, one of you come back here and tell me. Take a peasant or two with you if you need guides, but only if you do, and don't choose dullards. Move quickly. Any Saxon you might happen to meet, you make him talk if he knows British. I don't care how." Quirinius turned back and closed the door.

The abbot coughed again softly and Quirinius deigned to notice him, amused that his sanctimony was no defense to hunger. "Go ahead. Eat." He watched as the little man went to the table and, like

Quirinius himself, ate his bread in little morsels he tore off one by one. The remnant perhaps of a good upbringing. Or perhaps he was a sly little fellow and had learned to ape his betters. Quirinius' mind returned to the question of the missing Saxons, but, really, he had done as much as could be done to find them, and after a glass of wine, he felt somewhat less oppressed, more his usual expansive self. At the same time, he could not help but discomfit the little abbot. He had been irritated by the fellow's implication that he was too proud.

"I think we were talking about sacrilege a little while ago," Quirinius said.

Three: The Monastery, October 491 AD

"It was near the end of an April," Quirinius said. "Say, thirty years ago—thirty-three precisely. The abbot listened without a word. Ambiorus, who ate his soup with his elbows on the table, watched his commander with frank interest.

"My father was proud of his horses, and he had a special favorite, a stallion he'd brought from Spain. He named him, with a certain lack of imagination, 'Hispanus.' He'd cost a small fortune. My father had sold a small estate near the Cambrian Mountains to the Uortigern and had the animal shipped over.

"And he was a beauty, pure white and a mane like floss. Even though his hooves were white, they were not soft. He was fast—my father said Hispanus had come from stables had that supplied race-horses to the Circus in Rome. For the Blue faction, I believe. My father used him to cover his mares, and a good number of my horses are his descendants.

"He was bad-tempered, though, and many of the peasants were suspicious of him. It was the color, of course. He was white, as I say, and we've all seen white horses, but this one seemed to put off a sort of radiance when the sun hit him just right.

"That year my father sent Hispanus west to an estate we held about twenty miles away. In the direction I showed you through the window a little while ago, Abbot. He had a dozen mares there and he wanted some foals. Hispanus spent the winter there, and in the spring my father wanted him back at our estate, and so he sent for him.

About a week later—it was in the late afternoon and we were in the forecourt finishing dinner—the bailiff of the other estate arrived in company with the messenger who had been sent for the horse. The bailiff was in a panic; Hispanus was gone. He was terrified, even

30

though my father never had anyone beaten. No doubt he was afraid he'd be turned off the estate and made to roam the country with his family. He stood in front of us bending forward and twisting his hands like a beggar.

"'What do you mean he's gone? Gone how?' my father asked. He was a tall man, but slender and, because of his manner, not as imposing as he might have been. He stood suddenly, knocked over a glass, and let a servant-girl snatch it up without pushing her away, which would have been the right gesture. The bailiff was a big man and rough—his hands were big and battered as mauls, and his nose was flattened. Still, he put his hands up fearfully as if to push my father away. The messenger, a slight man, watched him to see what would happen.

"'I'm sorry, Dominē. He's been stolen.'

"My father said nothing, only put his hand to his chin as though there were a great deal to consider. His hesitation irritated me. I admit that I was wrong to judge him so quickly, but I was young then and sure of everything, so I turned in my chair and scowled at the bailiff. 'Why did you let him be stolen?' I asked him. The bailiff turned to me, uneasy—he could see where the conversation might turn.

"'Well now, Master,' he stammered. He should have expected the question in some form or other, but he hadn't prepared for it. He was off-balance now, and so I asked him another question to keep him that way. 'When was he stolen?'

"'Two days ago, Master.'

"'By whom?'

"'Jutes! Saxons!' one of my sisters answered, which was silly, though the bailiff watched me closely to see if I'd go for it. If it were Saxons, then maybe it would go easier on him; they were everyone's bogeys. But I didn't go for it.

"'I'm looking into it, Master.'

"'So then, you don't know.' By now my father was regarding me. His glance was quizzical—it was clear that he was at the same time amused by my initiative and yet uncertain where it would lead. I had no idea where it would lead either.

"'Were other horses taken?' I asked.

"'No.'

"Clearly something odd was afoot. Why else the theft of a single horse? On the other hand, he was the best in the country.

"'I wonder if any of old Maximianus' tenants are behind it,' my father asked no one in particular. He was growing distressed the more he thought of Hispanus' theft. A handful of servants stood about in the middle of their tasks, and so it was a mistake to have said this aloud. Although my father and old Albinius Maximianus had campaigned together years before under Ambrosius Aurelianus, we had had a running dispute with him over a village near the estate where Hispanus had been kept, and a disagreement over who had power over that handful of peasants who wouldn't declare themselves either way. Now the news would seep out soon enough, and our servants and tenants would expect my father to act, and it would be hard not to lose face if old Maximianus declined to cooperate.

"'I suspect it myself, Dominē' the bailiff said. 'Only I myself wouldn't go accusing any of the great men.' Sly bastard, joining my father in this speculation before the other servants. Putting the blame on the shoulders of those who couldn't be touched. 'A man like me can't stand against a great man like Maximianus.' He looked at the other servants and provoked a few nods.

"My father said nothing, merely scowled helplessly, perplexed about what to do. He could dispossess the bailiff, but if he did nothing more, then he would appear merely vindictive, and it would seem that he couldn't protect an officer of his own, even on his own property. And besides, he wanted this valuable horse back. He turned to me as if to say, 'Well, boy, you see how it is to be a magnate, caught three ways between chance, your neighbor and a canny peasant.'

"What could we do? Clearly some horse-thieves had been at work, perhaps they were even Maximianus' tenants, but were we to creep to him and plead that he hunt up the horse for us? Or were we to fan the dispute into a feud with the Maximiani like some British clan shambling back to the shaggy ways of its forebears?

"Now, my father had erred; he should have flogged the bailiff for his incompetence and planned what to do later. Instead, he had faltered, unsure of his next move. I loved my father and, though he had fought alongside Ambrosius Aurelianus with distinction, he was no tactician, a fact he admitted to me. 'I would let Ambrosius decide when and where to fight,' he said to me once. 'I just kept my men in hand and saw that they were steady. And that they never went hungry.' He was good at logistics, apparently. In fact, he was a man made for an earlier, better time. He'd have been better suited to writing dilettante history and judging frescoes—perhaps paying to clad some brick municipal building with marble. People liked him instantly; he was just wrong for the period.

"I watched him stand there uncertainly, arms crossed over his chest, chin down in thought. A moment or two passed, and I became angry on his behalf, so I spoke up impulsively. 'I'll get the horse back if he's still in the country.' I hid my anger, though. I leaned back casually in my chair and turned my spoon about idly, as though what I proposed were nothing much. No one could have told who was more shocked, the bailiff or my father. But, of course, my father couldn't deny me the chance outright—again, it was because of the servants. I could see him frown, trying to look as stern as a Danube general. In fact, he wore his beard cut very close like a Danube general. He admired Diocletianus, though he wouldn't admit it to anyone but me because he wanted to be seen as a good Christian, which he was. Still, he had a weakness for secular order.

"'After all, Father. It's time for us to talk with Maximianus about a number of things. I'll discuss Hispanus while I'm there.'

"He was staggered a bit by the brass of it all and by the specificity of the suggestion. And it yet seemed so reasonable at first blush, for it played into the misperception that some of the blame for Hispanus' theft might be imputed to Maximianus. 'Well,' he said, looking around at the servants—he worried about subordinates' opinions (not just their welfare; as I say, he was, on the whole, rather too sympathetic for the times). But he didn't say anything further. I'd outmaneuvered him; it was like a sharp move at tables that leaves the other man hopelessly searching among the points for a good reply.

"I had a feeling then—I don't mind saying so, arrogant though it makes me seem—that suddenly I was in command of the situation, and that it might be important—that I could make the situation important, anyway. Even the afternoon sun seemed brighter for an instant. I half-thought if I turned to look, I'd see a pillar of sunlight come through a cloud to the west.

"'All right then,' my father said at last. 'You can ask Maximianus what he knows.' He paused just the slightest instant. 'If anything.' He clasped his hands behind his back and glanced down at his shoes for a moment and waved the bailiff away. He didn't expect me to stick my neck out far. He was a dear man, really."

Quirinius held his cup in both hands and looked into it, studying the weak reflection of a lamp in the surface of the wine. The abbot glanced across the table, careful to mask his puzzlement with a look of faint interest. After all, where was this going, this story? Furthermore, he felt ashamed of his interest, mild though it was. Instead, he should have felt resentful at Quirinius' presumption in establishing himself at the abbey. He should resent being put upon, ordered about like a servant, dragged about by his habit, snubbed by the Count's subordinate. Better to have cultivated sullenness in the face of these slights, but he found himself oddly unable. Quirinius somehow provoked a feeling of sympathy that undercut resentment.

"Hmm, hmm." Quirinius hummed the start of a tune and rolled the wine glass between his palms. "I can't quite recall how it goes." He continued to play with the glass. "Do you recall it, Ambiorus?"

"No, Dominē."

"Ah, well, it's an old tune. Perhaps I alone recall it. My father used to sing it to himself sometimes. It had words that he thought were quite affecting. 'They're most affecting, Flavius,' he'd say. That was his word. 'Affecting.'"

Soldiers shouted outside the house, calling the end of the watch to one another. The three men listened as the calls went one at a time across the grounds and down the hill. The abbot glanced out of the window at the sky darkening behind the grey, featureless clouds. He wondered where the bishop was. He had said he would arrive today, by evening at the latest. Would he continue to travel after dark? Or would he appear the next day? The abbot was frightened of the Saxons prowling nearby, preparing to harrow the countryside just as they had so long ago when he was a child. The sooner the great men met in council to decide how to disperse the threat, the happier he would be. God might decide to spare the monastery, its forty monks and half-dozen lay brothers, but perhaps there was instead something less pleasant in store for them. Who could tell? He felt himself vulnerable, even with this bear of a man at the head of the table, who lorded it over everyone as though this were his stronghold. Men said that Quirinius had the strength of a bear—even the spirit of a bear—and that this could be seen in his ears, which were similarly rounded. Perhaps they were. The abbot looked and thought he could see it—just. But then perhaps it was only suggestion and shadow. But the question of his ears aside, had he enough men with him?

He drew a series of deep breaths and took some wine, all to calm himself. Perhaps Quirinius' arrival was, after all, part of some divine plan to smite these barbarians, his sudden appearance like an unexpected bolt of lightning that splits an oak and leaves it smoking. And who more fit to do it than Count Quirinius? Even the man's Latin was remarkably fine, smooth and well-shaped and pronounced in that fine way with v and c they way did in Italy, as though he were a teacher. Surely such excellence was a sign of other more immediately welcome excellences. For instance, he had not only commanded with great success, he'd killed men, and with his own hand. Say what you will, a man like that must be respected. Calmed somewhat, he took a drink of wine and awaited the rest of the story.

"I left the next day in hunting clothes, but fine ones. I wore a sword and carried a pair of javelins in a bucket on the saddle. I took three dogs and a dozen men, ones who could hunt and knew how to ride. Like me, they were armed. And I brought the bailiff along, who was full of false cheer. My father wanted a grandfatherly old peasant, one whom he liked, to travel along, but I knew that this would threaten my authority, so I refused. I was conscious of things like that even then, you see. Instead, I took Canidius, who, although he was only about my age, my father had made one of his lieutenants. He was the son of peasants on the estate, but steady and fearless as one of the old heroes, Patroclus, for instance. No horse could shake him. My father had insisted a year or two before that I drill the soldiers in his place, but he had Canidius second me on the drill field, and Canidius taught me to ride well.

"We reached the estate in the afternoon but stopped only to exchange horses and knock the dust from our clothes. We pushed on toward the main estate of the Maximiani and reached it in the early evening. I sent a rider ahead so that we would be received properly and to tempt old Maximianus to meet us outside of the villa's walls. I knew it would be better for him to see me with the entire troop—display would be better than any report. But he had his sense of dignity too and declined to do it. Instead, he sent his bailiff out with a gang of field hands to take the horses and show the men to a barrack. Field hands, you see? Faces tanned like leather from the outdoors, clothes so patched they looked shaggy. What a contrast to my men chosen from among our soldiers. So, it was a peaceful gesture, or perhaps a slight, his yokels a match for my soldiers. He was likely playing with me to see what I was made of. I could see a face peering out from an upper window as I passed through the gate. I'm sure it was Maximianus.

"I took Canidius and one of the other men as attendants—I don't recall the fellow's name anymore but, unlike Canidius, he was older than I and big as a menhir, and together they enhanced my authority. Of course, the display was transparent to Maximianus, but then he'd know that I knew and that was all that mattered.

"The front court, the yard really, of the estate was lovely. The grass had been scythed down to a couple of inches and was thick as an eastern carpet, and there were rectangular beds of flowers everywhere—orange-pink single roses for instance—and the façade of the villa and its outbuildings were whitewashed. Very pretty. Very civilized. I liked the place, felt quite at home there, really.

"Maximianus kept us waiting in the entrance hall for a good quarter of an hour. I'd have done the same. I unfastened my sword-belt, handed the weapon to Canidius, tossed my riding cloak to the big trooper, and then lounged casually about the hall pretending to judge the frescoes on the walls and the mosaic on the floor. It was very fine: a cornucopia in the center, one of the four winds personified at each corner, the whole in white, charcoal and ochre tiles. When an attendant entered to say that Maximianus would see me, I waved my hand casually. 'Good work, all of this,' I said, just as though I were some sort of connoisseur." Quirinius laughed at the thought of it. "I was cheeky back then. But, you know, there are times when cheek is what's needed."

Ambiorus nodded.

"Good man. But don't get above your station. No cheek to me." Quirinius leaned over and slapped him on the shoulder with a laugh.

"No, Dominē," Ambiorus said, startled at Quirinius' familiarity. He glanced to either side and blushed.

Quirinius took up the thread again. "I met him in the salon; it was in the east wing of his house. He sat in a chair and did not rise to greet me. Like a monarch. I advanced to the center of the room and, as I had done in the hall, I looked pointedly at the frescoed walls, as though to approve of them. The work was well done, by the way. The images were skillfully painted and fairly new, say, from fifty years before, and so the themes were Christian. The villa was substantial and old like ours, and I wondered idly what might lie beneath the new pictures. After a few moments I glanced over at Albinius Maximianus and nodded politely, just as I would to anyone else of my station. We exchanged formal greetings, and he waved me to a chair that a servant set down for me before leaving.

"'Well, young man, I cannot pretend to be entirely pleased to welcome you.'

"I smiled as innocently as I could—call it cheek again, if you will— and replied, 'Thank you, Senator, for your understatement.' He frowned at that. Let me tell you, flattery and frankness combined can work wonders. He sat up straighter and regarded me for a few moments with light, almost colorless grey eyes. They were off-putting, frankly, accentuated as they were by his white hair. But he wasn't so old, really; it was just that he was a pure Celt, I suppose, though the family had been noble for a hundred and fifty years. They had had some connection with Magnus Maximus and had taken their name from his.

"'I take it that you grasp your presumption in approaching me uninvited and with no good excuse?'

"'I presume upon your hospitality on behalf of my father,' I said. I spread my hands and shrugged. 'I'm dutiful that way.'

"He snorted and waved dismissively. 'I have a quarrel with your father and thus with you.'

"'I know it. Something small, as I understand.'

"'Oh, you understand it, do you?'

"'You are interested in a certain village, I believe.'

"'Dunmhor,' he said. I put my hand to my chin and frowned as though trying to place it, and then I called it by the Latin: Ripa Collinae. 'Forgive the lapse of memory, but it is sometimes difficult to recall such an insignificant place.'

"'That settlement was given us by Aulus.'

"'Who, it would seem from the outcome of things, had no good authority to take it from the Deciani, who had expressed their intent to deed it to us.'

"'They had no good title!' Maximianus said, leaning forward. I shrugged, as though indifferent to the point. He looked irritated, though he kept his voice flat. 'Remember that I suffer your visit out of respect for your father's station, opposed as I am to him in regard to the village. Don't presume upon my patience too far.'

"I could see that it was time to propose a solution, to unravel the problem. 'Your respect for my father—it is the desert of his station, certainly, but does it not arise too from the fighting you and he did years ago under the Count and Senator Aurelianus against the Angles and the Jutes?'

"'Yes, certainly,' he said, sitting back in his chair and watching my face, trying to guess where I was going, where a snare might lie.

"'That fighting was certainly a noble undertaking. People talk of it still.'

"'It was indeed.' Maximianus looked up over my head, as though seeing it all again. His voice had dropped.

"'You and my father, both of you senators, and Aurelianus, Count of the Britains. It must have been splendid.'

"He looked down sharply at me and said, 'Don't exaggerate,' but still his voice was soft.

"'Is it only the village that vexes you?'

"He considered the question for a moment and then nodded. 'Only that.' Some moments passed. Then he added, 'Those peasants want to come over to me. They say your father's too far away to protect them, in any case.' He looked at me, bluff again, but not so bluff as before.

"'Well, then, Senator, I think the breach can be mended.' You see, it was here that inspiration struck me! Who knows? Perhaps the idea had been rattling about it my head, unknown to me, but now out it came like a hatchling. The village was really of no interest to us—the squabble with the Maximiani had left it effectively free, so that we took no revenues from it, and it was true what Maximianus said. It did lie on the edge of our ambit and was difficult to protect. We could hand it over to Maximianus and lose nothing but a little face. And, perhaps, not even that.

"And did you give Maximianus the village, Dominē?" Ambiorus asked, eager for the story's denouement.

"Oh, yes, I did. And I turned the concession to good advantage."

There was more to the story, of course. Quirinius had gotten into an area that he preferred to keep private, so he kept the details to himself and only mulled on how he had turned the situation to his immediate advantage.

He stopped the tale there but recalled to himself the rest of the conversation.

"And how would you mend this quarrel?' Maximianus asked. He had a habit of turning his head slightly to the right and watching sidelong when he was suspicious.

"I understand you have a daughter.'

"Let's not get off the point. You're a distracting fellow. You take too many turns. Like Ulysses.'

Quirinius laughed. "Perhaps, but this is to our mutual advantage and involves none of the Ithacan's deceit. Your daughter?"

"Albinia Maximiana. What about her?"

"She's not betrothed?"

"No."

"Then, Senator, let me see her."

* * *

Quirinius stared at the curdled daub of the wall, and he recalled his first sight of Albinia. Maximianus' salon was edging toward dimness; it was getting to be that time of day when the light through the windows faded, but the lamps couldn't be seen even to flicker—there was still too much light. A threshold time—not day, not evening. The light was false somehow and caused Quirinius to blink unwillingly and strain; it was like trying to see under water or into a different realm.

Albinia stood with one foot over the threshold, hesitant. Quirinius regarded her, remarked her paleness, her skin so very white that it appeared distinct from her clothing more by texture than by color. Her hair, an ashy blond, was drawn back and disappeared into the gloom of the doorway behind her; it seemed, therefore, that her face hovered for a moment in the dimness like that of a spirit. Maximianus waved her in, but he watched Quirinius and not his daughter as she approached.

Albinia glided across the room, her back as straight as a rule, and Quirinius could see she was tall, but very slender, almost elongated like a figure in an eastern icon. Her father introduced her, and she curtseyed. She tugged up her skirts with the tips of her long fingers, and he could see a small missal half hidden in the palm of her left hand. She floated away. Quirinius could not remember what she had said in that brief meeting, or what her voice first sounded like, whether it was girlish then, or womanly, as it later was. He could only recall her cool, otherworldly appearance.

Maximianus watched her go. "She'll be a nun. Her mother's against it, but I know the girl's nature." He turned back to Quirinius and then looked at his feet a moment, embarrassed at revealing anything personal.

"Do you want that?" Quirinius asked.

He shrugged. "I must accept it. I have only a nephew, Moderatus, to follow me, and he's young."

"Then let us agree upon two things. We Quirinii will waive our claims to Ripa Collinae and..."

"And?"

"And you will give Albinia to me for my wife."

"Oh ho!" Maximianus tilted his head up in surprise and gave a short bark of laughter.

"I'm a rascal, you see, Senator."

"Indeed, you are. But clever, I'll grant you that. All the same, I say the village is too small a consideration for what you ask."

Quirinius took a careful, pedantic tone, and leaned back in his chair. "Is it? Well, now, let's do a little rough reckoning. The village and its dependent farmsteads in exchange for a daughter whom you will keep from the nunnery. A nunnery that you, as a great man, would be obliged to ornament at your cost."

Maximianus conceded this.

"And, if you marry her to me, you'll find yourself in alliance with the Quirinii."

"A costly alliance. You'll want one of our estates as a dowry."

Quirinius shrugged. "A small holding will do. One that would support, say, twenty soldiers and mounts. And then, of course, your support for us in the Council and ours for you." Maximianus sat silent a moment considering.

Quirinius went on. "Who are the great magnates of the Britains? Let's name some of the greatest: the Maximiani, the Quirinii, the Modestiani, the Aureliani and the Atres, and the most powerful, the Bassi. If we ally, even the Bassi must truckle to us. And we can defend ourselves. Your young nephew, for instance, will have a strong protector until he comes of age, if you should ever encounter a sharp reverse."

"Ah, defense."

"Saxons, Picts," Quirinius said. "We Romans must band together."

Maximianus grunted softly, thinking, but it sounded to Quirinius like assent. The matter was, for the most part, decided that evening.

* * *

Ambiorus, emboldened by this master's earlier chaffing and by his confidences asked, "And the rest of the tale, Dominē? About the horse?"

Quirinius, called back from his thoughts about Albinia, continued. "I won the old fellow over—I'll spare you details—and then told I him why I had ostensibly come. I said, 'Actually, I'm after a horse.'

"'A horse?' He leaned back and regarded me closely, as though he suspected another surprise. 'The horse is a mere excuse, surely.' He began to smile.

"'Not entirely, Dominē Maximianus. I'm after my father's prize stallion, that costly horse Hispanus. He's disappeared. My bailiff is incompetent, and so I'm here to see if any of your people know anything about it.'

"Maximianus didn't say anything for a moment, though it wasn't because he took any offense at the question. He was confident, not the sort to worry about what others might think of him. Then he said, after he'd thought for a moment, 'None of my people are horse thieves.' He was playing with me clearly, to see how I'd reply, to see if he could discomfit me. I smiled at his ploy.

"Maximianus sat back and rested his elbow on the chair arm, put his chin on his fist. I thought he must be thinking about me, but then he asked, 'How long has this horse been missing?'

"'Six days.'

"He looked up in thought. 'Four days ago was the vernal equinox.'

"I couldn't follow this reply. It seemed inconsequential, something that had popped into his head—like a forgotten birthday, for example."

"Why did Maximianus remark on the date?" the abbot asked. He was drawn to the story in spite of himself, but mostly he wanted distraction until the bishop arrived. He told himself it was Quirinius' distraction he wanted, but if he'd been honest with himself he'd have seen it was his own he craved. He caught himself sitting on his hands like a schoolboy.

"Oh, yes. Well..." Quirinius kept his eyes on the wall. "The date, yes." He sat silent a moment. "It became apparent later—that the date was important." The abbot watched Quirinius fumble with his thoughts.

"Maximianus lent us his best huntsman. 'He knows the country better than anyone,' he said. 'And he knows my holdings hereabouts

43

too, if you must cross them.' My men were suspicious of him, but I knew the old man had done it to show his good faith, and, besides, we took the fellow back with us to our estate where he had to do his best for us. He brought his own two dogs and made us leave ours behind so there wouldn't be any trouble between them. He let us know that because four days had passed we'd have no chance—or mostly none—of finding Hispanus. All the same, I decided that we would search.

"The huntsman—his name was Lugh, an old god, I believe—snooped around the stables and studied Hispanus' stall.

"'What are you looking for?' I had to ask him twice, the second time in British; he didn't know Latin.

"'To see if his hooves were nicked.' He was on his knees, sweeping away the straw. He didn't call me 'Dominē'. When my men muttered, I just laughed.

"'He was taken care of like a pet,' I said.

"'Too bad. Nicked hooves would help.' He rose, and we followed him to the paddock. He strode into it and stood a moment, taking in the ground. His dogs sat on either side of him and watched for a signal. The dozen grazing horses pulled up their heads and looked at him with brief, dull curiosity. Then he walked purposefully to the far end of the paddock, which was marked off from the field beyond with a low, loose stone wall. A boy sat perched on one of the rocks minding the herd. Lugh ignored him, only studied the stones in the low wall. The rest of us, six men and I, began to follow, leading our horses behind us.

"When we caught up to him, he said 'This wall's been mended.' He pointed to a small boulder near the top of the wall. 'It was facing the other way, but now...' He shoved it over. 'But now the moss is under the rock where it doesn't grow.' He kicked over another two or three rocks, and it was clear they too had been shifted not long before.

"'Someone's breached it to let the horse step over.' Lugh glanced around, looking for tracks. I told two of the men to open the gap up more so we could lead our horses through, but Lugh said, looking at the woods beyond the wheat field, 'You won't need them.' He added 'Dominē' after one of the men shoved him, then he stepped through the gap in the wall and trod across the field. He walked lightly through the young plants, never touching any; he left hardly more of a spoor than his dogs. I told Canidius to lead my horse despite what Lugh had said. One has to consider one's position.

"As he walked across the field, he stared intently at the woods a hundred and fifty yards away. They lay just across a road that marked the boundary of the field—a narrow road, but paved, that runs from Silva Durotorum and eventually to Glevum, with a fork, incidentally, to Caerbach, a place the soldiers had called Castellinum when a cohort had been posted there long ago. There'd been a village there even as late as my father's childhood; he told me so. In fact, there still is a bit of a settlement, though the soldiers have been gone eighty years. Lugh was scanning the woods as he went; he would turn his head sharply now and again, like a hawk. I think that he knew where he was going all the time, but he was shrewd and made it look like he was tracking. No matter. By the time we'd reached the embankment on which the highway stood—by the time we'd climbed it and stood on the roadway, he'd chosen where he wanted to enter the trees— along a game path in the scrub that formed the edge of the forest. One of the men squatted to pluck a blade of grass from between the road-stones. He bit the root casually and looked left and right, probably wondering what the traffic had been like a hundred years before. I wondered myself. Lugh already stood at the margin of the wood, dappled in shadows; he looked like a leopard.

"We crossed the road and went under the rustling green canopy of the trees. It was immediately clear that Lugh had been right about the horses. The men might grumble about leaving them behind, but leading my horse alone was a chore, and there was no riding among the trees. Once past the scrub at the edge, you could tell it was an old forest from the size of the trees, oaks with boughs that spread a hundred feet, grey-black ash that reached sixty. The trees met overhead and pleached a green roof between us and the world above. It seemed that we were going not only into the woods, but down into another, dimmer, cooler world. It was an older world with fewer colors, dark tan fading insensibly into a hundred shades of brown, and then above us the green of the leaves. That varied too. The highest were bright, tinged with yellow from the sun, those lower were any number of true greens, and the leaves suffused the light with their color—it seemed the light itself was green, the mark of an earlier world before cities, a world old-young without history, or without a past it could know.

"The whole atmosphere was marine—cool, greenish, supported by massive dark boles, great trees with leaf-slick avenues between them. You could think of nymphs here, just as you might at the bottom of the sea. And then here and there, as we passed, we would see a clear shaft of sunlight, like a finger, maybe, from God, probing into this early world. And more, there was depth to the forest, different levels defined by the leafy branches at different heights, and then the cool earth below where we trod, following Lugh's serpentine lead.

"It was true a horse could have been led this way—but only this way. Deadfalls and unexpected slopes on either side kept anyone to the path. Still, too many days had passed for anyone (Lugh perhaps excepted) to tell whether the tracks along the game trail had ever shown the prints of a horse's hooves. But if a horse had been led through these woods, he'd have been led this way. So then, was Lugh a fine tracker, or a fine guesser? And what was his guess?

"I called him back after a while. 'Where are you leading us?' Lugh looked bland. 'After the horse,' he said. 'What marks are you following?' Lugh said nothing for a moment and then looked around closely at the ground he'd already covered without a glance. After a moment he pointed to a broken twig and a shallow depression. 'A deer, perhaps,' I said. 'A bear?' 'I know my business, Dominē. Remember that I must answer to Dominus Maximianus.' I looked at

46

him. 'You know something, Lugh.' He shook his head, declining to answer.

"We followed Lugh quietly; we were all of us hunters, after all. Once we flushed a deer and a couple of times started a rabbit that flashed through the brush and left nothing behind but a quivering leaf and the memory of a sharp rustle. When this happened Lugh's dogs looked longingly after what had sprung off, but he'd whistle sharp and short between his teeth, and they would keep with him.

"It would be hard to say how far we went because we couldn't see more than thirty yards at a time. The tree boles, the leaves of bushes made a screen before us. Birds cheeped above us, invisible as wood spirits. Lugh proceeded, sure-footed as a hart, deeper and deeper into the wood.

"After a while we came upon a large stone, you know the kind. It was the size of a man—just as tall and narrowing toward the top. It canted a bit, its footing pushed up by tree roots, and leaned back like a man caught in a fall. In a hundred years, maybe fewer, it would topple and disappear under a blanket of leaves. It seemed the rock was caught falling in an older, slower world, and we quick men would not live long enough to see it through."

"It was a menhir," the abbot said to Quirinius, suddenly taking part in the story. "A monument put up before men knew about True Religion."

"Exactly," Quirinius said, cutting him off. "It was a relic of the world before Rome, before Celts even, when the place was peopled by small dark men who, the peasants believe, still live beneath the earth, or maybe on islands to the west.

"Soon we came upon others—first a line of six, like men on patrol, then thirty in a block like a troop moving up to battle. Here and there one lay fallen. It was an uncanny sight because there were trees sprung up among them and all around. They were so very old they'd been put up when the land had been a meadow and the forest had grown up in their midst. I felt that we were in the middle of a sort of weirdness, our feet in two countries, as it were, one of them ancient."

The abbot crossed himself. "Those stones may be different; they may be soldiers the druids enchanted. I have heard that many wonders occurred during the campaign of the Emperor Julius Clementinus, before the British kings were finally put down."

Quirinius looked at him with pity. "There never was such an emperor. They are pagan monuments pure and simple."

"We followed Lugh among the stones, as through a primitive double colonnade, into the heart of an older world. We put them behind us, but we weren't free of their idea, so to speak. The men were uneasy—they had probably heard the same idiot stories about the druids." Quirinius stared hard at the abbot. "I said, to no one in particular, that these stones were found in many places, really. Not uncommon at all. My grandfather had seen hundreds in a field in Armorica where they marched across a field in serried lines and down a bluff to the sea to disappear beneath the water.

"Lugh turned back to me. 'They are all around us here, Dominē.' He pointed to one side. 'A good twenty lie that way and then another score that way. He pointed over his shoulder with his thumb. He spoke with delight; he enjoyed the men's fear—his confidence, by contrast, exalted him. He needed to be brought back to his station, so I said, 'You can clearly find what stands still—can you find the horse?' He reddened. "Quite likely, Dominē.' He turned away and pressed forward.

"A short time later we came to a clearing, and Lugh hesitated at the threshold. He put a hand over his eyes against the sun. I thought in that moment—it was something about his posture, I suppose, his carriage—I thought in that moment that he was looking to see my reaction to what he already knew was there. I stopped too and didn't look at him. In the middle of the clearing the earth rose sharply and the top was rounded like a cushion. What we had before us were the remains of an old fort, some chieftain's stronghold from long ago before the Romans came. No one had lived there in centuries, of course, and so the rampart wasn't more than a soft grass-covered bank--an open ring with a gap where the gate had stood, say, four or five centuries ago. I saw that people still used it as a sheepfold because the grass was sparse near the breach, and the earth was bare right at the threshold.

"Although Lugh's attitude betrayed something, I couldn't hesitate before the men, so I went ahead toward the breach in the rampart. I waved both arms to bring the men up on either side of me, and off we went. Despite the sheep turds here and there, there wasn't any noise of a flock, only a few crow calls. It made me edgy, but I didn't draw my sword because I didn't want to appear alarmed.

"We passed through the breach and saw it was the usual sort of place: a ring-wall surrounded a broad circle of meadow. There were some large hummocks here and there where the chief's house and barn had fallen to the ground centuries ago. And there were a pair of old standing stones—monuments to the dead chief and his wife most likely, hatched with that vertical script no one reads anymore. All this was what you would expect, but there was something more I hadn't foreseen, something newer and at the same time older. And obscene.

"It was a wooden pale, a slender tree trunk sunk into the earth; it rose a dozen feet, and fixed to the top of it, was Hispanus' head. His forelegs were crossed and nailed below it and his tail was nailed below that. His eyes were gone, and his lips drawn back over his yellow teeth—he seemed to grimace at the world, to stare beyond it. The whole apparatus stood there like the trophy of some murky victory that had happened behind our backs. I could hear one of the men whispering a prayer. A breeze picked up and Hispanus' mane and tail floated toward us, and a moment later the smell affronted us. I stepped back involuntarily." Quirinius took up his cup and drank some wine. He looked pointedly at the abbot. "The peasants thereabouts had sacrificed the horse to Epona. They were turning their backs on Christ. Have you seen any sacrilege to match that?"

The abbot said nothing.

"Your objection to the wine seems quite paltry now, doesn't it?" The abbot still said nothing.

"Doesn't it?"

"Quite paltry."

Quirinius turned to his captain. "That's the trouble with ecclesiastics. They lack a sense of proportion." He smiled at Ambiorus and then, of a sudden, he stood up and left the table. He wandered to the other end of the room, pushed one of the shutters open and then leaned half-turned against the sill. He clenched and unclenched his hands behind his back and regarded the night sky. The abbot could see that something agitated him.

Quirinius had been angry at the waste of a good horse, but that came later. So did his anger at being led like a naïve on a traipse through the woods by this crafty, doubtless heathen peasant. What he felt first was outrage spreading from his guts to his skin, outrage at the paganism. His anger did not distract him from right feelings about the thing, dread and revulsion at this recrudescence of a dark worship. God, but the Romans had spent four hundred years dragging the province by the scruff the neck toward a life worth living, and when they'd found true religion, why then they'd passed that on too, along with law and roads and everything else worthwhile to these lumpish people. And here he stood in a district full of folk too cloddish to hold on to their advantages.

As Hispanus' head rocked in the breeze at the top of his pole, the shadows in his eyes shifted, and Quirinius conceived for a moment that the animal's spirit was looking back into the world he'd left behind. Quirinius forced the thought from his mind and looked at his men, who now stood in a half-circle behind him and waited expectantly. Outside the fort his horse whickered. He said to them, "This is evil business." And then he called Lugh up. The man had hung back, but now he came uneasily forward, unsure of his little victory now that he had it.

"Lugh," Quirinius said. "This is your country." Lugh did not reply. "Is this a heathen country, Lugh?" The huntsman shrugged, head turned slightly, keeping his eyes away from the pole supporting the horse parts. "Answer me." Quirinius' men moved slowly closer around Lugh.

"We're Christians, Dominē," he said at length, looking at the men on either side of him and then at Quirinius to see how he took it. Then he glanced up at the horse head.

"Does this look like the work of Christians?" When Lugh didn't answer right away, one of the men jostled him.

"No."

"You'll agree the smell is hardly like incense."

"Yes. No." Lugh watched Quirinius' face to see how he should answer. He sensed the young noble was dangerous—he wondered how he had missed it until now. One of his dogs came up to him, but one of the men kicked it away. Lugh heard the yelp but didn't look. He tried to think. "Now, Dominē, the Saxons..." But he trailed off. Like other peasants he could be cunning with his silences, but he wasn't a handy liar.

"There aren't any Saxons hereabouts."

"No, Dominē."

"That's better. Now who is the priest over these parts? And where is he?"

"It's Silverius at Castra Minuta. He's well-respected."

"Evidently his example isn't enough for some people." Quirinius found himself enjoying his own glibness. The men weren't frightened any more—his sarcasm calmed them, and they guessed he knew what to do about the situation. They were beginning to smile. "How far is the town from here?"

"Not far. About two miles. North across the meadow."

"Then lead us there, Lugh. You need to help us strengthen this weak priest."

Castra Minuta was thirty thatched houses huddling their shoulders close around the walls of an old auxiliary fort. The walls were of a stone as grey as a winter sky, as was the commander's old house— now the priest's—and close by was a daub and wattle church so weathered and colored that it seemed to have grown out of the earth.

It was on the cruciform pattern with a low belfry to one side. So, all quite civilized for this half-lost little place.

By the time Quirinius'men had entered the fort, a number of the townsfolk had gathered to consider them. Quirinius could see that his men's weapons made the people uneasy, and that was fine. He stayed upon his horse to impress them and rested his hand on his sword hilt. He looked over the crowd and reckoned that not everyone was there, so he ordered one of the townsmen to ring the church bell. When the sound came moments later it had a flat, thin sound—harsh, like a small man coughing; it must have been cobbled out of a sheet of tin, but everyone knew its voice, and it brought in the rest of the town, including the priest himself, who strode up followed by his housekeeper and a tow-head child with shocking blue eyes.

The priest was a man about forty, so Quirinius judged, a solid, cautious-seeming man whose face showed he had difficulty choosing his approach to the strangers. He had shaven, but not for a day or two, and his robe had two dark mud stains over his knees from working in the garden. He stepped up from the townsfolk who had crowded around him, either to protect him, or maybe to be protected. He said, loudly, "What is happening here?" At the sound of his voice the bell stopped ringing—the man who had tolled the bell came from the belfry. He looked sheepish and nodded at Quirinius for his excuse.

"That's a good question, Priest," Quirinius said. The priest scowled up at him, which took courage because Quirinius' face was hard. He had decided to do a harsh thing as he stood in the ring-fort in the dirty shadow of Hispanus' swaying head. The idea had come to him as sudden and unheralded as heat lightning reaching from one side of the night sky to the other—glowing forks or tridents rubbing their backs along the underside of the clouds and illuminating with a pale light the faces looking up at it. The suddenness and completeness of the thought convinced Quirinius that it was right even though, in later years, he had doubts.

He had had the pole knocked down and the head and hoofs buried; the men complained about digging with their spear points. He took the horsetail with him—lavish and long and white—draped across the saddlebow. Now he tossed the horsetail to the ground before the priest. The man stared down at it, puzzled. The townsfolk glanced at each other warily.

"Who are you?" the priest asked. "Do you come from Dominus Maximianus?"

"No. I am Flavius Quirinius Claudianus." He said this in a round, rich tone and heard a murmur of "Cuirann Beag!" go about the crowd as those who understood passed the news to their neighbors who knew no Latin. He enjoyed their respectful tone; he felt buoyed by it. "I have been searching for a stolen horse. I have found him—parts of him, anyway—not far from here. In the ring fort."

"Parts of him?" The priest looked at his congregation as though they could explain. No one spoke; several, abashed, grew red. "What do you mean 'parts of him?'"

"What I mean, Silverius, is that the people roundabout have sacrificed the animal to the Horse-Mother." The priest shifted his feet and rubbed his jaw, uncomfortable, perhaps that the young man knew his name.

"Epona," the priest said, rubbing his jaw. His eyes flashed from side to side—he was trying to take it in.

"So, you know about it, then."

The priest looked up, alarmed. "No! Not at all. But who doesn't know her name?"

"I wish no one did."

The priest scowled.

"The world's imperfect, Dominē Quirinius. There are remnants here and there of older things." He shrugged and forced a mild smile. "One works as well as one can." He spread his hands to show he was a reasonable man faced with a difficulty. His expression called on Quirinius to join him, but, like a young man, Quirinius knew what to do—no doubts trammeled him the way they did older men like his father, for instance, whom the priest's gesture recalled to him at that moment. Quirinius regarded him coldly and then he began to speak British—loudly and clearly. His horse turned her ears about, alarmed. She took a step back and Quirinius pulled the reins sharply to halt her. "There must be no heathens among us. None at all. Some of you have killed my horse, which is very bad, but you have darkly sacrificed him to one of the old gods, whose name I will not even pronounce, and this is worse, an evil that will not be repeated."

A few of the townsfolk mumbled that, surely, what he accused them of was untrue. But many of them looked abashed; surely, they were lying. "I will not argue; I have seen the wreck of my horse serving as a squalid offering not two miles from here in the old fort where you pen your sheep."

"Look, Master, they're like children." The priest then grasped his boot like a supplicant, and his face showed how hard for him to truckle. He was used to a high position in the town. "Leave them to me. Put the village under an indemnity if you like."

Quirinius looked over the priest's head and continued in British. "Your priest asks that I leave this business to him." He waited a moment, excitement gathering in him as he approached the threshold of his plan. All faces were on him now, the townsmen, uncertain, eyes squinting, heads rocking slightly as they shifted from foot to foot in their unease, Quirinius' men, mouths half open as they looked up at him on his horse. The priest turned back to stare at his flock. He scowled, angry at them now for bringing this trouble on themselves. No one would meet his eyes—it was clear he had a good deal of authority and they were fond of him. His housekeeper, a rangy woman of thirty or so but too pretty all the same for a housekeeper, stood a little aside and took the priest's part and frowned at the villagers. The little boy lurked behind her, trying not to be seen, but all the same time peeping with frightened eyes around her.

"But I cannot leave this matter to him," Quirinius said to the crowd. The priest turned back, disheartened, and sighed.

"You are Romans." Quirinius watched them closely, saw some frowns of puzzlement. "Romans are civilized and do not pray to demons." There was muttering from the back of the crowd. "Five hundred years ago Caesar first came to our shores, the precursor of a new and better way of life. He was followed by those who introduced fine houses where there had been huts, cities where there had been settlements, ports where there had been weedy banks and law where before there had been only the will of the strongest. Now, who am I to say this? I am perhaps not the greatest, yet neither am I the least of the—" He paused because in that moment he noticed that he was losing them through his pomposity. People glanced at each other, a pair of biddies began to whisper, a father was pointing out one of Quirinius' men to his little daughter. Even Quirinius' own followers were glancing over at him, like the yokels they were.

The thought of losing these people was like a barb in his side. "And so," he concluded vaguely, "And so, it is clear that you still worship heathen spirits in sight of your church. And this cannot happen without the connivance of your priest." The man shouted up at Quirinius as though to one of his own villagers: "Ho!" But Quirinius, who felt himself swelling with power, moved on, inexorable. "And so, we must convince your priest to redouble his efforts to root up this evil." He told two of his men to seize the priest because they were going to flog him. He chose the most stupid of the men and another whose religiosity he doubted. They hesitated until he yelled at them. The priest stood glaring up at him but knew that arguing would only demean him. The townspeople, however, were concerned about his safety more than his dignity, and their voices rose into a hum as each urged his neighbor to be brave. The crowd moved forward perceptibly. Quirinius drew his sword but kept the point low, down by his boot, and then rode close along the edge of the crowd, which quailed back. Some stumbled, and an old man fell and scolded a woman who helped him up, but they kept their distance now. Quirinius turned back to the priest. The men had tied his hands together before they realized that they could not pull off his robe now. "Cut it off!" Quirinius said sharply.

Here is where the men began to hesitate; they were more awkward than they might have been in cutting it. One of the men took his hunting knife and slashed the back edge of the collar, but he hesitated a moment and looked over to Quirinius for a nod. "Get on with it!" The man then sharply tore the fabric, and it came apart with a shriek. The other pulled the torn robe down around the priest's wrists. Now the grey robe, hanging from the priest's waist and wrists exposed his body, white, middle-aged, strong once, but now growing soft. The arms must have been powerful once, but they were growing thin; the robe had lent him dignity. The priest grimaced; he didn't show fear, only anguish and shame at being exposed this way before his flock like some doddering beggar at the end of his course with his rags all falling away.

And the villagers murmured in sympathy, a faint sound like lowing in the distance or thunder in the next parish. They inched back over the ground Quirinius had driven them from, so he held his sword up before him. It stood well in his hand—the hilt directly under the point—it floated perfectly balanced, ready as a hawk to stoop on whatever invited it. Seeing this, his men held their spears at the ready. Lugh, Quirinius noted, was trying to fade into the crowd, but someone shoved him forward.

Quirinius' heart spoke quietly to him; he heard the blood passing through his ears in susurrations like a surging wind. He felt as bright, say, as his sword and now and again fine dazzles skirted the edges of his vision like droplets of quicksilver. His head was hot. He could do anything—it was obvious to him. He turned to the men who held the priest. "Take him over to the wall." They did it and shoved his face against the stones. Quirinius walked his horse nearer the wall, and the crowd followed, but slowly, keeping their distance.

The dull fellow and the the doubter, as Quirinius thought of him, pushed the priest to the wall; he ordered the bailiff to join them. The priest, hopelessly trying to maintain his dignity, held his shredded tunic up around his waist with his bound hands, and his elbows stuck out sharply to each side—ridiculous. The bailiff didn't have a proper whip—only a length of cord, so Quirinius told him to use that. One of the men got a piece of cord from somewhere and Quirinius had the bailiff tie Hispanus' tail around the priest's neck, and then the bailiff started to beat him. The priest flinched after the second or third stroke, but he didn't cry out. The crowd moaned and moved forward, but then quailed when Quirinius' men waggled their spears. Quirinius could feel the burden of the crowd's despair; it hung over him like a fusty cloak.

The priest didn't yell or call out, even though the bailiff knew how to beat people. He waited several moments between strokes so that they would hurt more. Still the priest didn't yell, even when the bailiff swung with all his skill. Instead, he chuffed hard like a tired cart-horse, but that was all. The bailiff swung with a will, clearly disappointed that he had nothing heavier to work with, and at every second or third stroke he tried to catch Quirinius' eye, tried to get his approval, redeem himself, however slightly, for Hispanus' theft. Quirinius, however, kept his gaze steadily above the bailiff's head; he would never dignify the bailiff's glance. He wasn't ashamed; that wasn't it, but somehow things didn't feel right. The atmosphere was sour, like a breeze across a midden. The lichen on the fort walls seemed quite in evidence, and the daub on the buildings around showed itself half-ruined, a thing he hadn't noticed before, the lath behind it peeking through in many places. Everything about seemed rather more down-at-heel than he'd first noticed. The priest had half a dozen red stripes on his back; their color was somehow disturbing. The little towhead was waving his arms from the edge of the crowd and squalling. Most ugly.

The crowd was impressed, and that was the important thing, but Quirinius had expected them to take the priest's humiliation as a blow at their pride—that had been the idea, really. The priest himself was insignificant. Instead, there was groaning and, more irritating than that, even some tears here and there people, women mostly, thank God, were crying. Somehow things had not gone as they ought, even though they were going according to the plan. The events were as he had intended, but the effect of them was not.

Quirinius was startled by a sudden movement. The priest's housekeeper, his wife, really—he could sense it—ran out of the crowd. One of his men half-heartedly levelled a spear at her, but what could he do with it, really? She pushed it aside, ran to the priest and draped herself over his back to protect him. She circled his neck with her right arm and waved her left out behind her, confusing the bailiff's efforts. The other two men tried to pull her off, and the priest himself stepped back from the wall, confused. He lumbered awkwardly with the woman on his back, who screamed unintelligible things at Quirinius' men. Her dress crept up and showed her long narrow calves. It seemed that no one in the village had any gift for dignity.

"That's enough," Quirinius said. "Stop it." The woman—and his men—all looked at him as though they were uncertain whom he was speaking to, but everything had stopped anyway. The woman slid around to the front of the priest and tried to hang onto him that way, but he was conscious of his dignity and swore in low British and pushed her away. It seemed odd to Quirinius that he found this sad. The priest, keeping his robe gathered tight around his waist with his bound hands, walked through the crowd with his head up. The people opened for him, and he was followed by the furious woman, who turned back to Quirinius and flung a dozen scalding words at him. The towhead child ran after them. Many of the people crossed themselves.

Quirinius didn't talk to anyone as he rode back to the estate. The bailiff, naturally obsequious, tried to discuss the whipping, suggested that it had been an invaluable exercise. Who knew what good would come of it? And surely God would appreciate what they had done, keeping his servant on the strait path and abusing Epona to boot.

Quirinius slashed at him once, sharply, with his riding whip, and the fellow dropped back to ride in silence at the end of the troop.

Four: The Second Estate of the Quirinii, 459 AD

A full summer—the trees are in thick leaf and not one has a trace of spring-yellow in its leaves. They are a hundred shades of honest green. There are woods and copses all about, and far ahead the road goes through a little forest, indifferent to the wood that once stood discretely back, though now young brushy trees have sprung up immodestly close. The men have stopped on the high crest of a hill, for the Roman road goes brusquely to the top—there is no cutting, it climbs like a chamois, and clamber up it whoever will. It's a road that shows the old power of Rome; convenience runs a poor second to display. And the road drops down as directly too and cuts through a long meadow like the tonsure of an Irish monk. Yes, there are some, everyone agrees, encamped to the west and clinging like limpets to those rocks at the edge of the world.

And Quirinius sits his horse in the middle of the stone road at the very top of the hill and leans a bit toward his father, who is gesturing over the country they see, at the woods, which belong to the family by some ancient deed, and to half a dozen woods standing here and there at the distance of a dozen miles from them. They stand out of the downland like ships in a wide green sea. And though the land is green, much of it is cut into shapes, squares and rectangles, but mostly trapezoids of wheat and oats, each a different shade. Does Quirinius note the two villas to the north and east? You can hardly see them at this distance, but his father knows where to look. Yes, he does. He knows they are the family's; he knows the one to the north in particular, the larger of the two—the one with the statue of Constantius Chlorus' father in the forecourt. And the smaller estate, the one where Hispanus was taken from, but Quirinius says nothing about that—there was some disaffection between the two of them about the way he handled things, although his father, on the whole, is satisfied at the prospect of an alliance with the Maximiani. He chided Quirinius sharply for his impulsiveness, and this rankled him because it was just. But that was a year ago.

And from this height you could see not just the Roman road that dove down from the crest and cut the plain in two, but a dozen lesser ways—alleys from field to field and around pastures that linked this land like a web to the great road they travelled that linked all this land to the Quirinii themselves.

"And more besides. Places you can't see," his father said. "Holdings in Cambria and an estate across the sea in Armorica. A river dashes across it and drives a flour-mill. I've never seen it, and I never will, but, like a little foreign province, it keeps bringing us a modest income. They're all like provinces, really." His father looked around him in all directions. "I've often thought of it that way. All the estates. Some of them big, some not. Some raise wheat and some sheep, some make pottery, and on most you'll hear only Latin spoken, just like Italy." There was longing in his voice; Quirinius knew he had always wanted to go to Italy, but there was no reason to go, really, and, besides, things were so disturbed on the way there.

Quirinius nodded—he had heard all this a hundred times. His father sensed this and leaned gracefully from his saddle and patted his arm. He urged his horse forward; Quirinius followed and after them trailed ten family soldiers, helmets on the saddlebow and shields slung over the back. They looked like turtles with red shells ringed bright blue in the sun. Three wagons followed with a curule chair, three tapestries, a strongbox full of papers for the Council meeting later at Corinium Dobunnorum, provisions, and four trunks with whatever Quirinius and his father might need for their month away. Finally, bringing up the rear, another dozen horsemen, one holding aloft a cavalry banner, narrow purple and hanging from a crossbar. It showed Victory crowning Britain, the device of the Third Troop of Thracian Lancers, *Ala III Thraciani Contofori*. This was Quirinius' grandfather's command when Valentinianus had been emperor at Rome. It was a royal progress.

The column headed down the road, along that grey channel through green fields, a cut keeping one field from another, one pasture from another, and in time the walls of the estate came into view, their whiteness standing out gradually from the burned-off mist of the late morning until it seemed to Quirinius that they approached a small city. There were walls, yes, but also orchards on either side, a huddle of houses beyond the walls, barns, ricks, bins and, at a safe distance, tombs along the road, old ones mostly moldering through centuries of rain, covered with Latin formulas fading from the weathered stone, fading from local memory. The tombs of an earlier family, the Aureliati—married into the families of local chieftains and sunk into the sump of British tribes. But on the monuments, they wore the toga and stared with bland Christian eyes into a middle distance filled with rest or maybe God.

The road had a few people scattered along it now; the news was out. The Clarissimus, Senator and Dominus Marcus Quirinius was coming. He would be there to inspect his little world, to maintain it with his power, to right its wrongs, to smile on everyone, to suffuse the country with his right spirit. As they passed peasants, many of them shouted petitions or the wandery preambles to law cases they would bring before him later. He smiled benignly down at them and rode on. When people got too close, a soldier would brush them back with the flank of his horse.

Distance had cleaned the villa and polished its walls; nearness rubbed them with a smutched hand. Quirinius considered this, thought how much more beautiful things are at a distance, how perfection was always a dozen miles away and never closer. It was up in the sky like Plato's Ideas, or perhaps it was only in another time, say, a hundred years in the past or a hundred in the future. However long his arms were, they would never embrace the perfect—he could never race a horse fast enough to come up with it. Maybe on Hispanus, the ghost horse, he mused. Maybe Hispanus, unshackled from the world as he now was, could be so fast.

Quirinius' father was first through the gate. Some called him Old Quirinius; others at his holdings further west who had little Latin knew him as Cuirann Hen. Most often he was just The Senator. He raised his right hand in a benediction like a priest. Quirinius watched him closely, judging his style. Not bad—confident but not arrogant. He looked benignly down from his horse at the crowd, at least two hundred Quirinius reckoned, and waited until the bailiff of this estate, a certain Sequanius, came ahead and grasped his foot and touched his forehead to it. The Senator smiled benignly down at him. The estate's tenants stood in a half-circle, bareheaded and eyes down.

And there was the priest of the estate. Quite a young man and eager to please. He began with a prayer. After the second word of it everyone joined in. When it was done, the Senator nodded and then said, "Court tomorrow. Right here." He pointed to the ground, then slid from his mare and walked inside.

* * *

It was late at night when the Senator learned of the bandits. It was nothing so grim as a scampering survivor half-dead over the villa threshold, or a pillar of greasy smoke from a farmstead at the horizon. It was the account books that gave them away.

The Senator was patient. Quirinius hadn't realized until then what discoveries patience could make. He'd always regarded his father's patience as mere over-cautiousness, but perhaps he'd judged him a bit too hard; he was like that. Certainly, he himself could not have sat, as his father did, at a table under half a dozen guttering rushlights stinking of sheep's tallow and hemp that cast a dozen shadows apiece, all gliding and shifting at the margins of the room like spirits pressing against the light. He could never have sat, patient as a woman at needlework, poring over the columns of tiny black ciphers in their ruled tables, the totals underlined at the end of each page, but otherwise as obscure as any other figure you might choose to pick out. The ledger was like some holy text in an odd script that you could read, but only with great effort, and even then, you might be skimming over secrets, over trends and truths that really mattered. Like a bird flying over a village that sees two dozen thatched roofs, maybe two of tile, but can't imagine the things beneath them. Quirinius had always resisted learning bookkeeping. Maybe he would have to change his attitude.

The Senator sucked in his cheeks and lifted a rushlight over the ledger and squinted at the figures for some time. A drop of tallow fell on the page and he rubbed it away, leaving behind a circle transparent as dusty glass. "What is this, Flavius? Thirty-five?" Quirinius bent over his father's shoulder.

"Thirty-four."

"Hmm," the Senator said and put the rushlight down. He settled back in his chair and put his folded hands before his down-tilted face. Sequanius, the bailiff, shifted from foot to foot a moment and looked down too, afraid to meet anyone's eyes. "No," the bailiff said, so softly that he hardly said it at all.

"What? Repeat that!" Quirinius' voice was sharp. His father waved at him to be quiet, but the bailiff was frightened just the same. "Of course, it's very close, Dominē." He shrugged, tried a weak smile, but it faded. "Mice, you see. And the occasional theft." But he hadn't the mettle to tell good, convincing lies.

"Mice don't drink beer and they don't eat flour by the hundred-weight."

"Perhaps you need a cat, Bailiff," Quirinius said. But his father didn't laugh. Instead, there was a silence. Then the Senator went on, bending close over the book.

"Three barrels of beer and two hundred pounds of flour. And a half-dozen hams. What else will I find missing?" He looked up from the page at the bailiff. The flickerish lights cast a dozen shadows around the man; they hovered behind him like possible confessions.

"Well?" Quirinius said.

Sequanius shrugged and shook his head. He was young and close to tears. Quirinius could imagine his thoughts: *Here I am trained to read and write and do sums and I'll be sleeping in the woods tonight, and that's if I'm lucky.* Quirinius wanted to flog the man and put him in a harness and make him pull a coulter throughout the summer.

There was more silence. Quirinius could see that his father knew how to use it. Father and son listened to the man's heavy breathing for half a minute. And then, suddenly, the fellow knelt across the table and clasped his hands on the edge of it like a man at a prie-dieu. He looked anguished. "A bottle of rose perfume, a shovel, a dog and a dining chair. The one with the leather footstool." The Senator glanced the littlest bit toward Quirinius, who thought he was trying to cover a smile in spite of himself. His stomach tightened because his father was not angry.

"I had to do it, Dominē. For everyone's sake. They all look to me here. They ask my advice on things I've no business about—who should marry whom and so on. What to do about a bad son... I mean, one feels responsible, I, I ..."

"Be quiet," Quirinius said. "It's not your property to give away, even if you feel cowardice is a duty." He saw his father lean forward, his half-smile now obvious. Like Quirinius, he'd solved the mystery of the warped accounts, and it seemed to him that perhaps that was all his father was really after. That the answer itself would expunge the cost.

"Good." the Senator said. "Tell me about it."

Sequanius glanced over at Quirinius an instant but slid his eyes away when he saw no sympathy. He looked up at the Senator.

"Dominē, there are men in the neighborhood. Up in the hills somewhere."

"Go on."

"Desperate men and vicious. More like dogs, really." Quirinius snorted. The bailiff quailed but went on.

"They claim to protect us for a rent each month. Usually a barrel of beer or one of flour. . ."

"Protect you from whom?" Quirinius used his harshest tone, but it sounded practiced to him; he wasn't happy with it. His father shushed him.

"Sometimes a ham or two or a bucket of lard."

"Yes, yes. I see it now. And if you don't?"

"They might burn a hayrick. They've hamstrung a horse or two hereabouts, and they killed a man once from the Mauriaci property. They left him at the crossroads."

"And you decided this was the best way to avoid trouble?"

"Don't answer for him, Father."

"Why not, if it's the truth?"

"It's the cost, don't you see? The cost of fighting them. Who can say what it might be?"

"You're surely one who can't say."

"Be quiet, Son." The Senator looked back at the bailiff. "Why didn't you report this to me."

"Because he's damned incompetent!"

"Don't answer for him."

Why not, if it's the truth? Quirinius could hear this answer in his mind, but thin and whiny as he mocked his father. Still, he was too angry to be ashamed of it. The bailiff had unclasped his hands and was holding the edge of the table now as he knelt, and he looked to Quirinius like a child, or a dwarf perhaps, craning over a counter.

"It's become the custom, you might say, in these parts. The Spuriani pay, and the Trinovantii, the Siliviuri and, of course, the Mauriaci, as you might expect."

"They're insignificant people. All of them." Quirinius said. Which wasn't true, really. The Senator leaned back in his chair and covered his face with his hands and then pushed his hair back. Quirinius could see that he was tired—travelling was hard on the old fellow. Of course, in his fatigue and soft-heartedness he would make a mistake. Quirinius knew that. And he did, too, by Quirinius' lights at least, but—thank God—not a big one.

"We'll talk of this tomorrow," the Senator said. The bailiff's shoulders slumped in relief, and he got right to his feet in a bound. He bowed his way to the door, bobbing like a pigeon. As he went, he traced a curve around Quirinius, never getting within two yards of him.

* * *

The Monastery, October 491 AD

Quirinius hadn't spoken for some time. He'd risen from the table and taken over the abbot's chair once again, and now he rested his mouth against clasped hands like a man who prayed, yet the abbot doubted it. He turned back to his plate, where there was an untouched chunk of bread sitting in a puddle of thin mutton grease. He stared at it a moment, thinking that the bishop ought to have arrived long ago. The abbot said nothing.

Bishop Valerianus was approaching, however. Late, yes, but that couldn't be helped. He had had to settle a property dispute between a pair of whining, obsequious priests, a pair of fat men who, God knew how, had managed to inherit, so they claimed, land side by side. But the property line was as limber as an eel, to hear one of them tell it. The line's sinuosity managed to encompass all of his neighbor's property and then arc out to surround two of his own outbuildings and half an apple orchard before writhing back south to rest. The other swore that the line had run some other way for a hundred years—since Propertius had been governor, as Your Grace will surely remember. Any deeds? Of course not. Just a huddle of serfs on each side, each ready to contradict the other. Illiterates afraid of the priests and even more afraid of him, some of them very old men whose backs turned as sharply as the disputed property line, men with more fingers than teeth, whose age was supposed to put their stories beyond suspicion, or at least reproach. But only God knew what the truth was, or ever would know.

As he rode along, the delicate branch of a fir swatted the bishop in the face—the path led among trees and was dark and as narrow as a cat's back. He felt his face; there was a tacky trace of sap on it.

As he rode, his mind went back to the case. Because the truth could not be known, there was nothing left but to act properly. No priest should own land. Did the priests each have brothers? Yes?

67

No? How unfortunate for the one who had only an unmarried sister. Bishop Valerianus found a sheet of palimpsest on his desk and drew a rough map despite the priests' descriptions. Houses, outbuildings, orchard. And then he took a rule and a pen and, with one sudden stroke, divided it down the middle with a conscious disregard for landmarks.

"So much for boundaries. Now, for the dispute. You. . ." he pointed to the priest with brothers. "Your tenure is finished. Your brothers now have this land as tenants in common." He looked to the other. "And you have only the spinster sister. So, your land falls to the Church. It's now a dependency of..." Valerianus couldn't quite recall if there was a religious house nearby. He looked at Brother Merydd, his sharp little secretary. "The monastery of St. Ada?" he suggested helpfully, looking diffidently up and away. Perhaps it was, as he made it seem, the obvious choice. He'd have to look into it later to see if Merydd had some interest in the place. The priests were hurried out by a squad of burly lay brothers, and their remonstrations—execrations, really, he supposed—were soon faint enough not to be troublesome at all.

Bishop Valerianus' horse stumbled in the dark and he slipped onto its neck. Damned undignified that, but in this murk there was no one to see. He shifted back. The Saxons should leave him alone; that was the agreement. Therefore, he shouldn't have to take this path, but all the same only a fool would put the agreement to the test if he didn't have to. The Saxons were encamped to the north not far from the main road where it drove through the wood. And so here go Bishop Valerianus and thirty church soldiers on foot down this trail, parting the dark with their noses and listening for the mucky sucking sound that will tell them they have reached the bogs and swales around the Island of Apples.

* * *

And Quirinius still sits in the meeting house, thinking of that visit to the small estate so many years ago. As the senator had said, there was to be court on the next day.

Assizes in the morning in the villa-yard. The hope of justice for some, the certainty of entertainment for the rest; the best show since the Senator held court half a year before, wrapped in a wool cloak, copper leaves like curled hands trolling about him in the autumn wind. *At least the weather is better this time,* Quirinius thinks, as the bailiff bosses the servants. They make a platform from a pair of tables and toss an old arras over it to give it dignity. They put a footstool in front and the Senator's big chair from the wagon on top of it. Just below and in front sit another table and a settle for Quirinius.

"It's important that you're seen to take part in the doing of justice," the old man says to him, just as he's done for the last two years. And so, it's for him to sit there and call the cases and write his father's judgements down into the black-bound ledger. It's two feet tall and takes both hands to lift. This seems to give the hundred judgements already recorded there a wonderful immutability.

Quirinius sits and watches the bailiff resentfully. He's been forgiven—why else let him participate? Why else does he beam at Quirinius? Quirinius leans on his elbows and sharpens his pen with a small ivory-handled knife. He scans the crowd, his face showing nothing. Most of the hundred peasants standing in the yard watch him surreptitiously, glancing away out of respect when he looks up. But now they straighten, for here come the Senator and six of his soldiers to give him dignity. The priest walks alongside, but humbly; Quirinius stands. The priest goes to a stool to the left of the platform and waits there until the Senator has taken his seat. Soldiers stand to either side of the platform, the bailiff steps out into the yard to escort the first litigants, and Quirinius takes his seat and puts the sharpened pen behind his ear. He calls the first case and writes down the names in neat, curved capitals while the two peasants fidget, each worried over who speaks first.

What could have happened at the estate during the last half year? More than Quirinius' imagination could concoct and very trivial. It was always this way. He would sit at the table listening to the interminable accounts—the peasants could never get to the point. They'd wring their hands and look at their feet and you'd have to shout at them to speak up, or maybe they'd clench their fists and shake them at their sides and stamp their feet like children and shout at each other. But either way the stories wandered, turned back on themselves like adders, and were very long. It seemed they often started shortly after the Flood. It begins with something the plaintiff's wife had said to him that morning while she was scraping porridge out of the breakfast bowls. We eat a lot of porridge, but everyone agrees there's nothing better for a man in the morning. And in the evening too, if there's a bit of mutton in it. The story forges ahead to nowhere in particular—or nowhere Quirinius could see. You never knew where the buggers were going with anything—they lived in an eerie world of simultaneity where every event took place alongside every other and all were equally significant. Or insignificant.

And the Senator would sit forward in his curule chair and nod sagely while some confused peasant tried to explain why someone was his cousin and how this was somehow essential to the case, even though the matter arose from a dog that had been killed for hunting chickens. But even so, he was otherwise a good dog and worth a lot. And no, the cousin really doesn't come into the case now that My Master the Senator asks. Quirinius would sit there shifting on the settle, his back aching, waiting to write the judgement, any judgement, just to put the case away and move toward dinner. He thinks of something like this and polishes it in his mind.

IT IS THE JUDGEMENT OF THIS COURT, FLAVIUS QUIRINIUS CLAUDIANUS, PRESIDING, THAT one Rufinus, plaintiff and peasant, be stripped and switched thirty times for making a damned nuisance of himself to this court, and

IT IS FURTHER ORDERED THAT one Eburactus, defendant and peasant, shall be stripped to his spreading waist and switched thirty times for beginning the defense of his case with an excruciatingly detailed account of his ancestry modeled on the genealogies of the Old Testament, but longer than any of them, and

IT IS FURTHER ORDERED THAT the object of this case, to wit, one superannuated ewe (in the meantime wrongfully sheared by an unknown third party not joined in this case) be forfeited to this court and awarded to any litigant who can state his position in a hundred words.

Of course, there could never be such justice. No, the Senator would hear it all, listen to all the maundering, and then in the end would divide whatever was in issue; it was always the same—justice sacrificed to peace. Quirinius doubted what the old man believed, that peace could be rendered from simmering compromises.

But suddenly, unlikely though it seems, there comes a matter of moderate interest, one involving freedoms and rights rather than squabbles over theft or cavils over property lines.

All the same, what has caught Quirinius' attention is not the matter of the case, which anyhow took the Senator several minutes to winkle out and unwind from the clew twisted tight by a half-dozen dull parties and witnesses. What drew and kept his eyes from the pages of the ledger, in which he had been amusing himself by ruling a line as neatly as he could beneath the last decision, was a young woman. She was fair, nearly as much as Albinia, but with a tinge of color on her face. Her hair was red—copper, really—and struggled out beneath her head cloth. She was dressed demurely in a straight, shapeless grey shift and dreadful, tongueless British shoes dusty from her walk here, but her face was broad and full of delight; she glanced frankly at everyone about and once or twice smiled and showed a gap between her two front teeth, which everyone knows means a woman is lusty. A bit broad in the shoulders, her ankles muscular—she was some sort of peasant, but a better sort, Quirinius could tell. The humor in her face spoke to her intelligence. She didn't give the

71

sheepish smile that other peasants did when called up before the Senator, glad of the attention so long as there wasn't too much of it, warmed by the interest of the onlookers.

Now Quirinius, because he was only twenty-five, thought of women and coitus every little while, the way young men do, no matter what else he was occupied with, digging mud from the frog of a horse's hoof, combing his hair, answering the Senator's correspondence. He would imagine it vividly, recall it really, though in a rather repetitive way, for the Senator was a bit of a prig, and the servant girls in the villa were cautious with Quirinius and had not given him much experience. He had had relations with three of them in the summer in the nearby woods, and twice in his own room with Maura. She was thirty and a bit plain, but very buxom, and he hadn't slept for two nights after each experience, thinking how he had to have her again or he would die. But she was soon married and wouldn't come near him again, so he'd lain in bed with an erection for so long that his stomach ached. And he worried about what he would tell the Senator if any of them conceived, but they never did.

He looked at this copper-haired girl with real intensity, wondering at her voice, her smell, the texture of her hair, and rather soon his fascination had slid into that hot sort of love that young men have. They develop it in ignorance, and it is all the stronger for it. She was lovely, and she wasn't afraid to look him in the face and smile—just as though she were his equal. He saw the comical slot between her teeth and wanted to kiss her right there.

The red-headed girl was the object of the dispute, and she stood to the side of a bony nun of about sixty. Alongside the nun was another pair, apparently husband and wife, each more truculent-looking than the other, and then a few steps away another family, father, grown son and mother, a small, fretful woman wringing her hands. All but the young woman were agitated—they might have been the core of a riot. Now, here was something to see.

"Now what's the trouble here?" the Senator asked. Quirinius could tell from this that the Senator would start in his usual way, without method.

One of the litigants, a man, nearly bald but with a bristly red beard springing from his jowls, said "Master and Senator, this nun's got hold of my daughter and won't let me marry her off." The Senator frowned. "And who are you?" He pointed to the other family. "Why are you here?"

The father, a slight hunched man, said, "It's my son she's going to marry, Dominē. Once you hear the case, of course," he added and ducked his head in a peremptory bow. Quirinius marvelled at how common people could never answer the questions put to them. "This old woman's standing in the way." He pointed a finger at the old nun.

"Show some respect, you cur," she said to him.

"How can this old nun—" the red-bearded man began.

"Abbess," said the old woman. "I'm the Abbess of St. Constantia, and you can't even read or write, you boor."

"That's a lie! It's a lie, and you know it! Master, Master. . ." He was beside himself over her claim. "I'll see that you're punished for that lie. The Senator will never stand for this in his court." Quirinius could see that the Senator only rolled his eyes. "I have three books in my house." The abbess crossed her arms on her flat chest and harrumphed. She looked calmly up at the Senator.

"He may know what is the top of the page and what the bottom, but it can be nothing more."

"What are your names?" Quirinius asked. "They must be written down." Everyone spoke at once, and the bailiff shouted at them to be silent and then to speak one at a time or not at all. There came a brief lull as all of the parties looked at each other, and then again all of them spoke at once. Quirinius put his pen down and rubbed his face with both hands. The red-bearded fellow raised his arm as if about to cuff the abbess, but the old girl didn't flinch. One of the soldiers shouted, "Hey!" and took a step forward. There was some laughter from the crowd of peasants. The Senator pointed to the red-bearded man.

"What is your name?"

"I am Avidius, Your Excellency."

"And what is your trade?"

"Boor," said the abbess. The crowd laughed again, and Avidius glared at them and made an obscene gesture to a few chosen members. This provoked whistles and coarse taunts.

"Be quiet," the priest told the abbess. She turned to him and smiled blandly. She'd gotten her jibe in; it couldn't be taken back.

"I am Avidius, a freeholder near Collina Durotorum. My father was Macrinius and many of my cousins are your tenants."

"And you?" the bailiff asked the other man, assuming some authority.

"Dumnorigus, a free man also with a holding near Collina Durotorum. This is my son Cornovius and my wife Castina." The wife bobbed her head at the Senator.

"Do you have any complaint about the abbess?" the Senator asked.

"Pulcheria," the abbess said, identifying herself. Quirinius scribbled her name. Narrow as a slat, face as long as a sentence. Pulcheria. Her figure made him think of a shift draped over a saw-horse.

"No, Dominē," said Castina.

"Shut up, woman. The question was to me." Dumnorigus bowed. "Yes, Dominē, I do."

Quirinius spoke up. "What's the girl's name?" He reddened as everyone, the Senator included, looked over at him. "We should know it. First things first," he said, wishing he could have thought of a weightier aphorism.

"Quite right," the Senator agreed. "Well, girl?"

"Caelia, Dominē," she said. Quirinius wrote it down in his finest hand. "Daughter of Avidius and...?" he asked, just to hear her speak again.

"Varia," she said, turning to him. His heart jumped for a second.

"You're being pedantic, Quirinius," his father said.

"I'm sorry. I thought this was the place for it." The Senator sighed.

Caelia, Avidius, Varia, Dumnorigus, Cornovius (curiously, he too had red hair), Castina, Pulcheria. Quirinius looked up from his writing to the vane of the sundial that jutted from the wall across the courtyard. The smudge of its shadow would creep an arc of two hours before this matter would be done. And yet, for all that time, if he were careful how he did it, he could watch Caelia, as he might a flower, and this would lighten things. But in the end she would go to Cornovius; she was, after all, for her father to dispose of. Though she was a mere peasant and not for him, he winced as he thought of her lying on a straw mattress next to Cornovius, their red heads on the pillow in a shanty somewhere. Somehow, he felt it as his loss, but then, that was the price of his station. There was soon to be compensation, Albinia Maximiana. Surely after they were married, she would keep him occupied.

The Senator had a natural dignity, was well-spoken. He knew Greek, unheard of these days. In short, he had all the advantages and ornaments to be a judge, but his failing was obvious to Quirinius. He lacked that perfect, that definitive hauteur that caused men to cower and submit to him without any overt display of strength. Yes, he had dignity, but he was avuncular, and his courts always seemed to Quirinius rather unruly—they seemed to wobble along like a farm-cart with a warped wheel.

Of course, there was no one to take tyronian notes, and this villa-court was hardly one of record. But it went like this.

TRANSCRIPT OF PROCEEDINGS OF 12 MAY IN THE CONSULSHIP OF FLAVIUS RICIMER, THE CLARISSIMUS M. QUIRINIUS CLAUDIANUS, SENATOR, PRESIDING.

SENATOR: Now, once again, what is the trouble?

QUIRINIUS: I know it's hopeless, but I'm going to tell everyone to keep to the point.

SENATOR: That's enough, Flavius. Priest, please swear the parties.

PRIEST: Who are the parties? I mean, all of them who are up here...?

AVIDIUS: I am a party, Father. And so is Dumnorigus. We alone. After all, who else will need to speak?

SENATOR: I will decide that.

AVIDIUS: Surely, the women will not speak?

PULCHERIA: I will speak, woman or not. Don't be mistaken on that account. I will answer Avidius' scurrility.

SENATOR: She has a point.

PULCHERIA: But there is no need to administer an oath to me. I am an abbess and do everything in the plain sight of God.

QUIRINIUS: Everyone does. Let her be sworn.

SENATOR: Who is the judge here?

[Laughter from the crowd]

Silence, or I will clear the yard of spectators.

[Groans of disappointment from the crowd followed by shushing to silence the litigants.]

Let everyone be sworn.

PRIEST: Even the women?

QUIRINIUS: Even the women.

SENATOR: Even the women.

AVIDIUS: Oh, Dominē, please help us.

PRIEST: Be silent! Except to swear the oath.

[The oath having been given, the matter proceeded.]

SENATOR: So, what is the complaint?

AVIDIUS: I wish my daughter Caelia to marry Dumnorigus' son Cornovius, but she is in the Abbess's service, and she forbids it.

QUIRINIUS: Remarkable!

SENATOR: I don't take your point, Son.

QUIRINIUS: He has stated his case in twenty words. He's a marvel of economy.

AVIDIUS: Thank you, Master Flavius.

SENATOR: Now, don't be impudent, Son.

PULCHERIA: We leave that to Avidius.

CAELIA: [Laughs.] *And Quirinius finds her laughter delightful.*

PRIEST: Do not speak until spoken to.

PULCHERIA: Why does Avidius speak first?

AVIDIUS: Because I have been wronged!

SENATOR: Pulcheria! If you kick Avidius once more, it will go badly for you. Bailiff, stand between them.

[Chortling from the crowd.]

PULCHERIA: Yes, Dominē.

QUIRINIUS: I advise you to make it sound like you mean it.

SENATOR: You, Pulcheria, what do you say?

PULCHERIA: I will continue to speak in Latin despite the difficulty Avidius will have, because Latin serves the Senator's dignity better than British. I will, of course, speak as plainly as I can. I willingly relinquish any unjust advantage over my accuser because I need none. I am in the right, and God will see that justice is done.

SENATOR: Yes, yes. Get on with it.

PULCHERIA: Avidius indentured Caelia to me a year ago, and for a period of two years she is mine; that is, until the end of next winter. My abbey has paid a dozen sheep for her indenture, and I am within my rights to keep her until her time is up. And besides she may at any time decide to become a postulant.

AVIDIUS: So! You'd steal her! You admit it in front of everyone!

QUIRINIUS: Shut up.

PULCHERIA: Well said, my young Master. Commendable economy.

SENATOR: Continue.

PULCHERIA: Avidius had another daughter, God rest her soul, whom he had intended for Cornovius, but she took ill last winter and passed on. Now he wants to join Cornovius and Caelia and join his and Dumnorigus' freeholds too. This seems a good plan to him, you see, because he has no sons. I believe, Dominē, that his left testicle may not work.

[Laughter from the audience.]

PRIEST: No impudence from you, Mother Pulcheria. It doesn't become your station.

[Indistinct statement from Avidius to the effect that his left testicle is fine.]

SENATOR: Who is the judge here? I'll handle this.
PULCHERIA: Everyone knows that boys come from the left!
THE CROWD: They do! They do!

[Indistinct statement from Avidius, swearing in low British dialect.]

QUIRINIUS: Silence!
SENATOR: Whom are you addressing?
QUIRINIUS: It was a general admonishment, Senator.
SENATOR: I see. Quite right. Silence! Avidius, do you deny the Abbess Pulcheria's claim?
AVIDIUS: I deny that it is right that she should have the girl.
QUIRINIUS: Answer the question.
AVIDIUS: I have, Dominē, as well as I can.
QUIRINIUS: Did you indenture her?
AVIDIUS: Yes, but...
QUIRINIUS: Does the indenture continue until next spring?
AVIDIUS: Yes, but...
SENATOR: Let him finish.
AVIDIUS: But I am a Roman. We are all Romans here and have power over our children even unto life and death!

VOICE FROM THE CROWD: She's to go to the nunnery? Not much life there!

[Laugher from the crowd.]

QUIRINIUS: Silence!

DUMNORIGUS: But he did not send her to be a nun! Only to be a servant! He can take her back.

PULCHERIA: He cannot!

SENATOR: I am speaking to Avidius. How can you take her back? Does the contract mean nothing? Does the law only apply at your convenience? Valid when it suits you, invalid when it thwarts you? You see? You have nothing to say.

DUMNORIGUS: Dominē, may I speak?

QUIRINIUS: No.

SENATOR: No. Well, in a moment.

AVIDIUS: I have offered to return the sheep to Abbess Pulcheria.

DUMNORIGUS: And the offspring.

AVIDIUS: But this doesn't satisfy her. She's a hard, cruel woman.

CAELIA: Hard perhaps, but not cruel.

Her voice is like a bell and Quirinius is delighted to hear it. He wants to hear her sing sometime.

AVIDIUS: Be quiet, Daughter.

SENATOR: Pulcheria, is this true? That Avidius will return the flock?

PULCHERIA: So, what if it is true? Why should I oblige him and turn her away, and then waste a month finding a new girl? I'll never find another so clever. And besides, I've taught her to read and write. She's improved herself. Is that nothing?

DUMNORIGUS: I'll offer you an extra sheep of my own—for the reading and writing.

PULCHERIA: I am gladdened to see how you value those skills.

DUMNORIGUS: Two sheep then, but wethers.

QUIRINIUS: Is this a marketplace or a court?

SENATOR: Why can't you people wait a year? The girl isn't with child, is she?

AVIDIUS: No.

VARIA: No.

CORNOVIUS: No.

SENATOR: Well, then.

QUIRINIUS: Why doesn't the girl answer for herself? It seems to me she's the best witness.

CAELIA: No!

SENATOR: Very well. So, why not wait a year?

AVIDIUS: A lot can happen in a year, Dominē.

QUIRINIUS: That's no answer.

SENATOR: Then it seems clear to me that I must decide whether, if Avidius makes good Pulcheria's expenditure, he can exercise his right as a father to take back his daughter. Now, Flavius, write this down.

QUIRINIUS: Yes, Senator.

SENATOR: It is my judgement that. . .

CASTINA: I want to confess! I want the priest to confess me!

SENATOR: What! What is this stupid woman talking about?

CASTINA: These children cannot marry, whether you leave Caelia at the nunnery or take her away.

QUIRINIUS: We're getting off the point here.

SENATOR: Why not?

CASTINA: I cannot say. But you must believe me.

QUIRINIUS: Why?

CASTINA: Please believe me!

SENATOR: I can't just throw up my hands and render a judgement on the ground that some hysterical woman has invaded my court and asked me to resolve a complicated matter between a half-dozen parties in a way that suits none of them and on a principle that no one is aware of. You can see that--it's plain.

CASTINA: They may not marry!

QUIRINIUS: Senator, she's unhinged. Dumnorigus, get control of your wife.

DUMNORIGUS: Now, Castina. . .

PRIEST: Perhaps it would be best if you permitted me to speak with her.

SENATOR: Oh, perhaps. But be quick about it.

QUIRINIUS: Who's the judge here?

[Castina and the priest draw off to one side and mutter for a few moments.]

SENATOR: Well?

PRIEST: [Speaking quietly so that the crowd cannot hear] The woman has a good reason for what she says, Dominē. These young people cannot marry.

SENATOR: Why not?

PRIEST: I cannot tell you. It was a confession.

SENATOR: What?

PRIEST: A confession.

SENATOR: I heard you the first time!

PRIEST: Well, then, Dominē. There it is.

SENATOR: There it is not! So now you two are partners in mystery and want me to go along this hidden path with you!

PRIEST: Confession is holy.

SENATOR: So is the rule of law, you stupid bugger.

Quirinius delights to hear this from his father.

Priest, Castina, I am about to render a judgement, and you will not like it.

[Avidius claps his hands for joy. The crowd murmurs and inches up. The soldiers shove them back with spear-shafts.]

But you have one chance come up here to me and tell me privately what you wish, and if it bears on this matter, I will give weight to what you tell me.

DUMNORIGIUS: You ask her to speak, Dominē, but you will not let me hear?

SENATOR: That's it. Flavius, join us.

81

[A discussion is held off the record between the Senator, Castina, the priest and Flavius.]

The peasants wobble from side to side like strolling pigeons as each seeks to look over his neighbor's shoulder, but the soldiers keep them back, though even they too glance back hoping to catch a word or indication here or there, for nothing is as enticing as a secret. But the Senator is careful. He leans forward in his chair and looks down at Castina, the priest and Quirinius, who stand in a conspiratorial knot just below him.

"Well," the Senator says, "What on earth are you concerned about? Caelia isn't even your daughter." He's sophisticated, so he can keep the curiosity out of his voice, but Quirinius can see a hint of it in his eyes. Castina cannot, though--she's a naïve, more or less, and looks modestly at her feet. The priest looks away, feigning indifference, but his eyes are cocked back at the woman. She looks from side to side, at Quirinius, at the priest, and then down at the ground once more. She opens her mouth twice without effect, and then says, "Cornovius is Avidius' son."

A simple statement, but the implication takes a moment. The Senator frowns, taking it in and Quirinius needs an instant too. And then the thing that was hidden is obvious, like a hare under a bush once you realize it, invisible one moment and the next obvious and trembling.

"I was unchaste, Dominē, years ago, with Avidius. No one knows the boy is his, not even Avidius. It's why the girl and boy both have red hair." Her logic has missed a join, but the point is clear. The truth now out, the priest feels obliged to say the obvious: "They are brother and sister, then. Their marriage would be incestuous. Genesis, I think. Or Leviticus. Both, actually." The Senator was ignoring him. He had a hand across his eyes and was waving everyone back.

The senator hates the unforeseen. It's what brings the peasants out to watch the assizes, though he suspects there may be some betting on the outcomes as well, but it's something he doesn't tolerate well, and it makes his judgements difficult. What to do about this? Anything he wants, really; he has the naked power, but he wants judgements sopped in principle (or conforming to the law, at least), but how does he rule on this one so that next year, or the one after that, Caelia isn't married to her brother and at the same time Dumnorigus doesn't beat his wife? (The Senator is sentimental; he believes in love, misses his dead wife.) There's a way, of course, and of course it's imperfect, but then if his judgement in this case makes the law seem a mystery to the peasants, it is for the most part anyway.

[The court resumes.]

SENATOR: My judgement is this: that Caelia shall finish out her term as a servant at the Nunnery of St. Constantia. And further, her term shall continue for an additional three years. Only afterward shall her father take her back into his hand.

The crowd looks at him expectantly, waiting for a reason. The Senator calls to Quirinius to give him a book from the table, and he ostentatiously turns the leaves, runs a finger down a column and then across several lines of text, mumbling to himself only half audibly (it's all for show--the book is merely an account ledger). He looks up at the crowd and says, coolly. "A contract is a contract and cannot be unmade without the agreement of all parties or their successors, and so on and so on. The Twenty-Second Article of the Third Constitution of Theodosius I." He slams the book closed and sets it beneath his chair. Quirinius and the priest, who know it's a trick, look at each other casually and wonder how this solves anything.

Of course, that was only half of it. Pulcheria had to be snagged and brought into the villa through the kitchen door in the back and sneaked up a back set of stairs into the office while Caelia waited on a settle by the oven. Quirinius would have preferred to find an excuse to wait in the kitchen with her, to lean back against the warm bricks of the oven and gaze at her, but instead he had to lead the old abbess up to his father and the priest. She was spry and went up the stairs ahead of him so quickly that he found himself watching the backs of her lean white shanks as she took each riser.

The abbess had won more than she bargained for. The senator told her what Castina had said and then made her promise to urge Caelia into the nunnery where she wouldn't cause any accidental incestuous connections.

The Senator said, "I'm not happy about this; it's underhanded, but I think it's the best that can be done." Quirinius was flushed; he didn't like it either. Not because it was, as his father said "underhanded"—he was by nature more practical than his father—but because, in some way, this decision put Caelia at a greater remove from him than would marriage. Or so it seemed. His thoughts were a stew of the impossible and the unlikely in about equal measure.

Pulcheria shrugged her bony shoulders. "Everyone's a cousin of some sort in most of these little villages anyway. I suspect that you could have let it slip by this once."

The Senator shook his head. "The law is the law."

"You are a noble and can afford certainty."

"So, it's settled then." The Senator nodded at Quirinius to show her the door.

"Not quite, Senator,"

"What remains?" the priest asked.

"Why, the girl's maintenance," Pulcheria said.

The three men looked at each other. Quirinius asked the question to save his father's dignity.

"What do you mean?"

"It's all well and good to saddle me with the girl. And she's a good girl, mind you. But her indenture has been extended, and I must support her. I had no intention of accepting any novices so soon. We are a small abbey, and she'll be another mouth to feed."

"But you're feeding her already." Quirinius said.

"A small allowance would be helpful." Pulcheria's voice was suddenly wheedling, and she looked down at her clasped hands like a young girl.

"Don't be insolent," the priest said.

"Is it ever insolent to recognize the truth?" Her voice had taken a whiny edge.

"Yes," Quirinius said. "And at times like this." The abbess smiled slyly. But before Quirinius could take the matter further his father had capitulated, just as he knew he would.

"Yes, yes. All right. Next spring when her indenture would have been up, I'll send you a smoked ham and a barrel of flour. You'll get that twice a year."

"Thank you, Dominē. For five years?"

"For two," Quirinius said. And then again more loudly. "For two."

"We'll make that three, Mother Pulcheria," the Senator said. He waved his hand at her, and in an instant the priest had one hand on her arm and the other on the doorlatch. She gave her valediction from the stairwell, the priest rushing her down through the dimness and away.

Quirinius couldn't get away from his father, couldn't frame a good excuse for some minutes. Instead, he fussed with the rushlights and the lamps, setting them alight in anticipation of the sunset. He was clumsy at it and scorched a sleeve; his father wrinkled his nose at the smell and regarded him narrowly.

"The whole thing couldn't be helped, Son." He leaned forward across the table with his hands flat on it, as though steadying himself. "That halfwit Castina set the whole thing in motion, and years later there wasn't much choice about what was to be done. It's like that sometimes. This way the girl will be kept away long enough that those rustics will find the boy another wife. And she might leave the nunnery if she wishes." Quirinius turned to him and shrugged.

"You leave her there that long, she'll take the vows. Not that I'm blaming you—"

"I should hope not. The point is you'll have to make hard decisions when your turn comes."

"What's another nun, more or less?" Quirinius asked aloud, though really to himself. But of course, as always, a question is hardly a comfort.

"Quite right. She might be happier with a man, but who knows anyway? There were eighteen matters to resolve on this estate alone and there'll be another dozen when we get back home. Anyone who thinks he can put things right with minute precision is a fool. Especially the messes that people make. Anyone who thinks he can do that is the sort that'll hurt the world by trying. You need to know not to be that man." He sat back and smiled. "You'll see that soon enough."

"That to be a judge is to fail?"

"In a way." He leaned forward again. "But only in a trivial way."

"You need more light, Father. I'll get another lamp or two." Quirinius went to the other side of the house to fetch them from a room that faced west. He closed the door behind him, shot the bolt, and then crossed in darkness to the shutters, which he swung open. He looked down into the forecourt where the squares and trapezoids of velvet lawn bordered by low, clipped hedges were turning deep grey in the evening light. The lawns were divided into careful, studied angles by pea-gravel paths, which held their lighter grey immutable, the lack of shading speaking to their care with which they had been levelled and raked smooth as a carpet. Quirinius looked over them, over the villa wall to the road leading away. It was scattered with peasants walking singly, in pairs, and in little groups, going home enwrapped with laughter, resolution, anger or calm.

Too far away for him to see clearly was an oxcart with two figures on the tailboard, women, one long and lean. Pulcheria and Caelia. They were riding into the glow of the sun that set, red, ahead of him. The splendid ruddy light dazzled Quirinius and he could not make out Caelia's face, nor her copper, copper hair, though it glowed in his imagination bright and long as coals beneath white ash and he could see in his mind's eye her blazing head.

Five: The Monastery, October 491 AD

The autumn leaves, now almost hidden by the approaching night, still rustled softly in the thousands of trees all about the monastery, and the rustling seeped softly, like cold, into the meeting house. Against this soft, almost imperceptible sound, Quirinius heard calls, indistinct in the distance and muffled by the shuttered windows. He glanced at Ambiorus, who, younger and sharper of hearing, had noticed it too. The captain rose and crossed the room and, opening the door, exchanged a few words with the guards. He looked back over his shoulder. "Bishop Valerianus is at the gate, Dominē. With thirty men. Footsoldiers."

"And Moderatus? Pennomorix?"

Ambiorus shook his head. "Only the bishop."

Quirinius took a sip of wine. "Footsoldiers? A bunch of rustics supplied by his protector, Bassus." He shook his head. "The bishop alone and no one else to leaven the atmosphere?"

"Dominē?"

"He's a proud man. And so am I. Put the two of us in a room and it won't be large enough." He laughed without humor and rolled his wineglass between his hands. Ambiorus turned back to the open door and squinted into the indigo evening. The abbot rose to stand discretely in a corner and await the prelate. All three were silent some moments until Bishop Valerianus, tall and lean as a staff, strode through the open doorway and past Ambiorus without the slightest hesitation. Once in, he looked quickly about, taking in the meeting-room and those in it before approaching the abbot. He placed his right hand for a moment on the man's head in a blessing, then shrugged off his heavy brown travelling cloak, spattered with mud and felted with horsehair, and handed it to the abbot, who carried it reverently to the far side of the room and hung it on a peg. It was then that he deigned to regard Quirinius.

"Greetings, Flavius Quirinius, Dominus and Senator."

"And Count," Ambiorus added from the doorway.

"Of course. Let us not for a moment neglect that office." He nodded his head in the merest suggestion of a bow. His deep-set, dark eyes glinted above a forced smile.

Quirinius waved a hand casually in a half-salutation and pointed to the chair at the far end of the table before the bishop could decide for himself to sit there. The bishop looked around the room again, as though considering other choices, and then took the proffered seat.

"Your plans, Dominē Quirinius?"

"For the Saxons? I have none."

"Indeed? I can hardly believe that." He nodded vaguely as the abbot set a glass before him and poured wine.

"First, I must know the situation. What men you have brought, what men Moderatus and Pennomorix will bring. Where, precisely, the Saxons are. That sort of thing. You understand." He took the tone one uses with dullards.

"Of course." Bishop Valerianus graciously, so it seemed, ignored the tone.

Ambiorus took his place at the table once again, at Quirinius' right hand. He looked for an instant at the bishop and his distrust was evident. The abbot, emboldened by Bishop Valerianus' presence, said, "Count Quirinius has been gracious enough to share some of his stories with us as we awaited your Eminence's arrival." The bishop favored the little abbot with an unconvincing smile, his dark eyes sparkling in the lamplight. "Has he now? What a remarkable experience!" He turned to look down the length of the table. "Please continue, Dominē Quirinius," he said, his voice thick with hearty, false enthusiasm. Quirinius leaned back and scowled, suspicious that he might be outmaneuvered. Then, as though granting some trifle, he said to Ambiorus, "Now, where did I leave off?"

Ambiorus answered, though he looked at the bishop. "You had told us about your first visit to Dominus Maximianus."

"So I did." He looked down at his place in thought. "He was an important man, old Maximianus." He sighed. "As I said, he and my father had fought years before under Ambrosius Aurelianus."

"Count Ambrosius?" the abbot asked.

"Yes. Emrys Hen, the peasants call him now. The ones who remember. I met him once."

"Quite an honor, I should think," the bishop said, prodding him to speak further.

Quirinius smiled down the table. "Yes, it was, Your Eminence. An odd thing happened to me then." He looked at Ambiorus. "It was a year or so after the business with Hispanus that my father and I paid the old commander a visit."

"Hispanus?" the bishop asked.

"A horse. Just a horse." No explanation. The bishop frowned, puzzled. Quirinius continued. "My father had been charged with asking Ambrosius Aurelianus to come and attend the local senate. It was because of the Saxons, you see. They'd been ranging as far west as Eburacum; the peasants had seen scouts. And besides, Hengist's son had been making noises about cooperating with the Pictish chiefs if the Roman nobles didn't pay him off. The Council hadn't succeeded in drawing Ambrosius out, so it wasn't clear to me how my father was to convince him, but we went anyhow and took that spur of road north from the highway just east of Villa Claudiani. It splits there and heads north—straight as a taut string, so you know right away it's a Roman road though it isn't paved. Hard as iron anyway, the earth tamped down by four hundred years of trudging, man and beast.

"All the same it wasn't heavily settled in that country—the fields had gone wild: there was long grass and dark wild buckwheat that had spilled out of farmsteads ages ago, and here and there a house slumped into ruins. Late in the day, when the sky showed some pink along the horizon, we saw foot-tracks leading off into the woods to the west, so we knew there was a woodcutter nearby, and that meant we'd find a village soon enough, and we did. It was a dense settlement gathered two hundred yards from a fortified villa. Probably half of the inhabitants had moved there from other places in the neighborhood during the first troubles thirty years before.

"It was Ambrosius' villa, and while they're all fortified now, this was more of a stronghold than usual; it imposed on the country. The walls were double, as it were. He'd built an outer keep around the inner stone walls. The outer wall was a ring of wooden peels, split tree trunks set into the earth and weathered grey with the years. Here and there I saw evidence of a fire, black scorches at the foot of the wall and streams of soot to the top, but the attacker, whoever he was, had been driven off years ago."

"Saxons? Jutes?" asked the abbot softly.

"No. Vitolinus," Bishop Valerianus said, nodding to the seat beside him, which the abbot took.

Quirinius continued without a comment. "You could see the villa proper through a heavy wooden gate with a parapet over it. A pair of guards leaned against it and looked down at us casually. The inner walls were of grey stone, and the villa peeped over the top of them; it was of two storeys, and a tower at one corner loomed high enough to overlook the countryside.

"Ambrosius' men waved us in. We'd sent a horseman ahead of us so there was no surprise, but all the same it seemed to me that there weren't many of his men around, and they were rather casual and off-hand in their greetings. Our men were put in stables in the yard between the walls. Supper was already prepared for us, but Ambrosius himself declined to join us. This peeved my father, who sat at the head of the table scowling, but only now and then—he couldn't forget that he was a guest. Was the master ill? Away at another estate? The steward who attended us said, no, he was not.

My father looked pointedly about the room. It smelled of must. The table itself was covered with rings from wine cups. I judged it hadn't been scrubbed in a year, maybe two. The shutters had been opened to the dining room, but there was dust thick on the window sills and the light had an odd, weak and filtered quality. There were tallow-dipped rushlights on the table, but only two, and shadows were beginning to creep out of the corners. The steward, uncomfortable at my father's silent inspection, said, 'He sees very few people these days, Dominē.'

"'We're not just anyone,' I said. The steward nodded but shrugged at the same time to show that he was a reasonable man, but without power.

"'It's because of the Saxons,' my father said. 'But, of course, he knows that.'

"'The Saxons won't come this way, Senator. Dominus Ambrosius' reputation, you understand.'

"'Perhaps not,' my father said, leaning back in his chair and putting a hand flat on either side of his plate. 'But we come here at the behest of the Council. We ask his attendance on behalf of everyone.' The steward sighed, the picture of helplessness. 'You will, of course, put our request that he attend the Council to your master?'

"'Well, as to that, Dominē...' His voice trailed off, and a few moments of silence followed. 'He does indeed know the purpose of your visit. I do not see what I could add that would be of service to Your Excellences.'

" 'In other words, you are afraid,' I said. He did not like that, but half-acknowledged the truth. 'A man should know his place, Dominē. I know mine.' I stared at the fellow with contempt, and finally, he nodded. 'I will try, Your Excellences.'

"'Good man!' my father said. He slapped the table encouragingly.

"After supper we went to our room. The shutters had been thrown back to let the fresh air chase the stale, but all the same the place was gloomy. The sun had slipped down behind the villa walls, and the bedroom was only twilit. My father and I waited for some time, but Ambrosius never called for us, and my father made no complaint about it. He always slept well, for he wasn't generally troubled by conscience. Because of his plodding and his fair attitude to others, I suppose, he never made any great mistakes. But he also never took big chances, which, it seemed to me, was a path to nowhere."

Bishop Valerianus rolled his eyes at the ceiling, but the abbot, despite the bishop's signal, hung on the story.

"My father hadn't really expected to succeed in bringing Aurelianus to the Council—I see that now—though I think he had expected a conference with him. Well, he shook his head ruefully and climbed into bed like the good Christian he was and went off to sleep. But I was prickly in those days and was offended that Ambrosius disdained to see my father and thus snubbed us. He was a hero, true. Still he'd known my father years ago and owed him the courtesy of an interview. Even if he was a great man, the victor of the battles of Cuallop and Thamesis, who had dispatched a dozen Saxons with his own hand, he should have known it was best to meet with other Romans—his own kind—and discuss their mutual concerns.

"So, I sat at the foot of my bed until long after my father was asleep. I pretended to read by the creeping dimness (I remember I had to hold the book up at a comical angle to catch the last glimmer of light). It was the *Little Iliad,* as I remember. And the only noise was when I turned a stiff page or when the ropes of the bed creaked. When the darkness had grown too great for the lamps to overcome, and I could hear my father's deep breathing, I put the book down, took up a lamp and slipped out into the passageway, and began to walk through the house.

"Because night had almost arrived, and because the windows of the house (apart from ours) were shuttered, each room that I passed through was dark as a cave. My lamp pushed the shadows back, but not far, and each room, because the corners were obscure, seemed cavernous—shapeless, even."

"Could you not tell us what the great man's house looked like, Dominē?" the abbot asked, encouraged by the bishop's presence to ask a direct question of Quirinius. The bishop glanced ostentatiously at his fingernails. His mouth was turned down in distaste at the abbot's interest in celebrity.

"On the walls were frescoes, the usual subjects, garlanded heroes with bland expressions, trompe l'oeuil garden scenes, a city at peace seen from a distance. The floors were mosaic in black, white, tawny hues. Hunting scenes, dogs falling on roebucks, short-cloaked men on horseback, hares trembling in thickets. At another time I might have been tempted to study them."

But Quirinius had looked closely. The frescoes, yes, there are those. Perhaps they are skillfully done, perhaps they aren't distorted as they appear to be in the dim light of the single lamp, each figure edging out of the darkness as he passes with the light, hovering for an instant in the twilight of the lamp. A face here or there, elongated by the art or incompetence of the painter or perhaps only by the vagaries of the lamp-flicker. They materialize out of the dark like phantoms, these pictures, and float alarmingly without context in a world of gloom. They are soundless, these faces; their eyes seem to plead, but they are as silent as their models, dead a hundred years.

And Quirinius passes these frescoes slowly, shielding the flame of the lamp with one hand, for he knows that if it dies he will not find his way back. And so, as he saunters along the halls, forgotten faces peep out at him in blends of ochre and cream almost washed of color by the weak light. He is fascinated, but at the same time uneasy; the household is asleep, no one is about, like the dead it seems to him that it sleeps when others are awake. Yes. He stops and listens, strains his ears, hears nothing through the cracks in the shutters across the windows, unless perhaps now and again the delicate squeak of a bat as it cuts through the night. The single flame against the dark means that he must step careful and slow, thus complicit with the rules of this dark realm. He is forced into an unaccustomed caution.

One hall is much like another, which makes the house seem larger, and the rooms leading off are each a mystery, smelling faintly of must and too deep to see far into. There is an armory, though, the door left carelessly open, and lurking inside are shirts of mail, spears whose heads are too rusty to glint in the lamplight, a faded battle standard. All relics of campaigns thirty years past, Quirinius supposes. He goes on, turns a corner and enters another hallway and reaches the end where steps begin to climb. This at last is the way up to the tower. The steps disappear up into darkness, and yet Quirinius has the opposite impression--that somehow they constitute a descent. At the foot of the stairs is a huddle shrouded in a brown blanket, a white-headed old man sleeping on a thin straw pallet. A servant—a watchman if you like—as sound asleep as he can be. Quirinius pauses a moment and then steps over him soundlessly. He begins to climb.

The steps are soft stone and dished in the middle from a century of use, and the stair curves to the right, cramping Quirinius' right arm, the design according with conventional military practice. He switches the lamp from his right to his left hand and proceeds up, soundless, passing now and again a small window open to the night.

At the seventh or ninth turn there's a hint of light--doubtless it seeps from beneath a door, so that the steps in front of him appear without the need of a lamp. Quirinius knows he is coming to the end of his dim passage, that he's twenty steps, perhaps, from the Great Man. Now that he's so close, his indignation isn't enough to buoy him completely, and he grows more thoughtful of his place. He makes his steps heavier, audible, he slides his shoes on the steps to make a shuffling sound, he even coughs lightly like a servant to call attention to himself. So, when he reaches the landing beyond which is the room in which the Great Man sits, Quirinius has, he thinks, perhaps humbled himself a bit much. But then, reflecting on the slight to his father (and thus to himself), he steps up to the door and knocks boldly.

* * *

"And what was he like?" the abbot asks.

"Oh, a model man," Bishop Valerianus says before Quirinius can reply. "The very type of the Good Roman Noble." He stares meaningfully at Quirinius. Valerianus had risen to high position, in part, because of his voice, his tone, his faintly imperious manner. He can say almost anything, even with thudding irony, and get away with it.

"Quite right, Your Eminence," Quirinius says, ostentatiously overlooking the interruption. "But of course, that answer is quite abstract, one might say almost empty. What the abbot here wants to know is what anyone would like to know: *'What was he like?'* Were his dishes from Gaul or Italy? Did he scold his wife in public? What was his view of Divine Grace? Did he have one? What was the name of his favorite hunting dog? Did he abuse his guests by speaking too often of his victories? Did he bring you in with a dirty story and then make you complicit by drawing a laugh out of you?"

"These are trivialities," says the bishop.

"Are they now?" Quirinius turns to face the abbot. "Find out what makes a man laugh, for instance, and you know a good bit about him." The abbot says nothing, only brings his shoulders in, now worried, perhaps, about what his bishop thinks of him for his interest in worldly men.

"My last point is something that even Bishop Valerianus will agree with even though he never laughs himself."

"Laughter is coarse," Bishop Valerianus replies and crosses his arms, irritated to be made the subject of conversation.

"Well, perhaps it is," Quirinius says. "Perhaps it is. In any case, Abbot, you'll learn nothing about our Bishop here if you wait for him to laugh." There was a silence while Valerianus glowered at Quirinius, who in turn smiled at the abbot, who looked at his feet.

"Don't be abashed, Abbot. It is I whom the Bishop disapproves of because, he says, I rob the Church."

"You do, Dominē Quirinius. There's really no use denying it." Valerianus looked about vaguely as though half reflecting on a commonplace and searching for a more interesting topic.

"I have, from time to time, levied a few things from her, that's true, but in her own defense. As a practical fellow, Abbot--you are practical? Yes, of course you are; you are poor. As a practical fellow you may be able to appreciate this more than His Eminence, the Bishop. Paradoxically, though rich, he feels these pinches exquisitely."

The little abbot sat up straight with a childlike dignity. "Please, Dominē Quirinius, do not try to snare me."

"Bravo, Abbot. Say it again so that the bishop is sure to hear." The abbot reddened, but said nothing.

"But we digress. I can sense you want me to go on with my account." There was amusement in Quirinius' voice. He looked at the bishop.

"Go ahead, Dominē Quirinius. We do not expect Moderatus and Pennomorix much before the second watch has passed." He bestowed a fictive smile on Quirinius, who looked away from him. "We take it, from what you said earlier, that you met him in the end despite his..." Bishop Valerianus hesitated, choosing his word. "Despite his reluctance."

"Despite his snub." Quirinius sat back, nettled at the bishop's sardonic tone. "I found my way to his room up in the tower and banged on the door. After a few moments he said 'Enter,' in a resonant voice without a trace of enquiry in it, as though he'd expected a visit. I opened the door and stepped in. He was a big man—that's what struck me first. It seemed that when he stood up he would fill the room, that he must droop his head and brush his shoulders on the ceiling. It was partly illusion and partly suggestion because the room itself was small and hadn't been whitewashed in a while—the walls were smutted grey with lamp smoke and the ceiling beams loured over you. In short, the room was small and the stories about him very large. And so, as he sat there, he was dominating even at his age. He seemed older than I'd imagined, though perhaps he was only sixty. He was wrapped in a shawl worked with purple, and he sat in a fine old chair of dark wood with that tone and depth that only come with age. It had golden finials at the back and feet carved like a lion's. The chair was turned away from the door so that he could look out of the window into the deep night."

"Tell us what he was like, Dominē," said Ambiorus.

Quirinius smiled at the prompt.

"Big, as I said. Imposing as an obelisk, even as he sat. I was abruptly terrified of him and, finally, felt like the fool I was. He turned his head sharply from the window to regard me over his left shoulder for some moments. He had a truly terrific scowl, something it might take a good actor years to polish. He had flinty-blue eyes under bushy silver brows and a neat, trimmed beard like Emperor Zeno on his coins. He rested his arms calmly on the chair arms and then, when he'd had enough of me, resumed looking out the window.

"'Why have you come?' he asked.

"'I am Flavius Quirinius,' I said in rather a grand tone.

"'I know who you are. Do you think I don't realize what goes on in my own house?'

"'Then you know why I'm here.'

"'No.' He turned back to me. 'I know why your father is here.' He stood up and I was surprised to see that, despite his height, his legs were a bit short, like those of Ulysses."

"Who?" asked the abbot. Quirinius winced. Valerianus, by contrast, smirked, but at Quirinius.

"He walked stiffly to the window and leaned out with his big hands on the sill. He looked left and right into the night air. Who knew what he was looking for? He was practically a spook himself, lording it over the midnight countryside from his tower. He turned back, and I looked pointedly at a settle against one wall, but he just as pointedly ignored this.

"'Well?' He was marvelously rumbling.

"'To ask you to see my father.'

"'Really?' He put his hand to his eyes and rubbed them as though I were making him very tired. 'To let him plead with me to take my men and lead everyone against some Saxons somewhere.'

"'He has certain points to make.'

"'He has? Oh, yes. Yes. I'm sure.' He sat down again and pointed at me like a schoolmaster. 'Here's my point, boy, No one convinces me to do anything.' He took his hand down. 'I'm utterly free. Vitolinus and his friends and particularly those weak bastards in the Council. They freed me years ago.' He glanced out at the black sky for a moment and turned back. 'You haven't answered my question.'

"'I believe I have, Dominē Ambrosius.'

"'You're too young to decide something like that.' He looked down and then chuckled. I could see that he was cadging flattery.

"'Well, actually—'.

"'That's more like it, boy. Keep talking. You'll come to it.' He turned and smiled at me with half-closed eyes, drawing me on.

"'Actually, Dominē, to see you.'

"'I knew it.' He slapped his thigh and laughed. We were starting to get along."

"This is ridiculous," the bishop said. "Ambrosius was hardly so shallow and vain."

Quirinius looked over at Ambiorus. "His Eminence here thinks that only faultless men may be great."

The bishop put his chin up an inch. "To the contrary, a man is great precisely to the degree that he conquers his faults." He looked meaningfully at Quirinius.

"I'll try to remember that."

"Your wife understands these things better than do you."

"Because she's instructed by that little spy of yours."

"Father Custinen is not a spy."

"He's a lazy, greasy little spy that I keep on to please my wife, who, if she were more sensible, would interest herself in children or dogs or things that she might hope to understand." He looked about with irritation and settled his eyes on the abbot. He snapped his fingers. "Bring me some water. And be quick." The abbot's face clouded, and he looked over to Bishop Valerianus, who ignored him. After a moment he hopped down from his seat and went away. Quirinius got up and stood before the sitting bishop. "Don't think I don't realize that little bugger is a spy." The bishop smiled as though in pity. "I tolerate him because I've got nothing to hide, because I'd rather know who's a spy than guess at it, and because I think you're intelligent enough to understand that our interests are largely the same."

"He is merely your wife's confessor."

Quirinius nodded. "She hasn't a great deal to confess—she's too afraid of God to act."

"Others, however, might be well served to have a little more fear, don't you think, Dominē Quirinius?"

"Perhaps." Quirinius turned away.

"As to sin, well, let us say that, in certain circumstances, it might seem hard not to stumble."

"What are you maundering about?" Quirinius turned back.

"I speak with your interests at heart, Dominē Quirinius. Let us consider your wife. She has, of course, her duties. Marital duties. Not that she has been forced to submit to them for years." Quirinius scowled; Ambiorus pointedly studied a crack in the daub of the wall. "But I understand, from Father Custinen, that this doesn't trouble her, for her mind is generally on higher things." Quirinius said nothing. The bishop continued. "It is generally understood that you welcome the attentions of a servant girl now and then. A sin. Clearly. But, really, it's Caelia that you miss, isn't it? Caelia, Caelia. Now, that was a serious matter." He shook his head, as though sadly.

A moment passed, the door swung in on its grinding iron hinges, and the abbot came in with a pitcher of water. He glanced curiously at the men's faces, then smoothed his expression. He poured water for Quirinius, who said, "The Bishop necessarily interests himself in the Higher Things. So much so you'd think he that he'd forget that we ordinary men are mired in the world with compromise our only tool." He drank the water. "Of course he doesn't entirely forget—he's not a saint. You don't claim to be a saint, now, do you, Your Eminence?"

Ambiorus chuckled quietly in support of his master.

"I see you decline to answer. Very wise. Abbot, let us recall the Bishop's reticence in later years, you and I, when it might more easily be misconstrued as humility. A trait that seems required of saints. Humility. Ambiorus!"

"Yes, Dominē?"

"Have you ever thought how few bishops—men of power, really—have turned out to be saints?"

"No, Dominē."

"Or soldiers," Bishop Valerianus said.

"Or soldiers. But then my ambitions, like my life, are limed by the twigs of the world."

"How poetic."

"It is, rather." He turned from the bishop and looked at the paintings along the top of the walls and across the ceiling: angels, saints, evangelists elongated fantastically, and all in dull earthy tones. They looked to Quirinius in that moment like the work of a child. He closed his eyes and thought back to the Great Man.

* * *

The Estate of Ambrosius Aurelianus, 463 AD

Ambrosius Aurelianus had laughed, and it was short and abrupt like the creak of a dry hinge. "Was the door closing or opening?" asked Quirinius of himself in that instant.

"So, Quirinius, to see me. You're a bold young man. Years ago I'd have been glad to see that, might have asked you to join me. Where do you get it from? Not your father. Your mother?"

"Perhaps. I don't know. She's been dead a long while." He thought the poignancy of the answer might open the older man up further, but Ambrosius only sat staring, his elbows on the chair arms and chin propped on his folded hands. Finally his eyes took on a glitter. "Go ahead. Sit down."

When Quirinius had taken the settle, Ambrosius glanced to his right to a table with a beaker and food on it, eggs, walnuts, something red and leathery. A pomegranate? Here in Britain? It was almost magical. He tossed Quirinius a walnut, which he caught in the air without a glance. The old man grinned.

"Can you break it open?" Quirinius looked down at it, tan and hard. He wondered what the old man was getting at. He intended something; his eyes were crafty.

"Of course you can't. Not with your bare hands. Not even you. Here." He tossed Quirinius another one. "Now you can do it. Place one against the other and squeeze with both hands. They'll both shatter."

"Everyone knows that trick," Quirinius said and cracked them open deftly.

"Do they? Do they indeed?" The crafty eyes were on him. "Do you?" Quirinius, puzzled, held the broken nuts out for Ambrosius to see.

"Some things are known and other things, too, are *known,*" the old man said. Quirinius sat back and warily watched Ambrosius' sly expression. He began to eat the nutmeats to show his nonchalance. He'd suspected the man was a little mad, and he wanted to show himself that he wasn't alarmed by it, wasn't out of his depth. The two watched each other for several moments.

"Broad lessons can be drawn from particulars."

"I won't implore you to explain yourself, you know."

"You can see it would be useless," Ambrosius replied. "You can see that much—that's good for a young man. A start. And you have your dignity. You need that in this world too—don't let anyone tell you otherwise. But don't let it blinker you." Ambrosius turned to the window and regarded the night, giving Quirinius a good look at his profile in the lamplight. He turned back. "I'm going to tell you why I won't march against the Saxons. I hadn't intended to; it seemed too much bother, but there's a lesson in it. About dignity perhaps. And I like you, Boy. Perhaps we're alike. If so, then you're headed for great things--as great as this little corner of the world allows. And for trouble.

"The bugbear was the Saxons, oh, thirty years ago. They'd behaved themselves for a while after the Uortigern brought them in."

"I saw him once."

"Don't interrupt. I'm telling you important things. The Saxons were sent against the Picts. We set them like trained mastiffs on those painted savages, and they pulled them down and tore them up. The Uortigern sent a few Romans; I was one of the officers over them. There wasn't much for us to do—you couldn't command them much more than to lead them to the Picts and tell them to go at it. But they were willing enough and wanted to impress us, and we'd seen to it that each man had a sword and helmet. They love the man who equips them, you know. A Saxon'll die for you if you give him a mail shirt.

"It was a horrid, mucky kind of fighting, and they didn't give quarter. After a couple of years the Picts faded up into the crags and seemed to disappear like mist. They're still up there in the dark places, of course, waiting like goblins for their chance. But they're finished and the Saxons are here to stay."

"The Irish are settling north of the Wall," Quirinius said, to show he was paying attention.

"I've heard that. No matter. It'll take them another fifty years to strengthen. It was the Uortigern's hope that the Picts might stir up some trouble for the Saxons—he told me so—and keep the bastards occupied. But it didn't happen—wherever the Saxons had gone there was nothing left but those round loose-stone Pict forts with spirals incised everywhere. Empty, creepy places, otherworldly. So, now. Where was I?"

"You are the Count of the Britains. You still hold the post. My grandfather says that it was conferred upon you by Flavius Modestius when he was recalled to Italy by the Emperor Honorius."

Ambrosius waved a hand. "I relinquish the title. A mere name. Every clan chief to the west with twenty men, a strong house and a valley to look down on calls himself a king. They're hardly even kinglets. So long as he can speak British and claim his great-great-great grandfather was a king, why, then, he's a great man. Some claim their ancestors beat Claudius. As though Claudius and the legions never cut through them like an axe through lard and then built cities where their people had been squatting in marshes. And the common ruck believe them. The world doesn't know what truth is; it doesn't want to know."

"Or he claims that Carausius set up his grandfather."

The old man grimaced, but nodded. "Anyone's a good emperor so long as you can tie your legitimacy to him. Don't mention Carausius to me again." The old man was suddenly restless—he stood and looked as though he wanted to pace, but there wasn't room. He sat again.

"I fought the Saxons for many years, and I did pretty well at it. The trick is speed and concentration, you see. Get ahead of them or get behind them and outnumber them, at least at the critical point. Run away if you have to, but keep control of your men. That's the difference between soldiers and warriors. Soldiers can pull back, even run away, but they'll regroup. Warriors—for them it's just the fighting, and when they're beaten, or think they are, they dissolve like mud bricks in the rain. So, whenever I had enough men, and obedient ones, the outcome was pretty certain."

"As at Thamesis."

The old man shrugged it off. "Yes. But it was much like the other battles—just bigger. I had two hundred soldiers then, a hundred of them horsemen. Oh yes, a huge number, don't you agree?" The old man shook his head ruefully. "When we were in the Empire three thousand was a small army." After a moment he took up the story again. "The Saxons were crossing a ford. There must have been a good five hundred of them and so they'd taken a road. They wanted to move fast. And they do. Even though they're footmen they cover ground pretty well—not much armor and no supplies—they eat as they move along, stripping the country as they go. The peasants hate that. When you campaign, don't you do that to them. You need friends in the countryside, guides, informants and so on.

"I reckoned that half of them had waded across to the western bank. They were soaked to the armpits, cold and tired. We had come over to the eastern bank the day before, so they didn't expect us there, and we attacked the tail of their column. Got it to turn about and stop. All it took was a demonstration—some display and shouting. As I thought, the Saxons nearest the ford kept crossing, but in a hurry, stumbling. A few were washed away, and the others on the far bank couldn't cross back against the press still coming over.

"That left only about two hundred and fifty or so to face us, and we just swept along either side of their line, forcing them together, and then they broke, some running down the road, others running through us and crossing the fields for the woods in the distance. We ran them down and killed them individually. It's not hard when they break and run. You can kill as many as you like from behind.

"It's not that we annihilated them as the ballads say—perhaps we killed seventy, but the rest were so demoralized that when we crossed upstream later that day and reappeared on the road ahead of those that had crossed, they probably thought we were a second army. They made a shield wall and shuffled back to the river and crossed and went home. In the night we could hear wailing. I was jubilant about the outcome, but when I think of it it now, so many years later, it saddens me. Odd, that."

The young man watched the old man's face as he spoke, and, despite Ambrosius' last words, he noted a quiet, unwanted pride diffuse through it. "At the time how did you feel about it?" The old man stared hard at him for a long moment, and then smiled, harsh. "I felt like a lion—like a dragon, rather. I felt that the earth would shiver under my steps, that the stone roads would tremble like a quaking bog beneath my horse's hooves."

"Wouldn't you like to feel that way again?"

Ambrosius laughed sharply, harshly, like a dog. "No. Not at all." He crossed his arms over his chest and pinched his lips together, peevish. He turned to Quirinius. "You puzzle at the answer, but it's simple. Exhilaration is seductive and blinding as Calypso's eyes."

"But what does it blind you to?" Quirinius asked, trying to make sense of what he heard.

"To everything. In my case, to plots and plans. But you speak in a larger sense, don't you? Of course. Like all young men you're earnest. Well, so are your brothers, my son. So are your brothers."

"I don't understand you." In spite of himself, he was growing tired of the old man.

"Of course not." Ambrosius rose and went to the window. "I'll make it plain—less tiresome.

"For fifteen years I pounded a saddle with my rump all around the countryside running after Saxons. Occasionally Picts too. And when I wasn't doing that, I was settling my rump into a chair in some drafty council hall while important men-- men like me, to be sure!— maundered and havered about the state of the land. And what should happen to me for all my efforts? Vitolinus levelled one of my estates because I'd punished some of his clients. And before I knew it I had a war on my hands. He had the brass to attack this very estate—I've left the scorch marks on the wall to remind me of him and what he did.

"And he killed my boys, both of them. He knew they were headstrong, and he engaged them when I was up in the north on some pointless excursion. They were young—younger than you, and each was more impetuous than the other. I can just imagine them drawn into the wood where he killed them. Had them killed, rather. Here the old man shook his head. "They were good boys and I never had others."

Quirinius said nothing. He clasped his hands between his knees and looked at the floor. Things were not going as he had hoped, but he couldn't see where they had gotten tangled.

"And here's the point, my young friend," he said, wagging his finger once again. "I appealed to the Provinicial Council, but they did nothing. Useless." He sat musing for a few moments.

"But I killed Vitolinus," Ambrosius resumed. "I killed him. He imagined he could flee—elude me. Hide in the country in some dark niche. It wouldn't have mattered where he'd gone. I'd have pulled him from the cess of a privy in Rome if that's where he'd hidden himself. But that wasn't where he was. He'd gone to "castle" in Cambria, up in the mountains. It was a timber fortlet hanging from a crag, but that didn't save him because I burned the place and him with it. I remember the smoke was black and greasy. His men were burning, and Vitolinus himself appeared along the parapet smoking like a brand, and he screamed with a sound I could hear from fifty yards away, harsh like a sail ripping in a storm—so harsh I knew that his voice was gone forever. And then he burned with the beams of his fort. I had the ashes searched until we found his bones, and once they were gathered I had them broken and scattered. He was a Roman but he turned on his kind, so in the end he was worse than a barbarian and deserved nothing better."

Quirinius had listened quietly. Then he said, encouragingly, "You're modest: that fight—that battle along the Thamesis—kept the Saxons west of Londinium for a dozen years."

"But they are there now, squatting in the city that welcomed Constantius Chlorus. And what's worse, they took it without a fight. You can ask our Roman friends—they won't deny it. They're evasive, of course—they say, 'We don't need that old town because we live like kings in the country.'

"They do. And so they can turn their eyes from what's happening around them."

Ambrosius snatched up a pair of walnuts and cracked them in his hands. "You see the heart of the problem. You're astute for a young fellow. We live as nobles have always done—on the country. Oh, yes, we're a better sort than our British ancestors—whoever they were, proud illiterates burdened with supersition and broadswords. At least we read and write and don't sacrifice our criminals in wicker cages to savage gods. And now and then one of us goes to Rome to see what's there."

"There's more to it than that. Much more," Quirinius said.

The old man put the nuts uneaten on his table. He closed his eyes. "But is it enough?"

"We have to think so."

"Do we? Romanitas, that great aether, if you like, that suffuses the world."

"Yes, that is exactly it!" Quirinius said, who liked it very much.

"It was made of tougher stuff when I was a boy."

"It will be sturdy again. You see, that's the point. The Council—my father asks you as a Roman to join us, your fellows, and scourge the area of Saxons."

"I see, despite the vivid detail and intrinsic interest of my story, that you miss the point. The world is already too disordered, and we Romans don't stick by each other."

"Surely that's an exaggeration," Quirinius said. "Vitolinus can't have been enough to undo everything."

"Vitolinus could not have have acted without the connivance of others. He wouldn't have dared."

They sat in silence a moment.

"I gave everything up to my fellow Romans—and now I've got nothing left."

"You need some faith."

"Don't lecture me about faith in my fellows."

"No?"

"You're young, and so you judge it reasonable to pit your ideas against my experience. A common error of youth. Twenty years will teach you different."

Ambrosius gathered his shawl more snugly around him. The two of them sat silent for a few moments, glaring at each other. Finally, Quirinius sighed sharply and stood up. "If you will no longer fight, then whom do you suggest in your place?"

Ambrosius put his hand to his chin and looked down in thought. Then he looked up with a wicked smile. "I recommend someone who is simple enough to think he can fight and win. Now who might that be?" Quirinius shrugged and looked at the old man. Ambrosius stood up, once again filling the room. He turned slowly about, as though looking for something long neglected, something whose place is half forgotten. "Ah!" He stepped past Quirinius and threw up the lid of a trunk in a shadowed corner. He bent to rummage about in the disorder of its contents and pulled out pair of wooden tablets closed like a book on one another and joined along one edge with a purple silken lace. He opened the diptych and glanced at the writing on the panels, shook his head gently and chuckled to himself. He abruptly snapped the panels shut and handed them to Quirinius.

"I pass my office on to you."

Quirinius stared at the old man, baffled and silent.

"Try to grasp what I'm saying, you young fool."

"What is this thing?"

"Thirty years ago the Count of the Britains, Flavius Modestius Acindynus, was recalled to Ravenna with his troops. Some threat, Huns, Avars, Franks. The details escape me now. I was leading a hundred of my own personal soldiers under him as federates. Before he left for the continent he took it upon himself to elevate me to the office." He pointed to the tablets. "This is my commission, if you will. Thus I became Ambrosius Aurelianus, Count of the Britains. Read it for yourself. *'Potestate imperiale, officis Comitis Britanniarum, viri clarissimo senatori Ambrosio Aureliano, conferta est manu Flavii Modestii Acindyni...'* That kind of thing. Good Latin too, if you like officialese. Did he have the authority to so act? Perhaps. The Council accepted his decision."

Quirinius held the diptych out to Ambrosius, but the old man waved it away. "Get along with you, my young Count. Leave me to my little province." He indicated the fields beyond the window. "It's enough for me these days."

Quirinius, unable to think of a thing to say, left without a word. The old man watched him go with narrowed eyes, then chuckled to himself after he had gone. He sat down and turned to the window to watch the cold, impassive stars.

Six: The Monastery, October 491 AD

"The Council was a disappointment to me," Quirinius said. "It was a thorough disappointment, the sort that discovers itself to you immediately in some subtle way, not like, say, when a pretty girl smiles at you with bad teeth. No, more subtly, as when a physician comes to attend you with botched shoes and a mended satchel, and you know instinctively that there's despair—or sadness anyway—in his train. It was like that.

"The Council was held at Corinium, in the basilica on the forum. Not bad, I suppose, when it was built, but there were brown smudges here and there on the floor and a long dark flume down one of the walls to show the roof was leaking.

"About fifty men in attendance—a good number really; the fear of the Saxons had brought them out, though they weren't afraid enough, as it developed. There were fifteen true senators such as old Maximianus, men whose fathers and grandfathers had held the office in the time of Valentinianus or Anthemius. There was a pair of bishops as well. A stout little red-faced fellow round as a melon, Gerontius, I think his name was, and a weedy, sallow fellow with a cast eye. Now, what was his name? I'll call him Strabo.

"You could see at a glance that they loathed each other. There was some dispute simmering in the background. Ostensibly over doctrine, perhaps some concerns about free will." Quirinius glanced slyly at Bishop Valerianus. "I remember suspecting that it might have had more to do with parish boundaries where one jurisdiction faded into the next." The Bishop Valerianus studied his fingernails, declining to be drawn further into the matter, apart from the comment: "You do have a weakness for cynicism, Dominē Quirinius."

Quirinius shrugged, indifferent. He looked up in the distance,

111

recalling the two bishops. "Each had surrounded himself with a pack of black-robed priests to give him more dignity than the other.

"And a number of large landowners attended, curials, not senators, but Romans nonetheless—men with money and land and interests in protecting what was theirs.

"'The Guledig, Marc, was there. He claimed two dignities—to be a senator and a king. It shows you the state of the times that he could assert such an incongruity and people would accept it. He wasn't alone—two or three other kingkins had travelled from the west to attend as well. Gerren Llygesoc of Dumnonia and three brothers, kinglets of Gwynllwg, Penychen, Edeligion. Place-names that wrack a civilized tongue. They wore shaggy beards and checkered cloaks and pretended they could read. There was a sprinkling of even smaller chiefs who at least had the dignity not to claim royalty. And the young Uortigern was there, like an embarrassing memory. He kept pretending to his father's power, you know, but, with the Saxons in revolt, he was just a phantom, nothing more than a reminder of the awful mistake his father had led us into.

"So, there you had them, some Romans, each man complacent or suspicious or worried according to his nature; some Briton chiefs pretending to culture, and the ecclesiastics with their eyes to heaven and their hands on deeds. And somewhere, so it was said, three hundred Saxons hovered and sniffed about the edge of our country.

"The little forum outside was filled with retainers who trolled about the grass-plagued flagstones, happy to make a holiday in a city— more or less. You can imagine the great men in the basilica sitting in the fine old chairs they had brought, each with a secretary sitting below him on a stool. The kinglets from the west, in particular, needed them to explain the Latin they couldn't follow. The room, though large, was fairly light because the frescoes had been whitewashed over a hundred years before in view of the clergy's delicate sensibilities, and then no one could find painters skilled enough to execute anything worthwhile. So, there we sat, hovering, as it were, between two worlds.

"I couldn't help thinking of the great senate in Rome, as it is in Livius; even with all the bluster, slyness, bumbling and chicanery he tells about, it somehow always retained its dignity. By contrast what could be expected of this limping council? And yet, one works with what one has.

"The first order of business was to determine precedence. The Saxon Aelle had just spent the summer fighting and insinuating himself into lands along the southern coast, and there was real fear he might be about to snatch another parish or two of Roman land. All the same, there we were arguing over precedence. Who would sit where. Who would speak first.

"Ambrosius himself was partly to blame. He'd been head of the Council—he still was, nominally, but he had abandoned his fellows and snuggled into his aerie in the country, and no one had the humility to suggest another's name at the head of the council roll. Each senator felt equally entitled to assert his position, but only through indirection and by implication. Oh, those senators apart from my father and Maximianius were a genteel bunch and full of dignity. What a delay and marring of the whole congress until, by some glacial process, Nonianus Bassus got himself acclaimed head of the Council. He was old even then, though not quite doddering. That came later."

"Perhaps you are harsh to the memory of those men," Bishop Valerianus said, looking up from his fingernails. Quirinius chuckled ruefully, shaking his head as he cast his mind back twenty-five years. "Just understand that Aelle's men were sharpening their cutlery while we spent a morning deciding whose chair would be set in the place of honor near the back wall."

* * *

"The point, as always, was to mount a good defense. Now, we magnates could stay on our estates and, with armed peasants and retainers, wait to see what would happen. The towns could do the same. Knock down a derelict house or two, patch the town wall with the rubble, raise a militia, train it a month, and trust it to repel the

Saxons. Not always successful. No. But often.

"We Quirinii were powerful enough to have looked after our own interests, at least for the near future. We could defend the largest three of our estates with no one's help if we had to. Albinius Maximianus could, in all likelihood, have done much the same. The difficulty was this, that neither my father nor Maximianus had the military reputation of Ambrosius Aurelianus, the sort of reputation that inclines men other than one's own clients and retainers to follow. And, frankly, we had too few soldiers for raids and adventuring against Aelle's Saxons if a campaign depended upon us alone. We needed general agreement among the senators and magnates to band together a force large enough to discourage Aelle, and to stop him if he crossed out of his territory.

"When Honorius had written to the British councils years ago and told us to see to our own defenses, our family took on what remained of the Third Thracian Lancers—nominally five hundred men but by then about a quarter of that—and we divided them among our three principal estates. The Maximiani had private soldiers—bucellarii, or 'biscuit-eaters'—about as many men as we had at first, but then they'd reduced them to about sixty when the times grew quiet for a few years, and they felt the cost of so supporting so many men. And only about twenty of them were mounted. Despite their number, the Maximiani called them, rather grandly, a mounted cohort, just like so many of the troops that had minded the Wall for hundreds of years. The other senators had their own little private armies, but none of them had more than forty men, most of them foot-soldiers, if that's the right term for bodyguards and armed rent-collectors. Still, band them together and you might raise five or six hundred with enough equipment and nags to stare down the Saxons—even to raid south down to the Saxon Shore and keep them at home.

"The *reguli*, the kinglets, now they had men—most of them altogether savage—from the Cambrian Mountains. They had ferocity in their favor, but their equipment, when they had any, was poor, and they had no discipline. None whatsoever. Just like today. If we could levy some of these kings' men and join them with our own, equip them halfway like soldiers and teach them some discipline, then that would be splendid. Useful anyway.

"But the kinglets would have none of it when Maximianus proposed it. They declined in British—their secretaries translated their words into poor Latin in order to meet the dignity of the occasion. At first, I thought it was a desire to protect their followers. After all, these men came from the hilly west and were poor—they were hard for the Saxons to get at and not rich enough to be attractive. They would rather have us than Saxons as their neighbors, but they were less alarmed at the prospect of Saxon raiding, so we couldn't move them to join us purely on the ground of fear. No. Wealth had to come into it, and glory. They could be moved, but the lever was short and gave us little advantage. These kings wanted to lead their men into battle themselves because—to put it bluntly— that was their only excuse for being kings. Without battles they had no legitimacy. They were like Saxons in that regard, except that you could understand them when they spoke. More or less.

"One solution was obvious, at least to us, the senators. With enough gold or silver we could tempt a few hundred of these Britons—the common ruck, forget their leaders—and then, brigaded with our men under a competent Roman leader, we could face the Saxons with some confidence. But where to get that gold and silver? The answer, of course, was obvious." Quirinius stood and strolled about the room with his arms folded, smiling down at the abbot and the bishop. The bishop looked away in irritation; the abbot looked away in solidarity, but peeped over now and again furtively, held by the story. After a few moments Quirinius called out "Ambiorus!" very sharply. He had his back to the man.

"The churches, Dominē," he replied.

"Exactly!" He laughed a moment. "So, the plan was proposed: the church would give us twenty pounds or so of silver and ten of gold from various religious paraphernalia, and we would equip a little army. A couple of Saxon routs and we'd have recovered enough of the stuff that they'd plundered to repay the loan."

"You make it sound so easy," Bishop Valerianus said.

"Well, it would have been," Quirinius replied with some petulance. "I've proven that time and again. The hardest thing isn't to defeat the Saxons; it's to get people to pay for it.

"My father and Maximianus proposed and argued, cajoled and wheedled, but it was quickly apparent that there would be no consensus. The little kings were suspicious of us. In short, they distrusted their betters, though they couldn't admit it—probably not even to themselves. It's self-knowledge, I believe, that most men cannot tolerate. They crack under it like poplars in a storm."

Bishop Valerianus smiled and nodded almost imperceptibly.

"But to continue. Even with the kings so suspicious, we Romans might have prevailed if there'd been enough money at hand. But the church balked at this." Quirinius shook his head at the idiocy of it all. "The bishops made it clear that they wouldn't part with a single coin—not even a brass candlestick. And furthermore, one of them claimed he was suspicious of people who would beat a priest. Incredibly, he brought up the business about Silverius at Castra Minuta from years before. He utterly ignored the bolstering I'd given the church at that time."

"Indeed, why should he have opened the church treasuries? Your faith—the True Faith—is the very ground and frame of your world. He knew well that a man should hurry to defend it from his own substance."

"You idealists are all the same: simple men with dangerously simple ideas that you force the world into. You drive it into a mold with a wedge and a maul in a delirium of blows. Not simple men. Simpletons, really."

Bishop Valerianus snorted, stood, and crossed the room to a window on the side away from Quirinius. He opened a shutter on the night and looked out, then cocked his head to listen intently. He frowned.

"In the end, for all their principles, it came down to this--the bishops feared the loss of a little wealth more than they did the depredations of the Saxons. Of course, how could one expect perspective from men with their gaze only on God?"

The bishop swung the shutter closed with a sharp clack and drew his mantle about him closely. He ignored the Count's irony. Quirinius pointed at the closed window. "By the way, you didn't hear any Saxons out there, Your Eminence? No enemies hereabouts?"

"No. No enemies."

There was more to Quirinius' story. It was not merely the little British kings who were obstinate, not merely the bishops whose lack of foresight he could use to nettle Bishop Valerianus. In fact, the Romans themselves had been divided. He thought back about it, and kept his thoughts to himself. Why not? Times had changed, after all.

* * *

The Council at Corinium Dobunnorum, 463 AD

"Provocation must be avoided," a senator said. Quirinius had not seen the man before, but he knew by reputation who he must be: Eugenius Ater, a grossly fat man with buttery, curdled skin showing around his neck and an oily sheen on thin, but perfectly-dressed hair of an intense yellow impossible for a man of fifty. His hands were begauded with half a dozen rings, each with a polished ruby or emerald the size of a sparrow's egg, and his wrists were circled with gold bracelets. Quirinius supposed those gauds cost a good farm or two. His life was an open scandal, but one tacitly tolerated by the Church, to which he was quite generous. He was a comfortable man who declined to rise when he spoke; he knew his worth and made it clear to others. "It is to be expected that these Saxons or Jutes— whatever they are—when once they settle and improve their land, will be hostages to it as we are to ours. Then they will have something to risk, not merely the squalid little lives they are so happy to lose in glory. Let them develop a little comfort; that will hamper them more than ten thousand soldiers. In the meantime, we must let them have their way for a few years—"

"What? Ten? Twenty? A generation?" Maximianus crossed his arms and tilted his head against the back of his chair, his eyes closed, like a very weary man.

"Possibly, possibly."

"And at what cost?" Another voice asked from the back of the hall. Quirinius noticed a slight echo.

Eugenius waved a moist hand dismissively. "A few hundred acres—even a few thousand." He shrugged to show that, to great men such as they, this was nothing.

"And what of the people? Our tenants?" a curial called from the back.

The fat senator sighed deeply, as though with real concern. "The peasants are like weeds. One hates to see any of them rewarded before his time, but all the same they spring up numerous and hardy after every difficulty." He smiled showing his perfect, false teeth and turned his head about the room, pained at having to remind everyone of a sad truth that was, well, so obvious.

"Perhaps we should be certain what is meant by 'provocation.'" This suggestion came from Quirinius' father, who rose and spoke in a deep, loud voice. His son was impressed at the assertion in his tone; the threat of the Saxons had brought a streak of boldness out of him that he hadn't seen before.

"Reprisals, I should have said." Eugenius looked about significantly, carefully showing a note of impatience. "In order to be clear to everyone, let me say 'reprisals.'"

"Reprisals are the best weapon we have, Senator." Maximianus stood up as he spoke and looked over and down at Eugenius. He turned to the rest of the council. "Gentlemen, these people are savage. They are not Christian, they are not to be trusted at their oath, and they are provoked equally by weakness and by restraint, which they cannot distinguish."

"You are quite a judge of these people, Dominē Albinius Maximianus," Eugenius said.

"Oh, yes. Yes, I am. I have earned that. Some few of my holdings

118

lie to the south, and I have lost two of them. And in years past I fought these men under Ambrosius Aurelianus. These are things you have neither suffered nor undertaken."

Eugenius sighed to show how tolerant he was of Maximianus' trifling concerns. "I have sent men to fight."

"As few as you reasonably could, and the most unfit that you could dredge up."

"I owe a duty to my tenants not to risk them on casual adventures."

"What a tender concern you now express for peasants."

"The cases are easily distinguished," Ater said, looking away in irritation.

"The defense of our homes is hardly a casual adventure; even the short-sighted will see that." This from Quirinius' father, now taking up Maximianius' side.

"Let us not grow too personal, gentlemen," Nonianus Bassus said, coming slowly to his feet. "Let us remember our dignity, our accustomed courtesy."

Quirinius' father rose to confront the old fool. "We no longer have the luxury of courtesy, Dominē Nonianus. We are in difficulty, and over-refinement will leave us strangers in our own country."

"It appears to me that you are apprehensive of allowing life to present you with its beautiful mosaic," Ater said. Quirinius' father stared at him incredulously. "I prefer a mosaic of my own making, Dominē Eugenius. A true man does."

Eugenius clucked his tongue and looked down, shaking his head as though in wonder at the view. Maximianus sat down, crossed his arms and laughed sharply. Quirinius smiled at his father's boldness and at his family's new relationship with the Maximiani—no longer one of quarreling, or even indifference, but of alliance.

His father continued. "I doubt you will remain with us another twenty years, Dominē Eugenius, given your age. And you leave no one behind."

"Unless perhaps your sycophants?" Maximianus said quietly, but very, very clearly, pretending to study the clouds beyond the window near which he sat. There was some suppressed laughter from the edges of the council and a sighing like wind through a bush as the exchange was whispered in British to the west country chiefs.

The Senator went on, "Your world is circumscribed to the mere extent of your comfortable existence, which you hope to keep tranquil until your death." He hesitated for emphasis, and then added, "All at the expense of your neighbors."

Eugenius surged to his feet, and he was impressive, swaying in his anger. The other senators, now silent, shifted uneasily in their seats; there was more whispering from the Latin secretaries to their kinglets. "You are deluded. All of you." And he swung his massive oily head around to take in each face in turn. "Your world is exhausted, spent, gone, but you haven't noticed it. And what was so magnificent about it to begin with? What did it offer anyone that isn't offered now? I speak *sub specie aeternitatis;* I cannot help it. Men are born, live and die. This is reality and hasn't changed. All the rest was illusion, some thin and tawdry veil of philosophy draped around the unpleasantness of existence. There were a few nice toys, yes, but do we need them? Only a fool could stand like you men, with power and leisure at the brink of death, and yet strive to do more than enjoy what you still have." He stopped for a moment and looked around at the council, glancing into every face. "It is a slur upon me to suggest that my measured inaction puts us in danger. Quite to the contrary. Action courts danger. You may depend upon it. We reached an uneasy accommodation with the Saxons years ago—"

"And still they prick at us and drift west when they can," Senator Quirinius said.

"And that accommodation is worth the loss of little land. If we are seen to gather forces of any great strength, we will certainly provoke them to action. Let me make clear what should be obvious. Any man who promotes this idea of unneeded defense is more dangerous than the barbarian whom he claims to fend off." He stood silent a moment drawing everyone's attention to his next words, looked with some deliberation at the faces about him, and added, "Furthermore, I suggest to this council that it is unwise to slur the powerful." He beckoned to Bishop Strabo, who obediently approached him, and, putting his head close to the cleric, he whispered for several moments, while the council watched, curious and ignorant about what was said. And then, without a backward glance, Eugenius Ater, Clarissimus and Senator, left the council, his attendants in train.

"Perhaps we can get down to business now," Maximianus said blandly to the remaining councillors.

The weedy bishop, Strabo, still standing where he had conferred with Ater, said "You have offended a great man."

Maximianus snorted.

"A great man," the bishop repeated.

"Great? In what way great, Your Eminence?" Quirinius asked. He avoided his father's glance. The bishop turned to this unexpected quarter.

"The man's greatness is evident to all." Meaning, Quirinius supposed, that because Ater had birth, wealth and advantage he was, therefore, great in some transcendent way that had nothing to do with accomplishment, dutifulness, honor or sacrifice. It made Quirinius think for a moment of the heroes in Homer—Menelaus or Achilles perhaps, going about the world saddled with an epithet "godlike," for instance, despite their tantrums, vanity, cheating or simple brutality. But they, at least, were heroes—dangerous to their enemies and unashamed to try rendering the world a bit safer, no matter how many orphans they made along the way. Ater, by contrast, was not only prepared to gamble that, through calculated inaction, he could draw out his last years in vicious comfort before the sky fell in, but, further to this, he had the brass to suggest that anyone who took initiative was a dangerous fool. Quirinius found this an intolerable provocation.

Bishop Strabo continued to speak, his good eye on Quirinius and his lip flickering back in a tic from frustration or fear. "I do not attend this council to be questioned by whelps, no matter whose."

121

He sat down grandly and looked away with grace, speaking in an undertone to a young priest—his secretary—who appeared to take a note. The young man nodded slowly, as with great wisdom.

Quirinius' father rose abruptly to unsmutch the family honor. He made a perfunctory remark that even a divine of the highest should think most carefully before rebuking one of the Quirinii, be he ever so young. It was all formula, all gesture, but he was obliged to do it. He sat down, shifted himself until he was comfortable and then kicked Quirinius carefully and sharply on the ankle, all the while looking away and maintaining an admirably serene composure. Without looking at his son, he whispered. "You leave it to me to provoke the clergy."

The second bishop rose, the round florid Gerontius. He began to speak softly, and so the men gathered in the hall had to listen closely. Quirinius admired the man's technique. Some leaned forward unconsciously, some of the others—the older ones—put hand to ear and turned their heads sideways, listening like birds. "Eugenius would appear to be a quietist," he said.

"As should be any good Christian," the other bishop added, nodding his approval of the sentiment. It was evident that, at least on the score of defending Eugenius Ater, the churchmen could agree.

"Why continue to defend him?" A voice asked from the back. "He is gone."

"Because reports will fly from this meeting like ravens." Here Maximianus paused for an instant. "They may speak of our reverend bishops. May the reports be favorable." There was some muted laughter again, but only from the shadows at the back of the hall where faces were indistinct. From a handful others there came almost inaudible hisses of disapproval. A priest in Gerontius' entourage stood suddenly and looked back find the laughers, but the moment had passed. He sat down, huffing. Nonianus Bassus rose and called out "Gentlemen! Gentlemen!" to signal his enthusiasm for decorum, if not for the resolution of the questions at hand.

Quirinius' father took up where Maximianus had left off. "I

would understand Dominus Ater to suggest—and this is putting the best construction upon his actions—lack of them actually—and those of our reverend bishops—that we must wait and see what actions God takes in this world."

"It's in the nature of omnipotence, Dominē, that only his will is done." Bishop Gerontius smiled at the senator and then looked away as though he held no further interest. But all the same, he was listening. And his priest-secretary was watching, his eyes narrowed.

"Indeed. But still, it would appear that, through God's omnipotence, some of us, at least, might be compelled to act in his interest."

"You are presumptuous."

"No doubt. But perhaps that presumption is only a little push from God. Coming through the back door, as it were."

There was some noise of approval from the senators and curials. Quirinius watched his father with great pride.

"Some may recall that the Church over a hundred years ago, discouraged Christians from serving in the army. But, once the great Constantinus embraced the True Faith, this stricture disappeared as though it had never been. And Christians filled the armies of Rome and not, I might add, only to fight the enemies of God; the Church never spoke against their service, even in civil wars where Christian fought Christian."

"But the Church deplored those contests," the lanky bishop said, looking over the back of his chair at the elder Quirinius.

"As it should have. But now we face not only barbarians, but heathen barbarians. The Goths were Christians before they ever made their home in the Empire and carved out their kingdoms in the middle of civilization. And the Vandals. And the Gepids, for that matter."

"But not the Huns, you will recall, Senator."

Quirinius' father hesitated a moment frowning as though posed with a difficult problem. The florid, stout bishop rested a hand upon the back of his chair and gave the senator a hard, cruel smile. He thought the argument already won. "And the Huns—pagans that they were—have been utterly destroyed by their own subjects. Utterly destroyed. They have disappeared like a field of snow on a spring afternoon."

"By the hand of God, surely. It is, after all, in the nature of omnipotence."

"Certainly." Bishop Gerontius regarded him closely, uneasy at his concession.

"And God's instrument was, as I recall, the Christian Gothic people." He paused and let the silence draw the unwilling archbishop along.

"God acts in the world. Who can deny it?" Gerontius drifted around the point, playing for time, testing the ground like a traveller at the edge of a quaking bog.

"But does he not have his instruments, Your Eminence?"

"Well said, Dominē!" Maximianus applauded sharply.

"So, it seems to me, Gentlemen, that there is no real question about whether to mount a united defense. No, the real questions are two. Who will lead, and who will pay?" Quirinius' father looked about significantly.

* * *

Bishop Valerianus spoke from across the room. "The disappointment, Dominē Quirinius. Tell us about it. Was your father so terribly chagrined that Nonianus Bassus had been made head of the Council?" He took the tone of a schoolboy talking back to his teacher.

Quirinius shook his head. "No. Precedence was quite beside the point, as my father understood. It was the business of the Council that mattered. The wisest wanted to prepare for a likely war; the dullest hoped for an unlikely peace."

Bishop Valerianus clapped his hands softly. "What nice antithesis." Quirinius frowned. The jibe moved him to make his point clear, despite his earlier hesitation to reveal any division among the Romans. Clever fellow, this bishop.

"My father put the two ineluctable questions to the council. Who would lead an army if the Saxons moved north? And who would pay?

"The obvious solution was to appoint the richest man, to let him shoulder the expenses of horses, equipment, food, the inevitable damage to property. A tax could be imposed later to reimburse him, called by the old name, the annona militaris. My father and Maximianus jointly suggested it. Oh, but here things got sticky fast. The long, narrow bishop got to his feet and raised his right hand, lengthy as a ruler, to halt the proposal. 'Let us not waste time in vain debate.'

"'How can this proposal be vain?' my father asked.

"'Not the proposal, perhaps, but the debate itself, Dominē Quirinius,' the stout little bishop Gerontius said from across the room. 'If there is no real chance of raising the tax.'

"'No chance?' I asked, amazed. In those days I didn't understand the extent to which men will strive against their own interests.

"'In my capacity as Bishop of Glevum, I will not submit to a tax. And I doubt that my brother bishop will do so either, whatever our other differences.'

"'No, indeed,' agreed Bishop Strabo. Maximianus stood up, his face displaying cold anger, but he seemed at a loss about what to say. 'And let me state further,' Strabo continued, 'that Senator Ater has appointed me his legate, in the event that he could not be present for this council—'

"'But he was present!' a curial shouted from the back.

"'I think this point of procedure should be resolved in favor of the bishop's position,' Nonianus Bassus said, shambling away from the thorny issue of the tax. Oh, how he could use cunning in the service of his weakness.

"'What did Ater order to you say? How were you told to vote?' my father asked.

"'Be brief and to the point, as befits Ater's servant!' Maximianus said.

"Bishop Strabo, pale and bloodless as he seemed, still managed to flush at the slight. Then he drew himself up, if possible, even an inch taller, and said, with great pleasure quite evident in his voice, 'The Dominus and Senator Ater wishes all to know that he alone determines how his substance will be used.'

"'Then, he refuses to help his own people,' my father said.

"'He will not submit to a tax. And he stands in full support of any friend who joins him in refusing to submit.' The bishop looked meaningfully around the council room.

"'And he incites others to shirk their duty.'

"I looked over at old Nonianus Bassus. His expression showed him stymied midway between relief and unease. And why not? He couldn't decide which was the greater threat, the chance of the Saxons seizing or burning an estate of his, or the certainty of paying to avoid it. Of course, he wasn't alone. Ater was not to be lightly crossed. This would insure him of some allies, the hisses proved that some were present, and those few by themselves might have been enough to subvert the entire defense. And then there was the difficulty of the bishops by themselves--they could have been forced to submit, but each had his protector. Strabo was Ater's protégé. That was evident. Bishop Gerontius would call upon the Mauriaci to keep him from any obligation to the council and our defense. And this meant, of course, that the Mauriaci and their clients would not cooperate either. Bassus made one swift decision that day. Oh, yes, he had enough drive left in him to advance to a halt. He rose and spoke.

"'Senators and Curials, this is a difficult matter to decide. We face, as it were, a balance, but a balance quite unlike that with which we are familiar. The balance I speak of has two pans, but only one of them may we see.'

"'What is the old man maundering about?' I asked. My father did not kick me this time. He dropped his head and put his face in his hands in quiet frustration.

"'In one pan, call it the rightmost, we have the certainty of the military tax, a burden to be fresh laid upon a country still recovering from the necessary exactions of decades ago.' The old man straightened up in swelling pride at his metaphor. He leaned back a little, clasping his hands behind him, and rocked slightly on the balls of his feet in enthusiasm at the sound of his high, reedy voice. 'In the other pan, call it the leftmost, we have only the uncertainty of some Saxon raiding, and that, if it comes, from a people still striving to make and maintain their new homes and thus hobbled by a hundred obligations more likely to tie them to their farmsteads than to drive them to adventures.'

"'Make and maintain homes they have taken from us and our clients,' my father said. 'For that matter some of them were taken from you and your clients. And yet this provokes mere excuses for passivity. You sound like Eugenius Ater himself.' This was followed by both cheers and by hisses. The council was, as Ater and his friends desired, entirely divided.

"'The Clarissimus Ater's points are, I believe, determinative. We can afford to allow the Saxons a little play, indulging them, but only to a certain extent.' he raised his index finger as though emphasizing a reasonable, indeed unexceptionable point. 'Indulging them will, I believe—and I know that I am not alone in the opinion—incline them to be better neighbors.'

"'They are not neighbors; they are invaders.' Maximianus spoke loudly, sitting with his arms crossed, looking down at the floor to show his contempt for Bassus.

"'And,' Bassus blithered on, enchanted by the sound of his own voice, 'These Saxons are by no means certain to raid or make further incursions.'

"'Hah!' Maximianus shook his head.

"'There is no need for a tax.' Bishop Strabo summed up Bassus' and thus Ater's position.

"'Let those who fear see to their own defense. I suggest strongly that we put our trust in the Clarissimus Ater's judgement and follow his counsel.' Bishop Gerontius put his seal on the position.

"My father, stood up, slowly shaking his head at the council and spoke again. He judged the Saxons to be dangerous as, in fact, they proved to be, and it provoked him, he who was so generally conciliatory, to make it known in very certain terms that half of the council were fools. They deserved whatever evils might come and must not for a moment expect that taking the position of Eugenius Ater could turn out well or reflect with any grace or honor on their positions as senators, magnates or curials. Furthermore, they should know that their hesitation and lassitude endangered their entire civilized circle. I wish I could declaim his invective, but my father was a better rhetor than I, and, besides, it was so long ago. Half the council were incensed, as they should have been, but Ater was seen to be as reprehensible as, in fact, he was.

"And so, the Council broke up, and everyone dispersed, the wise determined to protect their holdings as best they could, the foolish hoping they would not have to. I could sense the bitterness in Maximianus as I stood with my father under the portico of the basilica. 'They'll pick us off in detail, Dominē Quirinius,' he told my father. 'One by one until we will be too few to resist.'

"My father sighed but smiled, prepared as always to see a glimmer of hope however rare and remote—like the reflection of the moon in a deep well. 'Have faith, Dominē Maximianus. If Aelle takes another parish, why then the magnates will grasp the nettle and act. There will be no havering once men grasp what they actually face. We have had twenty years of peace, and it may be that now is when we must pay for it.'

"Maximianus put his fists on his hips and faced south, where the Saxons were, and frowned. Then he turned back and said, 'We must agree, you and I, to band ourselves together and defend what is ours. I don't mean to see my world sink into some wild German kingdom.'

"'It won't come to that. You must believe it.' My father extended his hand to Maximianus, and they shook with ceremonial deliberateness."

Bishop Valerianus stood straight and then hunched and lowered his shoulders to ease his back, as though to indicate that the story had been too long. "Events proved, Dominē Quirinius, that you were never anything but inimical to Eugenius Ater."

"Did he not deserve his end?"

Seven: The Monastery, October 491 AD

"After the council meeting, my father wanted to return quickly. A bad decision, but he was in a hurry and susceptible. Nowadays it seems that half of one's decisions are bad. Trying to decide what to do in this disordered world is like trying to grow barley in spent land. Very little good seems to come of it. We've learned what the times are like, but things weren't quite so clear then. It was a late false summer in those days.

"At the suggestion of a peasant, my father decided to leave the Roman road with half a dozen soldiers at Fanum Minervae and head north to the estate where Hispanus had been stabled. It's in the old territory of the Bruttovani. The way north wasn't more than a deep, ancient track heading across a moor and then into and through some copses. The path was just wide enough for us to ride in single file. The guide assured us that, by the early afternoon, the path would take us out of the woods and down a slope to the Via Septimiana, where it passes our westernmost estate. The jaunt described a diagonal, and so should save us three miles, perhaps more. Peasants are not very apt, in my experience, with geometry.

"We couldn't take our wagons with us. They stayed on the road and would come the long way round and meet us at the estate at nightfall. And, besides, they were drawn by oxen and went slower than a man could walk. So, we left most of the soldiers to guard them and went ahead at a quick walk with the scrawny little fellow as a guide. He had wandered up to us in the forum and suggested the shortcut to us. He was called Uithyl, and he strode along to show the way. He wasn't much to look at, just a young peasant with a wine-marked cheek. His shoes were uncommonly fine smooth, rich chestnut, almost maroon. Odd what you notice. It's not so odd what you remember.

130

"Uithyl walked along ahead of us to show the way, sometimes jogging if the path dipped. He'd jabber back over his shoulder until my father snapped at him to keep quiet. 'Yes, Your Magnificence. Yes. Yes.' And he'd duck his head, all subservience. The man made me uncomfortable; it was natural—we didn't know him. He wasn't one of our peasants, and his dialect showed he wasn't from out our way, but it didn't seem much more than that.

"An axle of one of our wagons needed greasing and had been chirruping like a bird since we'd left the city. Soon, however, we lost the sound as we pressed north along the shortcut. The sound had irritated me all morning; now I missed it.

"Uithyl went on ahead, beckoning from time to time as though he wasn't satisfied with our progress, and then, as though he remembered his place, he would laugh and say pointless things as an excuse to call us by titles—senator, clarissimus, master, that sort of thing.

"So, we followed the peasant along the track and gradually the eight of us became strung out in a long line—perhaps fifty yards long. This meant that when the track dipped down from the hill and twisted into the woods, I couldn't see more than my father and two of the Thracian Lancers behind him. The other four were out of sight, if not out of earshot. The wood was quiet—now as I look back it seems that there weren't even birdcalls, and that should have suggested what followed, but it's just as likely I impose that on my memory, that I see things in view of the present."

"Like God?" Bishop Valerianus asked. "To whom like you, evidently past, present and future are all one?" He glanced at the little abbot with a smile. The abbot smiled too, but only for a moment and then looked down at the table and fumbled with his crusts.

"Perhaps His Eminence the Bishop is on to something. The facts count, not my impressions. So, then, let's say that even the birds didn't sing, and I was too absorbed to notice.

"But I did notice the tree across the path. Plain as the wall of a

131

fort, something not to be missed. The leaves of it were bright green, thousands of them, not one wilted. Clearly it had been standing an hour before, but no other trees were down, so I grasped in an instant that no brief, local storm had done it. All the same it takes a moment or two to work things out—especially things you don't want to grasp, and my horse, after she balked, kicked my father's horse when he rode up too close to her. There was a moment of confusion, and in that instant Uithyl leaped over the trunk of the fallen tree. He obviously meant to vanish like a deer into the bush, but he stumbled, did a pratfall and got to his feet with a muddy rump. Odd what you recall—often the most pointless and comical things—even in the midst of the deadly.

He disappeared.

"I drew my sword and shouted back to the men, but my father was slow to react and busy pulling in the reins and slapping his horse's shoulder to calm him. The two men who ran out of the underbrush easily pushed him out of the saddle. He fell heavily with a shout and didn't move—even when his horse stepped on him as he shied from one of the bandits grasping at the bridle. I tugged the reins sharply and got my mare to turn to her left, turning in one spot like a top, and she knocked one bandit over with her rump. When she'd made the turn, I was able to lean out of the saddle and strike the bandit trying to grasp the bridle of my father's horse. It wasn't a good blow, but his left arm dropped at his side, and he screamed and stumbled back into the bushes, leaving many of the leaves red.

"I tried to lean down and slash at the other bandit, the one who'd fallen, but he knew to stay flat on the ground, and I couldn't reach him. He slithered like a reptile away from the track and into the woods where I couldn't follow.

"The mare was heaving in excitement, and it took a moment to regain control of her. When I had, I saw that one of our men had driven his lance through an attacker who lay just off the path. He was swearing; he couldn't free his lance and was glancing around, afraid that other men might suddenly spill out of the woods at him. He let go the lance, drew his sword, and stared behind him over his horse's haunches.

"I dismounted and he did the same. We both felt better then, surer of ourselves, more confident that we could defend ourselves than we had been on horseback clinched in that rut among the trees. I stood listening. It was hard with the blood pounding in my ears. The soldier went to the body, put a foot on the chest and pulled the lance free with an odd, slick sound I'd never heard before. Then he looked to me for orders.

"'Put your helmet on. Tell the others to do the same. Get your shields.' He nodded. Vaguely, I heard him whistle with his tongue between his teeth to call the others to him. I went to my father, who hadn't gotten up. This gave me a bad feeling, a very bad feeling—shocking, like missing a step in the dark. He was very pale and shivering as with cold, though the weather was quite warm.

"His eyes seemed abstracted as though he were looking at things I couldn't see. I knelt to him and felt around his body; my right hand came back blood-slick. Somehow he had been stabbed—perhaps by another man I never saw, someone who had stepped out during the skirmish but then had disappeared when things hadn't gone quickly the bandits' way.

"It was clear my father was dying, and what seemed a very trivial thought came to me: 'Here lies dying the last man in Britain who knows Greek.'

"Thanks to the Blessed Jerome no one need know Greek," the abbot said. Quirinius looked at him in annoyance.

"Shut up," Ambiorus said quietly from the table, arms folded across his chest. The bishop smiled benignly at them both.

"It was just another rent in the world," Quirinius said. "We spoke for a few moments before he died. My father concentrated and could see me at first, and then he couldn't. He kept speaking, though, trying to tell me things he thought I must know."

"What sorts of things, Dominē?" Ambiorus asked.

"Oh, what to look for in buying a horse. How important it is to keep good accounts. He told me to always keep my mother's tomb well-tended. It was hard to listen to.

"When he was dead, I looked up and saw that the men, the half-dozen soldiers we'd taken with us, had formed a ring about us and faced out with swords drawn and shields out. The mottled woodland sun pointed up the grey of their helmets.

"We got to the estate in the afternoon—very late. We retraced our steps back along the rut and then made good speed along the road to catch up the wagons. Once joined up, the soldiers clustered about the wagon upon which we laid my father, and then escorted him with helmets on and shields held up against the world. Not that there was danger any longer. I had thirty armed horsemen with me, and the bandits had come off badly in a fight with only a handful of us. One of them was dead and lying athwart the wooded trail, and it was likely that the man who had taken the sword-slash was dead or would be soon.

"I thought all the way to the estate—and not just about revenging my father. That would come very soon, however. I thought of old Ambrosius Aurelianus and his dismissal of me and my request that he join the rest of us Romans. Saxons were coming; that was sure. And it was just as sure that, as things stood, he'd been justified, though only half-way, perhaps, in drawing apart and keeping to his own affairs. The council had been a fiasco—a farrago of evasion, mistrust and selfishness. The senators and curials—the weak ones anyway—deserved to be picked off one by one. But deserts were beside the point. A reckless idea was coming to me. I tried to dodge it—really, I did, but I see now that, somehow, I was confronting something unavoidable, and as real, if startling, as that great stone ring to the southwest."

"You knew, Dominē, that you were the new and true Count of the Britains." Ambiorus smiled with pride at him.

"It was coming to me, my boy. It was coming to me."

* * *

The Second Estate of the Quirinii, 463 AD

When they reached the estate, it was evening and the sun a red orb that, as it passed behind low trees, could almost be watched straight on. Quirinius was distracted, of course. He couldn't distinguish between the women who wailed because his father was dead, proof of the Senator's popularity, and those who wailed out of form or for fear of the uncertainty that follows a great man's death. In any case, he ignored them all. He drank a large cup of wine in the gloomy kitchen while the scullions and cooks watched mutely, the whole crowd of them inching back subtly into the shadows near the walls to efface themselves. Then he called Canidius to him and they walked to the Senator's office. Quirinius took care to sit in his father's chair and to strew an account book or two and a bundle of papers on the table. He sat behind it and spoke to Canidius.

"Captain, I will need your help more than anyone else's in the next little while." The man nodded. "Because, shortly, we must kill a number of men. We must kill them all. Anything less would be a very bad thing."

He nodded again. "Yes."

"First, however, you must take a half-dozen men and announce throughout the estate and in the neighboring villages that the Senator is dead, and that we will be preparing for his funeral, which will take place at the home estate on the day after tomorrow. Tell the village priests that they must each send twenty men as laborers to prepare things for our departure tomorrow."

"Dominē?" Canidius said. He used the form of address appropriate to the old senator. Quirinius found it jarring. "Yes, what is it?"

"You said we were going to kill those bandits. When?"

"Tomorrow."

"But the funeral? The journey home?"

"Just tell the peasants what I want them told. I want their minds occupied and I don't want those bandits to think we'll move against them for several days. Some of the peasants hereabouts are likely related to those men, and I don't want them to see what's coming." Canidius nodded slowly and deliberately. "Yes, Dominē. Just as you say."

"And then we will kill those bandits tomorrow. Every one of them."

"Yes."

"I will tell you later how we will go about it, but you must tell the men only to be ready. No one must shirk—everyone must do as he is told. No one must hold back."

"No, Dominē."

"You are good men, and you are tough. But the troop hasn't been in a fight in many years."

"The boys will do well, Dominē. They know you expect it of them."

"I will be with you."

The captain straightened and smiled. "The men will be quite content about that, Dominē. Quite content."

"You must find among the tenants two men who know the country."

Canidius nodded. "I will."

"And you must keep them apart from each other and from their families. Tell them that, if they somehow succeed in communicating with the bandits, they will, of course, be killed."

"Of course."

"And I will sell their families to the Irish."

"Yes, Dominē."

"And now, send the bailiff to me."

When Sequanius stepped into the room, the captain shoved him toward Quirinius in order to set the tone. Quirinius then informed him that his situation had changed since the days when Hispanus had been taken—since the days when he'd sent the bandits food and furniture to buy a little peace.

"Your conduct has encouraged these men to prey on the neighborhood—it has emboldened them, and they have killed the

Senator."

"Dominē..." But he couldn't go on. His mouth worked soundlessly for a few instants and then he gave up trying. Quirinius watched him passively, his arms along the chair arms like the statue of a consul. He observed the man shaking, noticed that his tunic was darkening beneath his arms as he sweated in fear.

"So, naturally, my first impulse is to kill you." Quirinius left it at that for some moments. Sequanius shrugged meekly, helpless.

"I have decided—provisionally, of course, to spare you because I believe that you can help me kill these bandits and thus atone, in some slight degree, for your criminal incompetence. If this is true—that you can help me—then, after the bandits are all dead, I will only dismiss you."

The bailiff said nothing.

"Do you know where their den is?"

"More or less, Dominē."

"More, I hope."

"There is a cave on the moor about five miles from here."

"I see. Help the captain here find two men who know the situation exactly. Bring them here, but do not tell them why or I will kill you."

The bailiff bowed his way out of the room backwards, instinctively avoiding the captain, but not the doorjamb, which he backed into. Quirinius fancied he could hear a nervous sob, but he was too preoccupied to find it satisfying.

Quirinius spent the night organizing. It kept his mind from a thousand other things—when, exactly, to bury his father; where all of the account books were, not just those of the major estates; how long it would take a bishop to arrive for the obsequies, what petty nobles would appear and maintain that the Senator had promised them something difficult or expensive—something now beyond proof but hard to deny them; where he could find a stone-cutter with skill enough not to make a hash of the Senator's tomb-inscription; how he would tell his sisters. Or perhaps winged rumor, as Vergil writes, was swift enough that they would know already by the time he brought his father's body home. And that would mean a different sort of greeting, a different situation. By contrast, planning the annihilation of the bandits was easy.

* * *

Quirinius left in the middle of the night—at the end of the second watch—with his thirty horsemen, two guides, a chastened, silent bailiff and a half a dozen fast gaze-hounds. They proceeded slowly under the weak light of a half-moon; the horses were uneasy, afraid of stumbling or breaking a leg in the dark, and the riders had to lead them afoot with hands on their bridles, slinking through the night. A mile from the cave the troop rested among trees that clustered along the top of a rise and waited for dawn. By report, the cave was approached by a path that dipped down from a height and then turned to pass along the foot of the rise.

Over the next two hours scouts crept near the cave to establish that the bandits were there, and to make sure that, as they had been told by the locals, there wasn't much in the way of escape for them. The reports to Quirinius were clear enough; there was a low sort of bulwark in front of the mouth of the cave made up of untrimmed tree trunks, but a determined man could clamber over it easily enough; in fact, it was meant as much as anything to pen stolen sheep. The scouts had heard bleating and the honking of a donkey. The bandits themselves were clearly in cave. There was some murmuring from within, and the glow of a cook-fire outside the cave-mouth that could be seen through a narrow gap in the bulwark.

The path up to the enclosure might be difficult to approach, uphill as it was and with no cover, but Quirinius' men had armor, shields and helmets. Determination ought to carry them there, even on foot, as they would have to go. The path had a sort of tributary track going away from it near the cave—the scouts supposed that a man who got out of the yard might try to slip around the brow of the hill in which the cave was situated, but he'd shortly be on open ground where the dogs would have no trouble finding him, and the horsemen would run him down.

Quirinius could feel the men's eyes on him even in the dark. He spoke very quietly, and the men enclosed him in a circle to catch his words. He reminded them of what he'd told them earlier, because he knew it would embolden them. He said that men who were bandits were so desperate they must lack forethought, and they must have been gulled and calmed by any rumors they had heard about the preparations for the Senator's funeral. Therefore, there was every reason to suppose they would be unprepared to meet an attack, even launched directly uphill at the cave-mouth. The bandits would have poor equipment, merely knives, cudgels, perhaps a sword or two. And they should melt at the onset because they had no discipline and honor, unlike these men of Quirinius, who were, after all, The Third Thracian Lancers. Quirinius himself doubted a bit the Lancers' discipline, but they did hunt and parade together and pride would compel them to obey. A few men might slip by, he told them, but they would be hunted down by dogs and men on horseback reserved for that. He called out the names of four men for that duty. They were to go down where the path ran along the foot of the rise and be prepared to chase any bandits who escaped, or to dismount and join in the fight if signalled. The rest of the troop would gather at the foot of the rise where the path crooked to go uphill and, when the word was given, make an assault straight up the hill in confidence that they could get to the bandits before they could make any defense. Quirinius thought it would be a bloody mess, but he was fairly certain that none of his men were likely to die. The bandits, though, would all die.

Quirinius descended on foot with the troopers to the path below. The four who were to ride down any escapees followed, leading their horses and arraying themselves on the right. The stood quietly, holding the horses by the reins and letting them drop their heads to the rank grass on either side of the path.

Quirinius stood quiet and expectant. He looked to either side to see that the men were properly ranged, and he waited until he might reckon that there was enough light that he could lead his men without disorder up to the cave, invisible here from the foot of the hill. He shifted from foot to foot and flexed his shoulders now and again, trying to settle his shield, which was slung across his back, into a more comfortable attitude. The strap was snug—it grasped him a bit and called attention to itself like an unwanted memory.

Eventually, the sky lightened enough for the men to advance without stumbling. He waited a few moments more until he guessed that the men, or he himself, could not hold themselves still any longer, and he gave the word to advance. There was the sound of shields being slung forward and a few dull clunks and scrapes where the men were standing too close to each other.

* * *

"Wasn't there some killing of bandits after your father's death?" Bishop Valerianus asked. "The first example of the famous Quirinius' sharp military skills."

Quirinius narrowed his eyes at the bishop and then looked down in a study. He was surprised that the bishop knew about it, surprised that he should allude so precisely to what he himself was thinking of. Odd, that.

"Quite uncharacteristic of you to have nothing to say about a given matter." Bishop Valerianus got up, put a hand to his back and walked in a tight circle, loosening his muscles. He wondered what the hour was, where Moderatus and Pennomorix could be. He turned suddenly. "Well?"

Quirinius shrugged. "Well, what?"

"Wasn't it this little fight that emboldened you to arrogate the office of Count of the Britains?"

"Not the fight. Not really. No. No arrogation either."

The bishop looked dubious.

"Tell us about it anyway," the bishop said, testy, after a few moments of silence had passed.

Quirinius shook his head. He gathered his cloak around him against the cold of the night.

140

He doesn't tell the story, but he thinks about that bloody morning.

* * *

The men advance in good order and, for the most part, quickly. There is some stumbling as the men in the rear crowd up against the men in front. There is a halt, some almost inaudible swearing, and then the men walk as quickly as they can two and three abreast up the steep path until the bulwark before the cave comes into view. They are close—perhaps fifty yards away. It is now fairly light, and Quirinius, whose ears are sharp, believes he can hear a voice or two echo in the cave, that, unseen, he knows is there. What he can see, though, is a long-eared donkey glancing over the bulwark, and, next to him, a sentry, a huge hulking man in a hide cape and with a squalid beard. He holds on his shoulder a club studded with rusted iron nails and is looking down on the troopers in dull surprise. His open mouth makes him look unutterably stupid.

Quirinius draws his sword and the others do the same. He glances back, half involuntarily, to be sure that the men are with him. Of course they are. The titan sentry continues to look, startled, at the two dozen men come to kill him, apparently sprung from the very earth like the sown men of Aëtes or Cadmus. He hesitates, scowling, as though he disapproves of the situation. Quirinius does not hesitate. He picks up the pace, but he doesn't run—no good in arriving winded—and the men surge behind him. A hundred feet more and they will be able to spill out of the path and spread out to good account.

The sentry puts his hand to his lips to whistle but seems unable to do it in his surprise. He looks stupidly at his hand as though it has failed him and then turns and shouts in a booming voice and glances back over his shoulder at Quirinius and the advancing troop. The bandit turns back to them, taking up his club in two hands, shifting from foot to foot like a boxer. Two of his comrades emerge from the cave puzzled, unsure of what he's getting at. He, however, knows quite well the mess he's in, and resolves how to face the troopers who have now spread out and are approaching the bulwark.

The big bandit rushes to the narrow gate to face the men that advance that way, yelling all the while for his fellows to wake up. A few scramble out of the cave into the pen; they can see what's happened, but at the same time they disbelieve it and seem bewildered. A couple of them have shields and spears, one a sword, another a hatchet, another a helmet and a butcher knife. Half a dozen sheep bleat and circle away in the confusion. The donkey watches solemnly from as far away as he can get.

Now the shouting is general—everyone is awake, but there has been enough surprise that the bandits are finished. Two troopers approach the gate under cover of their shields, swords out, and keep the giant at his post. The rest of the troopers climb quickly over the bulwark and, once they are in, one of them stabs the giant at the gate while he's occupied by the shouting troopers in front of him. The trooper sinks his sword into the man's side so deep he can't extricate it right away. The giant howls and falls; the others step over him and hack at him for good measure as they pass.

Quirinius has only scattered views of what's happening. The excitement is intense; he doesn't really recall climbing into the pen before the cave-mouth, but he's here now and sees two of his men go at one of the bandits—one with a shield and sword. One man faces the bandit and engages warily, trying not to expose himself. All the same the bandit manages to land a slash across the trooper's chest, but his coat of iron scales easily turns the blade away with a thin, drawing sound. Meanwhile the other trooper slips past the bandit's right side and slashes him in the leg, causing him to fall. While the bandit is struggling to get up, he stabs him carefully in the back and right to his heart.

The cave-mouth is narrow, a mere brushy slit really. Quirinius sees it expel bandits who, with unshorn hair and beards, seem more primitive than true men. They look to him as though they are of an older, coarser race or, worse, one that has turned back to some brutish condition from which the world ascended ages ago, long even

142

before Rome had put a polish on life. Even decked in clothes they can't hide their atavism from Quirinius. He can see the troglodyte right through the tunic and the cloak, and in that moment, he knows that he must expunge them from the earth before their example can spread. They must die, yes, but not as a revenge. No, Quirinius can see that he is cleansing a pollution.

He looks for an opponent, but he hardly needs to, the way things are going. There is a shriek, and a hand goes flying by; the bandit doesn't miss it long—a trooper kills the startled man with a single blow as he stares at his bleeding forearm. Still, Quirinius needs to impress the men, and so he chooses a large fellow with a shield in one hand and a spear in the other, and he goes after him. There's no real contest. Quirinius provokes a spear thrust which he turns with his shield and then steps in with the sword he holds high just for this. Once closed in, he slashes shortly and down and cuts the cords of the man's neck. He falls and there is a good deal of blood from the severed arteries. Quirinius bends to finish him off, but the man is no longer quivering; he is already dead.

Quirinius straightens and can see that skill and arithmetic have told. The bandits have no real ability with weapons. Clearly, they have always relied on bluff and numbers, but this time they are outnumbered themselves. It turns out there are only eighteen of them, and they have joined the fight piecemeal and are often killed two to one. Each time one falls, the odds lean harder against them and the whole matter accelerates to its end.

In two, perhaps three minutes, it was over. Quirinius sent two men with daggers to dispatch any bandit that might yet be alive, and found he had no more to deal with than three obsequious babbling men who had thrown down their weapons and who, kneeling abjectly, rubbed their foreheads in the dirt and called for mercy in British and remarkably crude Latin. Quirinius had them pulled screaming by their hair to the center of the yard where their necks could be stretched across a log dragged from the woodpile near the fire. He had their heads lopped off one by one with an axe he found lying about. The soldier he detailed to do this was unhandy and sometimes took two or three strokes. The convulsions were repellent, but the effect on the subsequent screaming prisoners was all he could have hoped for. He marvelled at how bloody it was, but he said nothing, making his face as hard, as chillingly bland, as a mask.

The cave was searched carefully, but there were no bandits hiding there. Quirinius had very much hoped to find Uithyl cowering in the dark, but all the men found as they stumbled in the darkness of the cave was mismatched furniture taken in raids or extortions, sacks of grain, and piles of rich but filthy clothing. Quirinius was distracted from these sordid finds by the arrival of the four horsemen who had been posted to hunt down escapees. They came up the trail leading their mounts. One of the bandits had gotten out of the pen at the start of the fight and had slipped off across the moor, but the mounted troopers had seen and gotten him. They had let slip the hounds, and after that the brigand had no hope—they ran him down like a deer, the troopers easily cantering after him. They took turns running him one way and then the other until he stood still in commingled fury and fear, and then one of the troopers walked his horse close to him and looked him over carefully for a while. There was more than a tinge of revenge in this. Finally, he deliberately drove his lance through the bandit. They left the body in the tall grass and were laughing when they reached the pen, where Quirinius stood, helmet under his arm, talking to Sequanius. He wiped his sleeve across his forehead and frowned in irritation as the iron scales just smeared the sweat. He shook his head to clear it from his eyes, and then stared a moment at the slender young bailiff. "Uithyl is not here."

The bailiff frowned, not understanding. "Our guide. The one who led my father into the trap." The bailiff mouthed a silent "oh" and nodded. "I want him found. I want him alive." The bailiff nodded again. "You are a lucky fellow, bailiff. Very lucky. Not only are you still alive, but I am seriously considering letting you retain your place."

"The Dominus is very kind."

"We shall see. Find Uithyl and hand him over to me. Do you undertand that this extremely important? So important to me that, if you succeed, I will not dismiss you?"

"I understand the importance, Dominē." He looked down and rubbed his jaw a moment in thought.

"Well?" Quirinius asked sharply.

"Do not consider it disrespectful that I state what is, undoubtedly, obvious to you." *Marvellous how well the fellow speaks,* Quirinius thought to himself. *An odd thing. How had he acquired an education? And some of his confidence is returning. Good. He will need that to succeed.*

"Tell me what's obvious. I've been occupied."

"The task will likely prove difficult. And will take time."

"Don't tell me that it's hard. Tell me that you'll do it. I'll give you twenty soldiers to sift the country with."

"Very good, Dominē. But I reckon that a small flock of sheep will do the trick."

Quirinius regarded the bailiff closely for several silent moments, and then smiled faintly. "Anything else?"

"A gold solidus, I think, Dominē. That too may be required."

"How long will it take?"

"I suspect that it cannot be done in a rush. It may need a subtle hand."

"And you have such a hand." The young bailiff flushed but didn't answer. Quirinius tossed his helmet to a nearby trooper and hooked his thumbs in his sword-belt. "How long might this subtlety take?"

"It may be half a year, Dominē Quirinius."

Quirinius nodded. "You'll have it all, soldiers, sheep, money and time." He turned back to the soldiers who stood about and ordered several of the bandits' bodies tied by the feet and dragged behind the horses into the heart of the nearest village. The corpses were difficult to recognize by the time they had been pulled over five miles of rough ground, especially the headless one, but identification was quite beside the point. It was all a lesson, a demonstration to the country of power and order.

* * *

"Perhaps the scuffle with the bandits was a fight beneath the dignity you've since obtained," the bishop speculates. "Perhaps that is why the story remains untold. I don't press you for it, oh no. I just supposed that it might explain what followed. I mean only that an unsympathetic listener might suggest that you grasped your opportunity with a good deal of, what shall we say? Enthusiasm."

"It began as revenge; that's true enough. Why deny it? But it didn't end that way. When I saw those men crawling out of the earth like beasts, everything changed. My father was dead; nothing I could do would remedy that. In honor of my father, though, I did something that surprised me. I left the bailiff in his place despite what I'd said. I did not turn him and his family out. I did it in some way for my father who, despite the bailiff's failures, sympathized with the fellow. I did not do it because he cringed or because he cowered when I told him what I wanted."

"What did you want?"

"'Want' isn't the word, really. I had to have it. It was an obligation, a sort of vocation, if you will. Something had settled on me willy-nilly." Quirinius leaned back in the chair with a sharp creak and smiled at the abbot. "You can explain to His Eminence the Bishop what a vocation is. Of the pair of you, you're the most likely to have an inkling."

"Your office as Count of the Britains, Dominē," the abbot said, steering around the obstacle.

"The bandits had power, but no authority, therefore no responsibility. But I could see what their naked power had done. It had cowed even civilized, good people who were, or should have been, stronger than they were. And I had some power now too—but I would be responsible. Not like the fools in the Council, who had authority or so they thought, but no power. I would have both—

146

because they couldn't stop me, yes, but that is only a trivial reason. It was because someone had to do it, they wouldn't, and I could."

"Rather a developed political insight for a young man of, what, twenty?"

Quirinius turned and waved dismissively. "Twenty-five. But you don't win your point, Your Eminence. I couldn't have articulated it then, no. But in my bones, I could feel that what I was doing was quite correct. My understanding came later, but my actions were quite, quite correct."

Eight: The Monastery, October 491 AD

Quirinius was peeved at the bishop's coolness. It rankled him, more than he would have cared to admit, that the confident bastard had so little respect for him. In spite of himself he felt driven to justify his position, though twenty-five years of holding it, even if merely by main strength as the bishop wrongly implied, should grant him a certain legitimacy. And legitimacy was important—that couldn't be denied.

Quirinius walked back to the heavy, dark table and leaned against it, his hands resting on the top. The bishop watched him with a faint smile, he could tell, even with his back to the man. Quirinius looked over his shoulder at him. "We should decide our dispositions for tomorrow."

The bishop shrugged. "If you like. It's your business anyway, active man that you are. But, as you implied earlier, it might be better to await the arrival of Moderatus and Pennomorix and learn their exact numbers."

Quirinius grunted. "In any case you've brought thirty men of your own. I'll second them to my troops."

"Of course," the bishop said. "In fact, I insist."

"How expansive."

The bishop opened his arms wide for a moment as though in welcome—or perhaps actually in welcome.

"I'll get more wine," the abbot said and slipped out the door. Ambiorus sat sharpening a knife in the ruddy gloom, the whetstone singing softly against the shining edge. He looked up incuriously to watch him go out, but Quirinius and the bishop ignored the abbot. Quirinius straightened up and turned to the bishop. "No monkey business, Your Eminence," he waggled a finger. The bishop looked theatrically shocked. Quirinius continued, "I've protected the church for twenty-five years—it's as strong as ever and, if I've made it pay, well, that couldn't be helped."

The bishop said nothing. For a moment his mind went back to a monk dead many years and buried in a churchyard forty miles away.

"I don't expect you to agree with my methods. But don't impede them." He looked hard at the bishop, who seemed about to speak when the abbot returned with a jug of wine, which he put on the table before backing away to the orbit of the bishop. The silence seemed to mollify Quirinius. "I'll tell you about my—my elevation—I suppose you should call it." Quirinius sat back down in the abbot's chair at the head of the table, put his elbows on the chair arms, interlaced his fingers and rested his lips on his hands. But he found, as he closed his eyes, that what came first to mind was not his elevation. It was not that moment when he stood rocking like a drunkard on the upraised shield and looked down into the upturned, joyous faces of his men, but something quite different, something of interest only to him, something that was, surely, more important to him than anything he was prepared to recount, though he could not say exactly why. And it troubled him that things so indubitably important could seldom be reduced to words. But if not so reduced, how could they be understood by others? Even by him? He shook his head.

* * *

The Principal Estate of the Quirinii, 463 AD
Quirinius headed west at the first moments of dawn. The wagons had been prepared during the night and the men, somber and armored, slipped into their saddles as one at the captain's command. Quirinius rode at the head of the column in a fine short horseman's cloak, his best tunic and trousers and a pair of scarlet boots that a servant had polished unceasingly throughout the night until they shone like ruddy oil. He surrounded himself with a dozen armored horsemen, at their head Canidius the captain and the ensign bearing the troop's dragon-head standard with open mouth and red silk tail. Next followed the rumbling wagon with the old senator's body on a

149

black-swagged bier, his head jiggling slightly on a plush pillow as the wheels ground along the way. At his feet were a helmet and an unsheathed broadsword to remind the peasants that in his time he had been a commander. The other wagons followed and then twenty-four horsemen brought up the rear.

The old senator would have disapproved, and Quirinius knew it. The old man would have had something to say like, "The sword gives way to the toga" or some such old saw. He was always full of those ancient aphorisms; no matter that the world had changed, and the advice was no more help than an incantation. All things considered, Quirinius would have preferred to give the old senator what he would have wanted, to have made the cortege a purely civil thing with no military tinge, however slight, dignified, not verging on something barbaric like a Saxon funeral or the obsequies of a Briton clan chief.

But first the world must be mended, the seams closed and so on, and the common ruck of people, and not they alone, must be shown who could do it and must be inclined to help. And so Quirinius had to ride in this military style through the countryside, seeding the idea that he, like his father, was first a commander and then a senator, and making it seem not only a truth, but one that people had always known.

The road was long—seemed long, anyhow. It was the same way that Quirinius had travelled a year before, but now the column plodded along at the pace of the oxen that drew the wagons, and the day seemed interminable. Quirinius made sure the axles were well-greased—no cheeping to recall at every moment his father's death-day. He had no need of recollection, but even so the massive wheels rolled slowly over the road cobbles with the sound of millstones. The road itself was straight as time, and for an hour or two, it might seem as though the troop made no progress, but then here and there would be a crowd of people gathered to see the old Senator's last progress.

Quirinius had meant to dispatch a rider to turn out people, but among the distractions of the night before he had forgotten, and so it was particularly welcome to him to see people at the roadside every two or three miles. Sometimes it was only a woodcutter in thorn-ripped clothes patched a hundred times, standing as straight as his gently curving back would allow. Other times it might be a farmer and his wife and a pack of muddy children hushed by their parents' reverence as they watched the black-draped bier. It was these people, the ones who came alone or in families, the ones who had walked of their own accord a mile or, perhaps, five or six, and waited without knowing how long, who impressed Quirinius the most. These people had not come out as an entire village—twenty or thirty cousins of various degrees and a priest to force them out, trying not to smile at the holiday the death had brought them.

No, these folk were pious; that was it. This struck Quirinius when he passed the first woodcutter and then, a mile away, another and then a shepherd and then, an hour later, a farm family and saw them all not hang their heads as the Senator was drawn by, but instead drop to their knees and stare at the body as though the old man had been holy. Had he been holy? For thirty years his father had kept these people as well as he could in his sentimental embrace, settled their disputes, defended them as far as he could, fattened their priests. Surely that bespoke a love of them and of his duty to them. Was that holy?

Quirinius frowned as he watched these simple folk kneel. Before his father's death he'd have thought it sacrilegious—mildly, perhaps, but still a thing to be discouraged. But now his heart was softened.

As the cortege passed, one old man who stood alongside a younger man—to judge by their great noses and chins they were father and son—hobbled forward to the creaking wagon that carried the Senator's body and reached up to touch the body for an instant. The old fellow barely got away from the wheel, which was as tall as he, before it could grind him into the highway. He stumbled back and the horsemen passed him, their eyes fixed ahead as though the

151

old man had done nothing—or perhaps as though the old man had done the most natural thing in the world.

But Quirinius never told this to Ambiorus, the bishop or the abbot. He did tell Caelia once long ago, but she could understand things such as this.

At midday, when the sun was at its height, and all the colors of the world were most intense—the way it is in childhood when everything is new and startling—they came to a town not far from the small estate where the old Senator had held his last court session. It was a small place, shrunken from what it had been a century ago when a set of walls had been put up around its center and the people moved in closer or away to the estates of the great men. All the same, it had a few hundred people yet and a church somewhere; although Quirinius couldn't see it, he could hear the bell tolling behind the walls.

The people stood along the road, the better sort closest, the town councillors, a senator, a pair of the big landowners from round about, the priest, a clerk. Behind them stood the rest of the townsfolk in drab clothes of russet and gray and colors close on tan, indistinct as autumn leaves seen too far away. These common folk stood among the tombstones and monuments of the Roman days, quiet at the passing of the column. The shadowed, carven faces on the tombstones looked on as the old Senator passed on his way to join them, and the monuments cast shadows here and there among the crowd. No wailing or kneeling here because the people were self-conscious among their neighbors and a touch more sophisticated, perhaps, than the rustics. But there was a certain solemnity that Quirinius approved of.

The column plodded past the crowd, soldiers staring ahead with their backs as straight as lances, dignity wrapped about them like a cloud. Quirinius kept his face impassive; he acknowledged no one. He did, however, see familiar faces—a senator, a pair of curials, even a number of the townspeople—in the crowd. As the old Senator's body passed the priest, he began to sing a hymn in a remarkably powerful voice, and from up ahead Quirinius was startled to hear it taken up by a dozen women who chanted with the confidence of practice. He kept his head up, but cast his eyes to the right and saw, to his surprise, that the nuns of Pulcheria's abbey had gathered by the roadside and there, in front of them all, was that shameless hard-bargainer herself, singing as bold as anyone, her hands wrapped together in prayer. Her eyes seemed calculating as she assessed him, the new master of the country in which her abbey stood, but all the same her cheeks were wet, and Quirinius was startled at her emotion.

But Pulcheria brought Caelia to mind, the girl who'd been the object of that petty suit a year before and, sure enough, she was still there among the sisters. She was not singing. She met his eyes frankly, lips pressed together, and then, turning her eyes to the body of the old Senator, she raised her hands to her head and pulled her head-cloth away. She shook her head sharply, and all her red, red hair stood about her head like a globe of flame. Quirinius started at her red, red hair and knew, just as certainly as he knew anything in the world, that this was her gift to his father. He stared at her a long moment and then turned sharply away, because that was the only way he could do it, and the image of her smoldered in his mind. Somehow it seemed that he had stepped into a place beyond time, as in dreams, and home and the end of the day came without an effort.

Nine: The Principal Estate of the Quirinii, 463 AD

The old senator's funeral was a small affair, if dignified. A handful of the local magnates hurried in, landlords on fine horses with servants on foot in train, and two senators besides Albinius Maximianus rolled up, jostled on cushions in rumbling coaches, their servants trailing on horses or mules. Once in the courtyard of the villa, they drifted, surrounded by their satellites, secretaries, valets, a half-dozen private soldiers, to the whitewashed chapel. They left their supporters and lackeys in the courtyard to hover and stare into the chapel's open door, while the tenants of the estate and of the nearest village meekly crowded along the walls. And when the obsequies were over, the important men made elaborate statements of condolence and left, all but Maximianus; he remained, for there was business to complete.

Quirinius waited for Maximianus early the next morning on a graveled path of the formal garden on the east side of the villa. The shadows were long but faint, thrown as they were by a low sun hidden behind a leaden sky that hinted at soft rain to come. He stood motionless, his eyes on the hedged entrance to the garden, but really, he was listening, not watching. He was straining, as though to hear, or somehow sense, the footfalls of Saxons gathering, mobbing up, before they headed north, great, round shields on their backs, spears on their shoulders, long knives across the front of their belts. It was only a fancy, of course, something that couldn't be done, and yet he felt moved to try it.

Behind him a rook, black as the firebox of an oven, called sharply from the top of a tree in the courtyard. He turned to look toward the sound, and, when he turned back, he saw Maximianus approaching him, stumping along, the result of a stiff ankle, an old injury, something he hadn't noticed before. He wore a Pannonian cap, as did Quirinius—a symbol of their station, after all—but Maximianus had pulled his down a shade too low, as though he faced cold weather, not the mere freshness of an early summer morning, and he wore a rich chestnut cloak clasped at the right shoulder but draped over the right arm as though against a chill. The outfit seemed to put a dozen years on the man, to render him, say, half as imposing as he had been when he had spoken just days before in council, much less alarming than the man Quirinius had met when he had intruded upon him in his hunt for Hispanus.

They nodded at each other in silence and then began to process slowly past hedges cut square as boxes and waist-high to reveal blooming single roses, red and white, brought from Italy so long ago that no one could remember when. The air was tinged slightly with the scent of grass scythed down two days before into dense green carpets. After half of a circuit through the garden, Maximianus glanced diffidently at Quirinius and, catching his eye, spoke casually, without slowing his step. "Occasions are important. They're to be respected."

Quirinius nodded but said nothing.

"And so I didn't raise any topics yesterday evening, after your father's funeral, which might have detracted from the dignity of that occasion." He looked ahead as he walked, clasping his hands behind his back, bobbing on his stiff ankle as he walked.

"I know what you're concerned with, Senator: my marriage to Albinia and the threat of Saxon raiding." Quirinius smiled over at him, encouraging him to speak. The older man took the prompt.

"I take it your father explained our agreement?" Quirinius, amused, noticed the implication, that the deal was done, that there was nothing to palter over. In fact, as far as Quirinius was concerned, the old man was correct only that the date of the wedding was to be revised. That date now had a certain urgency to Quirinius in view of the council's inaction and in view of his plan.

"I think I recall the terms, at least broadly. The marriage to take place at the end of November. Albinia's dowry to consist of the estate called Latifundia Vetus and its associated village? We are talking about a small walled villa, with grounds of what? Two hundred and twelve jugera?

"Yes, exactly."

"Eighty serfs, a dozen horses, three flocks of sheep. Swine, I can't recall how many, but quite a few. Forty cattle, six pair of oxen, half a dozen outbuildings, cottages for the laborers, four or five heavy wheeled plows, and the usual assortment of equipment. That's about right, isn't it?"

"It is." Maximianus stopped for a moment and studied him.

"And the village has another thirty households. What would that amount to? Another hundred and fifty tenants?"

"You've been thinking about it. I see that."

"I've been thinking what it means in view of the Saxons."

Maximianus started walking again, looking down at the graveled path. "The Saxons?"

"The estate—all of our estates, really—must be defended."

"Yes, yes, course."

"But the question is how we manage it."

"I don't follow you. We arm the tenants so far as we can and hold our walls."

"What I mean is simply this. Yes, we can barricade ourselves behind the walls of our villas. We can drag wagons up behind the gates and knock the wheels off to block them. We can order the peasants to set their scythe blades longways with the shafts to make spears of them, and we can set our soldiers to boss and scare the rustics in hopes they'll fight well enough. All the while they'll peep over the estate walls and watch as their homes are plundered and their cattle driven away."

Maximianus winced at the images, but he said quietly, "And still, it is just possible that Eugenius Ater may be correct about the Saxons—that there may be no incursion, or that it may be slight and bearable." Maximianus spoke as though embarrassed to speculate aloud that Ater might have a point. Quirinius understood Ater's position, the motivation behind it. At least to this extent, Ater was entirely unsuited to struggle; he could, or would, do no more than rely on his hopes. Twenty-five years of peace, more or less, had given him license, or so he thought, to gamble, through inaction, for what he wished. And license to draw enough of the magnates along with him into dangerous passivity.

Quirinius turned to Maximianus. "You don't believe that."

"That it is possible, yes. That it's likely, no."

"Like me, you appreciate the threat. So, let's not sit about like Ater and Bassus and the rest of their kind. Instead let's take men out and worry any Saxons that approach."

Maximianus said nothing, only strolled, rubbing his jaw.

Quirinius prodded him "Just as you and my father and the others used to do under Ambrosius Aurelianus."

Maximianus stopped walking and sighed. He looked about him at the light grey sky and the streaked whitewashed walls of the villa. He absently brushed his hand across the top of the low hedge and rubbed the dew from his hands. Finally, he looked up at Quirinius, squinting in the cool morning light. The younger man saw in his face and manner that, without the generality of the senators and magnates as allies, and with the death of Quirinius' father, even though only recently restored to friendship, Maximianus had grown cautious and the littlest bit smaller. Only recently he had urged others in the general defense, but since then he had grown uncertain in the face of the indifference of half of the senators and magnates. Quirinius could see that the trick was to reignite some of the old man's enthusiasm, shore up his confidence and call him back to the attitude he had had when he reckoned that the great men would move to protect themselves. After all, he had a plan, and Maximianus could help him a great deal.

The old man continued "In those days, my friend, we had the general agreement, for a while at least, of all who counted. No one stinted men or supplies; we could even tolerate the occasional defeat."

Quirinius took up walking again, pulling Maximianus along. He wanted to scold the man, even shake him to reawaken the anger and strength he had displayed in council, but instead he kept his voice soft, and his tone so very reasonable. "But surely, Senator, you don't mean that we should hole up and wait for them? Or trade them land for a short peace? You know that will only entice them to return in greater strength." He clucked his tongue and shook his head. A soft delivery. A careful tone.

"I suspect that even your father would have agreed to a rather..." here Maximianus hesitated, "A rather defensive approach. We were to support each other, of course, the Quirinii and the Maximiani. Your father and I agreed to that. Banded together, we'll have no real difficulty in protecting at the very least our two biggest estates."

They stopped and stood by a statue on a plinth. Quirinius looked up at it a moment. An old piece brought from Lugdunum. Well executed, a young man in a pointed cap holding a horse by the bridle. He looked back at Maximianus. "Surely we don't wish to just whinge at threats and hope for a lucky outcome?"

"So, then, you'd prefer to bring the fight to the Saxons themselves." Maximianus spoke with a flat tone. Cautious.

"In a way, but..." He searched for an enticing word. "... cautiously. I want to bring just enough of the fight to turn them away from any little adventures they might decide to undertake hereabouts."

Maximianus regarded Quirinius as though looking at something too distant to quite resolve. "You're an optimist, my young friend. A rare thing on this island." He gave Quirinius a tired smile. "But you were at the council. The great families only dither now. Petty feuds over boundaries, high-minded disagreements over Pelagius, a willing suspension of disbelief about the Saxons. The end of it all is that, in the absence of someone like Ambrosius Aurelianus, they are incapable of joining together to look after their own interests." He glanced up at the pewter sky and shook his head at the thought of it. He turned back. "It really pains me to say it, but I think we must accept their reluctance and the limitations it puts on us."

Quirinius waved a hand dismissively. "Let them dither. Ignore them. Here is what we do. We field a good troop of cavalry, say, a hundred and twenty men, and trail any Saxons we see in the district. Let's grant that they're as hardy and brave as their reputation; still, they're all footmen and can't move fast enough to force horsemen to fight. We'll shadow them, threaten them, distract them and hamper every action they take. We'll never have to risk a decisive fight. Instead, when it suits us, we'll run down any who drift from the pack or range across the country foraging."

Maximianus pursed his mouth, not convinced. "Not a bad approach, I grant you. But, really, it can't be done as things stand."

"It can certainly be done; there's no secret to it. Aegidius, the emperor's Master of Soldiers, is doing it right now in Gaul against the Franks."

"I grant you the strategy is sound and well enough known, but there is no troop as large as that, and the magnates have made it clear that they won't cooperate."

"Ah!" Quirinius raised his finger like a schoolmaster making a point. "I have fifty mounted soldiers, armed and armored, and I could soon equip and mount a further thirty."

"The expense. The speed..." Maximianus frowned. "And feeding a hundred and twenty men. So that means what? A hundred and fifty horses? Thirty attendants? A dozen pack mules?"

Quirinius said, "The estate that is your daughter Albinia's dowry will support a dozen soldiers—a few more if I squeeze it hard. I'll get the rest from my other holdings. My estates can feed them. And speed? We'll hurry." He spoke with all of a young man's confidence that enthusiasm trumps circumstance.

Maximianus regarded Quirinius with a certain care. He was impressed at the enthusiasm, even though he was doubtful.

"Could you deliver the balance, Maximianus? The other forty men? Equipped and supplied for, say, six weeks?"

Maximianus looked up in thought. He frowned like a man doing sums in his head and at the end said, "Apart from my tenants, whom

I will arm in a rudimentary way, remounted scythes, hatchets, nail-studded cudgels, that sort of thing, I have thirty proper soldiers—all fitted out, arms and armor—but only a dozen are mounted."

"Good. Could you deliver another ten men? They don't have to be soldiers, just tough, resilient men, but obedient."

"Men, yes. Certainly. But apart from swords, I have no equipment for them.

"And horses?"

"Oh, I could deliver a dozen. Mostly nags."

"They'll do.

The old man shook his head. "We'd end up with a motley band, half-equipped and half-disciplined. And don't think that I call attention to these difficulties because I'm too old for a field campaign. Because I hobble and can't make things out at a hundred yards anymore. What I mean is that large difficulties remain."

Quirinius ignored the objection. "How long do you reckon we have, if the Saxons move against us?"

Maximianus shrugged. "It has grown late this year, so next summer sometime."

"A month of exercises should be enough to keep a troop together and out of trouble, and a month is quite long enough for the blacksmiths on our estates to turn out a few helmets and some armor. We have a few extra pieces in our armory."

Maximianus stepped back from Quirinius' enthusiasm and shook his head. "Flavius Quirinius, my friend, you forget that I will need those men on my estate against the chance of a Saxon incursion. If I am stripped of them for reconnaissance or adventuring and the Saxons slip past you and call on my large estate..." He shrugged.

"They won't call on any of your estates if we move against them. The Saxons will curve and circle about the district looking over their shoulders, keeping to copses and ravines to avoid the horsemen. They'll soon grow tired, hungry and frustrated, never able to force a fight. They'll melt away."

"And if I find that I cannot help? If I must look directly after my own tenants and properties?"

"I'll take up the plan on my own with what men and horses I have. I can protect my own estates, but it's not likely I could shield anyone else." He looked Maximianus in the eye. "In that case, you can see that I would be helpless to extend any protection beyond my own estates. But with a hundred and twenty men—now that would be a nice little army and would do admirably. Oh, yes." He turned away from Maximianus and pointed with his chin over at the statue on the plinth. "Nice work, that, eh?"

"Well, yes," Maximianus answered, some mild surprise in his voice at the abrupt shift in topic. He squinted at the sculpture. "Your father had it imported? It looks to be Italian work."

"My grandfather. A rather good Gallic copy of Italian work. Not the sort of thing a Saxon would appreciate."

"Certainly not."

Quirinius waved his arm toward the villa and out toward the property as a whole. "This is how men should live. We know this."

"Of course."

"And the Saxons? Have you seen how they live?"

"Yes. On campaign a long time ago. When I rode with your father under Count Ambrosius we passed through some Saxon villages."

"I understand they live like badgers."

Maximianus smiled. "Some of them, yes. The common ruck. They dig a pit fifteen feet across, roof it with a cone of thatch, put rushes on the floor and call it a house. The better sort, the thegns, as they're called, have something more like a proper house."

"But I understand it's one long room like a barn, and that they stall their cattle at the far end under the same roof."

"Yes, they do."

"Well, then. Isn't all of this worth saving? Isn't all of this worth striving to protect?" He spread his arms again at the villa, the garden, the little Roman world around them.

161

Maximianus said finally "You haven't any real military experience, my friend. And yet it would have to be you who leads these soldiers." The old man had said the hard thing, but Quirinius noted how polite his tone was. The argument was over.

"I look forward to it. You say that I'm inexperienced? Well, yes. But the Saxons haven't any military science; boldness isn't a strategy. Now, given the press of time, I think that my marriage to Albinia should happen very soon, don't you?"

* * *

At evening Quirinius and his column approached, and the walls of his estate rose slowly into view, light grey verging on white against the bright green of the surrounding fields. The stones of the walls grew more distinct, and the touches of shadow broadcast across the face of the walls from the setting sun indicated the slubs of mortar between the stones. Six troopers had ridden a hundred yards ahead against the slight chance of bandits, but now they swung their shields across their backs, drew their mounts to a halt and then turned them about and waited for Quirinius to draw up with the rest of the column. From the gate in the wall, the bailiff approached with a crowd of tenants to greet Quirinius and his wife.

Quirinius came ahead, surrounded by another troop of his horsemen and followed by the carriage in which Albinia travelled, jostled along on cushions and hidden behind leather curtains against the misting rain through which they had started before dawn. After the carriage, came a light wagon onto which were loaded three trunks of Albinia's clothes and effects and another with her library, apparently all theological tracts. Sitting next to the driver was a coltish, adolescent serving girl in a mud-brown cloak, frightened at the move with her mistress to a new estate. She looked about constantly as though suspicious that, somehow, the twenty-mile journey would bring her to a foreign land, Dalmatia, say, or Mauretania.

Not Albinia, though. Quirinius glanced over at the carriage from time to time, but there was nothing to see, no hand drawing a curtain aside, no face peeping out to see the approach to her new home. Odd that she showed no curiosity. Had the last night been so bad? The consummation had been awkward, of course, because they were practically strangers, and Albinia had gasped and flinched. She hadn't really been at all ready for it, dry as sand and hard to enter. Nonetheless, it was to be expected, and things would improve, now that the first time was over.

Still, Quirinius was uneasy—he had to admit it. The marriage ceremony had put him off a bit too, like a badly played tune clearly recognizable, but not all it should be. Maximianus' wife pulled a long face throughout the brief ceremony, while Maximianus himself seemed relieved to see it go through. Their expressions seemed incongruous.

And then, at Albinia and her mother's behest, they brought a priest in after the ceremony to give a benediction. He was clearly a fanatic—you could see it in his eyes, which would now and again flash open too wide as though deep and hidden enthusiasms chased each other through his brain. And his voice would break into a sob now and then, when nothing called for it. But clearly old Maximianus and his wife, long and tall as her daughter, were impressed with him, and suffered him to address them each by name, as though he were their equal. Clearly, he had too much power in the household. But, Quirinius reflected, that was a problem for the Maximiani and not for him.

As Quirinius stood with Albinia in the salon of the villa, she shivered with delight as the priest intoned the benediction. At the end of it, his voice creaked, and he frowned as though unhappy at the marriage. And Albinia's mother shook her head subtly and turned away. Before he could reflect on it, old Maximianus had stepped between the couple and, taking their arms, led them into the dining room for the wedding feast.

Quirinius rode through the gate of his villa at the head of the column, and a shift in the breeze carried the smell of smoke to him for an instant, and he knew by the brush of it across his tongue that it

163

came from the forge. The smiths were at work. After a moment, a pair of hammers began beating a measured rhythm. The smiths were turning out plate for helmets and armor as he'd set them to do before he had left. These things drove the reflections of his wedding from his mind. Here was a thing he could grasp; he felt more assured.

Once inside the villa's walls, he reined in his horse and turned back to watch the carriage creak through the gate and pull up behind him. He turned back to see the bailiff advance from the crowd of servants. He'd apparently flushed everyone from the villa into the courtyard and made them stand, the tallest to the back, and the women to the front in their cleanest clothes, all with their faces and hands scrubbed. The bailiff nodded sharply to a boy who ran up to seize the bridle while Quirinius dismounted.

Quirinius waved a vague approval at the crowd and went to the door of the carriage, where he said, through the lowered curtain, "Domina Albinia, you are home." In view of the obvious, the four Latin words rang pretentious to him, and he sneaked a glance behind him to catch any smirks, but there were none. A few moments passed, and then the door of the carriage swung open. Albinia stood faintly shining, as it were, in the gloom of the interior. At an indication from the bailiff, another boy ran up with a stool which he set below the open door. He scuttled back, head down in respect, but eyes turned up for a peek at the lady.

Albinia extended her fine white hand to Quirinius and stepped down to the ground, graceful as a springing doe. He could hear behind him, like the soughing of a soft wind, the respectful sigh of the gathered servants. Albinia nodded graciously and swept her glance left to right, taking all in with a single, elegant gesture. Very good. He was pleased.

The bailiff said, in a loud, clear voice for all to hear, "We welcome the arrival of you both, Dominē Quirinius and Domina Albinia, with great anticipation and joy."

"Thank you, bailiff." He waved to the crowd and then said, "Give them a holiday tomorrow. Even the smiths."

Then Quirinius took Albinia's right hand and led her into the villa, which was pranked with garlands over the front door and begauded with colored rugs and swags of bright drapery over the sills of the open windows of the upper storey. The bailiff followed, and then Albinia's servant girl, who looked fearfully about, in contrast to her mistress, who took in everything with a calm acceptance bordering on indifference. Old Dobunica, head of the house-servants, stood awaiting them. She had managed the household for years, even before Quirinius' eldest sister had left to marry. For an instant he thought of his sister riding off on a fine white mule, their father beside her, on her way to meet her new husband and see her new home. She had turned back in the saddle and tossed kisses to him and laughed. She had met the man she was to marry and very much liked him. Quirinius thought he ought to write to her, to see how she was getting on. When had he last seen her? Six months? Eight?

Albinia stopped and stood still, like a creature without volition or, perhaps, like one indifferent to place or occasion, oddly close and distant at once, like a person in a report. Dobunica glanced at Quirinius, who nodded. Thus prompted, the old woman, small and black-eyed as a sparrow, took the heavy ring of keys from her belt and offered them to her new mistress. They jostled each other, the hafts black, the flanges glinting like silver or old gold from turning locks throughout the villa. Each clink a password to a secret place. "Domina, these are now yours. When you wish, I will show you all of the villa and tell you how things are done here."

Albinia stared for a few moments at the proffered keys as though seeing such a thing for the first time, and she made no effort to take them, even only briefly and to return them, as the custom implied. Dobunica stood motionless, not turning her head, but she glanced at Quirinius out of the corner of her eye, as though they stood unexpectedly before an eccentric. The bailiff's face settled out, flat and expressionless as a pond at dawn. Eventually, even Albinia noticed the strain and said, in a cool, measured voice, "No." She waved vaguely at the old woman. "Keep them. Keep them." She looked at Quirinius and said, "I prefer to occupy myself with other things." Dobunica bowed her head and slung the rattling cluster of keys back onto her belt. She put her hands together, "Dominē Quirinius?"

"Nothing more, Dobunica." He took Albinia's arm and led her up to the suite of rooms he had had set aside for them. A glance out of the window in the suite showed the sky darkening. He heard the hammers of two smiths striking slowly, one after the other, making hard, dark, slaps as they turned out a sheet of iron. Their work seemed to call him. He shook his head gently to clear it of idle thoughts and turned to Albinia.

Ten: The Monastery, October 491 AD

"Those 'quite, quite correct actions,'" Bishop Valerianus said in a musing tone that drew Quirinius back from his reflections. He turned back to the bishop and regarded him from across the dim room.

"Well? What about them?"

The bishop looked down and hesitated, as though considering how to begin. *His caution is a sham,* Quirinius thought. He growled at Valerianus. "Well?"

The bishop looked up calmly. "Let me say only this: opinion was divided at the time."

Quirinius snorted. "So you say now. The magnates and the little kings were happy enough with those first battles won and the peace that was gained by them."

"With the battles, certainly. But—"

"Tell us of that first one, Dominē." Ambiorus interrupted the bishop in a bid to head off a hot exchange. Oddly, thought Quirinius, the bishop did not scowl at the affront to his dignity. Instead, he settled back in his chair and smiled. "A good idea from your captain, Quirinius. Yes, tell us about it."

Quirinius scowled, suspicious that Valerianus was somehow maneuvering along his flank, but he sat down and waved at the abbot to pour him more wine. Where to start? Not with the preparations. No. Just the battle. And yet the preparations, the drill, the scouting, the strategy were really as important.

The Principal Estate of the Quirinii, 464 AD

The first weeks of that summer had sprung by quick as a startled hart. Quirinius oversaw the work of the smiths. He ordered twenty new swords and as many lance-heads forged, the sword-blades

167

turned out from ingots, the lance-heads fashioned three at a time from scythe-blades. Sheets of gray iron were cut apart to make helmets, the pieces hammered into shape in deep wooden molds to make half-bowls then joined by a band and a ridge. Smaller pieces were hammered to make cheek-plates and neck-guards. Yet other sheets were cut with great shears into rectangles that were fixed onto coats of scale armor. Carpenters, standing with fragrant curls of wood about their ankles, planed boards which, set edge to edge and bound tight about the circumference, made fine oval shields.

As he waited for the equipment to be completed, Quirinius led his men, both his old regulars in their armor, and the new men progressively armored as the weeks went by, on rambles and maneuvers throughout the countryside. They followed the dragon standards in charges, in retreats, in curves; they passed through streams and over the low stone walls that cut the peasants' fields apart until they had learned to move in organized troops of ten, twenty, fifty, a hundred, and finally, a hundred-twenty.

He drilled the new men with wooden swords from horseback, and all of them in striking wooden targets with a lance as they passed at a canter, but most of all he had them move in groups across fields, changing direction constantly at his order, dispersing and regrouping. By the late days of summer, he had a respectable troop—a bit unwieldy to command but, all the same, not bad. All with swords, lances, shields, helmets, almost all with iron-scale coats, a dozen with serviceable quilted coats that would stop a blade.

One afternoon at the edge of his estate, in the saddle and sweating in his armored coat, Quirinius took off his helmet, and watched the sun settle behind a wood to the west. After a time, he glanced over at Canidius, who sat his horse beside him. Prompted by his master's glance, he said, "The days are getting shorter, Dominē." Quirinius nodded. He looked over his shoulder at the horsemen milling in the field behind him, noting that they no longer drooped after a day of drill.

"The summer's passing. It's daily growing dangerous to wait," Quirinius said. He gave a single sharp nod at the troopers and turned to regard Canidius, watched his dark, calm eyes, and asked, "Can we trust them in a fight?" The question was disingenuous; the troop would have to move soon, ready or not. What he really intended by the question was not so much to learn the captain's opinion as to ready him for the campaign. Canidius looked away a moment, took off his helmet, and rubbed his damp scalp. He glanced over at the men, and then looked at Quirinius. "Our old troopers, yes. The new ones, just possibly."

Quirinius nodded. "That's what I think. But whether we're right or wrong, we have to try them."

"Yes, Dominē."

"We'll all rest tomorrow. The next day, we head south and patrol."

"Very good, Dominē."

"Come and see me after supper for orders." He waved at two of the old soldiers to accompany him and headed back toward the villa. He heard Canidius' shrill whistle behind him as he summoned the standard-bearers.

* * *

The Monastery, 491 AD
Quirinius looked about the room, drawing his listeners in, and said, "Saxons were heading north from the coast. A few small parties moved here and there, but there was one band of about two hundred and fifty that advanced bold as anything up the Via ad Ventum Belgarum heading, if no one did a thing about it, into the neighborhood of Corinium. They couldn't have taken the city, of course, but they could have spoiled a swath of the country fifty miles long once they had crossed the Fuscum."

"The Fuscum?" The little abbot asked, then reddened at his own impertinence in interrupting.

"The Abon Dub." Ambiorus gave the British name. The abbot nodded.

Quirinius continued. "The trick, in the end, wasn't to meet them for a fight, it was to draw them into a fight they couldn't win. And I had to do it outnumbered and with green soldiers. After all, even my troop of regulars had not been in the field since my father had fought under Ambrosius Aurelianus and, really, over the years most of the men had been replaced by younger. And the newest men? Those I had raised at the start of the summer or pulled away from Maximianus? Pretty well drilled given the rush but, in the end, only drilled. So that meant choosing my ground.

"There was a good stone bridge to carry the Venta Belgarum Road over the Fuscum, and the Saxons would head that way to cross there and proceed up the road to prey on the villas and towns to the north. Now, as Ambrosius Aurelius had made clear to me—and it's obvious when you think of it—there's a great advantage to striking your enemy when he's half-divided while crossing a river. You can strike when you outnumber those who have crossed and, if they fall into disorder, even their fellows can't save them by dashing into the confusion. That is, even if they can—or dare to. And it's better yet if you can do it where there's no bridge for him to get back to and defend himself on. So, the strategy was to take the bridge over the Fuscum before the Saxons reached it and hold it in their face. It would be easy to block the twenty feet across between the parapets. So, seven armored men across and six deep with their lances leveled, the rest of the men along the bank to discourage a rush across the shallows on either side of the piers."

"It sounds as though it should have sunk into a stalemate," Bishop Valerianus said. "You on the bridge, the Saxons at the approach. You would hardly dare attack two hundred and fifty men with your handful on the bridge; they would not dare to attack on a narrow front with no hope of flanking."

"No stalemate. It was merely a demonstration. I wanted the Saxons to move upstream a mile where there was a narrow ford and try a crossing there. That's where I wanted them."

"And, of course, they did as you wished." Valerianus rubbed his face as though in fatigue.

"Yes, they did as I wished. They're too bold to scout, and they get into trouble." He looked at Ambiorus, who grinned with delight and leaned forward in his enthusiasm at the story.

Quirinius thought back to the morning of that day.

The two hundred-and-fifty Saxons milled along the south bank of the Fuscum. They had earlier approached the stone bridge a mile downstream and had indeed found it blocked by a troop of dismounted cavalry who stood shield to shield, their lances set beside them in a thicket, steel points pricking at the sky. The Saxons drifted warily toward the bridge and then stopped a hundred yards away when they saw the first three ranks of troopers on the bridge level their lances into an impenetrable hedge. Beyond the bridge, horsemen patrolled the far riverbank, grand in glinting grey armor, ready to discourage any Saxon who might be bold enough to wade across the shallows on which the piers of the bridge stood. A handful of bold young Saxons jogged forward to show their courage with yells, with a clashing of spearshafts on shields, and with incomprehensible taunts, but the Third Thracian Lancers stood fast behind their blue and red shields, each man steadied and emboldened by the three glinting lance-heads that stood ahead of him, and by the calm voice of Quirinius, who stood among them reminding them that no one could pass that finely-honed, steel-tipped hedge. "Steady, boys. They'll keep away from those lance-heads; they're keen as a shrew's tongue." After a short time, the rowdy Saxons shouted their final insults and, unable to accomplish anything, ostentatiously turned their backs on the troopers and contemptuously sauntered back to the rest of their force.

Quirinius watched the little army of Saxons gather itself into a dense column and head back the way it had come, black- and yellow-quartered shields on their backs and spears on their shoulders. When they had distanced themselves a hundred yards he called, "Lances! Up and ground!" The men swung them to the vertical and

171

struck their butts on the stone roadway of the bridge with a clatter. "Shields down!" The men set their shields on edge before them and rested their left hands on the rims. Quirinius nodded in approval at how neatly it was done. The Saxon chief, sitting on a cart horse at the tail of his column and looking back, must have seen the crisp action. Good: it would be a lesson, a subtle threat. He stood and waited until the Saxons had disappeared down the road and over the rise beside the river to the south. From there they could not see Quirinius' next move.

They would doubtless try for the ford upstream a mile. He turned away and squeezed himself through the press of his soldiers and crossed back over the river to his horse and the trooper who held it for him. He mounted, waved a standard-bearer to his side, and shouted to Canidius, who stood at the edge of the bridge. "Hold the bridge with your men and wait for my word."

"Yes, Dominē."

"And you know what to do then."

"I do."

Quirinius turned his horse about and headed upstream. The standard-bearer dipped the flashing dragon standard and brought it up, directing the troop to follow, and seventy horsemen followed Quirinius at a trot.

Two hours later, as Quirinius judged by the late summer sun, the Saxons reached the narrow ford. That there was a ford here was quite evident, and Quirinius had reckoned that they would find it even if they hadn't caught a peasant or woodcutter to threaten into showing where it was. A spur must lead off to the northwest from the road proper because a path advanced encouragingly through a gap in the low bluff along the south bank of the Fuscum and down to the river, where it disappeared at the water's edge before reappearing at the north bank, above which Quirinius watched.

Many of the Saxons shifted up and down the riverbank, as though they distrusted the dark water that rushed over the ford. Quirinius watched them from the shadows of a copse along a gentle rise two hundred yards away across the river. A watcher lay flat on his stomach nearby, screened by a bush; Quirinius stood watching too, but swathed in a brown cloak to hide the glint of his armor, and he leaned against the bole of a great tree to hide his figure. At a distance he would be invisible, or at least unnoticed by any but the most astute observer, of which there seemed to be none in the crowd of barbarians across the river.

The Saxon chief mounted on the blocky cart horse lent a comic touch, since the animal had clearly been plundered from an estate in order to lend him dignity, but the chief was clearly no rider from the way he kept fighting to settle his seat, sacrificing what dignity he might have had. Four of his companions sat as awkwardly on bony, stolen nags. The rest of the men milled about looking at the ford, less than eager to wade into the dark waters in the cool of the late morning, burdened as they were with satchels, shields and spears.

The chief waved his arms angrily and shouted, impatient at the delay, but Quirinius could not hear him from across the river. He was pleased at this: the Saxons could not hear Quirinius' men either. They had been ordered to keep silent, but, though they did not talk, their movements, and those of the mounts behind him down the path that led up to this rise and then down to the ford were significant. Seventy horsemen, though they waited patiently, could not be entirely quiet. Horses whickered and here and there stamped out the odd, dull thud.

A young Saxon, just a boy, Quirinius judged, waded into the river and faced his companions. He raised both arms and waved to indicate where they should cross. Quirinius squinted to get a clear view; the water came almost to the boy's waist. Good, the river was high, even this late in the summer. The rest of the men began to mob before the ford as they prepared to cross. Some took off their shoes, some did not, all slung their shields over their backs. The first few stepped into the river.

Quirinius said quietly to the man who lay beneath the bush, "Count them. When thirty have crossed, come back to the path and call to me. Do not worry about silence. Be sure that I hear." The man nodded. "Do you understand?" The man nodded again. "Then tell me so." The man turned to look up at him. "Yes, Dominē. I understand."

Quirinius slipped behind the tree without a word, headed down the gentle slope behind the ridge, and tossed his cloak to one of the two troopers who stood holding the reins of three horses. He took the reins of one, mounted, and said to both soldiers, "Go to Canidius. Tell him to have his troop mount up and come to us now. He must be prepared to advance the instant he sees our standards. Do you understand?" The men nodded. "Yes, Dominē," they said in unison. Quirinius nodded and pointed to one of them. "You go along the river," he pointed to the other, "And you go back along the road and take the woodcutter's track through the wood." Both mounted, the scales of their coats clicking faintly, and disappeared on their errands.

Quirinius waved the standard-bearer to his side as he rode from the edge of the copse and down onto the beaten earth of the old footpath that led to the river. He kept at the head of his troop but was careful to stay always just below the highest point of the footpath where it topped the bluff and then went down to the Fuscum. No Saxon crossing the river would see a trooper before Quirinius' advance. After a short distance, he reined his horse to a stop, put on his helmet, shifted his sword in its scabbard, and took up his shield and lance. And he waited a short—but very long— time.

* * *

The Monastery, October 491 AD
Quirinius decided to take the story up here. "It was hard waiting, and I hoped that scout could count. Odd how these concerns seep up when there's nothing to be done. Soon enough, however, he came scrambling out of the woods, waving with one arm, holding his helmet against his chest with the other, shouting, 'Thirty! Thirty!' He seemed delighted with himself for working it out.

"I rode slowly to the top of the rise and looked down. By then about sixty of the Saxons had crossed, and they stood in a mob near the water's edge, half blocking their fellows who tried to finish crossing. Many of these stood waist-deep in the middle of the Fuscum, leaning against the current and stepping slowly, contesting with the river to keep their feet and holding their round shields overhead to keep them out of the water. There was a good deal of shouting, but it was clear they had no idea we were nearby. The challenge of crossing occupied them wholly, so the situation favored us even more than I could have hoped.

"I headed down the footpath toward the ford, and when I reached the mucky flat, I veered to the left, the standard-bearer close beside me. Too close, in fact, for we touched knees a time or two, but he carried the dragon good and high, and I could hear its scarlet tail snap. I could hear the hooves of the troop behind me as they wheeled left in a single line. In that way we could sweep alongside the Saxons, every man with a chance to use his lance or, if need be, his sword. To make the most of our numbers, you see. A shield is not helpful in an attack to the right, but it is easier to use a lance that way. So, I trusted in surprise, movement and armor, and, in any case, I had to leave the other flank to Canidius. At the bottom of the bluff, we shifted from a trot to a canter and passed in a line of single horsemen along the crowd of Saxons. I leaned out of the saddle to strike one of them, but only grazed his shield and sent him tumbling. I doubt that any, or more than a few of the troopers, did much better as they passed by, but no matter. Surprise and the demonstration of force was enough to crowd them together, to make them recoil into the river, and to encourage those who could not get back to the ford to flee in a thin column downstream.

"As I had drilled them, the seventy horsemen followed the standard and cantered past, turning a sharp left near the riverbank and then circling back to make a second pass. By the time the head of the column had described a circle and started its return, the mass of Saxons who had crossed the Fuscum were jogging upstream along the bank, and many of them had flung away their shields and spears to win a little speed. Their fellows on the other bank had stopped crossing altogether. The outcome for those on the north bank would have been certain even if Canidius' troop had not appeared, as it did, at that moment.

"There's little enough to say about the rest of it. The troopers cut most of the fleeing men down from behind with lances or swords. A handful of Saxons plunged into the river—who knows what happened to them? A little knot of them kept their heads and, crouching behind their shields, menaced anyone who advanced. One of the new men, a blitherer, urged his horse right up to them but, of course, the animal was more intelligent than his rider and stopped short of the spearpoints. A desperate Saxon turned aside the trooper's lance with his shield and seized the horse's bridle. His fellows followed up by tossing the trooper from his horse and killing him with a thrust from one of those great knives they carry. He was the only man we lost, and all because he couldn't learn that a man on horseback is in danger when he doesn't keep moving."

"Dominē?"

"Yes, Ambiorus?"

"What of the rest? What of those Saxons?"

"Did I kill them, do you mean? No. Here's the lesson: when you win, don't risk spoiling it."

"Dominē, no disrespect, but there must have been nearly two hundred left."

"Indeed, but they were sixty fewer, and it was enough to make them turn tail. Remember, my task was to keep them out of the country and to break in my men. But I see you're distressed. Listen. We headed downstream, crossed the Fuscum at the bridge, and then took the road down which the Saxons were walking home. We dogged them for a week at the distance of half a mile and picked off another dozen of them, stragglers and foragers. They walked home— a good fifty miles south of the Fuscum—with almost nothing to eat. When we turned back toward our country, we left them

176

downhearted and thin as wraiths. I kept patrols throughout our countryside, but no Saxons came back that year."

"It would seem that this little adventure of yours served a purpose quite beyond that of training your men and discouraging the barbarians," the bishop said.

"Oh, yes, Your Eminence. You're quite right. But what event does not offer several possibilities to the man whose duties force him to look?"

Eleven: The Monastery, October 491 AD

Quirinius' assumption of office took place a month after the Saxons had been sent off. He would have preferred it sooner, because that way it would have appeared spontaneous and natural, as inevitable, in other words, as, in his heart, he knew it to be. But if there was no spontaneity to convince everyone of the ineluctable and therefore legitimate assumption of office, then art must act where chance stickled.

"I assumed the office at Corinium Dobunnorum. I had sent Maximianus' men back to him after our return from the fight on the Fuscum and its aftermath, and my soldiers were told quietly afterward that Ambrosius Aurelianus had conferred the dignity on me of the office of Count of the Britains."

"And had he the authority to do this?" Bishop Valerianus asked dryly.

"Yes, he had put the office aside when my father and I visited him on the way to the council. He handed me the tabulae with the commission from Flavius Modestius Acindynus, his predecessor."

"Ah. I failed to grasp the extent of his power, that it was sufficient to promote you without even soliciting the views of the senators in the Provincial Council." The bishop smiled vaguely at the ceiling. He turned to Quirinius and raised a hand to stop him speaking. "Not that anyone doubts the rightness of the, ah, arrogation—a strong word, but I cannot quite think of another. And what is done is done—and a long time ago too. Tell, us, Dominē Quirinius, a little more about it."

Quirinius nodded. "All right. I dismiss your cavil; you stand at some distance from the practical concerns of the world. And so, I'll tell you about it, though I doubt it will much affect your views on the subject.

"Sequanius, the bailiff of our second estate, told Canidius and two or three of the men that I was to be the new Count of the Britains. I had to introduce the idea somehow. Why not use subtlety? Canidius sidled up to me the next day, diffident to know if it were true. A nod was enough to confirm everything."

"Something more official might have seemed called for," the bishop said. He examined a chunk of bread absently and set it back in the basket.

"Perhaps, but it's remarkable how often the slightest gesture will do. And isn't a sort of elegant economy one of truth's faces? And so, on a late afternoon the soldiers frog-marched me to the gardens behind the villa, tossed a red cloak of my father's around my shoulders and lifted me on a shield in the manner of the legions long ago. They wished to take part in an important development, to make it, in part, theirs."

"Now, I wonder how they knew the custom?" The bishop asked disingenuously.

"I stood on the shield, knees slightly bent, balancing. It felt, in a way, like drunkenness, the elation, the unsteady footing, the faces of the men looking up at me as if from a long way off. I'll admit it. Beyond the half-dozen men holding me up on the round shield stood the rest of the troop. And past them, a pair of minor senators with whom the Quirinii were allied, the bishop of the diocese—old and halt and faintly protesting, it's true. Our tenants too, and the nearby villagers. It had been the best showing we could do on so short a notice. And then the men gave The Shout, the barritus, by which the soldiers acclaim their leader."

"Their emperor," the bishop said. Quirinius smiled.

"The onlookers cheered, the senators excepted. The simpler among the onlookers were probably unsure of what it precisely signified, but they knew something important had happened. And besides, I clarified the situation a week later."

Corinium Dobunnorum, 464 AD

Quirinius came to town with a hundred and twenty soldiers—all he had—his forty new men and the entire Third Thracian Lancers with shields retouched, helmets and iron-scale coats gleaming from hours of polishing with fine grey ash. The horses had been curried, those of the captain and his lieutenants had their manes pranked with scarlet ribbons, and old silver medallions depended from their harnesses. The dragon standard flashed particularly bright in the afternoon sun; the villa's goldsmith had re-sheathed its gaping head with gold-leaf and polished its great, staring garnet eyes. The standards of the individual troops were particularly presentable, repainted where they needed to be, and the letters re-stitched with gold thread: Ala III Thraciani Contofori. His forty new troops had their own banner in mustard yellow with Bucellarii Quiriniani marked boldly across it in claret letters, all of them words that might work like a spell on illiterate barbarians, words that might cow unruly spectators. And then Quirinius came, proud and game as ever he had been, wrapped in splendor, confidence and his finest clothes.

As far as the ceremony went, everything had to be done all over again and on a larger scale, and Quirinius saw to it that this was done, at least as far as possible in this dwindling Roman world. His entrance was grand—he sent a troop of horsemen ahead so that the townspeople would not hesitate to open the gates, and the forum was presentable just the way he'd always imagined it should be. The soldiers had put a flock of sheep into the forum for an afternoon to graze away the grass from between the flagstones, and then a dozen serfs had swept up afterwards and settled any loose cobbles. When they were done, it looked as kempt it might have when Constantius Chlorus had passed through on his way to Londinium and the purple.

Quirinius' house, his house now, not the Senator's, fronted on the forum, and he'd had tapestries hung along the arcade on the second story. They were of russet and grey for the most part, but here and there a flare of red or purple sprang out, colors brought from Italy or the East, startling and richer than the common people would have seen, and they hung limp and heavy and therefore obviously rich, something impressive for the crowds on the next day.

Fitted together and standing before the house was a tribunal. It had been built quickly; the beams smelled strongly of fresh-cut wood, and drops of sap stood out here and there on the balks and glistened in the evening sun. And though the work had been done quickly, it had been done well and very exactly. Quirinius had forbidden nails, and so the tribunal had been constructed post-and-beam; though the structure was meant for an afternoon, it might stand a century. The beams were utterly square, the balks plumb as a statute. The carpenters' care was evident. They had done all they could to show that their master was a great man.

On the platform stood the old Senator's gilded chair and, at either side, a soldier in a bright white tunic and polished helmet, a new-painted shield posed on the flooring beside him and a spear straight up, tip to the sky. At the four corners were torches waiting to burn through the night.

There was a surprise the next morning. The townsfolk had turned out early to await Quirinius' assumption of office—nothing odd about that. Shortly after dawn they were milling about; no one had seen them drift into the forum, but the trickle of people from the countryside grew steadily throughout the morning. They trudged through the gates and into the forum and milled about, murmuring like wind in wheat. So far so good. But where were the nobles? The investment to come was as much for their benefit as for that of the common people, much more so, in fact.

Quirinius had notified the senators and the other magnates but had made a fine calculation in doing it. He meant to give them just enough time to attend, but not enough to react. But had he cut the time too fine? He was informed that there were, as yet, no nobles, no great men. He strode back and forth across his study, the captain watching closely, trying to anticipate orders and the bishop, old, grumpy, crabbed, sitting in a chair with a rug over his shoulders, even in the growing midmorning heat.

"This isn't even my diocese!" he said. Quirinius stopped pacing, turned and looked sharply at him.

"Be quiet," said the captain for his master. The old bishop shrugged and shook his head. Quirinius began to pace again. Should he go ahead with the public assumption of the office? There was no choice, really, he supposed. It would be worse to postpone it, to slink off to his estates, humbled by these men who couldn't even band together in face of a real enemy, like the Saxons. But to seize the office before a crowd of townsfolk and rustics, would that confer enough authority, enough strength, enough security?

Canidius coughed softly, more like a valet than an officer. And then he said: "They must come, Dominē. They may disagree, but they must come, if only to see how you do it and how the people take it."

"Hmm. So, it would seem. And yet." He stopped pacing. "I really didn't think they had the fortitude and unanimity to act as one—either for or against me."

"They don't, Dominē." The voice came from the open door of the study. Quirinius, the captain and the bishop turned to see a grinning soldier there. "They're approaching now."

"Who?"

"Well, the great men, Dominē. Ater, Bassus, Maximianus, Bishop Justinus. I have seen them from above the town gate. You can tell them by the banners."

"Justinus! Ha! And this isn't my diocese! It's his!" the bishop complained, raising his arms in sudden, doddery frustration. Quirinius didn't bother to look at him.

"And that means the young Uortigern and some of the kings surely, and all the landlords that matter, Dominē," Canidius said.

Quirinius scowled. "Don't you see? They aren't coming one after the other; they're coming together. They've all met somewhere—perhaps just on the road, but that doesn't matter. They're coming together. Now, men, what can that mean?" He looked at the scout from the wall, at the half-dozen soldiers and the bailiff.

No one said anything.

"Exactly," Quirinius said. "They've formed together like an army."

Within two hours they were in the town, Eugenius Ater rolling along in his splendid carriage with thirty horsemen and as many foot-soldiers, Nonianus Bassus with about the same, Maximianus with his twenty horsemen and half a dozen Atrebate chiefs with another hundred men between them, poorly equipped and going on foot but, all the same, horses were only a nuisance once in town. The young Uortigern came with twenty proper soldiers and a small troop of his father's Saxons, old relics who, for one reason or another, had stayed with his house. Habit perhaps, German loyalty perhaps. Perhaps they had been outlawed by their own people. Here they were, the last remnant of the men who had come to save Britain from the Picts and Irish. And then, surrounded by the local landlords, Bishop Justinus and twenty of his soldiers. A dozen of the lesser magnates followed them through the gate, each with about twenty armed men.

The nobles and their followers entered the town quickly, pushing the townsfolk and peasants aside, and, once arrived, they didn't mill about but gathered quiet before their lords, who stood opposite the tribunal on the porch of the church, from which they could see everything. Ater's and Bassus' men, in particular, stood at parade beside each other. Their horses snorted and balked here and there, but by and large they kept good order. The men slung their shields on their shoulders as though there might be action. They rested their lances upon their shoulders and waited. The sun brightened their helmets. Maximianus' twenty troopers waited, mounted at their flank, glancing about uneasily, as though unsure who their friends were.

Inside the house, Canidius reported to Quirinius the attitude and disposition of the nobles' men. Quirinius continued to pace, his hands clasped behind his back and his eyes on the floor. It wasn't the arming of the men that troubled him; of course, they'd come armed. It was the unity of action. That didn't bode well at all.

"Maximianus' men, they're standing with Ater's and Bassus' men, it's true, but off to the side and so, Dominē, I think they support us."

"They had better!" Quirinius said sharply. He wondered, as he had so often, whether he should have invited old Maximianus to join him in his plan. It been hard enough to winkle the extra forty men from him for the fight against the Saxons; it had seemed better to surprise him along with the rest of the great men and hope for the best. After all, their houses were joined now by marriage, so what choice did the old man have?

Canidius said nothing more because, no matter what he might say, Quirinius would be unappeased. There was a long silence until Quirinius shouted in frustration, "Oh, just come out with it! You're afraid if they attack, we might not come out on top."

"No, Dominē. Who can't have confidence in you? It's just, that, well—"

"As an ecclesiastic I know that I should be prepared for my last day," the bishop said in a thin voice. "'In the midst of life, we are in death' and all that. But all the same I feel uncertain that this would be a good day for me to die."

"Shut up," Quirinius said.

"The circumstances, I mean. Would I die blameless? Or with my soul smirched? I see your arguments for assuming Ambrosius' role, and yet should I be mixed up in this? And, you have to admit, I'm under compulsion. Does that exonerate me? Or does it rather tell against me that I've submitted when I, as a divine, should be made of sterner stuff?" He sighed and drew the shawl more closely around his shoulders.

"At least you have something interesting to think about." Quirinius turned away from the men and stared for a moment longer at the wall. Then, resolved to act, he turned and said, "Captain, send the men out and put them in position. Do not allow them to speak; do not allow them even to look challengingly at Bassus' and Ater's men. The rest I don't care about. They know what to do when I appear. Oh, and take this bishop with you and have him lead prayers for a short while as a prelude." Canidius hoisted the old bishop abruptly out of his chair like a bundle of sticks. His shawl dropped to the floor and lay there at the edge of Quirinius' vision like a doubt. The captain half-dragged the stumbling old man out of the room, the bishop's arm in one hand and his crozier in the other. "Don't forget the miter!" Quirinius shouted after them, and one of the private soldiers snatched it from a table and followed. The old bishop whined querulously, but all the same found himself, a few moments later, on the tribunal with his miter askew because the soldier had planted it on his head from behind as the old man struggled up the tribunal stairs.

Quirinius stood in the doorway to his house, waiting to ascend to the platform when he reckoned the moment was right. It would be difficult to decide that moment. He must improvise now within the framework of the ceremony. He listened to the bishop as the old man prayed in a high, rusty voice that carried over the forum a short distance and sounded remarkably like a mattock on a stone. No one was responding. That wouldn't do; Quirinius could see this. He said a few words to the steward of the house, who stood beside him, clasping his hands obsequiously, and the fellow bobbed his head like a bird and, first looking left and right, ascended half the steps until he could peep up at the bishop. He whispered, but the old man, nervous and half-deaf, heard nothing and continued creakily intoning.

"Just tell him!" Quirinius shouted. The steward looked down over his shoulder, nodded and then said plainly to the bishop. "Pater Noster! Pater Noster!" The old man, startled, hesitated a moment, and then, straightening his miter, began the prayer. Of course, just as Quirinius had known, his soldiers arrayed about the platform took it up and then the prayer was taken up in turn by the other soldiers—the most Roman first, those of Maximianus, Bassus, Ater and Justinus, and by the Uortigern's more civilized men. The voices had a muddy indistinct quality, like thunder at a great distance, and echoes from the walls about obscured the words, though not the cadences, and made the sound more indistinct, more powerful. Of course, the townsfolk and peasants joined in, and even the wild British warriors of the chiefs and petty kings. Quirinius now ascended the tribunal and strode forward, speed and dignity about equally mixed.

He waited until the crowd had finished intoning the prayer. He stood in fine clothes: white tunic with purple strips over each shoulder, fine trousers, a red commander's cloak. He wore a chaplet of oak leaves—gold of course—cut from foil by the goldsmith with a pair of fine sharp iron shears. Around his waist he wore a military belt from which hung a broadsword in a fine leather scabbard with a silvered half-moon chape. Quirinius was, of course, every inch a noble, but it was important that he be seen not as one among many, but as superlative. No wonder, as he stood looking across the forum, that he suspected the other magnates might try to kill him. Odd, he thought, that something so obvious hadn't occurred to him earlier. Still, he kept a bland expression and chose to regard this afternoon as a sort of battle which, whatever slippery and dangerous turn things might take, he could still win.

And so he stood still, statue-like, and stared over the heads of the crowd and into the distance like an emperor on a coin. In fact, however, he was concentrating, taking in the position and attitude of the other magnates' soldiers, assessing their postures, gauging their intent. Everyone had joined in the prayer, and that was good—they'd come with him thus far—not far, but a short way, and it would take something to draw them back, to turn them away. They had been drawn into the spectacle and made themselves part of it—it would take the magnates some effort to steer them from this useful rut. Time and, one might even say, rhythm, were important to the affair.

The prayer came to an end with a boom, as of surf, on the final syllable, and the silence that followed seemed unnatural, freakish. Quirinius still stood motionless and let the moments pass. Everyone watched him, and he drew the silence out like a skein until even he reckoned it would snap. He could hear his heart in his ears, speaking to him.

And then he raised his hands, palms outward, like a priest in benediction, always keeping his eyes on the distance. The soldiers, who had been told to cheer, but not when, and who waited straining at him, took instruction from the gesture and shouted. Then, a squad that had been detailed for it swarmed up the front of the tribunal with the shield. As with so many other things, it had been refurbished: new paint, gilding along the rim. The soldiers set it before Quirinius, who stepped onto it and felt himself raised up to the level of their shoulders.

He stood on the convex shield above the crowd, above the platform, halfway, it seemed, to the sky. The afternoon heat shimmered from the pavement, a breeze snaked between the houses and scurried around him as though the very world held him in its grip. He looked down, giddy, upon the guidons and standards of the troops and, further, upon the bright upturned faces of five hundred people and he could feel, then, that he was joined to them and that they knew it and would accept it.

The squad lifting him up gave the Shout three times, and each time they were joined in half a moment by the rest of Quirinius' troops below him in the forum. By the third Shout they had been joined by the troops of the other nobles. The nobles themselves, however, were less sanguine. They shifted uneasily on the top step of the church porch and cast glances among themselves. Maximianus' nephew and heir, Moderatus, scowled openly. "Uncle?" he said quietly, leaning toward the older man, then again "Uncle!" both sharply and quietly. Maximianus waved his hand negligently, not looking at the young man. Moderatus looked about cautiously, and then leaned in. "He's dangerous, Uncle. He's dangerous to our whole order."

"Perhaps. Perhaps. But we're bound to him now. We can't lightly set aside that tie."

Moderatus looked at his uncle as though about to wrangle with him, but then sighed sharply, stepped back, and watched the proceedings in glum silence. Maximianus watched the tribunal; he looked thoughtful.

The shield was lowered, Quirinius stepped from it and ascended to his father's chair, which had been set up on chocks to give it more height. He sat motionless, with the dignity of a consul. Two of his soldiers took up the shield, brilliant in its new blues and reds, held it up and balanced it on its edge along the tribune rail, to keep everyone's mind focussed. The rest of the soldiers stood about Quirinius on his golden chair. He extended his right hand and Canidius stepped forward and placed Ambrosius Aurelianus' old diptych in it, Quirinius all the while looking away, above the crowd as though he scanned important things beyond the clouds. He had added as flourish a new purple ribbon that depended from the diptych, broad enough for everyone to see. He held it aloft, but never looked at it. It was merely a thing. Like all other things, it was in his power, and he had no need to regard it. Instead, his eyes swept over the crowd as he turned his head slowly, ceremoniously, from left to right and back.

The people were with him now; he would live if he handled them well. And so, now, the personal touch. He slowly turned his head and cast his eyes across the crowd again, willing them to be silent, attentive, obedient. The magnates? No matter now what they thought. Without their men they were like snakes with their teeth drawn, splendid, elegant, menacing and harmless. It was time now for loft and elevation; it was time now for some splendor that the people could share.

"Senators, Clarissimi, Nobles, people assembled, I am here to inform you that I have accepted the burden so recently laid aside by the Count and Senator Ambrosius Aurelianus, that same burden which he has asked that I assume for the protection of all and the restoration of the state." He continued to hold the diptych aloft and motionless.

"There are Germans everywhere, Saxons, Angles, Jutes. The sea is more a highway than a barrier, and the Irish make their way across it to harry the west. The Wall, so long a bulwark between the World and Chaos, sits half-defended—No! Even less. It is all but undefended, its gates open as often as closed, a structure that beckons the Pict more than it repels him, that entices the Scot more than it rebuffs him. To the south the Channel Islands, once the handmaidens of Britain, are now the nests of pirates, desperate and heartless men, a scourge to Roman and Briton equally.

"All this is known to us. All this is known to the Dominus Ambrosius, who wearied and aged himself in your service and that of the state." Only the lords would have a glimmering of what "the state" meant, but its wonderful sound, its four rich syllables, should call out of the past to them like a mother's voice. Well, perhaps.

He looked grandly over the crowd but scanned from the corner of his eye the nobles gathered on the steps of the church. There were many who exchanged scowls and glances among themselves, but not old Maximianus, who watched things even more closely, if possible, than the rest. He must have been thinking, *Was what Quirinius said about his assumption of the office true? Was this Ambrosius' wish? Of what significance was this, even if true?* Or was it like one of those common half-truths that clutter the world, alternately greasing the ways and tripping people? And then, for those with a philosophical turn of mind, and Maximianus, like a good Roman, had some of this, there were truths and there were *truths.* Or perhaps there was no truth at all?

But Maximianus put these questions aside as he marked the glances of the other nobles, for it came in a flash to him just how they would regard the situation that young Flavius Quirinius Claudianus had thrust upon them. Ambrosius Aurelianus as the Count of the Britains was no threat to order, had in fact been the basis of a certain order for decades, and if he had effaced himself recently and had thumbed his nose at his fellows, well, that had been tolerable too, quite tolerable. But the situation couldn't last, of course. Politics, like the greater world, abhors a vacuum. Any thoughtful man could see that. And who would be drawn like Zeno's atoms into the void and fill it up? The old Senator's upstart son was more ready to cast the dice than anyone. And he was obviously both vigorous and handy in his actions. Not deft perhaps—the young man wasn't deft. He was a bear, not a fox, but competent in his heavy-handed way. Only God knew what might have happened if someone as ineffective as the young Uortigern had tried to assert himself as Quirinius was doing. There'd have been no hope for him. Maximianus stared fixedly at Quirinius. *But something passable might come from Quirinius' arrogant gambit. Possibly. The rascal should have warned me, though. No. Not deft. No fox. A bear.*

Still, Quirinius' speech was a pleasant surprise. His father, the old Senator, had been a better speaker—the local Romans had even flattered him with the nickname Quintillianus Minor. But all the same, the younger Quirinius' rambling, rumbling periods were worth a listen—he larded his speech with anaphora and threw in the odd transferred epithet, and he knew a bit of stagecraft. Where, by the way, could the young cub have learned that? His oration was pure melodrama, but, perhaps, Maximianus thought, this is the time and place for the rise of a great man. He crossed his arms and watched Quirinius with narrowed eyes. He listened. He was irritated, but he was open to things.

"In fine, voluntate Ambrosii Aureliani et pro bono proviniciarum, magna cum himilitate, dignitem accepto, ego Flavius Quirinius Claudianus, Comitis Britanniarum." Quirinius concluded in a booming voice, explicitly taking the office of Count of the Britains.

"It is very wrong of him to arrogate this title," Ater said, standing next to him. "At the very least he should have put it to the Council for a vote."

"At the very least," Maximianus said. "A month to get the conclave together, a few days of debate, and then an adjournment while we consider things."

"Exactly." The fat senator narrowed his eyes as he tried to decide whether Maximianus was speaking ironically. But Maximianus was beyond any concern with irony. He had begun to be caught up with Quirinius' arrogation. Just a bit. But enough. He had been swayed enough that, were there an effort on Quirinius' life, he would oppose it; he would intervene with his soldiers against it, despite the fellow's arrogance and failure to consult with him beforehand. *The rascal's gambling not only with his own life, but with my fortunes as well.* He shook his head, but half in that admiration that bold actions extort.

Quirinius' death had, of course, been Ater's and Bassus' and the Uortigern's hope. And who knew? Perhaps even the bishop's hope. And a good half of the rest would likely have connived for want of anything better in face of the situation. Not that the magnates had put it to each other in such terms. They hadn't quite blood enough for that, or perhaps they were still too civilized. Instead, they had met on the road to the ceremony. Quirinius had not allowed time for fully hatched plots, and so they decided to oppose him more gently—show him their displeasure by a muster of the troops. Perhaps the young man would back down. Perhaps his men would fail to acclaim him; perhaps there would be negotiation. And perhaps things would get out of hand, and he would be killed in a riot. Perhaps and perhaps and perhaps. The world was a loose, uneasy place, and a great deal happened unexpectedly, fortuitously even. And no one need feel quite responsible.

Other rash young men had destroyed themselves before now, and though Quirinius' fall and death was the half-hope of Ater and Bassus and half of the magnates, still it was only a half-hope, because their dreams were pale and filmy with indecision and would not coalesce. Maximianus glanced about him, saw his fellow nobles clustered in a gaudy gang, eyes narrowed, grimacing as though they had found vinegar on their tongues, but he could tell by their eyes and their postures that, in the end, they would not act. It was time to put the seal on their inaction. He bowed to them, stumped down to join his troops in the square and drew them up close beside those of Quirinius.

Twelve: The Monastery, October 491 AD

"The first thing after taking office was to get a look at the Wall. This was needed for two reasons. To see the thing itself, of course. That hardly need be said. The second was to let some of the men get used to me and to wrest some of them, or at least their loyalty, from the nobles. To—"

"To encourage those men to find a place in their hearts for you," the bishop said in a rich, honeyed tone.

"True enough, Your Eminence," Quirinius said. He turned to look at Ambiorus and the abbot. "But please observe that the bishop's irony doesn't render what he says untrue."

"It does affect the flavor, you might say," Ambiorus said from the back of the room. He now rose and stretched.

Quirinius laughed. "Quite right, my boy! But let's keep our eyes on the truth. Let's disregard His Eminence's sarcasms.

"So, yes, I wanted their loyalty—or at least their divided loyalty. For me? Somewhat, yes. But really—and this is the part it's hard to convince a fool of—but really because their loyalty was a tool I could use against the enemies of the province."

"And their loyalty—even divided as you say—was a protection to you." The bishop smiled with a touch of bitterness.

"Who better to be protected? The ninnies who wouldn't defend themselves from the Saxon raiders? The half-barbarian chiefs who could hardly be told from the Saxons if they didn't open their mouths?"

The abbot, who abhorred conflict, tried to turn the conversation back to its proper channel. "Dominē, was there no threat from the north at that time? From beyond the Wall?"

"There's always a threat from up there. Always. And then there was a certain propriety to visiting the Wall. As Count of the Britains,

193

I had to survey the Wall; it was simply part of my office. But it was a good thing I travelled there, because when I arrived with my men, I found we were needed. It was purely a matter of chance, but you can imagine how my visit was construed."

"As an example of your genius?" the bishop asked smoothly. "A sort of proof that you could see their danger from two hundred miles away?"

"Oh, better! Much better than that. I was the son of fortune, 'Felix.' Like old Sulla in his prime.

"You see, the Scots had come down from behind the Wall and troubled the king of Rheged—or a part of it, anyway. He called himself "Trifun" and maintained that one of his great grandfathers had been the tribune of a cohort of some sort under the second Valentinian. Who knows? It might be true. In any case, it seemed to him that the word, even corrupted as it was into his name, gave some shine to his house. From the days of his grandfather, his people had been given a free hand to rule the area as a sort of marcher state, a kingdom if you like, on the ground that they would keep the Scots and Picts behind the Wall, and we Romans would regard them as independent.

"His homestead was a refurbished hill fort, a great ring of earth on a height that let him look down on his subjects on the moors below and scan the territory for the approach of enemies so that he could shut himself up good and safe until the danger passed.

"We rode up the way until we came to the foot of his holding, and then I sent a man up to summon him. A stupid decision—I see that now. For what would have happened if he had declined the summons? I was pleased with the way things had gone so far, but still, I had little enough face to lose in those days, and a slight, even a mere slight from a little kingling like Trifun, would have been dangerous for me."

"You don't misstep now, though, do you?" The bishop's eyes glinted.

"Seldom, Your Eminence. Seldom." Quirinius spoke loud enough for all to hear. "But Trifun did not defy me; no, as I soon learned, he needed me. So, instead he gathered his most important warriors and walked solemnly down from the gate of his holding. He wore a huge and splendid bearskin cloak—it must have weighed twenty pounds—and a magnificent gold torque about his neck. I thought of Vercingetorix. As he approached, he gave off some of the savage splendor of the old Celt, but here it was fit and right beneath the cold, grey northern sky, in that land with nothing of civilization, the forlorn Wall excepted, for a hundred miles. He was as perfectly natural to the place, as fitted to it, as a fish to the sea. And, though he was barbaric, he reminded me of myself in some way I couldn't determine. He was a huge man—even taking the great cloak out of account, he was huge. Hands as broad as grain-scoops. Yes, he reminded me of myself somehow, even though his eyes were blue. His eye, I should say, for he only had one. The result of some old skirmish somewhere."

"In other words, he almost measured up to you?"

Quirinius laughed. "Indeed. That's it. For a daft moment or two I almost thought myself his inferior—at least in that wild country. The people there had been Brigantes when the Romans came. They are still, if I'm a judge, though of course they call themselves Rhegedati now. But does it matter?

"And then he spoke, and it was Latin. Rough and simple, true, but Latin all the same. He used a couple of complicated phrases he must have learned from some Roman who was old when Trifun was a boy. A grandfather perhaps. The records from Eburacum state that there had been a battalion of Batavian auxiliaries along the wall here for centuries. Maybe that's how the Cicero had leaked into his speech."

"How gratifying. But you were his superior all the same."

"And so, we greeted each other in the language of civilized men, and I could see his warriors swell up with pride like birds in winter to see him do it."

"And your reply?" The bishop raised his eyebrows.

"Simple enough. No future participles or gerundives, if that's what you mean." He looked slyly at the abbot. "You follow this, don't you?"

"Well..."

"Good. Very good." Quirinius said wryly.

"The niceties over, you slipped into British," the bishop suggested, slipping into British himself. He leaned against a wall and regarded the ceiling. He crossed his arms, but low, over his stomach, as though it pained him.

"Of course," Quirinius said, dragging the conversation back into Latin. "Though you might be surprised what British is like hard alongside the Wall. More like Pictish, I suppose, now that I think of it."

"You'll have to describe it to me. But some other time."

"We stared at each other, there at the foot of the hill. He was a tough old bird. As I say, he'd lost an eye somehow and had broken front teeth. But he was shrewd; I could tell. He looked me over carefully, and I'm sure he wondered how a man so young could appear at the head of such a troop, all obedient and well-fitted out. He knew it meant something. And so, he invited me to his supper, and of course I had to agree."

"Your instinctive grasp of diplomacy deserves remark." The bishop spoke without looking at him. Instead, he rose and began to pace slowly back and forth.

"You are clearly fatigued, Your Eminence. And so, I dismiss your scoffing. The meal was dreadful--mutton seethed in oatmeal. But I learned about the Scots beneath the Wall, where they were, and what they'd done. And even though they were too many for King Trifun, I told him I'd drive them away. I didn't need more fighters, not really. I had my Thracian Lancers, twenty of my bucellarii and two dozen others that I'd seconded from three or four of the lesser magnates."

"A test of your authority as much as a reinforcement?"

"Indeed it was. I was Count of the Britains and my authority naturally extended beyond my own domains. This had to be made obvious from the moment I assumed the office. What better way to do it?"

"The imposition of a tax, perhaps?"

"Ah, the annona still rankles, does it? Try for some perspective. But to return to the story. I wanted a few of his men; Trifun could lead them, or his son—but they must obey me. That was the condition. He saw the sense of it right away. First, it showed his subordination to the government of the senators further south and, second, the presence of his men, once we'd defeated the Scots—"

"The outcome was certain," the bishop said.

"It certainly happened. And second, their presence would give him enough to claim that he'd protected his people. This was important because a hundred peasants from nearby villages milled about within the stronghold waiting for the Scots to leave the country. They wondered how their homes fared, and Trifun took their looks as a deserved reproach. As we sat in his hall you could hear the voices of the peasants and the bleating and lowing of the livestock they had brought with them.

"And though he called himself King of Reghed, he was really only one of them. There were two others at the time, as I recall, grandsons of Coel. I think one of them was named Cyngar or something equally savage, and he had his seat at Corstopitum. Trifun's exact relationship to these kings escapes me, but whatever the details, it was quite an embarrassing situation for a monarch who couldn't keep order in his own state. He needed a victory and quickly; the details of it could be worked out after it had been won.

"After supper he took me to the guard-walk above the wooden gate, and we looked over the countryside. He pointed straight north across the moors and into the distance.

"'The Wall is there,' he said. 'You cannot see it distinct; it appears only as a grey stain along the horizon. But that is what it is.'

"I nodded. He pointed a bit toward the east. 'That smoke is a burning village.'

"I asked, 'How many have they burned?'

"'Enough,' he replied.   He was dramatic because he was bitter. But I could understand that.

"'Three? Four?' I asked. He nodded.

"'Four villages and several homesteads.' We stood for some time in silence looking out at the little column of smoke miles away. Finally, he said the obvious, because he couldn't keep himself from stating it 'There are too many of them for me.'

'How many?'

Trifun put his hands on the parapet and leaned forward. 'A hundred.'

"'I will beat them,' I said. Trifun turned to me, squinted a moment and then looked down at my troops resting at the foot of his stronghold. He nodded.

"'Well,' I said. 'Those Scots must be about ready to go home. Where is the nearest open gate or breach in the Wall?'"

* * *

The Wall: 464 AD

Quirinius and his men leave the next day as soon as the sun is high enough to see the margin of the road along which they trot. The men clutch their cloaks about them and lean forward into the clammy wind; their long, faint shadows follow them to the left, skimming over the road beside which they ride to save their horses' hooves. The road is not bad this far north, as Quirinius is surprised to see, until he considers that the land is poor enough that weeds find it difficult to push up between the road-stones and thus even the rare traffic along the way is enough to wear them away, and the peasants have found the broad five-sided cobbles too difficult to prise out for their shanties. Cold and inattention have preserved this stony way pointing straight to the Wall. The horses' hooves make a thumping sound as the troop trots along.

Quirinius rides at the head of the troopers. Trifun's son Patricius (how his father hopes) rides just behind him. The boy's hair is long, and his wrists are loaded with bracelets. He knows no Latin. Quirinius wonders who his mother could be, for he is small, his hair dark, and he bears the whorl of a blue-green tattoo on one cheek. Altogether too Pictish for the taste of the new Count of the Britains. But the boy is an irrelevance unless he manages to get himself killed. And Quirinius has already spoken quietly to the captain about this, and so now a fatherly old soldier rides beside the boy to watch over him like an angel. The boy's entourage is small; only horsemen can come on this fight, and Trifun hasn't many horses, let alone men who can fight from them. Only eight men follow the king's son, and they ride painfully, elbows flapping and rumps bruising. None of them, neither Trifun's son, nor the Rheged nobles, is properly equipped. A sword for each, yes, but only horn-plate helmets, and no other armor apart from shields. They'll be pretty useless in a fight, but, as a decoration for the boy, they do well enough.

By midmorning the column settles into a quick walk, and Quirinius can now see the Wall clearly for what it is, an amazing dike set up to let the barbarians to the north break themselves against it and slip back to their dripping cloudy homes at the end of the earth. Which can't be so very far away.

Under a high, pewter sky, the Wall lies quite like a dragon atop a line of hills and fills the dells between. It is a dragon with its tail in the German Sea and its chin resting at the Irish, and the mile castles and fortlets between them stand up like so many plates along the great beast's back. The scale of the thing strikes Quirinius only after he's watched it for a while, and he draws the reins sharply; the horse stops abruptly and branks. He stops for several moments, his gaze fixed on the wall because the thing is frankly amazing, sublime, even—in fact it is beyond the ability of anyone with imagination to take it fully in. And then of course he thought of Hadrian—the hard, scarred, determined old soldier with a map in one hand and a ruler in the other, an emperor, a man who could rule a line across a map

199

and, with a single stroke, call the wall into existence: *Fiat vallum!* And there it was.

And here he was, a little man with a little army scuttering in its lee.

The cavalcade moves, all orderly, after Quirinius and his captains and the Count's gold-headed dragon, its scarlet tail floating out behind in the cool morning air. Behind this is the purple guidon reading *Ala III Thraciani Contofori* and then Trifun's standard, sent with his son, some sort of rude disk on a pole. Quirinius disregards it; he hopes everyone does. At the rear ride twenty of the Bucellarii Quiriniani and, joined to them, the twenty-four horsemen levied from the magnates.

The troop moves along with an order that suggests the whole expedition has been planned. It has not, though—or not to the degree that Quirinius would prefer. All the same, he moves quickly, as though confident, deft as a juggler, or perhaps a sort of dancer, but like a juggler or dancer he expects to apply his skill to what chance brings and is confident he can meet it. This is his gift. Thoughts flash through his mind like clouds of silver minnows, but when the column passes off the high road onto the moor and picks its way carefully through the tawny brush toward a column of smoke two miles away, his thoughts gather on the smoke. It looks greasy. Is a cow burning in the middle of the hamlet? Or perhaps a man whose screams can't be heard so far away? Quirinius, bold as a bear, is confident in his power and in beneficent Opportunity—he will know what to do when he arrives. He is wrapped in The Idea and in ineradicable confidence.

In the meanwhile, he squints for the scouts he has sent ahead. There are glints on the rise ahead—scouts' helmets—and then the men themselves are suddenly visible, tall on their horses, as they trot toward him. Hurrying—but not too much, for they must spare their horses. As they approach, he notices, almost irrelevantly, that the scouts' lance-heads wink now and then, even in the glum northern day. The three troopers move in nice order about the circumference of the village, lances up as though in an exercise. The Scots in the burning hamlet will have seen the well-equipped scouts describing the edge of the settlement, displaying themselves grandly in their steel helmets and armor and moving together neat as gears. All quite disturbing even to the Scot chief and his nobles. These armored troopers aren't warriors—these men are soldiers, men who mean business, men who watch intently, men who don't course about pointlessly even though their horses are fine and worthy of display. The Scot chieftain frowns like a man who's heard a credible story about a ghost; he had thought the Romans were long gone, but now he can't be sure.

One of the scouts whistles sharp as a nick; all three scowl at the raiders for a moment and then turn and trot away, never looking back, even as the Scots shout at them and the youngest spit and toss clods in their direction to show how bold they are.

But they are not so bold as they at first think. When the scouts leave without hurry—for they too are bold—the Scots decide, wisely, that it is time for them to leave too, and off they go across the moor— not helter-skelter, no—but rather in quite good order at first. But they suffer worry; their minds are unquiet, and gradually they begin to rush. It's imperceptible at first, even to them, even as they cast the occasional sly glance about to see where their fellows are, each man considering, at the back of his mind, whether he's quite keeping up and whether he can get ahead without quite seeming to. And in time they string out in a longish column across the moor, the most anxious at the head, the more bold or circumspect at the tail.

The ninety Scots jog behind a dozen shaggy scantling cattle and try, even as they hurry, to guide them ahead. The better sort, the chief and a half-dozen of his nobles, ride ahead on long-maned, hook-headed ponies, and urge the men with sharp cries to follow at better speed. And soon, behind them, but never closer than a mile, is a single scout, watching, watching. Gradually the Scots spread out as they head for the wall, the faster passing the slower, the boys slipping past the men. Out of pride the chief will not allow himself to draw too far ahead, even though he believes that he can see what he did not expect when he crossed beyond the wall: a competent, mounted pursuit. He turns in his saddle, puts a hand on the pony's haunches, and squints back. Yes, certainly, almost certainly, the scout has been joined by another horseman, and behind them there is indistinct movement, more soldiers no doubt. But where from? He knows Trifun hasn't such men, and the Romans have been gone from the Wall for a generation.

He notes with irritation that his footmen are dropping their loot. They do it in a small way at first, a roll of homespun here and a ham there. Then one of them throws aside a bundle wrapped in a cloak, another drops a mattock and hurries on. Soon whole loads tied up in blankets are lying about and the moor is strewn for a mile with the shoddy possessions of three poor villages. And soon the Scots pick up the pace further and abandon the cattle, which shamble left and right away from the line of march and look reproachfully back past their bony, angular hips at the jogging raiders.

The Wall is close now, but so are Quirinius and his lancers on their well-fed, well-petted and strong horses. It's quite apparent to Quirinius what the Scots must do—head for the gate that lies two miles ahead and a bit to the west. Otherwise they will be trapped against the stones of the Wall itself and die there.

It is not a large gate, the one ahead—Quirinius has been assured of this. And this is a good thing because the gate will hardly be wide enough for more than three or four men to pass through at once, and perhaps fewer if they are frightened. And yet—and this is the dread part—the gate calls like a siren to the frightened raiders who will die as they try to pass through. Even Quirinius can hear the call.

The pursuit is long and slow. Quirinius and his men move at little more than a quick walk after the Scots. They spare their horses and never get close enough to provoke them into drawing up in defense. Quirinius knows what must be done. Follow, frighten, tire them, and then close in when they are sufficiently disordered. The trick is to know when that moment comes. He speaks to Canidius, who nods and then shouts to a pair of troopers with ensigns, and they move off, left and right and then ahead of Quirinius' force, and the ten men of their troops follow them, just as in a drill. The little troops advance at a canter and along the flanks of the now-distended line of fleeing Scots, and they keep their lances high and glinting against the grey sky, just as on parade.

Now the Scots have men on either side of them and behind as well; they are obviously on the edge of desperation—beyond it in fact, though the old chief can't admit this—they are unable to keep themselves from looking first at the gate. Its dark mouth is closer now, inviting. And the armored cavalry is about them.

Quirinius sees the gate as well, but he suddenly realizes something he hadn't considered, that the gate doesn't lead directly through the Wall. What he sees is an empty portal into an auxiliary fort built against the Wall, and he grasps the situation at once and swears. The fort was built against the wall and there will be another gate across the grounds of the fort. The gate the Scots are straining to reach opens into a fort.

He should have thought of this, he tells himself. Of course, the Romans didn't just put gates through the Wall, like holes in a sieve. Every one had been protected by a garrison in the old days. To breach a gate the Picts would have had to fight their way into a fort. And now this derelict fort could afford the Scots a little protection, if they could keep their heads long enough to realize it, and, even if they lacked the presence of mind to grasp their luck, there would be no room for a cavalry fight within the walls.

The situation calls to Quirinius for action.

From horseback he can see the gate into the fort stripped of its wooden doors and iron hinges, and it seems like the dark wailing mouth of an old man. It is still a good mile away, and he knows that he must cut the Scots down, or as many of them as he can, before they reach the gate where, if they are bold and steady, a half-dozen of them might hold off his men with levelled spears as he had held off the Saxons over the Fuscum. He is certain that he can prevail, but he must do it quickly and on horseback if he is to do it cheaply. Foot to foot will cost men.

Quirinius spurs his horse and gives a shout to Canidius, a deep ursine shout. Canidius nods at him, his eyes flash behind the nose-piece of his helmet, and he whistles earsplittingly loud with his tongue. Quirinius reflects for a moment on how important a minor talent can be. Up ahead, the ensigns of the horse-troops hear the sound, turn sharply in their saddles to glance at the captain's upraised hand, and then they dip their standards once and twice with great deliberation. The men of each troop now pull up sharply and stop shadowing the Scots. They wheel to face the raiders and level their lances. The troop to Quirinius' left advances, first at a walk and then at a trot, at which pace they pass through the Scots, and they transfix three of them who have turned their backs to run. Two of the horsemen leave their spears in the fallen Scots, one of whom rolls over and snaps a spear shaft. One horseman misses his man but knocks him a good six feet away with a brush of his horse's flank.

In an instant the horsemen have passed through the distended column of Scots and have even passed through the other troop of cavalry on the other side. They then wheel and join the other troop, and the two of them head back at the Scots again at a walk and then at a trot and then a slow canter, just as they have been drilled at the estate. All have lowered their lances save for the two men who have lost them; they hold their broadswords high.

Quirinius watches all this as he canters toward the disordered Scots. He shrugs his shield from his back and onto his left arm and draws his sword, all the while looking for a man to strike. By the time he reaches them, the remaining Scots have clustered together, each facing out, panting and big eyed, their spears out like the spines of a sea urchin. Quirinius' horse moves forward at them, and it seems they may break, but instead the hairy bellowing raiders only draw back into a denser crowd, and his mount swerves to the left and passes around them, just out of reach of their spears. He feels a dull blow to his back-- a Scot behind him has cast his spear, but it rattles harmlessly off the scales of his armor. Quirinius does not even turn to look; he just keeps on his way. As he makes a circuit around them, he hears hooves behind him, and he sees, at the edge of his vision, a few Scots stranded on the field, who throw away their shields and swords and run like hares for the fort. Immediately, a half-dozen troopers chase them, slashing down at them one after the other until a dozen of them lie in a line that approaches, but does not quite reach, the gate. A pair of men, lighter-footed than the rest, disappear into the fortifications, their tawny hair streaming behind them like horses' tails.

But, back where Quirinius rides, the whirl of horsemen has pushed the remaining Scots into a circle, and even the most fearful among them knows better than to leave the protection of his neighbors. Quirinius and his men draw off to watch them and circle lazily at a walk, observing, taking in the panting, glaring raiders. From the tail of his eye Quirinius sees a handful of Scots slink through the ruined gate. No matter. A few men to carry the tale of the defeat back home, a defeat even more dramatic and more dreadful in the telling and retelling than it has been and will become. A defeat at the hands of multitudes of Romans, all clothed in steel and blessed with arms that strike like drop-hammers and, like drop-hammers, they are stronger than any man. Six feet tall, all of them, and hard as rocks. Their eyes were dark as a mine at midnight, and whoever they glanced at, well, his blood cooled in the most peculiar way. No man could have stood against them, no. I'm lucky to be alive to tell you, though at night they call to me in dreams, and I stir like a poplar in the wind.

The Scot chieftain, however, cannot enjoy the luxury of survival. Only a good death will do now, a magnificent death to expunge the smirch of his clumsy, failed raid and elevate him to the realm of his great ancestors, the dark Celtic spirits whom Quirinius despises. He is probably convinced that Queen Maeve is his grandmother. The chieftain pulls up his horse and turns to face Quirinius. He is scranny, but his magnificent fading red beard gives him a certain flair, as does his dented helmet, an old Roman one. Quirinius notes that the cheek-plates are gone—lost in a bog somewhere, or perhaps hammered into spear points by a smith in a settlement too poor to get iron.

The chieftain's lieutenants hang back. They're brave men, of course. No one doubts it, but still they remove themselves a bit and watch his face in hope to see the glint of an idea that, like a lucky throw of the dice, will turn everything about and bring them home alive and respected to sit for years around their sheep-turd fires and tell the young fellows how they bested the Romans and left them dead on a heath below the Wall. They would be great men and alive.

But the chieftain knows better, knows what must be. He never looks at his men, but just fixes his eyes on Quirinius and squints slightly, like a man just making out the pole star on a light evening. Quirinius shakes his head gently a moment to be sure his helmet sits right, and then pulls his shield up a bit higher. It's a good shield, rich blue and with a red equal-armed cross painted on it for luck and to show he's a civilized man. He sheathes his sword and reaches his hand out to a nearby horseman. "Lance!" he says and feels it placed in his hand as he keeps his eyes on the chieftain. He takes the weapon and lets it slip a few inches through his hand until he's grasping the shaft where it balances. Then he levels it and turns his hand under the shaft, as he was taught in childhood. He squeezes his thighs and the horse advances toward the Scot. *No point in waiting, The old bastard might come up with something.*

He hears one of his men shout behind him, and he can hear the man's indecision in his tone; should he follow close, or let his master risk himself? But then, what's the risk? The chieftain's elbows bounce as he canters forward; the man is no horseman—he rides only to show his position. He can hardly keep his little shield in front of him. And his lance? Well, that's hopeless. He'll be lucky to touch Quirinius with the shaft, let alone the point. Quirinius, by contrast, sits his horse like one of Aetius' Huns. He's practically one with the animal, and he knows what to do. He keeps his lance level, but he's more interested in keeping his large horse bearing down on the Scot's small mount, and, as the men approach, the Scot can see that the mad Roman is simply charging straight into him. There is no science here, no art.

But of course there is. As the horses come within twenty feet they veer away from each other, as Quirinius knew they would, and the Scot passes him on the left. Quirinius pulls up his mount, turns it, and then chases the Scot, who is trying to gain some control of his frightened horse, which continues crabwise across the heath. He spurs his own larger animal and catches the chieftain up in a few instants, and for a while, they canter side by side, Quirinius now with the chieftain on his right. The man looks at him, puzzled and struggling to bring his lance over his horse's head for some sort of blow at Quirinius' unshielded right side. He can't do it, of course; he's not the horseman enough to handle the animal and the weapon and attack from the off side. *If he had any brains he'd drop the lance and try with his sword.* Or run away. That would be best. Quirinius squeezes the barrel of his horse sharply and cries "Ha!" to urge it on and, the moment he has pulled the littlest distance ahead of the Scot, he raises his lance and shoves the butt of it between the forelegs of his opponent's horse. The pony trips and is down in an instant; the chieftain flies over the pony's neck and pitches awkwardly to the ground to lie stunned and probably hurt, on the grass, while Quirinius pulls up, turns the lance around, trots over, and, leaning out from his saddle, studies the Scot for a few instants, chooses his spot, and stabs him carefully, once, to the death.

He looks up to see the captain and several of his men approach with a cheer. Fifty yards away the battle is over. The huddling Scots have thrown aside their weapons on the assurance they'll be spared, and they are, though Patricius and his father's men commence to rob them of their ornaments and shoes. The chieftain's lieutenants see this, observe their dead sprawling chief, and decide that he has covered himself in whatever glory was left. They wheel and head for the gate in the fort's walls, yip-yipping to urge their little horses on.

Quirinius moves after them, though not as quickly as he'd like—his mare is chuffing, and he sees the hair on her shoulders stand up damp like the bristles on a wet brush; he smells her sweat and his own. Still, he forces the horse on, as much by his personality as by the pressure of his legs, and Canidius and the ensigns gather just behind him; they have the grace to pace him and not to take the lead.

The men pass onto the roadway to the fort and, as they do, their horses' hooves hammer a cluttered high tattoo on the road-stones. Will there be any Scots in the fort to greet them? Certainly, when Quirinius and the troop approach they see no little phalanx of resolute men at the threshold of the gate, spears out like the fabled Spartans blocking the doorless portals of their city. In a moment Quirinius is through the gate and reining his horse to a stand as he looks about. He's not fearful, only prudent. The street he is on leads straight across the parade ground of the empty fort to the gate in the Wall at the far side. The timbers of its old doors lie tumbled in a heap beneath the lintel like ancient storm wrack with only a narrow way among the fallen balks, just wide enough for a single traveller or party of raiders in a file. All the same, the Scots are gone; they have passed through the gap to recede like shadows at dawn.

Quirinius starts his horse forward across the rammed earth of the parade ground, worn bare and hard as iron by the boots of drilling soldiers, though now sporting the odd cockade of tough weeds here and there. To his right is a line of barracks, doors stripped for wood a generation back, roof-beams silvered by the hard weather where the roof-slates are missing, which is a pretty general condition. The praetorium, utterly roofless, stands to his left and above the empty door is an inscription in stone to tell anyone who might still be able to read in this wasteland that this section of the wall is patrolled and kept in good order by the Cohors Equitata Dalmatica XXI. Who knows what had happened to them? Probably withdrawn by a usurper to blunder about in Gaul in his civil war a hundred years ago.

The fort had been stripped of power just as surely as of roof-slates, curtains, duty rosters, buckets, hams, door-hinges and boots. It was all of a piece, Quirinius reflected, and anyone could see it, should see it, if they had any sense, but, of course, in this disordered world, there weren't many who had seen it. No, only Quirinius can look about him and, in a glance, see what the derelict fort represented and represents: the Idea. Rome from right here, the doorstep of Pictland, all the way south as far as a bird might fly in a week or a thought in an instant to the edge of the Berber lands, and all of it ordered, civilized and productive. And here he is, Count of the Britains, no doubt of it now, passing through the silence, the swelling hollow left behind when the Idea had drawn back to the Inland Sea to huddle behind the walls of Constantine's city. And he'd heard disturbing rumors about even this, that Latin wasn't much spoken there anymore in the land of the Basileoi.

All the more reason to be resolute, stern, like the selfless Aurelius marching along the Danube for years at a time, a shield to the Empire. But Quirinius doesn't really have the philosophy for it, or perhaps his blood isn't so cool, his sight not so long, at least not where abstraction is concerned, and he feels a certain heat rising from his belly as he rides slowly toward the far gate. Odd, the heat, so local at first and then rising sudden as a storm along the horizon. He tosses aside his lance to hear it clatter on the hard gray ground behind him. He undoes the thong beneath his chin; off comes the helmet—he tosses it casually to whoever rides beside him. Now his head feels better, lighter, lighter even than it ought, but cool too, and that's good, or cool for a few instants anyway until the warmth rises through his chest and neck and he hears the sea singing in his ears. Odd, that—it's twenty miles to the sea but, yes, he can hear it plain as the creak of his saddle or the murmur of riders to either side. It's anger of a sort, he supposes. It can't be despair, no, not on a day like this.

He slips his shield from his arm and slings it without a glance from his saddle and, now that he has reached the gate, slides off his horse and strides to the stone stair leading up to the parapet above the gaping gate. The sound of the singing sea is louder in his ears, louder, louder; he cannot hear the steps of those who follow. He takes the steps quickly, takes each one with dignity, for they are his steps and were made for him.

On the parapet he stands between the battlements and looks down into the rough country below, a wild territory quite apart from civilization. He feels, as he surveys the land, that he is like a man at the edge of a cliff, or that he is a man at the margin of another, baser world.

And his head is warming despite the sharp north breeze up here above the Wall. He sees below him the half-dozen Scot nobles sitting on the roadway just beyond the gate. He looks down at them without surprise; it seems somehow, he knew they would be there. They are turned in their saddles and look back up at him, sitting motionless. Only their brick-red plaits stir in the breeze, or the shaggy fur of their garments. They are tied to Quirinius; they wait for him on the doorstep of their own land, and he looks down upon them, aware, somehow, that he knew they would be there.

His head is burning with a rage like that of some ferocious fever, and he knows that if only his men had the gift of true sight, they would see that his head is actually burning, putting out flames, scarlet, yellow, orange, and that the air about his head quivers like the air above a forge. He can feel the flames swathing his head, leaping up toward heaven in jagged spear points and forked dragons' tongues. The Scots, simpler men that they are, surely do see it, for their cold grey-blue eyes are open and their mouths, too, in the delight of horror. And then, in his rage at their temerity in crossing into his provinces, in a rage at their very primitiveness, Quirinius shouts. It is a shout, he knows, of a kind that hasn't been heard for an aeon, a shout to chill blood as they say or to freeze a pond or to crack stones or to cleave a man's ears and leave him deaf. It had in it all the anger of a man and all the strength of a bear, and when they hear it, the Scots turn away and blanch. They cower and shrink, oppressed by the clamor, down upon the backs of their mounts. Startled, one of the ponies starts forward, stumbles on a cobble in the roadway, and tosses his quivering rider, who dashes his head on a stone in the roadbed and lies dead. His fellows sweep him up and rush off into their fastnesses. They will remember Quirinius.

And so will his men. The fire is gone—his head is cool, and he is so very tired, but when he turns to face his soldiers, they step back uneasily and watch him with wide eyes for long moments. But the moments pass, and it is time to set out for home.

* * *

"When I got back, I learned that I had fought a particularly great battle, the Battle of the Caledonian Wood. That's what they call it. That forest is nearby, you see, and so now it has that name and people think we fought there. Galloping among the trees, I suppose." Quirinius looks down and laughs at the power of words. "You'd have to ask a peasant."

"And you killed two thousand Scots," the abbot says, who doesn't wish to let the legend go. He wishes it confirmed with the precision of a great number.

"Three thousand, I think. And I've since learned that I killed most of them myself." He doesn't chuckle now; he's grown sober, thinking of the shout and the dead man on the road stones.

Thirteen: The Monastery, October 491 AD

Bishop Valerianus, who knows things and is tired of waiting and tired of Quirinius, risks a question. "And it was after this triumph of yours that you returned to your holdings and to Albinia."

"Ganufara. The White Lady," the abbot says in British, for he venerates her, and her epithet falls from his tongue as naturally as any prayer. Quirinius scowls a moment.

"Yes, things happened thick and fast in those days."

"I'm sure the marriage brought you as much happiness as it did land and advantage," the bishop says as he wanders into the dimness at the back of the room, his hands together and hidden beneath his sleeves. He wishes he could see Quirinius' face but must be satisfied only to hear a slight tension in his voice.

"Oh, more. More, of course. Much more. Some say I wed her for the dowry alone because of my growing establishment, because I needed to support another forty soldiers."

"Ah, yes, economics."

"Exactly. You cannot ignore economics any more than cold weather or wheat rust or a leak in the roof."

"Or disloyalty," the abbot says, musing, and then looks up, startled at himself. He's not the only one. Quirinius looks hard at the little man and then to the bishop. Finally, he speaks again.

"Or disloyalty. I'm a bit too preoccupied to discover your allusion, Abbot, but no doubt there's something at the back of your mind."

"It was only a figure of speech."

"A simile," says the bishop frowning at the abbot.

"So, I would be less than honest if I didn't admit that I valued the marriage in part for, well, for what one might call reasons of state."

"That's really quite a noble motive, as should be apparent to anyone thoughtful," the Bishop says. "You sacrificed love to duty. And children." He watches Quirinius stiffen. "Perhaps this sort of sacrifice is not so unbearable for one, like you, who sees his duty and knows it."

Quirinius now stands up, looming grey in the glimmering lamplight; his shadow covers the far wall like night. "The weak may cavil—it's their consolation and reward, but the strong must accept burdens for, otherwise, what would the world come to?"

"Indeed. Although perhaps the strong misjudge their strength from time to time and would serve God better by letting him direct things freely."

"Perhaps." Quirinius sits again, but this time on the bench, and leans back against the table and faces away from the bishop. "I take it you believe he would be as content to hear our prayers in Saxon as in any other language." He smiles wickedly. "I eagerly await your answer."

"Your concerns are misplaced; that language will never prevail. The Saxons are too low a people, and God will keep them from us."

Quirinius grins at this, turns his face to the abbot and raises his eyebrows. "Amen," says the abbot.

"Amen," Quirinius agrees, still smiling. "And yet, I've travelled through the Western Hills and into the land that lies under the shadow of the Wall. And I've ridden through the Jute and Saxon lands, my friends. And when you see a peasant at fifty yards you might be forgiven for puzzling whether he's Saxon or Briton."

"All men are equal before God," murmurs the abbot.

"Quite right. We'll have to remind ourselves of that when the Saxons take our next diocese from us." Quirinius is growing about equally peeved at the bishop and the abbot—at the one for his knowledge and the other for his ignorance. Or is it at the irony of the one and the simplicity of the other? But who cares what their opinions are? The facts had unrolled themselves before young Quirinius with the ineluctability of Aristotle's logic. He needed more men because his office and his responsibility, not to mention his dignity, required them. He needed more men, particularly the best of those he had drafted from other lords. And he needed those whom he'd led up to the Wall, because they strengthened him and weakened the nobles from whom he'd taken them. That would come in handy in the Council.

So, when he returned from the wall, he kept twenty of the men he'd arrogated from the other magnates—those who were tractable, apt in maneuver, and willing. The rest he sent back to the other lords. He had not taken any of Maximianus' men; they were already broken in and warm to him from the summer exercises and the fight on the Fuscum, and their master was in his camp already and must cooperate now that Quirinius and Albinia were married. Her dowry was enough to support the extra soldiers and their horses, and, beyond this, Albinia was lovely enough, in an insipid way. Quite attractive enough to appeal to a young man.

So, these days, it is not hard to see Quirinius' star rising, shooting even, like a spark from the flue of a forge, high into the sky, for two weeks later he is back home again and entering the north gate of Corinium at the head of his men in cavalcade. Behind him and his immediate entourage trudge thirty-seven gaunt Scot prisoners too exhausted from their long march south to show more than a bleared curiosity at finding themselves in a town with citizens in well-made clothes peering down from the painted windowsills of two-storey houses as they parade through the square, followed by the rest of the Thracian Lancers and Bucellarii Quiriniani. In contrast to the Scots, they look splendid. Quirinius has made them clean their tack and mend their clothes, polish their helmets, and wear them for display despite the unseasonable late-summer heat.

It's quite a little triumph, for Quirinius has ranged through the north and swept an uncountable horde, uncounted anyway, of barbarians back to their dank, dark holdings beyond the Wall, and he hasn't lost a man doing it. The townsfolk, local nobility and churchmen mustered to stand along three sides of the forum have this explained to them by Quirinius in fat, periodic sentences delivered from the tribunal upon which he'd been proclaimed Count of the Britains. He notes with some satisfaction a half-dozen of the magnates watching him cautiously from the steps of the church, but with only a handful of attendants and only two or three soldiers apiece to prop up their pride. They have acquiesced in his dignity and office.

When he is finished, the people set up a howling and call for the death of the Scots, but Quirinius doesn't kill them. A promise is a promise, after all. Neither does he enroll them in his troops or put them to work on his estates. Oh no, there is a more expedient solution. Quirinius has found a canny Italian merchant who has sold a shipload of wine. He will purchase the sinewy little Scots and take them far away; they will disappear as surely as if Quirinius had slaughtered them beneath the Wall and left their stiffening bodies for the crows. And this way he gets a little money to distribute to his men and to those he means to take into his service. They snatch the bright silver coins avidly and polish them on their sleeves; they stare at Majorianus' head stamped on them and ponder whether that emperor was as glorious as Quirinius, Vir Spectabilis et Comes Britanniarum, Dominus Quirinius, who is big and powerful as a bear. When out of earshot, they sometimes affectionately call him Ursinus.

* * *

The Principal Estate of the Quirinii, Spring, 465 AD
In the early spring of the next year, a trooper from the western estate trotted in, a second horse on a lead and his clothes glistening from a soft rain. He left the animals in the care of a boy in the courtyard and sprang up the steps of the villa, his cloak following his hurry like a sail. He had a message for his master.

Comite Flavio Quirinio salutationes felicissimas ago villicusque servus tuus Sequanius, et spero ut salus tuus optimus sit. latro Uithylus captus est praemio gregis solo, ergo solidum tibi mitto in mano militis. si placeat, domandate eum de milite. latro in vinculis transfertur hodie. venebit ad te in pocis horibus cum custodibus septem militibus.

So, the canny Sequanius had done as he said he would. Uithyl had been caught and was on his way under the guard of seven soldiers. At the mere cost of flock of sheep. "And the coin?" he asked the trooper. The man bowed and took the solidus from the pouch hung around his neck beneath his tunic and presented it, the gold gently shimmering in his palm. "Good man. Tell Dobunica to give you a good dinner and all of the beer you can drink." He went off to find the bailiff and give orders to have the blacksmith ready to rivet a chain to Uithyl's ankles and fix it to a ring in a cowshed just outside the walls of the villa.

And that is where he found him in the early evening, sitting in half a foot of straw with his back to the wall and his knees drawn up in a shadowed, stinking corner. Sequanius stood near the doorway, and three troopers loomed nearby, thumbs in their sword belts, hulking and glowering at the little prisoner, who seemed too fatigued to cower. Quirinius entered, more imposing even than his soldiers, and regarded the glum little man for a long moment. He looked back and nodded his satisfaction to Sequanius. "Well done." Sequanius bowed.

"How did you get him?"

"I offered the flock for him. The husband of a distant cousin of his informed me where he was, and I sent a half-dozen horsemen to Venta Atris one night."

"Venta Atris." Quirinius scowled. "That is one of Eugenius Ater's villages, isn't it?"

"Yes, Dominē. Just as the name suggests."

Quirinius turned back to Uithyl, and it seemed odd how the fellow had brightened. A certain slight slyness had settled in his eyes. He rose, slowly, unprovocatively, with a sidelong glance at the troopers and gave a mild, obsequious smile. He bowed his head, and murmured in British, "Meistr?" as though awaiting an order.

Quirinius replied in British. "You are the last of those bandits who killed my father. The only one still alive." Quirinius said it as though musing. He looked to one of the troopers, who put a hand to the hilt of his sword and stepped closer. Uithyl flinched but managed, with a mild, slightly whining tone, to speak. "A good work, Dominē. Killing those men. Admirable! They had pressed me into their service, as you might imagine, perhaps the least of their malefactions, but all the same a degradation such as I could never have imagined." One of the troopers snorted. Uithyl went on, searching Quirinius' cold eyes. "To put it plainly, Dominē—and I'm sure you will see the truth in what I say—I was no bandit. Merely one of their victims. In fact, if I may dare to say it, as much a victim as your great father, Cuirann Hen."

Quirinius nodded at the trooper and then at Uithyl. The man struck Uithyl such a stout blow across the mouth that the little man staggered back against the wall. The chains at his feet clinked as they stirred the chaff. When he had regained his balance, Uithyl bowed very low and continued, "Forgive my overstepping. It was very wrong of me to compare my suffering with that of your noble father. Deepest apologies, Dominē." He sighed and touched his mouth gingerly, and rubbed his cheek, where the wine-mark flamed. "But who is the man who can entirely ignore his..." he hesitated and stepped back beyond the reach of the trooper. "His own suffering? Even if it's only that of a little man such as I?"

"Have you questioned this man, Sequanius?" Quirinius kept his eyes on the prisoner.

"I have not, Dominē. I leave that to you."

Quirinius nodded to himself and gazed on Uithyl. "Lying will not save you."

"Oh, Master, what I say—"

"You were, or made yourself, one of the bandits. You chose to engage in their vicious work."

"Master, no!"

Quirinius went on as though the little man had said nothing. "When you came to lead us into the trap you could have told us everything and put yourself under the protection of my father and all of our soldiers." He turned away and looked through window into the distance. "And yet you did not." He glanced over at Sequanius, who stood watching him. "He made a choice, this little bandit. But why? A mere lack of foresight? A failure of intelligence?"

"I do not know, Dominē," Sequanius replied, unwilling to guess.

Quirinius turned suddenly back to Uithyl and asked, *"Esne stultus? Aut credesti ut nemo te inveniat? Mirabile credu."*

"Quod te placuit ut dicam, magister? Quomodo innocentiam probam?"

"Ut dicam? Cur non 'debeo dicere,' latronicule?"

"Melior est, Domine."

Quirinius turned back to Sequanius. "You see how fine his Latin is? Correct anyway. He's not a peasant, or not exactly. Not so bright as he thinks he is, but cunning just the same, and he must have relied on some protection."

"Protection, Dominē?"

"Yes, but not from the bandits. From someone with real power." He turned back to Uithyl, crossed his arms and watched him for a few moments. "I'm inclined to have you killed right now."

Uithyl gritted his teeth and wiped his forehead with his sleeve.

"Can you think of any reason why I should not?"

Uithyl started to speak, stammered for a second, took a deep breath, and began again. "I don't plead my innocence. But as a proof of my good intentions toward Your Honor, I will appeal to your own interests and hope for mercy."

"And how will you do that, my little bandit?"

"Your Honor may not know that those bandits were protected, were clients, of Dominus Eugenius Ater. Now, Dominus Eugenius had perhaps let them get out of hand. Yes, out of hand—well, no use denying it, really. Your Honor has eyes quite as good as the next man. Better, no doubt.

"But consider now. Dominus Eugenius, right or wrong, when all is said and done, he's got his obligations to meet. Show me a man who doesn't. You're a magnate, a noble. You understand these things. But even a simple man like me—I have inklings. And Dominus Eugenius, well, he has his obligations and a hundred men too. Good fighters, all of them. There are songs about them; I've heard them—we all have. Dominus Eugenius, well, he could be much more than just a threat. He's a power in the land, and people bend to him."

Silence from Quirinius. Uithyl, who seemed to have been calmed by the sound of his own voice, now licked his lips, shrugged, and continued with forced calm. "Now, Master, you are justified. More than justified in what you have done. And Dominus Eugenius can be made to understand this, particularly if, well, as a gesture of your esteem to him, you would consider availing yourself of someone who knows him, to speak on Your Honor's behalf."

More silence, and then Quirinius replied. "You suggest that I send you, a murderer of my father, to Eugenius, and by this timid, ignoble gesture I will keep him from doing what? Launching a vendetta against me for killing his bandits?"

Uithyl, who saw that he'd gained nothing through indirection, now judged that he must try a threat.

"Your Honor, Eugenius Ater is a great man. He will not suffer to have his clients harmed without taking action, even against a magnate such as yourself."

"Let me understand you. If I treat you as I ought, and kill you as I should, Ater will be stirred to anger at losing such a valuable lackey?" The three troopers chuckled. He smiled grimly at Uithyl. "Upon reflection, it doesn't seem very likely does it, little man? I killed those two dozen bandits a year ago, and Ater has done nothing. In fact, I suspect that he's pleased. I think he didn't have it in him to do the job himself, and so he connived in their banditry and flattered himself by calling himself their 'patron.'" He turned to the troopers. "You. Get an axe. Have it sharpened, if necessary." The man turned to go but halted when Uithyl called out.

"Wait! Wait, Master!"

"What is it, little man?"

"Dominus Ater..."

"Yes? What about him?"

"Much of what you suspect about him is true."

"You presume to tell me what I know?"

"Dominus Ater did not confide in me."

"Of course not. Why would he?"

"But he did have me work as a go-between."

"Between whom?"

"He sent me to ask the bandits to favor him with a... with a certain task."

"To ambush my father and me." He turned to Sequanius. "You see? Now we are getting somewhere." He looked at the trooper standing near the door. "Wait on the axe a bit." He turned back to Uithyl. "I am correct, of course, about the ambush."

Uithyl shrugged helplessly. "You great men have your conflicts. They're not for the likes of me to judge. Perhaps there was an old quarrel, perhaps a new one." Quirinius thought of the squabble in Council months ago, the possible affront to Ater's dignity. The fear that he quite evidently showed that preparations for defense would provoke a Saxon campaign. He looked back at Uithyl, who seemed unable to speak further on the point. Quirinius repeated in a flat tone. "I am correct about the ambush."

"You are, Your Honor."

"And why do you tell me this?"

"If this could, in some way help you, you might consent to spare me, Your Honor."

Quirinius sighed deeply, as at a profound disappointment. "I had really intended to kill you, little man. This evening, in fact." He looked again out of the window at the darkening sky. He turned back. "You must testify against Ater before the magnates at the next Provincial Council."

"Testify?"

"Tell the senators and magnates what Ater has done."

"And you will spare me?"

"If you can do it, I likely will. I'll sell you to the Irish as a slave. But only if you testify."

"A slave of the Irish?" He grimaced.

"I'd judge from the quality of your Latin that you can read and write?"

He nodded. "A little."

"That might just keep you out of the field. Who can say?" He shrugged indifferently. "Or perhaps you prefer the axe? An end to your troubles in this difficult world?"

"I will speak."

"A sound decision." He strode out of the cowshed, Sequanius at his heels. On an impulse he said, "I'm tired of running this estate. I have other matters to contend with and need a steward for this estate. Send for your family; I appoint you." Sequanius bowed to the waist as Quirinius went off to the house.

* * *

Corinium Dobunnorum, Late Spring, 465 AD

A month has passed and Quirinius is halfway to setting things in order, the sort of order that lasts. He has chastised the Scots to the very limit of his power and with great success, but he must set his own house on the best footing he can. It's best for everyone. Yes, the Scots have been cowed, the dragon battle-standard has floated his tail over the moors of Rheged, Quirinius has settled into his father's estate, and most of the soldiers he'd taken from the other nobles and led to fight by the Wall have chosen to stay with him. God knew quite how he'd support them, people said, but Quirinius knew at the very worst there was always the possibility of levying a tax. Perhaps it would never come to that. All the same, he had the soldiers—imposing a tax would be easy.

Now is time to set things in order, time to show the world that young Quirinius is serious and means to stay the course. His position is secure—never better, but all the same, as Aristotle teaches, a body in motion will slow if no more impetus is imparted. So now is the time for further action and, more important, now is the time to satisfy the craving for justice that has been gnawing at the back of Quirinius' mind, like a mouse at the rye in a granary. In this way he'll deliver more impetus and do justice and, what is more, do it in the way demanded by The Idea.

Quirinius arrived impressively at the head of a cloud of horseman. The animals were glossy from combing, and the men well turned out—their armor polished, their uniforms cleaned and mended and the officers' helmets gauded here and there with a horsetail on the crown. Against this splendor, the crowd hardly noticed the peasant who rode a nag near the end of the troop. He was sallow from weeks without sunlight, his hair squalid and full of tangles, and there was straw here and there in his beard as though he hadn't seen his reflection or a friend for a long while. His hands were bound together, and a lead came off them, held by a trooper riding beside. Quirinius dismounted and headed up the steps of the basilica. When he was gone, the trooper slid off his mount and jerked the peasant, Uithyl of course, off the mount by the lead and dragged him up the steps to the porch, where he and two others watched him. Quirinius stopped at the threshold and glanced over at them all. "Come immediately when I send for you." The men nodded. Meek, Uithyl squatted down in the shadows against the wall and waited for the call.

As Quirinius entered the basilica that morning, he made real use of the greening, bronze-clad doors, which were swung back on their hinges, each standing twice as high as a man and as broad in proportion. He entered at the point of a triangle made up of two secretaries, two attendants, and three soldiers to carry and assemble

222

the parts of his chair. As he stepped from the autumn sunlight into the dim of the Senate chamber, he was careful not to squint—he passed gracefully into the hall as one confident and not too troubled by the vagaries of atmosphere.

He had come later than the other senators and councillors, as befitted his station, and strode to where his seat would be. Good, it was in a prominent spot. As the soldiers fitted his chair together, he stood, turning slowly right and left, and nodded blandly at the other men, measuring their expressions, noting whether they looked at him frankly, or whether they shifted their eyes toward their neighbors as Marcus Volutorius and Clementius Dumnorius did, to give just two instances. Some of the men shifted from foot to foot or, seated, casually avoided his glance. A few smiled, but most seemed uncommonly grave.

"Good morning, Senators and Magnates," he said to all and no one in particular. A murmured greeting floated back. Sequanius, acting as his secretary, coughed softly behind him--his chair was ready. He sat back confidently and without looking. "Gentlemen, let us proceed." He said it grandly, as though his name were first on the roll. The senator with that honor, stooped old Nonianus Bassus, said nothing, only rose and read the names off, squinting and holding the list so close that he hid his face. Quirinius looked down, seemingly thoughtful, but he was glancing at Sequanius on his right, who, sitting on his stool, had opened his tablets and was writing down the names of the men who were present. There were fewer of them than Quirinius would have liked to see, but Eugenius Ater was among them. He would watch the business of the morning and spring his trap toward the end.

As usual, the Council soon became enmired in trivialities: amending the order in which business could be dealt with, arguing about what had been tabled from the last meeting, and whether there was a quorum, and whether Bishop Marinus should be present. Some implied—though it wasn't said directly--that he hadn't sufficiently purged himself of suspicions of Pelagianism. Quirinius grew weary at the smallness of the council's concerns, but at the same time was fascinated by it. The Saxons and Jutes waiting to carve off further slices of the provinces of Britain like so many collops from a ham, and these stooped, effete old men troubled themselves over whether they would have to listen to the political opinions of a churchman who might believe in free will. But he left them at it for a good hour, to show how reasonable, how patient he was. He could wait.

Eventually, the dodderers faltered, exhausted by their own cavilling, and Quirinius rose and flashed a pleasant glance around, holding silent a few moments until he had everyone's attention, even that of Eugenius Ater, who cocked an eyebrow at him and then turned away and pretended a close interest in polishing the ruby of the ring on his left hand. "Gentlemen, you'll permit me this interruption, I don't doubt, even though you haven't resolved the myriad issues before you—precedence, procedural questions and so forth. You've got them well on the run, though, wouldn't you all agree?" No one did, though. The councillors stared, some trading glances with a neighbor, and after several cold, silent moments, Ater, satisfied at last with his ruby, spoke up. He held up his left hand, palm out for a long moment, judging the claret glint of the gem in the late morning light. "Pardon me, Flavius Quirinius, if I remark upon your presumption in breaking into the deliberations of your elders. It ill suits you to act this way when wiser heads are at work here. Oh, yes. Laying the foundations of the sort of measured discourse that you, so full of your self-proclaimed Romanitas, claim to value so highly yet, in practice, erode through your... ah... what shall we say? Callow enthusiasms."

There was a soft rumble, as of uneasy approval from the others. They disliked Ater, as Quirinius knew, but all the same they accepted, with a certain insipidity, Ater's mockery of him. That rankled, even though their tepid support for him was, for the most part, a vague resistance to be driven from their accustomed rut. As he looked about, Quirinius sensed this and began to see it plainly enough. Could it be that his recent rise, though well-deserved, discomfited the old men? Ah, yes. That was it. They would prefer him in a lower place. It was natural, of course. But they would have to accept him and his new position. He was the youngest man on the Council—at least the youngest of any significance—but he could see what the others would not: that he had the judgement and drive to override the little opinions of the old palterers. Their views were unimportant and, besides, his station, office and accomplishments demanded their acquiescence. All the same, he could seem deferential if necessary. Let the councillors and Ater do as they wished—he would play them like a flute. He stood as he went on.

"I will let the councillors decide how they take my interruption. I will let them decide, after they have heard me, whether I have abused their patience." He smiled all around.

Ater looked up at the ceiling, pretending to think deeply. "May we not simply assume the abuse, Gentlemen? Simply assume Flavius Quirinius' abuse and then press on with a certain condescension and silent indulgence?" He sat up in his chair and looked about at everyone with a sad, indulgent smile.

Quirinius lifted his hands like an actor. "Toward what, may I ask, are we to press on with such determination? The defense of our provinces, perhaps? It might be a good idea, but there doesn't seem much interest in it these days. It's apparently better for us to decide whether there are any grounds to the suspicion that Bishop Marinus may judge works to be on a par with faith." There was some shushing at this and some laughter, and Quirinius thought he might have heard a quiet hiss at the back of the hall. Good. He was stirring them up a bit, and they would pay attention. He finished: "With respect, I would observe that we have spent half the morning in trivialities and, if all goes according to plan, these trivialities will be followed by a heavy lunch."

Ater gave a loud stagey laugh and applauded, and the sound of his clapping splashed off the walls. "Very good, young fellow! You are more of a wit than I'd have imagined. Your father was the better speaker. Gentlemen, you'll recall his extremely polished diction, and what turns of phrase! Ah, the province will miss him. But the son has a bit of wit in him, don't you agree, Gentlemen? And, accordingly, I suggest we indulge him by passing over his outburst without remark."

There were some murmured sounds of agreement.

It was evident to Quirinius that Ater's easy manner and inviting lightness were drawing the councillors to oppose him, even if they weren't aware of it, and all this before any issue had even been mentioned. He said, "If the Council suspected that the business I have with it concerns you, then they would see how your little maneuvers are meant to direct attention away from an important matter. They must believe instead that your paltering's nothing more than a reflection of your trivial nature."

"Hmm!" Ater said, frowning, his chin in his hand. "Your correction is hard, Quirinius, very hard." His secretary and attendants laughed obediently, joined by many of the Council. Quirinius beamed all around as though indifferent to their opinion.

"It's nothing to the correction, Eugenius, that you deserve and that, one may hope, you will soon get." Quirinius sat down and glanced about the room, taking in the puzzled expressions of the other councillors, even that of Maximianus, who scowled his bafflement. Ater shifted his bulk in his creaking chair and turned to look at Quirinius for the first time full in the face. He narrowed his eyes, like a short-sighted man, or one who looks for something important in the distance.

He's worried, Quirinius thought with some satisfaction. He looked about at the other councillors, whose attention was now about equally divided between the two men. None of them were smiling. Quirinius turned his glance on Nonianus Bassus, and nodded, prodding the old fellow into action.

"Perhaps Flavius Quirinius Claudianus would favor us with a clarification of his last point," Bassus said with mild and evident irritation.

"Certainly, Clarissimus Bassus. Your request, as always, is a duty." He slouched back in his chair, rested his elbows on the arms, and propped his chin on his interlaced fingers. That should suggest enough insouciance to render his message the more shocking. "Let me be entirely clear." He paused to strain the attention of the councillors, Bishop Marinus, and the three or four kinglets whose attendance made ruling the western hill country easier. And then abruptly he sat up and leaned forward. "I formally accuse the Senator and Clarissimus Eugenius Ater of murder. I lay an indictment here against him for the murder of Senator Marcus Quirinius Claudianus."

There was a silence of the sort that comes when no one moves at all. A long pause, and then Quirinius watched Eugenius Ater stiffen in his chair and flush pink beneath his face powder. He gained control of himself in a moment, however, and forced a short barking laugh. He then looked around at the assembled councillors. "Forgive my laughter, Gentlemen. It was not meant to encourage this young man in his tasteless humor. It was merely the product of surprise. But, before this tasteless joke is pressed further, I might suggest," and here he looked about the room carefully, scanning every face, "that any reasonable man would fear to make such an accusation. Or to support it."

"The old Senator Quirinius was killed by bandits," someone called from the back of the hall. There was a slight echo as the words died away.

"So he was. The facts are well known—I might remind the Council that they were put about by you yourself, young Quirinius," Ater said.

"Count Quirinius."

"Count then." He flapped a hand in indifference. "By bandits," I repeat. "And of course, we thank you for ridding the country of them." He pushed himself to his feet by the chair arms, shifted uneasily, and glanced over the assembled councillors. Despite his bravado, he had grown cautious. His face was grey, and he

227

unconsciously rubbed the back of his head as though to dislodge a thought. Quirinius was pleased to note this and felt sure that all who cared to could see it, although a surprising number of the Council were looking down or studying the cloudy sky through the windows above them. "You did kill all of them, I believe?" Ater turned to Quirinius.

He nodded. He had killed all the bandits, strictly speaking. Ater seemed to relax at the response.

"Let us not stray from the point. I repeat my indictment. That on the seventh day of August, in the consulship of Caecina Decius Basilius, in a forest some ten miles from Corinium Dobunnorum, you caused the death of Senator Marcus Quirinius Claudianus through minions and hirelings."

Ater took a deep breath and, deciding on his tack, said, "I will not answer this charge. It is absurd and therefore an offense to my dignity."

"Your reticence condemns you." Quirinius said quietly. He looked about the room, not at Ater.

"It does nothing of the kind," he said, levelly, folding his arms.

"You insist on your indictment?" Maximianus asked. Quirinius turned to see that his father-in-law had risen behind him.

"Indeed."

"Then, Senator Nonianus Bassus, as leader of the Council, you must insist on an answer." It was clear from his father-in-law's flat intonation that he was cautious, that Quirinius' accusation made him uneasy. He was speaking from duty, and unhappy to do it. *It had to be this way, I could not show anyone my hand, not even him. He will understand later.*

Bassus held his chin, thinking hard. "Well, as to that..."

"You have my reply—that I refuse to answer," Ater said, glowering at Quirinius.

"Yes, but on what ground? Do you have some ground for this position?" Bassus' voice went up at the end, betraying his hope that Ater's reply would somehow avoid and thus end the issue. His

228

attitude to the man was deferential, and in that moment, Quirinius decided that Bassus not only respected Ater's position, but feared him. He wondered whether Bassus was alone in this.

Ater explained, "I do not submit myself to the jurisdiction of the Council as a court. Gentlemen, great as your powers are, I decline to accept that they extend to exercising jurisdiction over and trying a fellow member, a senator no less, which I am, if you'll forgive me telling you what you know. This Council contains senators, great men, and even kings." Oh, how flattering he could be! "But there is none here with the jurisdiction to prosecute a senator."

Bassus showed his relief when he warbled like the old man he was, "I take it, Senator Eugenius, that you stand on your right to be tried by no one but the Emperor or his Consistory? You assert that only the Emperor, or that body, has jurisdiction of this question?"

"Precisely, Senator." Ater said with theatrical gravity. "I realize that this position precludes any chance to join the issue in question, but really..." He shrugged and put his hands out, palm up. "The charge is inane."

Quirinius was pleased--it was an effort not to grin. Any trial would come to nothing, and he did not actually want one. His demand had been nothing but a sham, to gull these cavillers into acting in accordance with their weakness. He had levelled a deadly charge against Ater in open council and they were doing just as he wished, yammering and paltering about procedure. Things could not have proceeded more to his liking.

Bassus was droning on, "... not at first apparent, Gentlemen, but what the Senator raises is a valid point. He asserts a protection enjoyed by all of us with the good fortune to share his rank. And if I may say so, what he asserts is no mere privilege of rank, but an important prop to our society—that no one be judged except by those with the stature, capacity and perspective to judge justly. Why, if I remember properly what I learned in my school days..." Here the half-toothless old bastard chuckled as though he were reminiscing at a dinner party, and Ater stood beaming at him, full of encouragement, as soft murmurs of approval materialized like phantoms at the back of the chamber.

Bassus bowed his head and clasped his hands behind his back in a broad pantomime of deep thinking. "The Emperor's Consistory would certainly have jurisdiction; no question about it, none at all. And the Vicarius—he too, if there were one still. The governor? Well, that is less clear. But as there no longer is a governor—"

"But let us not lose sight of the fact that the question is entirely hypothetical," Ater added for the benefit of any dullard who couldn't see where this was all going. There was sage nodding among the councillors, particularly the dotards. Quirinius thought, *They ape sophistication, but it is a sham—they are abject men, all of them, men whose lives are streaked with fear they cannot face. Instead, they truckle to this shifting, oily mountain of a man. But, and this is the thing, none of the defense they supply has any backing; he has no true friends.*

Quirinius stood again and said, as though he wished to cut through the knot of procedure, "Gentlemen, I have evidence."

"Evidence. Well, we hardly get that far, do we?" The young Uortigern said this from somewhere behind him. Quirinius recognized his thin voice and was surprised—he didn't think the fellow had the temerity to take a strong position.

"Consideration of any evidence would seem premature." Another voice from the rear of the chamber. When he glanced around to see who spoke, all he could see were serious, weak faces.

Maximianus, who still stood before his chair near the wall, took a deep breath like a man about to put his shoulder to a cartwheel, and said, "Some fifty years ago the Emperor Honorius, by letter, conferred on the councils of Britain the right of self-government. Implicit in that charge is the right to police, investigate, judge and punish those in these provinces of Britain."

And now Quirinius takes a gamble and jumps in to finish this train of thought. "And, I submit, that such power necessarily extends to jurisdiction over all persons of whatever station, so long as that jurisdiction is asserted by those of the highest station, the senators and curials of this Council. There is no longer Imperial jurisdiction over Britain, and so to suggest that a senator of Britain may be judged only by Emperor Libius Severus is an absurdity—because it cannot be done, it means he is above the law. Consider a world where the great men may, legally speaking, commit no crime. Consider a world where anything is permitted to them, so long as they are bold enough to do it and strong enough to avoid the consequences. We have a word for it this: 'barbarism.'" He looks about, hoping he hasn't swayed many of his listeners, for, after all, a trial would be a defeat for him. To win this round of the contest against Ater, he must fail to win a prosecution.

Ater, spoke in slow and heavy tones, as though expressing a general exhaustion with the subject. "I am sure, Gentlemen, that an interesting disquisition will follow if we let Flavius Quirinius persist. I don't intend to puzzle over the legal question. Rather, I would remind the Council of what Quirinius said earlier—that he ridded the countryside of all these bandits that he accuses me of employing. So, there can hardly be any evidence for this absurd charge. Are we to discard well-settled principles of jurisdiction in order to entertain a charge that cannot be premised on anything but double-hearsay taken from bandits now dead?" He looked about, chin down and eyebrows raised, asking everyone to follow his thought. "If there can be no convincing proofs of this preposterous claim, then why institute novel—and quite possibly dangerous procedures—and entertain jurisdiction? What would be the gain? What the purpose? Shouldn't we turn our heads to better questions?"

Quirinius turned to his Sequanius. "Give me the statement." He held it aloft. "I have here a detailed confession from a man, a servant of Eugenius Ater, a certain Uithyl, who worked hand in glove with the bandits. They are dead, yes, but not this man who was their confederate." He studied Ater's face and saw the man was unmoved; Ater felt he had already won the day.

Bassus spoke up. "What could a mere commoner have recounted that could furnish the premise for exposing Senator Ater to a criminal trial?" He was bold now—he could feel the approval of the other councillors, cowards all, who supported him in his calculated timidity. "No, I think we see the wisdom in cleaving to the old way here. Despite recent changes, we can see it to be peculiarly suited to our situation, can we not, Gentlemen?" This was followed by many bland "indeeds."

"In fact, I think I may be pardoned for not even bringing this issue to a vote." There was a long silence. And then he spoke again "Yes, I can sense your approval." Quirinius noted in passing that the old man was too ashamed to look anyone in the face as he spouted this nonsense. He glanced up, as though contemplating eternity.

Quirinius handed Sequanius the document. "I have the man himself who was the go-between in the plot. He is waiting outside and will answer the questions of anyone who cares to know the truth of the matter." It was the highlight of his gamble. Quirinius turned to his captain, Canidius. "Bring the man here." The captain swept out of the room, his cloak flowing out behind him like wings, and in a moment returned to thrust Uithyl, stumbling into the hall, hands tied together, mouth agape as he looked with ducked head at all the great men. *The bastards had better not relent,* Quirinius thought. *They'd better cling to their timidity and protect Ater.*

Bassus stiffened and glanced at Ater, who frowned, pursed his lips, and shook his head the littlest bit. No more than a hint, but enough. Bassus turned to the Council. "There is no need. We have decided, and the matter is at an end. In my capacity as president of this Council, I declare this meeting adjourned." He turned on his heel like a bad dancer and hurried out as quickly as he could hobble. He was followed by the rest of the Council in a press, the younger men first, and then the rickety old senators and curials leaning on staffs or attendants as they hobbled out, pitching and yawing like skiffs in a storm as they made for the doors, their attendants following. Some of the old men hadn't moved so fast in a decade, and in a minute or two Quirinius stood in the chamber surrounded by his secretary and soldiers and by two dozen empty chairs. He stared in relief and amusement at the doorway clogged with backs and elbows, and then relapsed into his own chair. He could sense that Maximianus still stood by his chair near the wall, but he didn't look.

But he did turn at the sound of Ater's voice. "Well, young man. You don't seem to have handled this at all well." The great, fat man stood quietly watching him, flanked by a soldier, and a boy, a little smirking fellow with hair dyed the same false yellow as his master. "I have not yet decided what action to take in regard to this so-called charge of yours. It is clear enough that there is no support among our peers for its pursuit, and yet it will hang in the air like some bad odor."

"It will," Quirinius said. "It is just as it should be."

The immense man rested his fat white forearms on the back of his chair, and it creaked at his weight as he leaned casually forward. He narrowed his eyes at Quirinius. "And I can't say I'll forgive you your trespass, my friend. I'm not like that. No, no. But I might suggest a very long stay at some estate far in the country. Perhaps a couple of years. No need to trouble yourself coming to the city to deal with matters in the Council. After all, it is plain that you've squandered your father's influence. How you thought you could sway them is beyond me." The boy snickered. Ater straightened up and put a hand on his shoulder and drew him close, for support. "And you, Maximianus, you might profit by keeping your son-in-law from any further rash decisions. Who can say upon whom the sad effects of his actions may repose?"

"Don't threaten us, Eugenius Ater," Maximianus said simply.

Quirinius said nothing. He simply watched the fat man without expression until he had left the chamber.

"Flavius!" Maximianus burst out, trying to keep his voice down. "What was this about? What was the cause of this idiocy? What did you think to accomplish? Any sensible man would have known that, law or no law, Ater could never be made to stand a trial. Those days are gone. They're finished."

"I was not after a trial."

His father-in-law stood motionless in his bafflement. Quirinius waited until the old man could speak. "Ater's a powerful man and you have set him against us."

Quirinius shook his head. "He was always against us, as we've learned. Nothing has changed. He is not inconsiderable, but then he is not so powerful either. I have driven a wedge between him and his allies. I have weakened him. They have always disliked him, now they distrust him, they will stand aside. Some seem to support him, but they'll stand aside when the test comes."

"Stand aside? When will they stand aside? What test?"

Quirinius stepped up to the old man and encircled his shoulders with his arm. He looked about the Council chamber to be sure they were alone, and he said, very quietly, "They will stand aside when I attack him."

And then he walked out onto the steps of the Council house. Just outside the door Canidius stood with two soldiers and Uithyl between them. The peasant looked up at him hopefully. "Well, little man, you present me with a challenge. I agreed to spare your life in return for your testimony, but you were not permitted to give it. Now, what shall I do?" The trooper to the left of the little man drew his dagger and raised his eyebrows questioningly. Uithyl began to shudder uncontrollably, and the wine-mark on his cheek flashed scarlet. Quirinius watched him closely for a few moments, and then said to the trooper, "Cut his bonds. Let him go." And then to Uithyl: "Don't go to Ater's holdings; he'll kill you now. And don't let me see you again or I'll kill you. Go far, far away." As he turned away, he could hear the footfalls of the little man as he sprinted from the forum.

Fourteen: The Estate of Albinius Maximianus, Late June 465 AD

It is a warm June afternoon and Quirinius sits in Maximianus' garden with him. His father-in-law insists that they meet out here to discuss the attack on Ater's villa. "Away from the ears of the servants, Flavius," the old man says, and that's fine—no argument about that though surely there are any number of private rooms in the old man's villa. And so, Quirinius and the old man sit on a lichen-splotched stone bench in the afternoon sun, just in the shadow of a pollarded elm. A trio of servants set up a low table and pose a jug of wine and two fine, light-blue stemmed glasses on it. After he waves them away, Maximianus pours wine into each glass and hands one to his son-in-law. They each take a sip. "Pleasant out here," the older man finally says. "The wise woman at the south end of the estate says we'll have a long summer." Quirinius nods but says nothing. He doesn't want to draw out the preliminaries. He has his news and wants to tell it. Maximianus really had no reason to be uneasy about Ater's threats. No. In the end, his power was a mere sham, empty as a conjurer's trick. And Quirinius wants to move on, get back to his own estate. It seems things just fall apart when he's not around to mind them. So, he sits impatiently in silence for a few moments sipping the wine. Maximianus lifts his glass up to the light and squints at the sun through it.

"Marvellous taste this wine has, and a color to match." He sighs. "And so hard to come by these days. For all I know this may be the last for some time—perhaps for good. It comes from Aquitania, but these days most of it stays there. The Visigoths are drinking it, I suppose." He takes another sip, closes his eyes, and sloshes the wine thoughtfully around his mouth. He opens his eyes to see Quirinius looking dubiously into his glass. The young man takes a swallow and nods. *Yes, it's good. Now can we move on?*

"I can see you're not of a mind to discuss wines." The old man sets his glass on the table, leans forward with his hands on his knees, his elbows out, gets to his feet. "Let's have a game of bowls, son." Quirinius, startled, watches him a second, unsure that he's heard correctly.

"Bowls?" He narrows his eyes suspiciously as he sets his glass down.

"Yes, bowls. Marvellously relaxing. I expect you haven't had an opportunity to play for quite some time. Come along." He waves Quirinius to his feet and draws him out to the middle of the sward and away from the pollarded elms and box elder hedges. In the middle of the green are the bowls, a half a dozen heavy wooden balls the size of a man's doubled fist, and the little target-ball they call the "pig". Quirinius stands on the short grass, springy as a sponge, and looks down at them. He wonders what Maximianus is playing at. This old game was a triviality his father used to engage in, delighting whenever he pitched a ball close to the pig or knocked an opponent's away, but Maximianus had always struck Quirinius as being made of quieter, somberer, stuff.

Maximianus snatches up the pig and tosses it a dozen yards away. "There's a good mark," he says, and stoops to gather up a ball, which he hefts in his hand a moment to gauge its weight. Quirinius notes that the old man has chosen from the set one of the three stained with dark madder, leaving the lighter set for him. When Maximianus is satisfied that he knows its weight, he lobs the ball lazily at the pig. The heavy wooden ball sails in a low arc, lands with a thud and rolls a dozen feet, ending up a yard beyond the pig and to the right.

"Not bad," Quirinius says politely.

The old man shrugs. "Your throw," he says. Quirinius looks at him pointedly, and then stoops for one of the three buff-colored balls. He squints a moment to get the distance to the pig and then lofts the ball very high. The sphere drops almost straight down to settle close to the pig and rests there without rolling, the result of the backspin he has put on it, as his father had taught him years ago. It sits much closer to the pig than Maximianus' ball.

"Very good, Flavius. Do you play much?"

"No. Not since my father's death and, frankly, not often before."

"It's clear he taught you well."

"It was the sort of thing he was good at, if you understand me. He was rather a judge of wine too."

"I quite understand. Yes." He smiles enigmatically. "You lead, and so the throw is mine." Maximianus takes up another ball and tosses it; it lands beyond the pig and rolls a good yard farther before it stops.

"I thought you might like to hear about my recent—actions." The old man turns to watch Quirinius for a moment in silence.

"Instead of playing bowls, you mean?"

"Frankly, yes."

"I can see that. Well, Ater is dead, isn't he?"

"Yes. Quite. I thought you'd be pleased. In the end, his threats were mere vapor." Quirinius' voice shows some irritation at the old man's indifference. Maximianus ignores this and turns away to survey the game. He squints a moment to bring the lie of the balls into closer focus, but after a moment turns back to Quirinius. "I need a better look at the dispositions. Old man's eyes, you understand." And he hobbles on his bad ankle out across the green to the pig and the three spheres sitting about it like Ptolemy's planets around the Earth. Quirinius follows the old man halfway there, tossing a ball from hand to hand in impatience.

"I see that you still hold the lead," Maximianus says. "But I know just where to place my next ball. Don't be surprised to find in the end that the game is mine." Quirinius just shakes his head, whether in impatience or in wonder at the old man's whimsy, he couldn't have said himself. He turns to walk back to the mark from which they were throwing, and, as soon as Maximianus sees the young man turn his back, he gently kicks one of his balls just close enough to the pig to put himself in the lead.

237

When they are both at the mark, Maximianus crouches slightly and swings his right arm, releasing the ball in a gentle arc. He clearly intends to knock Quirinius' ball aside and solidify his lead, but, once again, the ball lands just beyond the pig and rolls a yard. "Go ahead," he says, keeping his eyes on the game. Quirinius sighs philosophically, and then pitches his remaining balls quickly, one, two, to show that, though polite, he won't be made utterly complicit in this foolishness.

"Hmm. Good throws, both of them." And they are, though his first is still the best. Maximianus, apparently satisfied not to bother counting up the score, takes his son-in-law by the arm and leads him back toward the bench. The young man looms over the elder as they walk in the late afternoon sun, and he still puzzles over his father-in-law's sudden interest in a trivial game. Seated on the bench once again, Maximianus asks Quirinius about the raid, and so the young man describes it to him.

* * *

The Estate of Eugenius Ater, Early June 465 AD
Speed was the thing. Speed had been Caesar's great weapon, and it would be his. Quirinius had urged his horse across the forum at a good trot and then down the street toward the west gate, his men scurrying to their mounts to follow.

As he rides down the ruler-straight highway, he goes over in his mind once again what he will do. Canidius rides silently alongside and knows better than to interrupt his master's thoughts. He directs his attention to the men, keeping them quiet with occasional gestures or sharp glares. He does his work so well that Quirinius hardly knows the men are there. He mulls over his plan one more time and steeps his mind in the project of killing Eugenius Ater.

It would have been better if the world were still ordered in a such a way that Ater could have been properly tried and put to death, but, at the least, he would die, both to expunge his trespass in murdering the old Senator and to uphold, if not the majesty of the law, at least the principle of justice.

Though he knows that Ater must die, he has said nothing of it, even to Canidius, his captain; he keeps his plans to himself until the time is right to act. Only when he must will he tell the men their part. And there's no one else to consult in the matter anyway. He spares Maximianus the details because it's clear that the old man has grown cautious. Better to leave him out.

There is no sense in lurking in the countryside to attack Ater on the highway. Though their entourages are about equally matched in number, he'd certainly prevail; his men are the harder and more practiced, but he doesn't believe he has the numbers to win without any loss. In fact, he prefers a battle less than a sort of arrest. Or, if there must be a battle, he must win it overwhelmingly—he owes that much, at least, to his soldiers. He heads back to his estate to gather the balance of his men. He speaks only to tell one of his lieutenants to go up a side road to one of his small estates and gather a dozen of his men. Bring them to Voxullodunum by noon the next day and have each bring a spare horse. The man nods and rides off.

Quirinius is at his estate by noon the next day and is pleased to see those men awaiting him outside the villa. The captain already knows to muster the rest of the troop—he drifts off quietly as Quirinius enters the villa for a meal. When he has finished, Canidius comes into the loggia to say that the Thracian Lancers and the Bucellarii are all accounted for, and all but two are fit to serve. One has fallen from his horse during an exercise and seems to have broken a rib. Nothing serious, but he won't fight for a month. Another is drunk but should be sober the next day. Should he be flogged? Canidius is ready to order it. No. Just put him in his armor and make him stand guard through the night—that will be harsh enough.

"And the new men? Those I winkled out of the other nobles?"

"What about them, Dominē?" Canidius looks grave.

"Join them to the Bucellarii. Make them take an oath."

"Very good. But..."

"Yes?"

"You mean to move against Dominus Eugenius, don't you, Master?"

"Yes."

"Very good."

"Choose one of the new men for an ensign and have a standard made for him. They'll be the third squadron of the Bucellarii."

Canidius bowed and hurried off.

* * *

That night Quirinius lay in bed with Albinia. There was just enough moon through the window that he could see the curve of her forehead glowing faintly white in the night.

"I'm going off tomorrow," he said. She said nothing, or nothing that he could hear. He sensed her lips moving soundlessly next to him. Another prayer, no doubt. He repeated himself and waited for her to finish.

"Yes," she replied, neither approving nor judging.

"You could tell?"

"Yes."

"Hmm."

"The men, the officers all scurrying. And the artisans."

Anyone should have properly construed the activity, seen what it forecast. The saddler with two men to help him mend some tack, the cutler at his wheel sharpening half a dozen swords. From his study, Quirinius had heard the bright cheeping of blades drawn across the edge of the turning wheel. He'd leaned out his window to look down into the courtyard below and watched the sparks fly away, dazzling and unreal, from the swords' glinting edges.

Albinia had drawn the right conclusion—when there was no hurry, the men sharpened the swords themselves with whetstones. She didn't say anything more, however. She seemed utterly uninterested, so perhaps he should have told her earlier of Ater's involvement in the Senator's death, but as with anything important that didn't concern her immediately, he'd kept it to himself, like some costly bauble that only he could appreciate. Because it was appreciation, in the end, that Albinia seemed to lack. When she wasn't immediately occupied with something, her eyes fixed themselves on things at a great distance, like the eyes in an imperial portrait, and the fingers of her right hand slowly gathered themselves one by one then and relaxed as though she were counting something to herself, perhaps prayers.

"I'll be heading south early tomorrow to..." He searched for a word. "To confront Eugenius Ater." Albinia turned her face to him on the pillow and watched him incuriously.

"Yes." Her tone was too flat for him to tell whether it was a question.

"I will fight him."

"Why?"

Quirinius rolled over onto his back and closed his eyes, frustrated. It was too late to explain things now. He could recount the facts, but of course the slant of them, the real meaning behind them—it was too late for that. There had been some whispers on the estate that Ater had been behind the bandits and the attack on his father. You can't keep soldiers from talking, but Albinia had been entirely oblivious. He might have told her days ago, and let her mull over it as he had, and let her reach the inevitable conclusion. But would she have reached that conclusion? Or any?

"Because he killed my father, and the Council cannot do a thing about it."

"That's why you attended the Council."

"Yes."

Albinia thought a moment. "The Lord says that vengeance is his."

"Yes, but it will set a bad precedent to wait."

"Will it be dangerous?"

"Of course. And that's why I'm telling you. So that you may be prepared for whatever happens. I don't want you to worry."

"I won't worry. Everything is in God's hands."

"That's reassuring." He pitched into sarcasm because, of course, Albinia's incessant religiosity irritated him. Not that he didn't believe in God like everyone else, but wasn't it enough that he believed and acted rightly? Couldn't one then properly move beyond whatever speculations and preoccupations filled her days? Clearly God needed men to get out in the world and put a lever under it from time to time. And what was more, it wasn't only her incessant devotions that grated on him. It was that she believed that whatever became of him in a day or two was part God's plan—some event the Deity had kept hidden in his pocket since he'd made the world. Fair enough—she'd doubtless heard it from some priest somewhere whose business it was to hold such opinions, but her indifference made him suddenly, desperately, lonely. He could see that if he were killed later in the week, she'd stand by his sarcophagus quite unmoved and see in his death nothing more significant than a collapsed millwheel, say, or a lucky guess, or lightning on a distant hill. She had so much perspective that nothing could move her; she had so much perspective that she had moved quite beyond feeling.

As he lay next to Albinia and felt her cool body along the length of his, he realized with great force, and for the first time since the Senator's death, that he was completely alone, and he thought how much he missed the old man, even with all of his irritating foibles. Quirinius would rattle around the big estate rubbing shoulders only with soldiers and his otherworldly wife and pore over the accounts with Sequanius. He supposed he could talk to Sequanius—he was a sharp enough fellow and had read a few books somewhere, but their stations were entirely different.

He felt the urge for sex, as would any man of his age, but the thought of lying atop Albinia--the only position she knew or would accept--while she turned her head and lay here, eyes closed, was not appealing. She would let him raise her shift and would obediently open her legs, but from then on, he was alone. Quirinius rolled away from her and tried to sleep. He could hear her mumbling prayers in the background.

* * *

The Estate of Eugenius Ater, Early June 465 AD

Albinia was far from his mind two days later as Quirinius approached the bounds of Ater's great estate. He had led his men openly along the Roman road that ran south out of Corinium. He knew it would be plain to anyone along the way that he was leading a raid, but he reckoned that he could arrive at Ater's estate before the senator could arrange an effective defense. As Quirinius saw it, Ater had two possibilities. He could meet him along the road and engage him in the field or close himself up within the walls of his villa. Quirinius was prepared for either.

He was convinced that he could defeat Ater in the open field if their numbers were anything like equal because his men were experienced and bold, and because he knew he could keep them in hand. By contrast, Ater's men had done nothing more military in twenty years than stare down the peasants as they paid their taxes to his villas. Furthermore, Quirinius' sudden approach should have left Ater with no time to muster any men from his smaller estates to reinforce himself. All in all, it seemed unlikely that Ater would dare meet him in the field, and after the session in the Council, he was confident none of the magnates would hurry to help him. Quirinius had a half a dozen scouts reconnoitering ahead, and there was no sign of Ater's men. Speed had proved its virtue.

It was clear that Ater would barricade himself in his villa and rely on his men to hold the walls. There his troops—perhaps fifty or sixty men—would see their strength multiplied, and that could pose a problem. However, Quirinius would trust again in speed. It might take Ater only moments to shut the gates of his villa, but he might not have time to gather all of his men before Quirinius' appeared. Some might be dispersed on the estate. And Quirinius' sudden approach might be demoralizing.

If Ater's men did succeed in holing themselves up in sufficient numbers, then Quirinius had an answer for that as well. He would round up his enemy's peasants and make them dismantle the wall at one or another point while he stood ready with his men to storm any too-lightly defended point. He'd set up a gin before the main gate and swing a ram from it against the portal. There had to be a stand of trees near the villa to furnish what he needed.

The troop turned off the paved highway and stopped along the hard-earthen road leading away from it, and they had crossed onto Ater's estate. Quirinius supposed that the villa would stand not far from the road to ease the transport of the grain that had for generations been one of the bases of the Ater fortune, and when a pair of scouts swept back up along Ater's road, they told Quirinius what he already suspected, that the villa itself was only a mile ahead. Most of the estate's land lay behind it. What was more, there was no sign of soldiers awaiting them.

"Not in the woods ahead? Not even a scout in the brush somewhere?"

"No, Dominē. Not even there."

Quirinius nodded at them, and they moved back to the rear of the column. He donned his helmet, and the others did the same. Each man slipped his shield onto his arm, found the balance point of his lance and waited until Quirinius gave the signal. When they saw him nod to Canidius, they moved forward without waiting for a command. The troop trotted down the road, which swerved first left and then right through the small wood.

Quirinius scanned the woods on either side as he led the troop, for, though he trusted his scouts, he was careful, but the wood was old, even older than the villa ahead, and, though the canopy was dense and the ground beneath it dark, the boles were wide apart and the underbrush sparse. It was just as the scouts had said—there was no ambush. After half a mile, the road came out of the wood and led gently down into the large meadow in which Ater's villa stood, surrounded by an earth and timber wall coped with grey stones. No sentries were visible. Odd. A field of low weathered stumps lay along one edge of the wall; an orchard had been cut down fifty years before to accommodate it. He could see the upper story of the house behind the walls, its red tile roof brownish in the early summer sun, its windows open and black-dark.

At first Quirinius was concerned only with bringing his men up on either side of him into a pair of broad flanks, so that they were free to wheel and meet any opposition, however unlikely. When it was evident that none of Ater's men were there to meet him, he turned his attention to a settlement a mile to his right, where most of Ater's tenants lived. Even at this distance he could see that the place had been emptied. He could see no activity and no large livestock; the peasants had fled into the country ahead of him, or perhaps some were on the villa grounds, though Quirinius doubted this—he suspected that Ater wouldn't encumber his defense with two hundred awkward peasants and a score of shambling oxen. All of this meant that Quirinius' approach had been noted at some point, and yet there was nothing to show any real defense. Why not?

The answer came to Quirinius after a little observation. The road down which Quirinius had led the Thracian Lancers and the Bucellarii continued straight ahead until it entered the gates of the wall that protected the great house. Oddly, the gates in the wall appeared not entirely closed—a thin band of light stood out between the portals, and Quirinius couldn't discern anyone along the top of the wall, or on the guard platform above the gate. The place seemed unnaturally quiet. The troopers saw this too, and Quirinius could sense them glancing sidelong at him, trying to see what he made of it.

He studied the villa's situation. It had been built on a plain, and the land about it was in cultivation—had been in cultivation for two or three centuries, for the hedges that defined the fields were thick and well-established. And though the land was gentle and rolled only like the sea at early morning, there was a tall, broad ridge a half-mile behind the establishment, which led away to the north and into a wilderland of hills and low trees. The top of the ridge seemed to undulate, as though alive, or as though it held a stand of poplars that shook, although there was no wind. He squinted a few seconds more and guessed what it meant. He slipped his shield from his arm and slung it on his back.

"Canidius, send a scout close to the ridge and have him tell us what he sees." The captain nodded and waved one of the troopers forward. "Be quick about it," Canidius shouted. The man handed his lance, shield and helmet to comrades and cantered off toward the ridge. Quirinius watched the man for a few moments and then advanced down the road at a walk, his men fanned out at either side, until he'd come just a hundred yards short of the walls, just out of effective bowshot. He stopped there and waited for the scout to return. He still saw no one on the walls around the villa. The only sign of life was a thin plume of smoke going straight up in the still air, probably from the kitchen or the forge. The air was so quiet he could hear the ringing calls of a million insects. Yes, at this distance it was quite apparent that the gates had not been properly closed.

"A trap, Dominē? Some trick?" Canidius frowned.

Quirinius stared ahead at the gate. "Possibly. Though I doubt it." He turned his head when he heard the scout approaching from the ridge.

"Well?"

"Ater's soldiers, Dominē. They're all up on the ridge. I can tell they're his by the standard—the white tail on their dragon. Some are sitting their horses up there and watching, but most are fading away from us into the trees, I'd say. They've brought some carts up there, and I saw a loaded pack mule or two."

"They're coming against us—against our estate." Quirinius heard a soldier say quietly in the background.

"No," he called back at them decisively. "The path they've taken leads nowhere. They're heading off into the wilds to hide." He thought a moment, then gave a command. Twenty horsemen trotted down the road another thirty yards, slowed, and then veered off to the left and began to circle the walls of the villa at a walk. Another troop headed to the right and sat their horses in the field to watch the walls until the others had made the circuit. After a few minutes, the circling troop joined those waiting in the field and rejoined Quirinius and the rest of the troopers.

"Did you see anyone? Did anyone see anyone?" He asked generally. All of the soldiers shook their heads; there were a few quiet "no's".

"Well then, let's see what goes on." Quirinius slid from his horse, took up his shield again, drew his sword, and advanced on foot toward the gate. He was surrounded immediately by his men, though he made sure to keep at their head to embolden them, and, as he approached the gate, he presented his left side so that he could keep well behind the shield, which he raised slightly against any arrows or other missiles that might come from the walls. But nothing came.

He stepped into the shadows before the gate. The portals had been shoved closed, but the bar had not been set, and, putting his shield against the right portal, he leaned and pushed. After a moment the oaken door shuddered and swung back sluggishly a foot or two. Other men put their shoulders to it, and when it had swung back, the entire troop spilled in afterward and drew itself together shoulder to shoulder in a tight phalanx, swords out and ready, heads turning about to look for Ater's soldiers. But there were none.

Instead, they stood in a wide court of rammed earth with nothing active but a dozen chickens wobbling and scratching at the side of the great house. The birds looked stupidly at the men, and then, burbling and ruffling their feathers, shuttled off indignantly a few yards. Quirinius put his hand up for silence and watched the scene a few moments. He tilted his head and listened, but there was nothing to hear. The still air brought only a faint, faint odor of smoke.

The window shutters on the second floor were all open—clearly no one had prepared to defend the house if the outer wall were breached, though the great front doors of the villa stood closed. The most prudent move would have been to scout around the outside of the great house to see whether a handful of Ater's men might be lurking somewhere, say, beyond the far corner of the villa, but even if that were so, they could not be many—probably not even a dozen.

He considered a moment longer and decided that the matter had tilted to the point where it was better to display boldness rather than caution. He ordered a squad to the doors. They were barred.

"Get it open," Quirinius told Canidius. The captain nodded and signaled the men to seize a two-wheeled farm cart that rested propped against the inside of the wall with its shafts in the air. At his orders three men grasped and leaned into each shaft and ran it backwards against the great front doors. The tailboard splintered at the second stroke; on the fifth or sixth the doors buckled in the center and shifted back with a crack, the bar holding them closed quite broken. The men pushed the cart aside. Quirinius noted idly, as one sometimes does in high moments, that one of its wheels had been knocked out of round and it listed as it rolled away. The men put their shoulders to the door and forced it wide open.

Quirinius went ahead, and his men surged forward, clustered about him as he stepped past the riven doors into the foyer. He paused inside and stood mottled in the shadows as he looked about. It was a fine foyer with good frescoes on the plaster of the walls, the seasons personified in good Hellenistic style daubed by a master-painter a century or so ago, if Quirinius could judge the work. The shading was well done, the figures well-proportioned, and their expressions convincing. The floor was a skilled mosaic, Europa carried by the bull across the sea, the whole surrounded by a border of blue and white waves. Again, it looked like fine Italian work or, if not that, the best work by an artist of Narbonensis. Cupboards stood here and there on well-turned feet, shining deeply from decades of polishing, and a chair sat to one side of the doors for the porter and even this, though sturdy, was well made to show that the master of the house valued a visitor's impression in even the least particular. But there was no one in the foyer. The only faces Quirinius saw were the wax funeral masks of the Ater family staring at him from the right. They watched from the shadows of their cabinet, the doors of which had, oddly, come ajar. Two hundred years of Ater's family peered out of the gloom at him, these relics of Ater's ancestors watching silent and eyeless as he passed with his men.

And there was no one in any of the rooms that Quirinius and his men passed through. At first they went cautiously, sweeping back curtains with swords' points and kicking doors open against the chance of meeting a soldier, but there were none, and gradually Quirinius and his men began to sweep through the great, fine house with confidence, the sound of their footsteps splashing about them off the beautiful painted walls. Here and there a squad of men veered off to explore a side corridor as the rest of the troop hurried ahead.

After the first flush of excitement, the emptiness of the place became even more striking, and Quirinius noted what surely had been there to see all along, that many chairs were tipped over, that some of the drapes covering the doorways to the various rooms had been torn away, that here and there were shattered dishes lying on the floor and that the doors of cabinets stood open. When they did, the shelves behind them stood half-empty, and oddments lay like dross on the floor all about. In the middle of one room an apple with a bite out of it lay on a mosaic floor. Ater's soldiers had not only abandoned the place--they had ransacked it. The meaning of it was clear. Ater hadn't fled with his men—he'd lost control of them.

Quirinius sheathed his sword and handed off his shield. He undid his chin-strap, lifted the helmet from his head, and put it beneath his arm. He turned his head now to listen closely, for he thought he'd heard a noise in the depths of the echoey old villa, and indeed he had.

For there was a faint keening sound as of weeping at the back of a deep cave. Quirinius frowned, looked about him. Canidius shrugged. He heard it too but couldn't construe it.

"Someone's here," Quirinius said. "Let's find him." He set off walking confidently. He wasn't all that confident, though, even as things were going, for, frankly, it was afternoon and the house was growing dark. The gloom and shadows were mixed with the hollowness of abandonment into a sort of spooky stew that would unsettle any man who didn't have soldiers to impress. But he moved with a confidence that grew more real as he strode through the house, studiously ignoring the furnishings more lavish than those of his estates—richer, older, even better made and more numerous, even after the looting. Passing through an arched doorway and up two broad steps, he came to the door of Ater's personal apartments. The sound was louder now. No doubt it was sobbing, but thin and high; it could not be Ater. He nodded at the door. "Open it." Canidius tried it, but, of course, it was bolted. He waved to the men and two came forward and kicked at it together. The beautiful door, finished to look so solid, was only trompe l'oeuil upon flimsy boards, and it buckled like pasteboard. It took nothing to sweep the litter aside.

Quirinius stepped inside to a fine room with fantastic wall-paintings griffons, hippogriffs and other fantastical creatures who have never lived. In the center of the room was a very fine bed, unmade, but covered in yards of expensive fabric. It had polished gold finials on the posts and a little gilded footstool to help the sleeper climb in. It was finest bed he had ever seen, and there was a band of unpleasant erotic pictures low on the wall quite near it. But still, the sound of sobbing was what interested him, and it came from behind a draped doorway straight ahead.

Quirinius swept the drape aside to look into the bathroom, and he hesitated a moment before stepping inside because the sight was unexpected and horrible. The bathroom, like the bedroom, was very fine, the walls well-plastered and decorated with cupids fluttering between geometric borders, the whole room very light, for the shutters had been flung open, and the windows looked south. Perhaps this was the last bright room in the house. Standing in the room was the blond boy who so annoyed him at the Council meeting, but now he wasn't smirking. Instead, he was sobbing and clearly hysterical, breathing fast and shallow and keening like a girl with irritating repetition. He looked absurd, standing with his back against the wall in elegant clothes, but with a butcher knife waggling in his hand, no danger to anyone but himself.

But it was what was next to him that was disturbing. In the bathtub, a wonderful deep alabaster tub of fine Italian work with a rope-work rim and claw feet that somehow suggested a sarcophagus, was Ater himself, floating dead in a scarlet pool. The dead man looked immensely fat, fatter even than he had in life. He was clad in a sheer white tunic, now red, and floated in the bloody water like a great dead carp with its glistening belly turned upward. His face remained white, but now it wasn't powder—there was a grayish cast to it. Ater's mouth was open, and Quirinius noted that the man had few teeth and those remaining were dark. He could see that Ater had been older and weaker than he'd supposed. He was relieved that the man's eyes were closed; even so, the sight was jarring. Still, he couldn't turn his gaze away. He knew his men had joined him only because he felt them brush his shoulders as they took their places beside him. A shield scraped against the door jamb, and then he felt it held against his chest. Canidius had stepped up to protect him from the absurd boy and the knife that he clearly didn't know how to wield. The scent of smoke came to Quirinius, but he dismissed it.

He looked at the boy and raised his eyebrows.

"Dominus Eugenius Ater has passed on," the boy said unnecessarily and with banal gravity, as though he had no talent for speaking, but had practiced all the same. He took a few heaving breaths, and fixed his gaze on Quirinius, trying not to regard the soldiers all about, who clearly terrifed him. "As did Seneca, he chose to take his own life in the bath, a noble Roman and stoic to the end." He gestured to the floor beside the bathtub, where a blood-smeared razor lay, the instrument that Ater had used to cut his wrists.

"What do you know of Seneca?" Quirinius asked.

The boy stood silent, shaking.

"Nothing. Nothing at all," Quirinius answered for him.

"He taught me everything," the boy said glancing over at the body. He turned back, shuddered in fear, and said, "You are a danger,

Dominē Quirinius. You are like some wild bear that brings nothing but destruction. Dominus Ater said it to me a hundred times. And now you have killed this great man—he was very afraid of you. You've killed a man with a great soul." Quirinius heard a soldier behind him hawk and spit.

"He was a degenerate and a languid killer. He worked the death of my father and then sought to hide it, and, when called upon to defend his country he refused. He had a petty soul. And when danger came to him, he removed himself. I regret that he was dead when I found him. I'll confess my disappointment to you. It's no wonder his soldiers fled when they thought he might lead them."

"His men are cowards, all of them."

"Perhaps. Perhaps not. But I can say they have standards."

The boy took a deep breath, screwing up his courage. "There's nothing left for me now." He squared his shoulders and brought the knife up to an ineffectual position that signaled his intention. "Die!" he screamed. But, before he could take a step, Canidius sprang forward and quite flattened the boy against the wall with his shield. Quirinius noted the stunned surprise in the boy's wide eyes as he dropped the knife. Canidius raised his sword high in the air and struck the boy hard on the crown of his head with the pommel, and he dropped straight to the floor.

Canidius knelt down and glanced at the boy. "It looks like I've killed him. I didn't mean to." He stood up.

"Don't trouble yourself, Captain. He was Ater's parasite, and he had no future without him. It was better for him this way. Ater had made him unfit to live in the world."

The smell of smoke had grown stronger; it made Quirinius uneasy, like a symbol in a dream. "Let's go, boys." And he turned and walked away.

As they passed through the foyer, Canidius put two fingers in his mouth and gave his piercing whistle to call any soldiers back who might have been prowling or loitering in the great house. Once in the courtyard, Quirinius had the men sound off so that he could account for all of them, even though there had been no real action. The rest of the troop stood about the gate in the outer wall, and Quirinius, hearing a shout, looked at them and saw a good deal of pointing in his direction, but higher. He turned and regarded the great house and then saw what was the matter; the place was on fire. Smoke curled over the roof like a malevolent spirit, and the crackling grew louder.

Canidius, who had seen his master's face, shouted at the men. "Who fired the house?" Murmured denials, much head shaking.

"Let them be, Canidius. An overturned lamp, an untended kitchen fire. It was something of that sort." He watched the fire grow, listened to its greedy voice. It might indeed have been as he says, some domestic accident, an oversight, the casual result of desultory looting. Or perhaps Ater's men had set it as they left. This seemed the most likely to him, for the progress of the fire was greater than he'd otherwise expect.

The men were disappointed—there could be no looting. Good. The fire made discipline easy—there was nothing to forbid them now, and, after all, pillage would have blurred the judicial character of the expedition. It might have made appreciation of the Idea more difficult.

Almost absently, he neared the entry and looked through the great doors to see smoke wash in a grey flood across the floor of the foyer; it began to fill the room and rise to hide the masks of the ancient Aters who watched him with a steady blank regard until they faded away in the grey atmosphere. When he couldn't see the images any longer, he shouted for the men to leave the courtyard and mount up, and he followed them out, the heat at his back, and he wondered how many books would be lost in the fire.

* * *

The Estate of Albinius Maximianus, Late June 465 AD
"So old Ater killed himself, eh?" Maximinianus said, reflecting.

"He didn't have the fortitude to defend himself," Quirinius replied.

"He didn't have the men."

"It's all the same. They sensed, even if he didn't, that he lacked the power to lead them. It was all of a piece."

Maximinianus mused silently for a moment and took another sip of his wine.

Quirinius felt compelled to speak in the silence. "Oddly, it was the masks that I found disturbing."

"The masks?"

"Yes. Ater had the old funeral masks—the ones molded in wax from the very faces of his dead ancestors. The old pagan custom."

Maximianus nodded. "Yes, I see. He always claimed his family were true Romans—from the City itself, I mean. And patricians. Actual patricians in the old sense. What an old custom. I wouldn't have expected any such masks outside of Italy."

"Someone had left the cabinet open, and they stared out at me. I've thought about how they must have liquefied in the heat and sunk into the earth. The images of the Aters lying deep in the earth like ghosts of some sort. Like the ones Odysseus met."

Maximianus shrugged. "Ah, well, we're all Christians now."

"They looked out at me, the faces of these vigorous old men from a vigorous old time, as I went to meet the last of their line, a man who hadn't thought his life or his honor worth the struggle to keep."

"Then perhaps they approved." He shifted on the bench and straightened his back. "You understood, of course, that the Council would never indict Eugenius Ater."

"I understood it quite well. A trial was never my intention. I made that clear to you at the time."

"You made it clear afterward."

Quirinius shrugged his indifference.

"It matters that you did not forewarn me, for I might have counselled you."

"Counselled me against taking the actions that I did."

"Perhaps. Clearly you didn't trust me."

Quirinius looked away, uneasy. "All the same, it all turned out well enough. The gamble was worth the taking."

"Again, I say 'perhaps.' But it seems to me that you failed to learn something very important at the Council meeting."

"I was not there to learn."

"That's evident. But try to learn now. Think what the magnates did when you accused Ater of murder."

"They did nothing."

"And why?"

Quirinius shook his head in exasperation at Maximianus' playing the schoolmaster. "They did nothing because they feared him."

Maximianus looked Quirinius in the eyes for a moment. "I think not. I tell you this; they did nothing because they feared you, Flavius."

Quirinius scowled, baffled. "Make yourself clear."

"The magnates and nobles, the senators and petty kings fear you in your swift rise, and they wanted Eugenius Ater as a counterweight. Allied with him and the Bassi, they believed they could defy you if need be. And now he is gone. You present them with a problem, Flavius. Perhaps you are my problem too, because I am inextricably linked to you. I always wished you success, but now I must depend upon it."

"Still, I say that the nobles feared Ater. There was no true support for him in the Council."

"That changes nothing. Let us agree for the sake of argument that you are right that they feared Ater. What of it? A man can fear one thing and yet turn to address another. Consider that Ater is dead, and you remain the single object of their unease."

The two men sat in silence regarding each other.

"We never tallied the score," Maximianus said.

"What?"

"The bowls. We never determined the winner." The old man hobbled over to the game, and Quirinius found him bent over judging which balls were closest. *But why bother?* he wondered. He had unquestionably pitched better than the old man.

"Ah, a close game, yes, but somehow I am the winner," the old man said with a certain gravity, as though discovering an unsuspected truth. Quirinius, in mild surprise, looked more closely. It was true. The old man had a single ball closer to the pig than any of Quirinius'. He'd won by a point.

"But how..."

"I'll show you a useful technique, my boy. Don't let it be used against you again." And, so saying, he pretended to study an elm at the end of the green and casually tapped the ball even closer to the pig with his foot. He looked back at it and then at Quirinius. "Why, it's an even better throw than I realized."

Fifteen: The Monastery, October 491 AD

"Where are Moderatus and Pennomorix!" Quirinius asks no one in particular. "At my age I should be in bed at this hour, even with a battle in prospect. Especially with a battle in prospect."

"They will come," Bishop Valerianus says. "Travel is difficult at night, even with a full moon."

"If they knew how to marshal and move their men, they wouldn't still be shuffling through the middle of the night. The only way to move men at night is along a road, and the Saxons could discover them easily and stop them, perhaps even destroy them piecemeal, first Moderatus and then Pennomorix."

"The Saxons won't stop them."

Quirinius sat down on a bench against the wall, leaned his head back and crossed his arms. He closed his eyes and said, "You claim to know a good deal when you say you know what the Saxons will do. It's a good deal for a churchman to know."

"You must have faith."

Quirinius snorted. "I have faith that the Saxons can surprise you." And as he says this, as he thinks back to his second encounter with them—one he doesn't bother to recount, because it is after midnight and he's very tired. And the importance of the encounter is not what another might suspect.

The Estate of Albinius Maximianus, June, 465 AD

It was about midday on the journey back from Maximinianus' estate following the raid on Ater's villa. The weather had turned cool as though autumn had taken an early step into the country, and the sun was colorless in a watery sky. Canidius glanced with studied casualness at Quirinius from time to time to see when it would be right to ask for a halt. Let the men eat. The question was written in his eyes. Quirinius meant to press on another hour and pretended not to notice. He looked lordly about the countryside as though it were all his, and perhaps, in a way, it was because he had undertaken to defend it.

Glancing about, he noticed smoke in the sky to his right. It climbed from behind a stand of trees in a plume too thick to rise from a forge or a pottery. He pulled up to a halt and pointed. "Is there a settlement that way?"

Canidius looked back at the troopers behind. "Well?"

"A small town," said one of the soldiers. "Silvania."

"Colonia Silvana," another shouted, proud that he knew the right name.

Quirinius couldn't quite place it. "How far is it?"

"Not far," came the unhelpful answer.

Quirinius had already urged his horse forward before he asked, "Where is the road to it?"

"Just ahead, Dominē. A half a mile, no more." Quirinius recalled a side road—a mere wagon track, really—of iron-hard earth leading north. He found the road just past the end of the copse and led the troop at a trot toward the town.

Colonia Silvana had shrunk; it was hardly a town. An unwalled villa lay to the left a half-mile away, but even at this distance he could see that its roofs had fallen in. There was no great man to protect the adjacent town, and it did not have walls. The fields on either side were fallow until the immediate outskirts of the town, and even there the low stone walls demarking the plots were half tumble-down. When Quirinius had led the troop into the outer precincts he could tell at a glance that almost no one lived there any longer. But apparently a handful of monks still tried to, for there was a burning church ahead and a large house beside it. The figures of two black-robed monks lay on the pavement before the house. Quirinius led the troop forward at a walk, cautious of ambush. He was quite aware that an enemy on foot would have the advantage of them here in the streets where there would be no room to wheel the horses and maneuver.

There was no enemy, however. That was plain enough when the troop reached the house beside the burning church and encountered no one. The house had been the former town residence of some great man, but monks had squatted in it and made it a monastery. A trooper dismounted and examined the two fallen monks and shook his head to show that they were dead. A handful of men slid from their horses and stepped cautiously through the splintered front door of the house. The horses feared the fire. Some skittered, others shied from the heat. Quirinius ordered each man to dismount and hold his animal by the bridle. The soldiers who had stepped into the house soon came out.

"Well?"

"No one's inside, Dominē." A short old, bearded soldier spoke for the group, an old lieutenant from his father's days, a steady man, older than Canidius, but not astute enough to rise as high.

"No bodies?"

"No, Dominē. No bodies. Not much of anything. Of course, they were only monks, but no lamps, no plates—not even tin ones. Nothing valuable. If they had it, Dominē."

"What about their treasury?"

"I can't really say, Dominē. If they had a proper one, that is. There is one small room with a broken door that's filled with empty shelves. But who knows how they used it?" He looked pointedly at the burning church and then at the skittish horses. "The horses, Dominē. They're getting hard to handle."

"I can see that."

"And the house is afire too. At the back on the second floor."

Quirinius led the troop down a side street and away from the burning church, all the time looking around for any inhabitants, but everyone seemed to have fled or found a good hiding place. Frustrated, he sent three squads of men to search the houses nearby and promised money to whichever first brought back someone to question. The town had lost most of its population, but the men cleverly looked for houses with doors closed against the street, and soon Quirinius could hear them kicking these in. After a short while some troopers brought him an ancient monk.

The old man quailed in terror, even as Quirinius assured him that they were Romans. He cringed, raised his hands, and bent at the waist as though he expected a beating, and he kept his eyes closed, afraid of what he might see. He burbled incoherently because he was afraid and because he was too old to have any teeth.

Quirinius repeated himself, this time in British, and the man opened his cloudy eyes and regarded him for the first time, squinting to get a good look.

"Romans?" He asked the question in British. Quirinius continued in it.

"I am Quirinius, Count of the Britains."

"Cuirann Guledig," Candius said, glossing it for the hysterical monk.

At first the old man said nothing, as though he couldn't take it in. Then he took a deep breath and chuffed like a tired horse. "They killed several of the brothers. The rest of them, I don't know where they are." Quirinius wondered who the old monk was talking about— the other monks or the attackers?

There came a crash as the roof of the burning church fell in; horses and men surged at the sound, and cinders flew like burning locusts down the street. The bell tower shuddered, and the bell of sheet-iron clapped tinnily for a few strokes, as though some hand were on the pull.

"Who did this?"

"Saxons," the old monk said. "Who thought they could come so far west? Can no one protect us?" He turned creakily with little steps until he faced the smoldering church and began to weep. "This was my whole life! It is gone and now I am old."

"How many were there?"

The old man only wept and wiped his eyes on his black sleeve.

"Did they have horses?"

The old monk only shook his head as though Quirinius had asked about geometry.

Quirinius got up on his horse. "Canidius, tell the men to mount up."

"Dominē, do you know where they went?"

"They'll go east to their homes, and they'll choose to take a road now that they're burdened with loot. We'll cross the forum and go east along that street. Whatever road it leads us to, we'll find them along it somewhere." He started off. Behind him he heard the monk wail, "Holy Christ, but the world is getting dark."

* * *

The road out of town wasn't paved, but it soon joined one of the great raised, stone roads. The troop continued east, and Quirinius kept the pace alternatively to a trot and a fast walk to spare the horses. He wanted them as strong as they could be when the fight came. He permitted only a pair of scouts to ride hard, and about an hour down the road he saw them cantering back toward him.

"Dominē! Saxons!" the first scout to approach called out.

"How many?"

"Perhaps thirty," he answered. The other cantered up and spent a moment reining in his horse, which turned a circle in its excitement.

"How armed?"

"A few have axes or a sword, the rest have only spears or those long knives of theirs. A chief on a horse leads them, but the rest are on foot. He has armor, and perhaps a dozen of them have helmets, but the rest have only shields."

"They saw us, Dominē," the second scout said, when he'd regained control of his mount. "It's broad daylight."

"Don't fret," Quirinius said. "Are they far ahead?"

"A mile, no more," the first scout answered, reaching for his helmet.

"You men go to the rear. Your animals are tired." The scouts glanced at each other unhappily but nodded and walked their horses slowly back to the end of the column.

Quirinius tied his helmet under his chin, took up his shield from where it hung behind him on the saddle and slung it over his shoulder where he could assume it quickly when needed. The men behind followed his example. He kicked his horse into a fast trot.

The road went straight, a wood soon springing up a good twenty yards away along its left margin. To the right was open scrub. Soon he saw figures ahead on the road and, as he approached, he could make them out as individuals, some blond, some brown-haired, one showing a great red beard as he turned to face them. Quirinius drew up and slid his arm through the loops of his shield. As he stood watching, gauging what was best to do, the Saxon chief on a glossy, fat black horse slipped back among his men to face his pursuers. Like Quirinius, he wore a Roman officer's helmet with wide cheek plates and a nose-piece that half-hid his face. It was a vulgar affair, though, begauded on the crown with glass gems in red and green, some gift, perhaps, dating from a generation before when the Saxons were first hired. Behind his circular shield there was a glint of armor.

The rest of the men were poorly equipped, just as the scouts had said, and even the chief was improperly armed, carrying an axe on a long haft, a footman's weapon, instead of a proper lance. When the chief had regarded Quirinius for a few moments, he shouted something to his men, who drifted back behind him and then brought forward a light wagon loaded with whatever spoil they had taken on their raid. The chief pulled back behind the men, who cut the dray horse free of the wagon and drove it with slaps down off the highway and into the adjoining field. They put their shoulders to the wagon and skidded it about until it blocked the road. A half-dozen men stood behind it with axes. At a command, one of them struck out the spokes of two of the wheels, and the wagon slumped into an immovable wreck.

"Clever, don't you think?" Quirinius asked Canidius. The captain merely frowned and then turned to squint at the Saxons, as though by sharpening his glance he could see some solution to the problem.

And the Saxon chief was clever. At this point, the Roman road was higher than the surrounding terrain, running almost like a low wall through the countryside, and the Saxons were standing on it behind their impromptu bulwark. With the ruined wagon across the road, there was no way to charge down at them, and there was no way to sweep close to them on either side, because, while the troopers could descend into the field, they couldn't then ride up to the raiders, who would stand above the level of the fields.

Quirinius had to decide quickly—he could feel his men's regard on him quite as much as the gaze of the enemy, and hesitation could lose him whatever chance he had to win the fight. Even if his men were less accustomed to fighting on foot than the Saxons, he had advantages in numbers, élan, and equipment. He waved his arm, the standard bearer dipped the dragon, and Quirinius led his men to the right and down from the highway into the grass alongside.

He rode until he was just alongside the knot of Saxons who stood, round shield to round shield in a tight clump, their chief sitting his horse behind and looking down over his men's heads. Quirinius' men obeyed their standards and disposed themselves in wings to either side of him. He looked to the right of the Saxons and saw that the chief had ordered a pair of handcarts set up to form a barricade on their left flank as well. Yes, he was a clever fellow—he had arranged things so that Quirinius and his men must come directly at him and on foot. Well, so be it. The bastards had a good position, it was true, but he did outnumber them.

He slid off his horse and signaled to his men to do the same. He then drew Canidius, the standard bearers, and a pair of lieutenants a few steps ahead, spoke to them briefly and quietly. There were nods all around. Quirinius harangued the men for only a few moments, reminding them that they had never let him down, that they had never failed him, that they outnumbered the Saxons, and that they were defending the provinces, the Idea, and the Church. He turned to face the raiders, drew his sword and advanced afoot. He was immediately surrounded by the troopers, who hedged him around with their oval shields and made a hedge with their levelled lances.

Quirinius and his men advanced at a walk, covering the few yards to the Saxons quickly, and then everyone slowed to be sure his neighbor was beside him, and the line moved on again at a walk until they met the Saxons.

The enemy had the advantage of the slightly higher position, and they were stalwart—one could tell by their faces and bearing, but the larger number of the Romans clearly distressed them, and when the men met, a few of the troopers with their lances and long Roman swords got under the round shields at the legs of the Saxons and a few went down.

Quirinius had trouble seeing; he tried to stay in the front rank to inspirit the men, but Canidius elbowed past him, and he found himself in the second rank with his shield raised to protect him from downward blows. He could hear shouts and screams and a terrifying cracking sound which he supposed was the sound of a Saxon axe splitting a shield.

In a few moments, however, it was largely over. A half-dozen Saxons were lying dead, and the rest had drifted back off the road and down onto the ground behind it. Quirinius clambered up the embankment and onto the highway, and he could see the remaining Saxons still clumped together, red shield to red shield, withdrawing in surprisingly good order to the woods behind. The chief stood in the center of them, shouting encouragement. His fat black horse ran free to one side, trying to flee the tumult. A half-dozen of the troopers had regained their horses and ridden up over the highway and down the other side in pursuit, but the Saxons soon melted into the woods, sifting through the trees, where horsemen could not follow.

Quirinius turned when he heard a man screaming and was sickened to see a trooper who had lost an arm to an axe blow. The man was wailing, his eyes open and fixed on nothing. His shattered shield lay nearby, covered with blood.

As Quirinius approached him, Canidius stepped up and raised his hand. He shook his head and said "No! He doesn't know anyone now. It's the blood—he's lost too much."

Quirinius didn't know what to say. Two troopers knelt beside the man and started to cut apart a cloak for strips of cloth to bind the wound, but before they'd driven their knives the length of the fabric, the man was dead. They knelt and looked at each other over the body, bright blood up to their elbows. Quirinius turned away, dazed.

Another man had died too—one of the new men he'd taken from the other nobles, a man whose name he had never learned, but now wished that he had. He undid his helmet, took it off and wiped the sweat from his brow with his sleeve, and, when he could see clearly, he scrutinized the woods into which the Saxons had drifted, but there was no sign of them. He thought of them slipping among the trees like woodland beasts, drifting east to their homes, unencumbered by loot, but prepared, like the tide, to return.

The Saxons hadn't seized much loot—the ruined wagon wasn't really needed to carry it—the wagon, which had been extremely well made, had itself been plunder. A good wheelwright had made of the wheels perfect circles, the spokes had been turned on a lathe, and an excellent smith had made iron tires and slipped them onto the wheels while they were red hot—they'd cooled and shrunk to fit. The work was exquisite, really, not at all what Quirinius would have expected to find outside of a handful of estates, or in Corinium or Glevum. But of course, the Saxon warrior had turned the work to litter when he had smashed the spokes of the wheels, and the tires had twisted as the wheels collapsed.

The troop's spare horses could bear the loot, however, which turned out to be church property: lamps, a cross, a eucharistic service, censors, a coffer, all of it silver and more valuable than Quirinius would have expected. The bodies of the dead troopers, which concerned him more, were put across the backs of their horses and tied so they could not slip off. The unceremoniousness of their treatment bothered him.

They rode back through the evening toward the east and Quirinius' second estate. Oddly, so it seemed to him, he heard the occasional chuckle behind him, despite the deaths of the two soldiers. He realized that, although he felt burdened by the men's deaths and thought the soldiers would hold him responsible, this was not so. It was as though the deaths of their comrades had confirmed the high and dangerous nature of their calling and exalted the survivors in a way that their previous skirmishes had not. Now the men will truly swagger, he thought. And he was happy about this, but all the same distressed and sad.

* * *

He presses the men hard, though they are tired from the fight, and he begins to recognize the countryside toward the end of the afternoon--the disposition of a stand of trees here and there, or of an abandoned farmstead, recalls to him the journey he made with his father years before, after the old senator had held court at his second estate, just ahead. Indeed, it does, because the beaten track that will take them to the estate veers off to the right, and he leads the column down from the roadway and onto its surface, earthen, but beaten iron-hard from centuries of travel.

The track slopes down to a small river, Quirinius remembers this, and soon he sees the flowing water bordered with shrubs and slender poplars as it runs slowly past the edge of a low hill. There is a gentle wind, and the leaves of the poplars turn silver as coins in the breeze or perhaps silver as the fish in the stream. Many of the shrubs along the river are clothed in white sheets or swatches of faded brown cloth because a half-dozen women are washing clothes. Several kneel and beat sodden clothes on boulders worn glass-smooth by three centuries of washing; another squats in the shallow stream soaking a garment with each hand. They are, of course, nuns from Mother Pulcheria's little abbey on the top of the low hill behind them.

Quirinius glances up and can see the abbey above them. The establishment is a large old farmhouse--he can just see its roof. The red tiles have been replaced with thatch, and its outbuildings and a daub and wattle church are all encircled by the farmstead's old wall, grey and crumbling at the top, but still for the most part sound. Overtopping the wall is a simple open belfry made of timbers, from which hangs a sheet iron bell. He thinks for a moment how a new sort of life had filtered into the crannies and crevices of the old Roman way.

He returns his gaze to the women as he rides toward the stream. Somehow the women have failed to notice the column, and in moment the wind brings a snatch of song—the women are preoccupied with work and singing, but in a few moments the nun soaking clothes in the middle of the stream looks up, and then stands up, drying her hands on her skirts, which are gathered up around her in her belt. She's a sturdy girl, and her wet, shining legs are naked almost up to the crotch. As though absently, she keeps the clothes she has left in the water from drifting down stream by gracefully placing her right leg before them and letting them gather and cling around her glistening calf.

Quirinius is startled to see her strong, well-shaped legs and feels a sudden sensation in his gut, as of falling a foot or two. She smiles frankly at him. He sees red hair escaping from the cloth tied about her head; it's the young woman Caelia. He feels as though he has suddenly remembered something quite important that he'd unaccountably forgotten—the sort of thing common in dreams.

The other nuns look up now that Caelia stands so straight, and they scatter into the bushes with the brief shrieks of alarm they owe to modesty, and in a moment Caelia is alone in the stream. Quirinius watches her as he rides along, and she watches him in turn, as bold as anything, and then, just before he can no longer watch her without turning in the saddle, she raises her hand and waves half a dozen times with a joyful enthusiasm. Quirinius sighs sharply, turns away, and, with his eyes closed, tries to direct his mind toward Albinia, whose vigor drives her only to the chapel, whose knees are calloused from her devotions. But he finds his mind drawn back to Caelia and to the memory of watching her, fiery-headed in the setting sun, as she rocked and jostled in the back of the wagon on her way with Mother Pulcheria back to the nunnery.

As though his recollection has prompted it, the abbey bell begins to sound. Quirinius looks up and notes that the slapping sound of the bell seems to follow its movement, always late by the merest moment. It's odd, he thinks, how much mystery there is in the world. He turns his glance back to the road carefully, so as not to see Caelia, and lets his mount plod ahead toward the estate.

Although he keeps his face turned away as he rides along, he can feel Caelia's lambent head, warm at his back like the sun. He closes his eyes and scowls as though against a bright light and doesn't open them until he has succeeded in smoothing his expression into something very bland. Does she wave at him still? His face doesn't reveal any of his concern for the answer.

With a sudden jog the path turns left and climbs gradually up the face of a broad rise along the top of which a stand of weedy trees stoop toward the east—mulberries, perhaps—Quirinius cannot concentrate, cannot say. He knows, though, that beyond those scrubby trees is an open heath a good three miles broad which, when he has crossed it, will slope gently down to the eastern estate where the Old Senator had held court and settled Caelia's future three years before. Suddenly everything seems tied to her.

At the top of the ridge, Quirinius looks back over his right shoulder at Canidius and, while doing it, casts a glance down at the river below. It flashes silver in the sun, silently at this remove; the women, even Caelia, are all gone from it. He rides into the midst of the weedy bending mulberry trees and glances back at Canidius. Quirinius decides quickly, as is his way, and, having decided, rides a little more quickly, gradually pulling ahead of the column. He waves his right arm for the captain, in a low and languid way--just as though some little, unimportant thing is on his mind. The captain rides up up beside him.

"In that nunnery is a tough old harridan of an abbess named Pulcheria."

Canidius nods. "She is well-known hereabouts."

"She's hard-headed. Don't argue with her or you'll be at it half the night. Just tell her what to do."

"Yes, Dominē. And what is that?"

"Take three men so that you'll look impressive and give her my regards. Ask how things are going up there; remind her of my father's generosity—and therefore of mine. Remind her how much she depends upon it."

"Yes." Canidius, naturally polite, shows no curiosity.

"Tell her I'm too occupied to visit her holy establishment."

"Of course, Dominē."

"This won't cause her much relief because she'll be suspicious of you anyway."

"Should she be?"

Quirinius looks at him for a moment and then smiles. "Why, yes. In fact, she should be."

"There will be no argument."

"Good. Instead, you must ask her how one of her nuns is doing. A girl named Caelia."

"Very good."

"I believe that our priest, old Remigius back at the estate, could do with a new housekeeper. Tell her that I think Caelia would be a suitable choice." It's an inspiration, this idea. A moment before he'd had no idea what his excuse would be but, in a flash, he has his answer.

"I understand." Canidius' voice is wonderfully neutral.

"I want you to bring her to me. Let her gather her things if she wants, but don't let her dally—she won't have anything much to speak of anyway, and I don't want to give Mother Pulcheria time to maneuver or interpose any obstacles."

"No, Dominē."

"Go and do this now," Quirinius says. Both turn and look down across the shallows to the nunnery across the river.

"She'll come, Dominē." Canidius turns his horse about, and soon Quirinius can see him crossing the little bridge upstream from where the women were washing. He leads three of the troopers, the last one with a spare mount on a line. Quirinius turns and shouts at one of the ensigns to tell him he's in charge of leading the men to the estate, spurs his horse into a trot and, leaving the men behind, finishes the last three miles alone.

Sixteen: The Second Estate of the Quirinii, June 465

Quirinius sat in his father's fine old chair in a corner of the room where, five years ago, the old Senator had settled Caelia's future. He'd sat behind the table to Quirinius' left, on which sat the estate's ledgers, some wax tables, an ink pot, and three beautifully cut reed-pens; he noted the style—his father had made them himself. This equipment had lent the situation a sort of official ordinariness, as though any judgement the old Senator might render was simply a matter of common sense and thus beyond dispute—beyond any sort of reflection, really. Quirinius hoped that the echoes of that scene would confer the same unexceptionability to his business.

So, he waited, alternately calm and alternately tense, for Canidius to return. Time passed, the day darkened, and a servant came in to light the lamps and make himself available for any duty, but Quirinius waved him away without a word. He bowed, stepped out of the room and drew the door closed behind him with remarkable silence.

The sky through the open window darkened imperceptibly until it was a rectangle of violet sprinkled with a half-dozen stars floating in the center of the silver-grey wall. He absently noted this play of colors as he sat motionless, his chin on his fist, until he heard the muddled clopping of hooves in the court below and knew the men were back. When noise stopped, he leaned forward in his chair, shifted his feet, and listened for the footsteps of a woman, but, of course, Caelia would step too lightly to be heard, wouldn't she? He listened to the indistinct voices down below but couldn't catch what was said, couldn't divine from it whether the men had brought Caelia or not. He wouldn't lean from the window and look out, as some love-struck boy might do—he had that much dignity, at least.

But if he had dignity, he had little patience. Why didn't Canidius come directly up? The stairs from this office led down to the central hall and the horses must be no more than a dozen steps away from it. He did fancy he heard a sharp voice, an old woman's. Surely Canidius wouldn't allow himself to be stalled by some old retainer? He stood up in impatience and paced in a tight circle once around the small room. He rubbed his jaw absently and wished that he'd shaved. Well, when you're busy you can't think of everything.

There's clearly some squabble on the stairway; Quirinius can hear the sharp tones of an angry woman, but the sound is confused by altogether too many sets of footsteps, some from boot-shod feet. Ah, Canidius. But what's up?

Quirinius waits for the polite knock at the door, but instead it swings open suddenly with no warning, and in rushes an infuriated Mother Pulcheria. Quirinius steps back involuntarily until he feels the edge of the table along his backside, and he reaches down involuntarily to steady himself. Over the old woman's shoulder, he sees Canidius step into the room with a look of mild chagrin: he couldn't keep the old battleaxe away. To Quirinius' relief, he's followed silently by another figure who, when she steps into the lamplight, is revealed as Caelia. She steps back against the wall and watches events with demure interest.

Quirinius looks at Canidius for an explanation, but he only puts on an improbable stone face as a defense against laughter. Quirinius wonders at his levity and notes that, in defense, he's pointing in Caelia's direction, apparently to a small bundle that she holds in her hands before her. Quirinius is too preoccupied with the unwonted appearance of the abbess to work out the implication.

Caelia is as amused as the captain. She takes one hand from the bundle and puts it to her mouth to hide a smile. Quirinius, too, tries to see the absurdity of the situation. Here he is, just back from fighting Saxons, and here is an old nun, little more than a slat in a grey drape trying to bulldoze him into a corner and who knew what else. She pointed her finger at him as though menacing a child, and her anger was so great that she forgot dignity so far as to speak British.

"Who do you think you are, Cuirann Beag?" she asked, more or less answering her own question.

"Cuirann Mor," Canidius attempted a correction. She ignored him. "Sending minions to my abbey and seizing one of the sisters? By what authority do you do this?"

"Did you seize her, Canidius?" Quirinius asks, drawing himself up. He towers over the abbess, who only seems tall herself because she is so thin. Sure of her rights, however, she doesn't quail. He waits for Canidius' answer, all the while trying to think of an approach to the situation.

Canidius coughs gently into his fist to show politeness and says, "No. Not at all. I only told the sister—and Mother Pulcheria here—that you, well, you thought the sister would make a particularly good, um, housekeeper for old Father Remigius back at the big estate."

"Well done, Canidius."

"Thank you, Dominē."

Pulcheria tossed her thin arms into the air as though all of this were the most ridiculous thing she'd heard in a decade.

"Just that you wanted her as Father Remigius' housekeeper," Canidius repeated, to fill the silence. "That's all."

"A priest's housekeeper!" Pulcheria yelled to the ceiling. "You must have fifty girls on the estate to place in that position. Why one of my nuns?"

"Well. . ." Quirinius said.

"You see? You have no answer."

Caelia laughed a moment at this and pursed her lips to keep herself silent when the three others glanced at her. Her eyes were very, very lively.

"She'll understand the sorts of things that concern a priest. I don't want to saddle him with a bumpkin."

"You think that I didn't notice the way you looked at her at the trial years ago? Oh, yes, young man! I see things and recall them.

And the way you look at her now? And the circumstances of all this? I can add simple sums—it's not difficult."

Caelia looked modestly down at her shoes but, even so, Quirinius could see her flush. That was a hopeful sign.

"I wouldn't suggest you say anything bad about Dominus Quirinius. That's my advice to you," Canidius said.

"I don't fear any civil authority when I act in accordance with my sacred duties."

"Perhaps you ought to," Canidius said, and he was not smiling any more.

Quirinius decided to tack. "Caelia," he said in what he hoped was a warm tone. He was edgy—he had to admit it.

"Yes, Dominē." She looked up at him, and he felt suddenly warm.

"Would you like to come to my great estate and help Father Remigius?"

"That's not for her to decide!" Mother Pulcheria turned toward the girl, the better to show her anger.

"She can decide whether she would like to do it."

The old abbess spun back to face him. "Her wishes don't come into it. She's made her vow. She made it a year ago."

"You mentioned the trial. When was it? Five years ago? Her wishes didn't come into that either, as I recall. And she's decided as my father had hoped she would decide. I suppose you helped her in that decision? In view of the discussion you had with the Old Senator?"

Pulcheria slid her eyes to Caelia for the barest moment and then watched Quirinius carefully, as though to see how far he might go. No one spoke for a few moments.

"Surely you recall the interview you had in this very room?"

Pulcheria scowled, crossed her arms and looked down as she gathered her thoughts, but she said nothing.

"I think the Old Senator made the observation that, if Caelia were to take a vow, it would ease a predicament that everyone faced. He was very unhappy with the prospect, though, because he didn't properly take Caelia into consideration. He was a sentimental man."

Pulcheria still said nothing, still looked down.

"But you seemed less concerned about sentiments, anyone's sentiments, really. As I recall, you expressed that in quite strong terms. It's your way, as we all know. Instead, you expressed an interest in the matter of Caelia's maintenance."

"It wasn't just about her. The terms helped everyone at the abbey." Pulcheria looked at him boldly.

Quirinius, happy at gaining the upper hand, pressed on. "Of course, of course. All quite selfless. Or very nearly. But still, there was Caelia always in the background and never consulted. And my father couldn't see a better way out of the situation, but I've always felt it was a bit hard on Caelia."

"Hard on you," muttered the old woman.

Quirinius ignored this. "And now I can see a remedy."

"I haven't the authority to release her," Pulcheria said, drawing herself up straight as a soldier.

"Can that really be true?" Quirinius asked, as though of himself. "But we won't trouble ourselves on that point just now, will we? And we won't trouble ourselves about the maintenance either. I'll just continue to send that on, no matter what Caelia decides. Doesn't that seem best? I don't want to influence her."

Pulcheria snorted. Finally, defeated, she turned to the girl. "You'll keep house for that old priest, sure enough but, mark my words, there's another man who comes into this. You understand that?"

Caelia just looked demure.

"Well?" Quirinius asked.

Caelia stood up straight herself and answered in Latin. *"Multum volo."*

* * *

The bundle she brought was a sign that she had already made her decision. Quirinius could simply have had the old abbess ejected if he'd been rude enough. He could see that now. But, at the very least, he'd taken Pulcheria down a peg, and that might make his dealings with Caelia easier.

Quirinius had his supper in the dining hall. A servant stood behind his right shoulder with a cloth in his hand, ready to reach to the sideboard for whatever his master might want. At the end of the table the new bailiff and Canidius stood attending him in their capacities because there were a hundred small decisions to make about the management of the estate and the results of the raid. Quirinius had difficulty keeping his mind on these things but recognized what a good thing it had been to encounter the Saxons on the way back from the raid on Ater's estate—it had confused certain issues rather helpfully—perhaps it would have been better to say that it had alloyed Quirinius' punitive campaign so that it was not merely one of internal order, but also one of defense of the provinces from barbarians. And the church treasures recovered from the Saxons could be distributed where they would be most helpful to Quirinius' plans, which were, after all, intended for the benefit of all the province. A closer look at the Saxon plunder had turned up a pair of gold reliquaries holding indeterminate bone fragments from two obscure saints whom Quirinius had never heard of. Any cleric would be happy to have his church graced with these relics. Yes, one of them, at least, should go to the monastery at Avalonia.

In this way, a number of important things would be accomplished. The Romans would be in no doubt about Quirinius' right to assert the office of Count of the Britains, the Saxons would be wary of him, and the Church would be grateful. But even with these goals assured, it was difficult for Quirinius to keep his mind on the business at hand; how many acres should be planted in wheat next spring and how many in millet? Could Canidius draw from this estate two horses to replace those that had gotten lame on campaign? Was there enough lime to make mortar to repair the bake-house, or must it be done in daub and wattle? The smith's son wanted to become a soldier. How could he be dissuaded? A good smith was more valuable than twenty soldiers.

When he had finished with the interminable dinner, he went down the main corridor toward the east wing of the house; it was up there that the old senator's bedchamber, now his, was. A grey-headed servant woman preceded him, driving the shadows ahead of her with an oil lamp. She kept her face expressionless, although, Quirinius thought, as he passed the various open doorways along the hall, that servants glanced up at him as he passed. They had probably always done so, though the women hadn't seemed so interested. He was sure they were watching, interested in the situation now.

Quirinius followed the woman up the stairs and to the door of the bedchamber where she stood gravely with her head down. She made no effort to open the door. Quirinius waited a moment and then himself lifted the latch and cracked the door open. At that moment the old woman blew out the lamp and faded back, like a ghost, into the darkness. He stood alone in the pitchy black hallway wondering obscurely what he was about to find—what he was about to do—and why the question worried him. The edge of the opened door was a faint yellow line from the lamplight within, so clearly Caelia was there waiting, as he had ordered that she be. All the same he was uncertain—not about her compliance—but about the nature of it. He grasped at that moment that he feared her compliance would be like that of Albinia—dutiful and cold. Perhaps that was what one most often got from women after all, nothing more than that. What would he do if it were once again the case? He turned his mind from the concern and resolved to let events decide themselves.

He swung the door open and, when inside, and dropped the latch, all the while keeping his back to the room. He stood there for several moments and heard the ropes of the bed frame creak as Caelia, still unseen, stood up from where she had been sitting. He took a breath and then turned to see her standing in the light of a pair of lamps on a table by the bed. Her habit was changed. She wore a servant's simple white shift and stood barefoot. Her copper hair was uncovered and down and, though thick, was roughly shorn and came down only to her jaw. Of course, she would keep it cut to a length that suited her headdress. Still, he thought, it was lovely hair.

He went over to her and looked down into her face.

"Caelia," he began, but couldn't think of another thing to say. She waited a moment in calm patience, and he said her name again, "Caelia" and again stopped. He simply could not explain the situation—the hundred subtleties of it that ran variously through his mind—but silence seemed wrong too, perhaps even brutal. Though the silence did not strike Caelia that way, she put her fingers to his lips to enjoin him not to speak, and then, crossing her arms above her shoulders, she pulled she shift from herself in a single motion and stood naked before him.

Quirinius' heart suddenly slammed in his ears as though he'd run a mile; Albinia had never unclothed herself entirely, even when she slept with him. The sound of his heart was like something outside of himself, and he had to shake his head a moment before he could look down at her. Her form was tremendously appealing, just as he had hoped it would be and feared it would not. Her arms and legs were strong from work, her breasts were actual, not mere suggestions like those of Albinia, and the shock of hair below her navel was red and thick. In a word, she was vital and alive, and here before him in a way that no one else had ever been.

Caelia helped him undress and they climbed into the bed. Some time later she shrieked—it was her first time—but laughed just then too and deeply, showing her delight. And when they were done, Quirinius slept hard and long as though after a good day's work.

* * *

The Monastery, October 491 AD

Bishop Valerianus knows something of Quirinius' relations with Caelia and has from time to time spoken of it allusively, but it's not clear exactly what he knows, for, really, he is younger than the Old Bear, and what he's learned is by report. But he has enjoyed the reports—he likes to think from time to time of Quirinius' moral failings—even though he suspects that, somehow, they are exaggerated or, in some important way, unimportant. Still, whatever the cast one might wish to affix to the situation, Caelia was Quirinius' mistress for eighteen years—indisputably a bad thing when looked at from any of a half-dozen perspectives. And though Quirinius had the decorum not to flaunt the relationship, he was still offended. It especially irked him that the old priest Remigius, now long gone, had never grasped what was going on.

"It is not only the Saxons that can surprise one," Bishop Valerianus says, taking up the thread of conversation where Quirinius had laid it down a quarter of an hour before.

"And what does that mean?" Quirinius asks.

"Let me get at it this way. Eugenius Ater was one of the first to— pass off the scene—as the result of your rise."

Quirinius rankles at the euphemism. "He killed himself. It's that simple."

"You didn't kill him with your own hand and burn his house? That's how the story goes." He smiles to think that he knows enough to disbelieve it, but that most do not.

Quirinius turns his head sharply to look at the bishop sitting, eyes closed, on the bench along the wall.

"He killed himself. I found him floating dead in his bath."

"The mere news of your progress toward his estate was enough to undo him."

"He was decadent, hence weak. His position at the Council made that abundantly clear. As for the fire, his men probably caused it, looting as they abandoned him."

"A pity that this isn't widely believed."

"Well, it was, when the event was fresh, what, twenty-five years ago? The senators and the nobles and the little kings all knew the truth."

"Many of them are gone, and stories change and grow."

"I don't care about the stories."

"Don't you wonder how they can change?" He opens his eyes and stares back at Quirinius. "They can change so much, so very much."

"They change because there aren't enough literate people to write a decent account of what goes on."

"True," the bishop says. "And because so many of the old generation are gone and those that remain share, if not the knowledge of what you've done, at least an appreciation of your pre-eminent position."

"What is that supposed to mean?" The abbot does not understand either and turns from one to the other trying to guess what the bishop means from their expressions.

"I mean that the nobles have for years grasped a certain truth."

"And that is?"

"That you are a most dangerous opponent."

The abbot speaks up from his seat at the table, trying to force a happy construction on this. "Of course, Your Eminence. Ask any Saxon, Pict or Scot who has met Dominus Quirinius."

"Our bishop is not talking of barbarians, Abbot."

The abbot, defeated, sighs.

"There has always been a certain attitude toward me on the part of the great men. How shall I characterize it? As—"

"Envy? Timidity? Perhaps a certain resentment?"

"They have no cause for those feelings. Let us call it 'respect.'"

"Of course. That's just the word for it."

"No one has anything to fear from me."

"Wasn't Ater the most powerful man in the province?"

"The richest, perhaps. And besides, even old Nonianus Bassus had more soldiers than I at that time. And Marcus Paulus Rufinianus about as many. I was no threat to any of them—or anyway, to anyone who followed the law. To anyone who was a true Roman."

"As you judged it."

"Yes. As I judged it. And every man must judge a thousand things a day. 'Judge or die.' I've often thought that one of the most basic tenets of survival."

"Ah, you reckon yourself a bit of a philosopher!"

"And yet I will act, and that is what makes men uneasy. I will act, because it is my nature to act. I cannot change that. But any man who acts must judge and act rightly. I have always tried to act rightly. I would like to think of my entire career as a proof of that."

"Ater's death was a proof of that?"

"An especially good proof of it."

"So, Ater dead, his estate house burned to the ground and his soldiers moving in a drift across the country to practice banditry."

"Only a handful turned bandit. The rest went west into the service of Guledig Marc. What your predecessor regretted and, therefore, you too, I'm sure was the loss of Ater's tithes when his peasants turned freeholders or went under the protection of other nobles and kinglets.

"There are many kings now," the abbot says, to no one in particular.

"And many are the sons of two hundred years of senators," Quirinius says. "But because some dimly remembered ancestor was a king or chief in the countryside, they take the title."

"It can be useful to take a title," the bishop observes drily.

"It can indeed. *'Comes Britanniarum'*—that's what you allude to. But take the title of 'king,' —make yourself a petty king along the marches, and I assure you that your children will be mired in barbarism by the second generation."

The bishop laughs.

"The nobles have said for years that I am proud—and of course it's true. But they say it while hiding behind my shield."

"But truth is truth, isn't it? Regardless of the speaker's standpoint."

"You have never cared for me, Bishop Valerianus."

281

The bishop says nothing. The abbot squirms on his bench and looks away at the crude paintings along the edge of the ceiling.

"You needn't deny it—needn't answer. I'm indifferent to your feelings, really. I'm puzzled not so much at your dislike—we're different men with different tasks, different characters, but I am puzzled at the depth of it."

The bishop leans back against the wall again and looks up and away from Quirinius. "You flatter yourself that you are the special object of my concern. It's an example of your self-absorption, that's all."

"I wonder." Quirinius pauses. "Is it just the levies I've imposed upon the churches from time to time?"

"Let's not discuss those, Dominē Quirinius. There's no point."

Perhaps the bishop's comment about self-absorption isn't so wide of the mark. Perhaps Quirinius' attention is too often centered on his own difficulties and schemes, and he fails not so much to notice things as to miss their import. For example, only if pressed would he remember a little incident woven into the events that led up to his greatest battle and, were he to recall it, would he understand its importance?

* * *

Glevum, 482 AD

Quirinius was ready for any contest. He was as quick to decide as ever, and he was stronger than ever. His estates supported two hundred soldiers, and three small kings were his clients He protected each from the other and joined them in driving off Scots. He could thus field nearly eight hundred soldiers, three hundred of them mounted, without even dragooning any of the Roman nobles into the business. And, if it mattered, he could levy a score of private soldiers each from a dozen of his fellow magnates. He'd learned his strength from the willingness of the kings to obey him, and he'd learned something about fighting from the half-dozen battles and raids he'd engaged in against Saxons, Jutes, Scots and Picts. And he'd learned how much it cost to maintain his little army--they ate up a good deal of what his tenants produced, and the barbarians were too poor to plunder. The occasional tax made up the shortfall, but, oh, how the nobles and churchmen whined.

Aelle was stirring, that vigorous Saxon in the great old Channel fortress to the south. Aelle had stormed ashore years before, driven the local nobility north, and subjected the peasants to himself shortly before that council meeting after which Quirinius' father had been killed. Rumors now drifted north that Aelle was setting things in order for a raid, perhaps even a conquest. The rumors weren't hard to substantiate—there were a few British or Roman merchants who would trade with these Saxons, and they could see that Aelle made no effort to hide thirty wagons in a park before his great hall, twenty long ships drawn up on the shingle round about the crumbling fortress and the hundreds of happy, brawling warriors who had come in them from the eastern British shore, some perhaps even from Germania itself. The peasants grumbled at bringing sacks of grain and wheels of cheese down to the king, and a few, who had heard of Quirinius' reputation, drifted from their holdings north into Roman Britain to talk of it.

Where would Aelle strike? That was as uncertain as his final object. Was it plunder or conquest? He'd had an easy time of it around Anderitum, so why not an easy time a few days march to the north? As Eugenius Ater had suggested, the Romans had let him stay untroubled where he was—surely this was a mark of weakness? Surely it was time to move forward?

Quirinius knew that Aelle must soon march and fight. He had no choice, for how else could he support his men but on the Roman countryside and on plunder? He had no economy. Quirinius could feel the potential, like electricity in the air in the moments before a thunderbolt. And so he sent small troops of riders to the churches and monasteries throughout that part of the country that he directly administered and had them each bring back as a war tax some silver or a gold medallion or candlesticks so that he could buy another thirty horses for the campaign. A few of the poorer places gave a sack of flour or a ham or a barrel of beer. Good enough—it showed their allegiance to the Count of the Britains and would help feed the army that he would field against Aelle.

But one rich place gave nothing, the church at Glevum and the monastery attached to it. Bishop Severianus, surrounded by an entourage of priests and monks, stood at the brink of the steps of the church porch and thundered at the three troopers as they stood looking up at him, holding the reins of the horses they'd dismounted from out of respect. "You tell Dominus Quirinius to trouble the Church no longer. He has his province..." and he hesitated here for emphasis, "Perhaps. But his sway is limited to a certain civil authority, however murkily he may define it." Valerianus, then a young priest, stood behind the squat old fool and kept a bland face throughout the old man's blathering. He was convinced that Bishop Severianus was daring more than he knew. Even though his brother was Nonianus Bassus, he was inviting danger. Not immediately, of course, for the troopers frowned as they tried to follow the bishop's elevated diction and, once they grasped that they were getting nothing, they looked at each other, scowled back up at the bishop, mounted and rode slowly away. Most of the younger monks jeered at them, and they could see he was pink with pride even to the very top of his bald head. He waved a hand for quiet and stumped grandly back into the church.

The others drifted away, but Valerianus remained in the church porch, arms crossed and leaning against a pillar. He stared across the little forum through which the troopers had passed before they disappeared around a corner. He was still smarting from the chiding the bishop had given him for his advice that they accommodate the soldiers.

The two of them had stood in the gloomy vestry listening to Brother Guin report that soldiers of Dominus Quirinius were in the forum demanding a war tax.

"It's little enough, Your Eminence."

"Little enough!" The bishop turned to Brother Guin as though to force him to share in his amazement.

"Well, yes, Your Eminence." Brother Guin could see where things might lead, so he just stared over the bishop's head.

"This is not a question of degree, Valerianus. It is a question of an, an..." he grasped for a word. "We are talking about the dignity and power of the church, against which nothing can be matched."

"Of course, you are right, Your Eminence."

"I don't care for your tone, Valerianus." The squat prelate glared up at him.

"Forgive me, Your Eminence."

"You propose to advise me—and in front of another, no less." The bishop nodded at Brother Guin, who had somehow moved away toward the door. "So, I take it there is something in your meager experience of which I am unaware which licenses someone of your frankly low origins to advise me?"

"Certainly not, Your Eminence."

"'Certainly not, Your Eminence' indeed." Severianus imitated Valerianus, but in a humiliating nasal tone. "I seem to recall that your mother was some sort of menial on one of my estates. What was she? A...?" He prompted Valerianus with a feigned lapse of his very good memory.

"A cook, Your Eminence."

"A cook, yes. And your father was, I believe, a peasant of no particular note before his death."

"I don't remember him."

"No one does, really."

"Brother Guin, get on with your duties." He scurried out with a nod.

"Now help me on with my robe."

Some time had passed and Valerianus leaned against the pillar, smarting at the bishop's criticisms. Valerianus knew he was right, of course. The old fool wasn't nearly as secure as he thought. "My estates." He'd heard that often enough. It was Severianus' expression

285

for the estates that his brother, Nonianus Bassus, in fact, possessed. But he would never have the satisfaction of pointing out to the bishop that Nonianus had the power in the family and had likely chosen Severianus to be bishop because he was easily spared from other duties.

"Will the soldiers come back?" Valerianus turned to find Brother Victor looming at his side.

"More of them will come back, I think." Brother Victor watched Valerianus blandly and in silence with deep doglike eyes. After a while Valerianus added, "No one seems able to thwart Dominus Quirinius."

Brother Victor frowned. "Who?"

"Flavius Quirinius. Some call him the Bear."

"Why?"

"Because, Cousin, he is big like you."

"As big as I am?"

"No, not that big." He turned to look back across the forum with its shocks of grass growing up between the uneven blocks.

"I have swept the church, Valerianus."

Valerianus nodded but kept his eyes on the forum. After a moment his huge cousin tapped him gently on the shoulder, as he had done ever since they were children, and showed him the broom as though it proved his assertion.

"I see." He smiled encouragingly although his mind was still on Quirinius and his soldiers. They must return. Everyone agreed that Quirinius had two hundred soldiers at the very least and, if he took them all on campaign, he couldn't do without a tax. The bishop could see that as well as anyone, but in his pride he had swathed himself in his office and resisted. For two or three pair of silver candlesticks they'd have had peace. But now what? When the soldiers came again, they wouldn't be denied, and the bishop would be humiliated. Severianus' humiliation would be enjoyable, but would that be the end of the business?

He felt Victor's childlike tapping on his shoulder again. "Yes?"

"Cousin, you must teach me to read. The abbot says I must learn."

"Must you, now? This has proven to be a hard thing."

Victor rested one hand on top of the other on the end of the broom shaft and frowned. "I know the alphabet, but I cannot learn to read."

Valerianus sighed. His cousin knew half the alphabet, perhaps, but couldn't learn more.

"The abbot says he despairs. He says I cannot learn things."

Valerianus considered this a moment and then said, "You know your duties."

"I do."

"And you know to obey."

"Yes."

"And you know the offices."

"Yes."

"And so, you don't need to learn more things." He watched Victor think about this a moment and then grin happily, showing his great yellow horse-teeth. But a moment later he was frowning again as he tried to think. "But the abbot says I must learn to read as the other brothers have done."

"Listen, Cousin..." Valerianus began and then caught himself before he could say the plain truth, which was that, aside from learning a dozen letters of the alphabet, Victor wouldn't go further, and Valerianus couldn't do more. He felt guilty even at the thought, and so he took Victor's broom from him. "Later this afternoon we will try again, and then I will speak to the abbot and see what might be done. Now go back to Brother Guin and tell him you've done the sweeping."

"Yes, Valerianus." His cousin lumbered off, smiling.

Valerianus reflected, sadly, that the brothers said Victor ate twice what another man could but thought only half as much, and that it was true. Still, he consoled himself that he had prevailed with the abbot to admit Victor to the monastery, where he was largely protected from the vagaries of the world, even if he was the victim of the occasional unkindness. Valerianus swung the broom idly in his hands, finding the point of balance, and then walked into the gloom of the church to sweep where the floor met the walls. He took up all the dust that, as usual, Victor had missed.

Seventeen: Glevum, April, 482 AD

A week later, on a cold and rainy day, Quirinius approached at the head of a column of his horsemen, put out by Bishop Severianus' refusal to pay the tax. The bishop sat eating his dinner enshrouded in gloom, for the shutters were drawn against the rain, and only a few bars of light crept through them to fall across the table. Valerianus stood beside the table reading aloud a list of accounts from a waxed tablet. He squinted in the dark.

"From Vicus Camulodinensis, twenty bushels of wheat."

"We had twenty-two from them a year ago." The bishop said, chasing some boiled meat about his plate with a silver spoon. Valerianus "hmmed" noncommitally.

"Any excuse?"

"I didn't ask the carter."

The bishop sighed theatrically.

"The harvest was rather better last year than this," Father Valerianus said.

The bishop took this as a mild remonstrance. He put his spoon down slowly and turned to Valerianus, but, before he could speak, Brother Guin came running into the room. He ducked his head to show modesty and danced from foot to foot in agitation. Valerianus was relieved by the interruption.

"Well?" The bishop shifted his truculent look from Valerianus to Guin. He reached out for a chunk of bread.

"Soldiers, your lordship." He was so alarmed that he blurted this out in British.

"Soldiers?" The bishop drew his hand back and licked his lips nervously. "My brother's men?" he asked hopefully, but he looked worried.

289

Of course, the answer was no. The bishop's question reflected a foolish, forlorn hope, and Valerianus knew in a flash what Brother Guin would add: that the Bear's men were coming for the war tax, no doubt in greater numbers and in no mood to be denied. And that was substantially what Brother Guin did say, his head drawn deep into his cowl like a frightened turtle. Two troopers standing in the church porch said that Count Quirinius himself, at the head of his men, would arrive shortly to collect the tax. Bishop Severianus seemed to melt like fat in a pan. He blanched and then flushed from his cheeks to the summit of his shiny head. He looked involuntarily at Valerianus for guidance, but the young man held his tongue in feigned respect.

The three men regarded each other silently for a few moments, and Valerianus, despite his own misgivings, savored the bishop's sudden fear. He looked directly into Severianus' face, then raised his eyebrows inquiringly, and asked—but only with a view to fanning the bishop's fears, "Whatever should we do now, Your Eminence? Tell us, that we may do what is needed." He allowed some irony in his tone, and then the hint of a smile. The bishop looked about helplessly for a moment, as though some hidden advisor were lurking in a corner, and then surged to his feet. He turned to Brother Guin and said, "Have a brother take the soldiers behind the stables and give them something to eat. Talk to them, distract them. Then have my horse saddled and ready, and have the monastery's mules waiting in the alley to the north side of the church. When you have ordered this, return with three of the brothers and join us in the treasury. Bring capable men—none of the dolts." He said this last over his shoulder as he hurried from the room. Brother Guin bowed to the bishop's back and ran after him.

Valerianus, the bishop, Brother Guin and three monks were soon in the church treasury pulling out anything of value and tossing it any which way into coffers and sacks. The treasury was not entirely dark—the shutters of the room were thrown back to let in the watery afternoon light, and one of them banged dully back and forth in the wind. Rain spattered and slickened the grey stone floor beneath the window; Brother Guin's backside was dark with dust and water; in his hurry, he'd slipped in the puddle beneath the window. The monk had shrieked in surprise as he'd fallen and hugged a golden salver to his belly as he'd flopped down, and it crossed Valerianus' mind that Guin's misadventure was all in keeping with the bishop's haphazard, dangerous actions.

After a few minutes Valerianus heard the slipping of mules' hooves on wet stones and their snuffling in the alley beneath the window. The wind carried in the sweat-and-urine smell of the animals, and just knowing that the mules were there caused him to wonder whether Bishop Severianus' idiot plan to fly to his brother's estate might not come off after all. Brother Guin heard the sounds too, and he shook out and threw a fine cloak over the bishop's shoulders while Valerianus slipped out of the treasury and through a side door to the alley, where five small brown mules stood placidly in a line, each with a grey-robed monk holding its halter. Animals and men blinked in the steady rain.

At the head of the line was the bishop's white horse, his bridle held by the abbot himself, but the animal pulled at the bridle and swung his hindquarters this way and that to avoid the saddle that a little old monk tried to throw over his back. The monk's head hardly came up to the horse's withers, and so even if the animal had been obliging enough to stand stock still, he could hardly have managed it. Valerianus paid this little attention, though, because he had been ordered to oversee the brothers as they tied various coffers, reliquaries and sacks onto the mules' pack-saddles.

"Hurry," he urged one of the brothers, who nodded but continued making his knots with alarmingly slow deliberation. In the background he could hear Bishop Severianus upbraiding the abbot for being stupid enough to bring his horse, a contrary animal, but very fast, out of his stall before he'd been saddled. Valerianus shrugged to shift his robe about himself—it had already become rain-sodden and hung heavy and cold from his shoulders. He wished that he had thought of snatching up a cloak himself, but the bishop's thinly concealed panic had been contagious, and he'd thought of nothing but how to empty the treasury and load the mules before Quirinius and his soldiers arrived.

Still, he was no more unfortunate than the rest of the establishment. The entire monastery had emptied, and the brothers stood in the alley down which the bishop intended to leave. They stood blinking whenever a shift of the wind drove the rain into their hooded faces, and Valerianus could see his cousin Victor in the middle of them, a head taller than anyone else, his cowl down, rubbing the rain from his face with hands as big as shovels.

The bishop waved his arms at the brothers, calling on them ineffectually to clear the way. His ten half-equipped guards, the poorest of his brother's soldiers, men whom he was willing to spare, tried to assist with threats and shouting and the occasional prod with a spear-butt, but the drift of monks only flowed here and there, not resisting but always continuing to be in the way. As often happens in times of stress, Valerianus noted small, irrelevant details--a patch of rush-matting on a wall across the alley where daub had fallen away, the faint glow of the sun behind the clouds for an instant before the sky resumed its uniform grey. He noted too that, despite the bishop's haranguing, the shouting of his guards, and the swerving of the fine white horse, the abbey's mules stood patient and still, blinking against the rain, showing no concern. And then, quite suddenly, they turned their long ears back in alarm, and in that instant Valerianus guessed what this meant and turned to look down the alley. It was dark with horsemen. Quirinius had arrived.

Valerianus felt his arrival like a blow. No reasonable person could have thought the bishop would get away to the Bassi estates, but, caught up in action, he had half-believed the cleric might do it. Now he stood afraid for having abetted Bishop Severianus in his scheme, but, even as he stepped back from the mule-train and faded against the wall, he could see that Quirinius had no interest in him. The Bear had glanced at him for just the merest instant and then looked past him, clearly in search of the bishop. Valerianus narrowed his eyes against the rain and stared at Quirinius, whom he was seeing for the first time.

Quirinius was a big man, seated on a blocky sorrel horse, and the effect he made was much like that of an equestrian statue—slightly larger than life. He was not dressed in finery; he wore a sheepskin cloak to shed the rain, and, for the same reason, a flat, oiled, broad-brimmed hat like a common traveller. Valerianus recalled for years these images he had gathered as he swept his eyes between the squat bishop and the big man on the powerful red horse. It was most often words that Valerianus recalled, but this day's images were, if anything, more powerful than any words said that day.

"I'm here for the tax," the Bear said, plainly, but in Latin to show that his business was official. *"Veni, ut impostum colligam,"* or something close to it. *"Annona aut argentum. Et comprehende id habebo."*

Bishop Severianus, who had shrunk when he first saw the horse-troop, now puffed up in anger. Brother Guin approached with the bishop's miter in both hands, and Valerianus could see it softening as the starch melted in the rain. Ridiculous. Bishop Severianus knocked Brother Guin's hands aside with his crozier, and the hat fell to the ground, collapsed entirely, and darkened with the mud brought up from between the cobblestones by the rain.

"Tribute, you mean!"

Quirinius reached up and tilted his broad hat to shed the rain, and then settled it again. Then he urged his horse forward a few steps until he was right before the bishop. He put one hand over the other upon the saddlebow and leaned forward to loom over the cleric. As he did this, a half-dozen of his men drifted past him and herded the bishop's soldiers away. This done, the troopers drew their swords and left them casually balanced across their saddlebows as they watched the bishop's soldiers closely.

"Construe it however you will. How you take my action is of no interest to me. But I will have the tax."

Valerianus looked up with fascination into Quirinius'eyes. They were deep brown—perhaps too dark, really, for those of a man. Were a bear's eyes of that shade? And his ears—were they, as the peasants said, truly round like a bear's? The hat made it impossible to tell. He was imposing, in any case. He was clean-shaven like an emperor or a consul, and his imposing size, exaggerated by the sheepskin cloak, lent an additional threat to his manner.

"It's a question of jurisdiction. You willfully misapprehend the extent of your authority."

Quirinius looked down at the bishop a moment and then laughed. He glanced over his shoulder at his troopers, who joined him.

"If you attempt to seize church property..." But here the bishop's voice faded. He had no argument to offer, not even a florid clause or cliché.

The two men stared at each other for a few instants, and then Quirinius called to one of the troopers and pointed to the first of the mules in train. "Lead that one out and see what he's loaded with. It may be enough."

"Why not take them all!" One of the bishop's soldiers shouted.

"Because this is taxation, not robbery," Quirinius said to everyone in a loud clear voice.

As the trooper he'd detailed turned his mount toward the line of mules, the bishop broke out suddenly in British. Valerianus became, if possible, more uneasy—it was a clear appeal to the bishop's soldiers, who knew little Latin.

"This is no tax! You are a bandit and nothing more. A mere despoiler of church property, an opportunist and..." He stopped, searching for another accusation.

"And?" Quirinius asked quietly.

"And a murderer. You are the killer of Eugenius Ater and the despoiler of his property, as everyone knows! You..."

Quirinius is clearly surprised at this accusation; Valerianus can tell. And he can tell that the bishop is pleased to have angered the

Bear. But of course, it's just another of the bishop's mistakes. Although he had always known his master was incompetent, now the depth of the man's inanity strikes him. The bishop argues from weakness, he provokes the powerful, he fails to prepare for the obvious. It wasn't as though he couldn't have fled a week ago to his brother for protection or have asked him for more soldiers. If his brother had refused, well, then he'd have known where he stood and could have found some way to submit to the Bear and just, perhaps, retain some shreds of his dignity. The man is an idiot, and Valerianus sees it now with perfect clarity.

But the damage is done. There is an inarticulate shout from a few yards away; the bishop's words have had their effect. Valerianus looks at the bishop's soldiers, backed against a wall, but they only stand motionless and sullen, watching the horsemen who watch them. No, it is his simpleton cousin Victor who has cried out in frustration. He comes charging out of the crowd and through the horsemen, who at first keep their attention on the bishop's soldiers. In a moment the huge Victor is past these troopers, screaming incoherently and hefting a road cobble in both hands over his head as he moves toward Quirinius. The Bear swings his horse about to face the surprise, but it is unnecessary--the trooper who'd ridden to the lead mule lifts his sword from the saddlebow and, as Victor passes by him, deftly swings it backhanded to strike the monk solidly on the back of the head with the flat of the blade.

Victor stops instantly, stunned, as the trooper has meant him to be, and he drops the cobble into the alley with a clatter that alarms the Bear's horse and causes him to back into the bishop and send him stumbling. Valerianus sees a splash of mud appear across the hem of Victor's habit as he drops the stone, and then he watches his cousin stand for a short while, eyes wide open, but, really, seeing nothing or, perhaps, not understanding what he perceives. The huge young man totters a moment, drops to his knees in a faint, and then sprawls forward onto his face.

There comes a deep collective gasp from the crowd of monks, and then suddenly everything is in disorder. Bishop Severianus slips away through the side entrance back into the treasury, the Bear's troopers turn their horses and fade back the way they have come, and meanwhile a score of monks pass among them toward the fallen Victor. In moments Quirinius and his men, and of course the lead mule, are gone. Valerianus pushes past Brother Guin who stands with his hands to his mouth in horror and then sees what has shocked him. Blood is welling up from a terrible wound on the back of Victor's head. Despite his skill, the trooper has cut Victor's head, and badly, and the blood seems to go everywhere in the rain. Valerianus joins a half-dozen monks who pick up his cousin, huge and inert, and carry him into the abbey. He notes, even in his distress, that many of the other monks are kneeling in the alley and dipping their habits into Victor's blood. "He is a martyr!" someone says.

Victor died in the middle of the night, and there came a wail from the monks as the news spread throughout the establishment, even from those who had earlier mocked his simplicity—perhaps especially from those.

* * *

The Monastery, October 491 AD
"You rose rather quickly, as I recall," Quirinius says to Bishop Valerianus. "Upon the death of that foolish old bishop, Bassus' brother. What was his name? Severianus. Yes, Severianus. Suddenly, there you were, a bishop, but of no great family. And, as far as I can see, no great holiness. So, in the absence of wealth or connection, I must construe your rise as the result of mere competence."

Bishop Valerianus ignores him.

"The bishop's cousin is St. Victor," the abbot informs Quirinius.

"Ah, so you're the cousin of a saint. I suppose that plays into the situation. I can't say that I'm familiar with that particular saint. However, there are so many these days; the times seem to turn them out in goodly numbers."

"Is this levity, Dominē Quirinius? I had not heard that you were much concerned with levity." Bishop Valerianus thus turns the conversation to a new topic. He doesn't really care for the old one. It's true enough that Brother Victor's death smoothed his path. In fact, there's no doubt about it. It bothers him, yes, on a number of fronts. For one thing, he can never settle in his mind whether Quirinius or Bishop Severianus is the more guilty of his cousin's helpful death. And he can never quite rid himself of the suspicion that, were it not for Quirinius, he would be eking out the meager living of a priest on one of Bassus' estates. Is he, really, a creature of Quirinius?

Eighteen: The Monastery, October 491 AD

The thought that somehow he might owe something to Quirinius has troubled the bishop for some time. The pointlessness of Victor's death rankles him and, though he is a bishop, thoughts have flitted through his mind from time to time about how that death might be recompensed. Yes, his early rise is generally attributed by cynics who have bothered to learn his history to the relationship to his cousin. However, Quirinius has forgotten the entire incident.

But Valerianus' memory of the incident is vivid. Had it not been for Quirinius, Victor might still be alive and reciting the Creed. True, he'd be doing it with the blandness of incomprehension and no grasp of it, but he'd be saying the words. Or, if he were dead, his death might have come about from bad luck, an accident, say, or as the result of the plague that had killed, among others, Bishop Severianus. And the plague had helped too; the old senator Nonianus Bassus had no other brother to put in Severianus' place and had acquiesced in Valerianus' elevation. After all, Bassus couldn't exercise control over that bishopric—Quirinius' taxation had shown that. Why not concede the office to the priest Valerianus?

"As I suggested earlier, Dominē Quirinius, you suppose I have taken a greater personal interest in your career than, in fact, I have." He's seeing even now, in his mind's eye, Quirinius' trooper leaning out from his horse and transmuting Victor from monk to saint with a touch of his sword.

"I suppose that ought to be reassuring," Quirinius replied. "That you dislike me without interest. And why not? It's done all the time." Quirinius looked about the room and asked, "What time is it?"

"About the end of the first watch."

Quirinius nods. "I'm tired." He lies down on a broad bench along the wall and closes his eyes. "I'm not as young as I was."

Valerianus turns his attention back to the matter at hand. Creature of Quirinius or not, he could remind the older man of a few indisputable facts. "No, indeed. What is your age, Dominē Quirinius? Fifty?"

Quirinius nods. "Close enough, fifty-three."

"The concentration of power in your hands has always presented certain—how might I put it—difficulties. As the years pass, those whose duty it is to anticipate the future—"

"Men such as you?" Quirinius speaks with his eyes closed, his hands clasped on his chest. His posture reminds Valerianus of a dead man. "I thought you churchmen concerned yourselves with the eternal, or the immanent, or whatever the terms are. But then I forget you are a bishop."

"However much a bishop may regret it, he has truck with worldly matters."

"And what worldly matter is it that concerns you?"

"Your succession." He watches Quirinius closely for any signal that he's hurt him. "You have no children. No line."

Quirinius lies motionless and silent for a few instants. Valerianus thinks, *Good. He's unhappy.*

Finally, Quirinius says, "I'm not a king."

"And yet the kings do as you say. And so do the Romans. Call yourself what you will, everyone knows what you are. Like Julius Caesar, a king in all but name."

"How flattering. I think." Quirinius sits up and turns his head about to loosen his stiff neck. "I will be around for a good long while yet. Who, and what, comes after me should hardly concern you." But it does concern Quirinius, who wants the topic shelved.

"And yet it does concern me. Say what you will, even where the civil authority has devolved in part to the church, the demise..." he says it with a certain relish "... of civil authority is a matter of concern."

"In other words, if I had sons—"

"But you don't." Quirinius flinches at this; Valerianus can tell he's hit the mark.

"If I had sons, then things would go easier in ten or twenty years."

Valerianus shrugs. He has nothing to add to such an obvious statement.

"You miss the entire point of my efforts," Qurinius says. "I am first among equals, like the head of the Senate in Rome. A senator like all of the others and yet, in some way, first among them."

"The other Romans are your equals?

"I'm only the Count of the Britains." But it is Quirinius who is misses the point. He thinks Valerianus is talking politics, and not merely to wound him. "I've worked twenty-five years to restore and keep order in this province, and I'll hand it in good order, along with my title, to whomever I find fit to carry on the work."

"You make it sound so plausible, Dominē Quirinius." He pauses dramatically and then asks, "Who might be your successor? Moderatus? Someone else?"

Quirinius waves away the question with feigned carelessness. He's thought about this many times but can never come up with a name. "He'll be evident when the time comes." He stands and walks out of the door to stand beneath the black night sky. Oh yes, Valerianus has troubled him.

The lack of children bothers him—has done so for years. It's a burden not lifted by a pair of nephews. His sisters married Romans, but the boys have somehow failed to get the right sort of education—they haven't gotten the Idea. It is not the sisters' fault—you can't find good teachers anymore. You might find the odd Gallic or Spanish cleric, but books are hard to find, and everyone seems to be accommodating himself to the twilight, as it were. The boys weren't barbarians, exactly, but barbarism didn't alarm them—they had grown up with it, they had never known a time when Latin wasn't receding like the tide and pulling so many good things with it. They'd never known a time when battle poems in British were not as immediate as Catullus or Vergil.

The Principal Estate of the Quirinii, 470 AD

Of course, he'd tried to have children with Albinia. When it had become obvious that the thing was going to be difficult, he'd worked hard to compensate. He'd lain atop her with such regularity that he came to dread the chore. What seemed odd to Quirinius, however, was that she did not. Not that she had any enthusiasm for it—no, that wasn't it. But she had no distaste for his increasingly mechanical attentions either, only an irritating indifference to the sex, one so perfected that she seemed not there at all. Her presence-absence made Quirinius uncomfortable, as though he were engaged in a private sexual activity onto which she had stumbled.

No wonder, it seemed to Quirinius, that she never conceived. When he was finished, she'd pull her shift down past her knees and roll over. She was asleep in moments as though nothing more significant had happened than combing her hair. Quirinius actually wondered whether her indifference rendered her sterile.

And so, of course, he'd high hopes for Caelia. Albinia's sterility furnished him with a sop to his conscience—and he felt he needed one in support of his affair with her; Quirinius took vows seriously. But not so seriously that he could not break this one in the face of Albinia's indifference. If he could have children with Caelia he might justify his affection for her in purely practical terms.

In fairness to Albinia, Quirinius would have admitted that she was indifferent to most things and not to him alone. Devoted to religion, and particularly the observance of it, her single aim on any given day was to hear mass in the chapel; everything else was of scant interest. Her indifference to Quirinius wasn't a result of distaste—wasn't a judgement, really. It was just that, in her view, he didn't measure up well in comparison to God. But then, who did?

And so, by gradual steps, Quirinius and Albinia reached a tacit understanding. As the months went by, and then a year and then close on two, he found himself spending more time traveling between his estates and working into the night when at home at the big estate, Villa Quiriniana. He would sit up very late working, or just dozing, in his fine chair behind the table of his study on the second floor and, finally, he had the little room next to it whitewashed and fitted with a bed. He had left Albinia largely to herself by this time. Neither of them could be said to be happy, but from Albinia's viewpoint, happiness was nothing to be concerned about.

"Really, Quirinius," she'd said to him once, when he'd hectored her into talking in bed late one night. One of the last. "I don't understand your talk—anyone's talk—about happiness. What can it mean, really?"

From Albinia's perspective there was this one good thing at least, although she had not managed to maintain her virginity as those holy women had done in the stories she avidly read, at least she was untroubled by children and, eventually, not much troubled with Quirinius. It gave her more time to write letters to the surrounding bishops and to study their replies. They always replied to the wife of the Count of the Britains on the vexed theological questions she would pose them. Bishop Severianus, for example, was forced to appreciate her attentions, but had his assistant, young Valerianus, frame the replies. The young priest, overworked, simply copied out marginally relevant passages from obscure religious texts he suspected, rightly, that Albinia hadn't copies of.

It wasn't difficult, a few years into their marriage, to slip Caelia into the household and, further, to slip her into the bedroom by the study. And, frankly, Quirinius didn't see any point in hiding this as long he could maintain a certain decorum about it, a certain thin pretence that nothing was happening. And so Caelia kept the old priest Remigius' little house, turned up every inch of ground around it that she could for a garden, and slept in the little whitewashed room on the second floor.

Quirinius doesn't think much about this history despite the bishop's gibes; his mind runs over these facts in only the most cursory way until he recalls a night with Caelia years before.

"It's you, Bear," Caelia said to him quietly as they lay in bed. Quirinius shifted slightly and laid his head on her shoulder. He could feel her chin rest along the top of his head.

"What is?" He was half asleep, lulled by her hand passing through his hair. He wished that she didn't keep her thick copper hair clipped so short. It was some nunnish practice, he supposed, that she'd grown used to. He'd have to put his hand up to run his fingers through it because it only it fell below her jaw. He began to raise his hand to do it anyway.

"That you have no children," she said softly.

"Albinia says it's because I sleep with you. She says it's a judgement on me."

"No, Bear. That's not it."

"I know. I could never have any with her either. So I asked her whether that was a judgement too, and which of us was judged. But she wasn't amused. She can't be, of course. I think she's a little mad."

"Perhaps." As always, when Albinia came up, Caelia was circumspect.

"Don't concern yourself with it."

"I know you love me, Bear. And you've never been careful about when you sleep with me. I know you'd like to have children. Even with me."

"Especially with you." Quirinius got up on one elbow and looked into her face. "Don't worry about children. Don't worry. I'll take care of them. I'll adopt them or legitimate them—some such thing. There'll be no trouble. Don't worry about Albinia or her family. There's no one who can oppose me."

"No. There won't be any trouble." Caelia's voice dropped off sharply.

"You sound sad."

"For you. There won't be any trouble; there won't be any children."

Quirinius narrowed his eyes and turned his head a bit, as though he hadn't heard right. Through the louvers in the shutters there was just enough light for him to see the gleam of Caelia's eyes as she watched his face. "It's been nearly two and a half years and I've never conceived. And we have never, ever been careful."

"Ah," he said, beginning to grasp what she meant.

"And I was never careful. I never used any tricks. Never said I was tired. I wanted your children too, even if you'd sent them off to be peasants."

"I would never do that."

"I know. I think I always knew that. And, for a long time, I'd dream of what they would be like. But now, I know that we'll never have them. And what's saddest, I think, is that you'll never have them. I know it's hardest on you."

"Why do you even say all of this?" Quirinius knew, suddenly, that she was right, that the flaw lay in him and nowhere else.

"In a way, because it's true. The hardest things to say are true ones and many shouldn't be said. But I have to tell you this."

"Why?" He shook his head.

"Because I want you to be content." Quirinius couldn't follow this. He frowned, puzzled. "Because I want you to stop longing for what you will never have. You can't be happy doing that. No one can." They lay in silence a long while. "It seems to me you often fail to see what is there to be seen. It's as though you sometimes take the world to be what you would like it to be and not what it is." She broke into British at the end as she tried to get the verb in the right form—as though, somehow, that were very important. "Would like it to be."

"I'm a realist. Consider my career."

"Esne? Me domando, Urse. Forse." She'd gone back to Latin, sensing his disquiet. "Are you? I wonder, Bear. Maybe so. Can you be content? You must know what is true, if you're to be content."

He didn't reply, and, in time, he could sense that she had fallen asleep. He slipped from the bed and went to his study where he sat wrapped in a cloak and watched the stars until they faded into the morning sky. He didn't think of much of anything. He didn't touch Caelia for a good week but then, in the watches of a cool night, he reached for her. But they never spoke of children again.

* * *

The Monastery, October 491 AD

Quirinius feels a chill as he stands before the meeting house in the night. He rubs his hands and wonders idly whether he'd have been so cold if he were younger. He has to face it—he's no stripling anymore. He turns back into the building where Ambiorus, the abbot and the bishop are waiting. It is a bit warmer inside there, though still not quite warm enough. Quirinius picks up another cloak and wraps himself in it before sitting once again in the abbot's chair.

"Shall I make up the fire? In the brazier, Dominē?" The abbot is solicitous. Quirinius shakes his head. No good showing weakness.

"If Moderatus and Pennomorix don't arrive soon, I'll begin to wonder whether something's gone wrong."

Bishop Valerianus sits up a bit straighter. The abbot looks over at him curiously.

"I'll wonder whether the fools have taken the wrong turning, whether they're off somewhere unintended like Deva Victrix. Or maybe Pictland."

Valerianus relaxes. The abbot, who has noticed this, frowns, trying to work out the cause.

"Perhaps they're not eager to come."

"Why not, Bishop Valerianus? This whole expedition is because of them. I've marched here because of them. It'll be Moderatus' estate or Pennomorix's "kingdom"—as he calls it—that will suffer if, as you say, there's a raiding party hereabouts."

"Perhaps Pennomorix regrets his walls," the bishop says, trying to prompt another story.

"Ah!" Quirinius says, with a sound of irritation. "That was years ago. Remarkable how long some men's memories are."

"Indeed. Some men's."

The abbot looks at the bishop but says nothing.

"He was disobedient, Bishop. Pennomorix began to wage a private war against Guledig Marc."

"A 'private war'? You make it sound rather serious. Surely it was, at most, a mere feud."

"'A mere feud?' Is it 'a mere feud' when a magnate—call him a king if you will—plunders his neighbor and torches a village? It sounds a good deal like war to me. That's what makes us so unhappy when the Saxons or the Jutes indulge themselves in it. And besides, I'd forbidden it."

"Of course."

"Either we unite against these barbarians or we don't. Don't you think Aelle and his Saxons see these things? Don't you suppose this sort of disorder calls them in?"

"I suppose."

"You suppose. When Aulus stripped the north of troops for his little jaunt into Gaul—the one where he fought as a usurper for the throne of the Empire and lost—when that happened, we soon had those barbarous Picts down on us like weasels in a chicken house."

"That was long ago."

"You think it can't happen again? That history has no value? I thought you were more intelligent. Perhaps you're merely cunning." Quirinius looks away from Valerianus, shaking his head as though in disbelief. The abbot glances over at the bishop and sees him, oddly, smiling.

"But there were no Saxon or Jute depredations, were there? As a result of Pennmorix's squabble with Guledig Marc."

"No, because I moved quickly. I'd have dragged Pennomorix by his collar to the Council and tried him before the senators and the magnates if I'd thought it worthwhile. But I'd learned it was pointless by that time."

"You did something else."

"What I did was little enough. I went to his stronghold and showed him who was master."

"His stronghold."

"One of those old ring-forts from the days before the Romans came. The usual hill with an earthen bank around the summit and a palisade. A timber gate in a gap finishes it off. Just a little fortlet."

"A rath," the abbot said.

"That's the British for it. You know how the chiefs have been re-fortifying them for the last fifty years. Just like the one Trifun had up near the Wall. Or the little one I'd found Hispanus in."

"What, exactly, did you do?" Valerianus asks. The abbot, who has been listening closely these last few minutes, suspects from the bishop's tone that he already knows the story. So why the question, then?

"As I said, what I did was little enough. I went to the ring-fort with a hundred men, summoned him out of it, and made him watch while I had the gate dragged away. It took a team of four oxen even after the pins had been struck out of the hinges. And I tore down twenty feet of the palisade on either of side of the gate and burned it in the meadow below along with gate itself. I forbade him to rebuild the gate or the palisade for a year."

"I see."

"It was clever of me, I think. A little humiliation, which he needed, and then a little fear. He sat perched on that hill in his windy little fort praying none of the other kings would find an excuse to attack him until he could rebuild."

"The fear and humiliation doubtless taught an enduring lesson."

"Doubtless."

"Of some sort."

Quirinius looks at the bishop for several moments with narrowed eyes. "What do you mean?"

"I mean that I wonder exactly what the lesson was."

Quirinius snorts. "It should be obvious—even to a dullard. And still more to you."

Uncharacteristically, Valerianus rankles. "I was pondering a different question, who learned the lesson."

The abbot dares to add his piece. "As in the old proverb. 'Happy is he who learns from others' mistakes.'"

"What are you implying, Your Eminence?" Quirinius asks, ignoring the little abbot. "That the lesson had a broader application than just to Pennomorix?"

"Time will tell."

Quirinius, though, is tired of the conversation. "It was ten—no, twelve years ago." He closes his eyes as he tries to recall exactly. "It's no longer worth worrying about." But Quirinius is more fatigued than he knows, and, upon closing his eyes, he slips into a dream.

But it's a beautiful dream. He is standing on the gravel path of his villa's formal garden on a warm, bright summer day and, beside him stands Caelia, who is, somehow, his wife. They hold hands and watch their children leap and sprint after each other. How beautiful they are, how much they resemble Caelia, and he delights to see their copper heads pop up from behind low box-hedges that line the garden paths as they play hide-and-seek. They call out to each other in a flawless Latin that sounds like music. He listens closely and, incredibly, what they say is in meter, as though poetry were their native speech.

Quirinius' eye is caught when the shutters of a second-storey window in the villa (how nicely whitewashed the building is) are flung open and a man looks down upon the garden. Of course, the window should be opened. Quirinius then realizes that the sun is newly risen, and that this magnificent day has only begun. The man looks down upon everyone, and Quirinius sees that the man is his father. Yes, he recalls now that the Old Senator has been gone a long while—obviously on a journey somewhere. How could he have forgotten this? And where has the old man been all this time? Far away, that's clear. To Ravenna, where the beautiful palaces are, most likely. Or perhaps even to Rome. But the details aren't important; he's back home. Framed in the window, he smiles solemnly down upon his grandchildren, proud of his whole line, really; he can tell. And Quirinius feels a contentment new and full. Caelia looks up at him, all of the children somehow instantly clustered about her. "Bear," she says. "Bear..."

Quirinius awakens with a start to find Ambiorus shaking his shoulder. He closes his eyes and sits back, desperately trying to see Caelia's face and to hear her voice again, as he has not done in seven years, but the dream, as all dreams, is evanescent and fades away like the pink of a late evening sky.

Ambiorus is speaking. "The Domini Moderatus and Pennomorix have arrived."

Nineteen: The Monastery, October 491 AD

Quirinius sat up slowly and cocked his head toward the open door where the monk stood who had brought the news. Yes, if you listened carefully you could hear the indistinct murmur of voices in the distance, the sound of Pennomorix's warriors as they approached the monastery's outer wall and dispersed outside the gate. A shift in the wind brought the smell of sweating horses—Moderatus' troop of cavalry, thirty men, the remnant of the mounted cohort that had served under old Maximianus, now ten years dead.

Quirinius eased himself back against the wall to wait for the two. He was so very tired—surprised at his tiredness, in fact—and, besides, it would affront his dignity to await them standing. He closed his eyes, hoping the men would dawdle, and fell again into a doze from which he was startled awake by Ambiorus' hand upon his shoulder. He shook his head to clear it and found Bishop Valerianus watching him closely and with an inexplicable smile. He frowned and worked to puzzle out the cause but got nowhere for, sooner than he'd have expected, Moderatus strode into the room with Pennomorix right behind. *As always, at his heel, like a favorite dog,* Quirinius thought.

As Moderatus approached, he rose slowly, to hide his stiffness.

"Where in hell have you been? It's the middle of the second watch."

"Dark night," Moderatus said. He nodded at the bishop and ignored the abbot, who had stepped out of the way. "No moon. You know how it is to move men in that kind of darkness. And horses are worse—especially in strange country."

"In fact, I do not."

310

"No, I don't suppose you do—you don't take risks." He glanced over his shoulder at Pennomorix behind him. The other's bony face was, as always, eerily expressionless.

"I take risks, but not unnecessarily. What if the Saxons had been waiting for you along the way? Say, in that wooded bank over the road just to the south?"

"They'd have been as blind as Dominus Moderatus," Bishop Valerianus said. "Everyone on an equal footing."

Ambiorus spoke softly. "No. They'd have learned the country ahead of you and known how to use it against you."

Moderatus didn't turn to look at the captain. He kept his eyes on Quirinius, smiled, and said in a most reasonable tone, "You shouldn't let your men abuse their betters."

Quirinius laughed harshly. "I don't."

Moderatus' smile disappeared for a moment and then, inexplicably, it returned, as though he had heard something extremely amusing, something quite hidden from the others.

His smile seemed incongruous to Quirinius, not only because he couldn't fathom what had provoked it, but because Moderatus strongly resembled his humorless cousin Albinia, who did not smile. Like her, he was tall and slender, even in his armor. And pale like her—almost colorless, and, seen against the grey iron rings of his armor, his wan face seemed, like them, a thing of pale metal, perhaps latten.

Pennomorix showed no expression during the exchange. He stood motionless and indistinct in the gloom in a long cloak of grey checks that hid his scrawny body and gave it the appearance of greater bulk. Only the chape of his scabbard peeped out below the cloak hem and glinted a dim orange in the lamplight. He was unusual among the British chieftains in that, like a Roman, he shaved, but he was bald, and his flattish face, with its dark, sunken eyes, stubby nose and high prominent cheekbones was utterly expressionless. He put off a rather macabre air that Quirinius found unsettling when he bothered to think about the man, which was seldom. Pennomorix hated him, but this was of no importance, for Quirinius was indifferent to his opinion. He was a contemptible little barbarian, useful as a buffer against the Irish raiding down from the north, and not worth a thought beyond that.

"Let's get down to business."

"Yes. Let's." Quirinius took the abbot's chair, the bishop to his right, Moderatus to his left. Pennomorix clambered onto the bench next to Moderatus and turned his blank eyes on Quirinius.

"A hundred and fifty Saxons? The number is certain?"

"No more than that," Moderatus said. "More likely about a hundred and ten, so it won't be like Mons Badonicus. We're certain to outnumber them, and they'll be overmatched by the cavalry."

Quirinius said nothing. The mention of the old battle tripped the little abbot's heart for an instant, even though war was hardly his province. He knows the story of how Quirinius fought three days and nights alongside the kings of Britain with the cross upon his shoulder, and he knew that five hundred Saxons had died and no one had slain them but the Bear. He had read the account in the abbey's annal

proelius montis badonis in quo quirinius ursus dux bellorum tribus diebus et noctibus pugnavit saxones, cruce in humero, et brittones fuerunt victores. cadunt quinque centum gladio ipsius.

Corinium Dobunnorum, June 483 AD

There was, perhaps, some exaggeration, but whatever the exact truth, the Saxons had not come back.

The mention of the battle calls back memories for Quirinius too, but they are poignant, which would surprise those present. These memories form sides of the story that the abbot has never heard.

On an early September afternoon eight years before, Quirinius came into the Council, taking the steps with long, easy strides. He waved carelessly at Canidius to indicate that the captain should wait under the porch and then went in, looking right and left at the gathered representatives, as his eyes adjusted to the dim interior of the room. There weren't as many magnates as he would have liked, but those who mattered most were there: Albinia's cousin Moderatus, standing in for Maximianus, who had visibly aged these last five years; the young Uortigern with a troop of dependable, if second-rate foot soldiers; Bishop Severianus; a handful of Roman senators; Guledig Marc; and Nonianus Bassus, older and more frail. Quirinius took his seat and waved at him to start the proceedings. Bassus glared at the affront, and he spoke without preamble and without mention of the taxation imposed on his brother's see. Though anxious, he could not keep his resentment hidden, but from Quirinius'perspective that was good; it's always useful to know who your enemies are. Quirinius put his elbows on the chair arms and rested his chin on his joined hands.

"Aelle and his men are about to cross into our province." Bassus said to the assembly. *Our province,* Quirinius smiled sourly at the turn of phrase. *All three provinces, all three Britains, were ours once.*

"What is his aim?" one of the Romans called from a seat in the back.

Bassus shrugged. "Does it matter, precisely? Destruction, plundering."

"Of course it matters," Quirinius interrupted. He spoke to the Council generally, not watching Bassus' reddening face. "If we know his aim, then we can thwart it."

"He's coming north on the road to Aquae Sulis," said the little west country king, Vortiporix, in very bad Latin.

Quirinius closed his eyes. "And why would he do that? No one has lived there in twenty years."

"Perhaps he doesn't know. He is, after all, only a barbarian."

Quirinius shook his head slowly, thinking of the old expression *ipse dixit.* He took a deep breath and gathered his patience. "Aelle is too shrewd for that. Even if Aquae Sulis were still a town, he wouldn't head there—he couldn't storm it, particularly if it were still a town."

"Tell us, Dominē Quirinius, what Aelle is after. And please, don't hesitate to condescend." Bassus' tone dripped with false humility. He sat down in such a bony heap that he might have rattled. Quirinius waited some moments to reply and noted that, despite Bassus' invitation, there was no laughter from the assembled senators and nobles. They were uneasy. Thus they could be handled, even driven if need be. He nodded to himself in satisfaction and then stood.

"First, I will say that, whether you agree with my view or not, you must agree that Aelle's broadest actions were anticipated." He paused for a few moments as he looked about at the assembly. "I see by your expressions that you do not quite grasp the implication of what I say, so I will make it plain. As Count of the Britains I was entirely justified in levying a war tax, always in the face of resentment, sometimes in the face of resistance." Here he looked pointedly at Bassus and his brother, Bishop Severianus.

"In other words, when this difficulty is past, you expect us to submit, with grateful hearts, to any further taxation," Bishop Severianus said.

"Let us not wander from the point."

"And that is?"

"That half of the money has been spent to equip and enroll soldiers."

"Your soldiers."

"Largely, yes."

"And a good sum remains to encourage the kings to the west and north to help us resist."

"As federates," the Roman voice came from the back.

"Exactly. And so, my point is that we are in a fair position to resist this Saxon. We have soldiers and we have money. But still, we must do it with real success. This is an opportunity for us—a great opportunity. But also a great danger."

"Why?" Moderatus asked. Quirinius glanced over at him and forced himself to smile, even though the man reminded him of his cousin Albinia.

"Because I think Aelle's plan is very simple. I believe he wants to clear a swath of territory and settle his followers on it. What do these Saxons call them? Carls?"

"Thegns, I think," Moderatus answered. "How would he do it, though?"

"It is very simple, and that is where the danger lies. Peasants don't care much who their master is. Ours prefer us, of course--they're used to us, and we're all Christians. But they'd accommodate these Saxons if it came to it. Therefore, what must Aelle do? Well, he can ignore the peasants. He need only turn his attentions to us, the nobles, the great men—we are the only men who matter. So, he must burn and plunder as many villas as he can. Persuade, if you like, as many of us as he can to remove ourselves from that land, perhaps go to Armorica or Aquitania, perhaps just move twenty miles west or up into the mountains. With the villas gone, with our way of life gone, there's no reason for us to stay, and the peasants will rub along under their new masters. It's happening in Gaul. And the danger, as you can see, is that, because, he has so many men, it will be easy for him to do this if we don't dog him and keep him from the villas."

"What is this great opportunity?" Bishop Severianus' tone that suggested he doubted there was any.

"It lies in this. Aelle has so many men his of his own, and a great number of Saxon adventurers from the east. Some say two thousand."

"Two thousand!" Bassus squawked in surprise like an old hen.

"Don't fret over that figure, Senators. Aelle couldn't handle or even feed half as many in one place for any length of time. The number is only a figure of speech; it means only that he has a great many of them, perhaps five hundred. But think. If we destroy them, really destroy them, we will have stopped not only Aelle to the south, but gored and hampered the Saxons to the east because so many of them have come here adventuring. We will be the best position we have been in for half a century."

"And how do we do that?" Bassus asked. "How, exactly?"

"I will attend to that. I have sent messengers to the kings and chiefs whose land is nearest, and I have marshalled my men."

"Is there anything, then, for us to do?"

"Oh yes, Senator Bassus." And Quirinius turned to look at the rest of the Council. "And you as well, Senators and Magnates. I'll be passing Corinium on this day a week from now, and I expect you each to have a number of your bucellarii fitted out and ready to follow. Each man equipped and enough food for twenty days. I expect sixty men and thirty spare horses. Good men and good horses." There was some murmuring at this. "Twenty days. We must get out and back without despoiling our peasants as the Saxons will have done. My captain, Canidius, will tell each of you what troops I expect. Gentlemen, good day." And with that Quirinius swept out onto the porch of the senate house and called to Canidius. "They're ready for you." He walked off without looking back.

* * *

The Principal Estate of the Quirinii, July 483 AD

"Of course, I would rather go south and strike Aelle on his own holdings." Quirinius sat in his old chair in the corner of their little room as he mused to himself and Caelia. He stared ahead at the streaks in the white-washed wall as though waiting for them to come into sharper definition in the growing grey light just before dawn. Caelia sat quietly on the bed, looking down at her hands in her lap.

"But the difficulty is this: no one has the mettle for that anymore— at least not the Romans, not most of them. The kings are game for that sort of thing, but they haven't the skill or the economy to do it and, besides, they're poor and they bumble. They lose a fight and then just sing about it for years."

"Please tell me that you'll always look after yourself, Bear."

He turned to her and smiled. Even in the mild glow of the rushlights he could see that Caelia's hair was no longer the bright copper color it had been eighteen years before. Coarse white strands shot through and dulled it. Her bare white feet, dangling a half foot above the floor, were broader too. He flushed warm, surprised as he realized that, if anything, he loved her more now that she was older.

"Why 'always,' Caelia? I expect the whole business to be done before the month is out." But she only shook her head and continued to look down. In that moment, the shadows thrown by the rushlights rose around them, growing suddenly as if by magic as the flames bent under a draft slipping through the shutters. The summer breeze relented, and the shadows crept back to their accustomed places behind the furniture at the perimeter of the little room. He settled back in his chair, laid his head against its back and regarded the ceiling.

"Aelle has the advantage of the raider—the advantage that I might have if I could force the sluggard senators to raid south instead of waiting for him. His advantage is simple. We don't know where he's headed. Yes, he wants to the torch the villas, but there are many of them. Which will he head for first? And which second? And if he's chased but not handled properly, he can still do a great deal of harm by striking at whatever is offered unless we force him into a fast retreat. In other words, a raider's movement and uncertain goals multiplies his threat, as it were. Aelle might head anywhere and do anything. It's the raider's natural advantage.

"However, I've done what I can. Maximianus is too old to fight himself, but he's sent a troop of horsemen under a captain to find Aelle and dog him as he comes north. They're too few to fight him, but they'll force him to keep his men together; they can run down stragglers and make them uneasy about exposing themselves to attack from behind if they raid villas."

Caelia nodded but said nothing. Quirinius didn't note her silence.

"But Maximianus' captain has another charge when he finds Aelle; he's to send a messenger toward Corinium. I'll be there, or heading west from it down the road toward that river—what do they call it? Abon something? Abon Mor? And out onto the plain. I'll lead our troops toward Aelle, mine and those I've taken from the others. That will amount to two hundred and sixty cavalry and a good hundred and fifty footmen. Meanwhile Marc and Vortiporix are to head down from their territories to join us. They'll bring another two hundred with them—all footmen and half wild, but they'll do. I'll try to force Aelle into a set-piece battle. With luck, we'll be finished with war for a long while."

The two continued to sit in silence a while, Quirinius staring out at the early morning sky, grey as tin. Finally, Quirinius rose and sat next to Caelia on the bed; frame squeaked at his weight. He took her hands and chafed them gently, noting small crescents of dark blue beneath her fingernails.

"Why do ask me to *always* look after myself, Caelia?"

"Because I worry about you."

He leaned over and kissed her cheek. He patted her hands.

"You think it's because of the campaign, Bear. The battle."

"Isn't it?"

She shook her head. "Not really. Well, yes, in a way. In a way." She stopped for a moment. "I don't mean that I'm indifferent to what happens to you."

"Like Albinia."

"Everyone dies. I hope you die in happiness."

He frowned at this, and then his expression grew quizzical. "Why talk of death? Why now?"

"I think that the real dangers you face are from things you cannot see. And I just can't believe that the Saxons will ever kill you. Yes, I can tell myself that it's because you are too clever, too bold, too organized for them. I don't want you to die fighting, Bear, I don't. But if you did, then you'd meet death doing what's important to you. And would that be so terrible?"

"And so, why should I be careful? What are you getting at?"

"There are so many things to say, and I've never said them." She turned to smile sadly at him. "I've had, what, eighteen years to talk, and yet I've never said some things." He began to feel uneasy. She continued. "Well, I suppose that for the first several years I had nothing really to say."

"We've always talked."

She nodded.

"It's because you have no children."

"Oh, I suppose if I'd had them then I'd be too busy to think. Perhaps. But I'm not too busy."

"What are you thinking of, then?" He put his arm around her.

"You're dutiful."

Quirinius nodded.

"You have this Idea, of yours."

"I don't have it; it exists apart from me." He felt pretentious putting it that way. But, of course, it was true.

Caelia nodded. "There are things apart from us, no one can deny it. And you must do what you think is right. And so must I."

Quirinius was puzzled. "What must you do?"

"You fight because you must. You do believe it's right to do that— that it matters."

"Of course it matters."

"I suppose so. But sometimes I wonder how." She shook her head. "But the thing is this--you have decided your course and you act as you must. You don't fear any judgement about it."

"Of course not."

"And that's right. We must all decide what to do, and then we must do it. It's the acts, you see, by which we are judged."

Quirinius' frown dissolved, and he chuckled. "You're a Pelagian. You've talked about that old scoundrel, Morgan, before."

Caelia smiled at him too, but sadly. "Faith is important. But so are acts. I believe that, yes, just as Pelagius taught."

"Morgan."

"Morgan, then."

"Caelia, what is this all about? For years I've listened to Albinia mutter about God and duty..."

"Her duty is only ritual."

"Granted, but you've never troubled me with any of this. And you were in Pulcheria's old nunnery. By the way, was the old girl a Pelagian? Is that where you picked it up? Or was she just an opportunist?"

"She's dead now. *Nihil nisi bonum.*"

"That's a task. Still, I always admired her brass."

"How can I explain it, Bear?"

"Explain what? Free will? I love you, but educated men have debated it for centuries, and Augustine's against the idea. Can't we just move on?"

"When I was summoned to your father's court session years ago, I saw you for the first time."

"Yes. I remember it. Because of you. You know it; I've told you."

"You were so handsome. And decked in your spotless white clothes with the purple and blue stripes over the shoulders—I still recall them, how they ended in beautiful roundels to each side of your chest. The sewing and the embroidery of the roundels was finer than any I'd seen, apart from that on a bishop's alb. I thought, 'This is what a prince of the Imperial House looks like.' You see, you were so elegant and serious that day." She brushed the corner of her eye with the back of her hand. "At the end of the day I travelled back with Mother Pulcheria to the nunnery. I hadn't been happy at the thought of marrying that boy; I had resolved to accept it because God's plans are hard to fathom and, if it had to come to that, I knew there would be some good in it."

"Or some good if you went back to the nunnery," Quirinius said with some irony.

"Yes, that too. But, though I'd grown accustomed to the nunnery, I wasn't happy to go back. I was thinking of you, of course. I couldn't help my thoughts, but I could do the right things. The rituals, feeding the poor, that sort of thing. I could choose to act rightly. And then I saw you again, when you passed by leading the Old Senator's cortege. And that was hard too. And finally, when you rode by with your men mounted on that big horse and covered in armor like a hero. Well, you were a hero. And I stood in the stream and watched you go, and I thought I would die just from longing for you."

"But I sent for you that night."

"Yes, you did. And I came. I thought, 'He's been on my mind for so very long that it must mean something. It must be that I should go to him.'"

"I recall the first thing you ever said to me. *'Multum volo.'*"

"Oh, yes. Very, very much. But I wanted to believe just as much that it was a good thing to do, and I could believe that. I didn't decide to marry that boy. My father decided it. I didn't ask to go to the abbey—he and Mother Pulcheria decided that. And I didn't ask to be taken to you, so, when it satisfied my longing for you, it was easy to justify. And I was a help, a prop, however insignificant, to an important man doing important work. And, what was more important to me, really, was that I was a comfort to you who'd been saddled with a wife like Albinia. Don't misunderstand. I loved you. I love you yet, but it was easy to justify."

"Why did you think that you should justify love?"

"Because the whole thing was . . ." and she hesitated, searching for a word. "The whole thing was irregular. We knew that—keeping house for vague old Remigius, but then sleeping here with you. At first, and for a long, long time it felt right despite the irregularity. Very right. And then I was less sure that it was entirely right. Not very wrong, I suppose, really. Not at the start and not for a very long time. But, as the years have passed, I have been somewhat troubled."

Quirinius tousled her hair. "So, that's why you won't grow your hair out!" He laughed. "Keeping one foot in the nunnery, as it were. More than that, in fact. I should have kept you from visiting the place. I think the visits upset you."

Caelia smoothed her short, thick hair back with both hands. "Perhaps."

They sat in silence a little longer, and then Caelia drew a deep breath, put her shoulders back and looked at Quirinius. "Bear, I'm going back to the abbey tomorrow."

His eyes widened. "Pay your visit later—I don't want you away from the estate while the fight is on. I have men who'll protect you here. You can go later."

"You don't understand. I'm going back to the abbey to live; I am not coming back here."

Quirinius thought for a moment that he had misheard, but when he searched her face he could see from her expression that he had heard quite well. He began to open his mouth, but could think of nothing to say, and, for a second, he felt dizzy, if struck in the head. It passed, but Caelia's expression was the same, and he knew he was losing her. "You can't," he said, but couldn't go further.

"I must. We must all do what we should do. Perhaps I should never have agreed all those years ago, because now it is all so hard. But that is done and doesn't change my duty. And I despair for you because you are so alone. I love you." She blinked back tears. "Find someone else if you must."

Quirinius wanted to be angry but couldn't think how to come at that feeling—it was as though he'd forgotten all but the name of the emotion. Caelia stood up from the bed, and, to Quirinius' surprise, hugged him. "Oh, Bear." The door shook suddenly to a brash knock, and he recognized it as the crescendo of a hundred noises just outside. The men and horses had been gathering below for some time, and he was needed. He flung a cloak over his shoulders and turned to Caelia and said, again, "Don't do it," but it sounded to him less like a command than a plea. He didn't wait for her answer but opened the door to join Canidius in the hallway and closed it behind him so that he could not hear her answer. Down below, in the courtyard among the milling men and nickering horses, he looked up at the whitening wall, at the window of his little room, and he saw Caelia looking down at him. They stared at each other for a few moments, and then Quirinius had to turn away and give the first of a hundred orders sending his little army into the long shadows of the west.

Twenty: The Stone Ring, July 483 AD

Just beyond Ambrosius Aurelianus' villa was an old ring fort. It was the usual sort of place: a green earthen wall slumped over the ages to a gentle, circular bank with a broad gap where wooden gates had once stood. Even without gates it made a good bivouac for the cavalry, more than two hundred sixty horsemen, his own and those he'd levied from the landholders. A hundred and fifty footsoldiers were joined to them, gathered from town militias or from chieftains in the hinterland. They could be used for pickets and, perhaps, could be trusted to hold the center of a line for as long as it took to make a cavalry sweep. Watch them on the march. See how they do.

The bank at the top of the hill, though now low, broad and gentle, kept the horses from wandering, hid the cooking fires at night from any watchers that might lurk on the plain, and gave the sentinels high points from which to scan the countryside. Quirinius knew that, apart from the chance of an odd scout, the Saxons could hardly have reached the area, even if it were their goal, but it was good to get the men into the habits of war. He climbed the northern bank and looked down on the plain, just to show how it should be done, but the only object of interest was the great stone ring a mile away. Canidius, who was up disposing the sentries, walked over. Quirinius continued to look down on the primordial structure. As he'd been told, and as he'd seen earlier as they had travelled toward the fort, the ring was made up of enormous, roughly-cut standing stones twice as high as a man. Many still bore huge lintels joining their tops, making rectangular gates of them. He judged the circle of portals to be a hundred feet in diameter, and there were many other stones, tumbled over, inside. It was an odd structure, imposing despite its crudity, and chilling to Quirinius because it was so alien. The idea struck him that the very breeze might be chilled as it passed through those stone gates. He shook his head to clear it of the fancy.

"The druids built it," Canidius said. "The stones don't come from hereabouts. That's generally agreed. They could do most anything."

Quirinius didn't reply; he merely stood observing.

"The druids had hidden powers," Canidius said, continuing to stare.

"Or perhaps oxen, sledges, men and a very long time. Look at it, Canidius; it's older than the druids."

Canidius said nothing for a few moments, and then, "Yes, Dominē."

"You sound doubtful."

"No, Dominē."

"Of course, you doubt me. You don't want to believe your eyes— like most men you prefer to believe what your heart tells you." He slapped his captain on the chest with the back of his hand. "Well, druids or not, it's a thing to see."

"I don't like it, Dominē."

"Makes you uneasy, does it? Such a great, weird thing. So much labor and planning and for what? All that work and all that mystery. But don't fear it. It's just a ring of stone." He turned back to the interior of the ring fort and rubbed the sweat from the back of his neck. "This armor's hot. I'm going to take it off." He walked down the gentle batter of the bank, headed for his tent.

* * *

Quirinius' shield hung from a hook on the tent pole, a Roman shield, gently elliptical, dished out, and a little more than three feet tall. It had been refurbished for this fight. The old canvas stripped off its face and a new layer applied. A new rawhide binding stitched and shrunk around the edge to draw the boards tight, but the shield-boss, though dinged and nicked in earlier fights, had not been replaced, only polished. But what Quirinius regarded, as he sat on his camp-stool, were the fresh, painted face and insignia, which gleamed faintly, even in the light of the single lamp. Though the darkness of the interior of the tent muted the colors, he knew them well; he could see them in his mind with the same clarity that he could see Caelia. The binding was painted blue so that a ring of that color encircled the shield as the Ocean encircled the world, and painted across a deep red field was the bright blue Chi-Rho of the Imperial Army. It was very finely done: the proportions were balanced and the edges remarkably sharp. The painting itself was subtle too. The brush-strokes had been scarcely evident, even under the full noon sun when Quirinius had first examined the shield closely on the road west. The paint had been carefully blended so that the shield glistened like a jewel. On the back of it, above the boss, was painted in Caelia's careful hand *protego*.

The shield's fine finish accounted for the littl dark curves beneath Caelia's fingernails that he had noticed two nights before. She had painted the shield for him. And so, of course, he thought of Caelia as he regarded it in the shadowy tent, and she, like the colors of the shield now muted in the glow of the single lamp, persisted in his thoughts. She couldn't return to the abbey, really the thing was inconceivable. She might be dissatisfied, but then, who wasn't? The world was not a place laden with satisfaction—that shouldn't come into her decision.

After all, there had been many towns in Britain once, and some fine cities too. They had all been excellent places knitted together by fine, clean roads without a stone loose or a ditch blocked. He'd often dreamt of that time, Quirinius had, when the provinces were in their best state, but he had never seen such a world and never would. And yet he pushed on. There were fine cities yet in the south of Gaul, so it was said, and in Italy. And there was still New Rome, Constantine's city to the east where a splendid Emperor commanded a gleaming army and a great navy of narrow, fast-running ships that beat the water with countless oars as they cut and surged through the azure waves of the inner sea. And this emperor ruled in robes of silk and cloth-of-gold from a marble hall, and he walked in scarlet shoes through high, porphyry corridors and frescoed chambers pranked with gilt and mosaic, lighted by bright shafts of sunlight striking through windows of glass and alabaster set in the walls of his gleaming palace by the sea. And, what was more, that palace nestled in a splendid city of elaborate churches and of fora studded with the statues of great men and heroes in bronze and marble, amid which strolled civilized people in flowing robes splashed with purple, vermillion, green and yellow. And Quirinius would never see any of it. No matter his successes, he would never see any of it. And yet he soldiered on. And so could Caelia; that was all there was to it. Of course, she would see her duty in the cold light of day—there was nothing to worry about.

Quirinius put his elbows on his knees and rested his face in his hands, as he tried to imagine a forum in Constantinople, its churches, triumphal arches and memorial columns glowing pink in the rose-light of sunrise, the long shadows pulling back across the smooth cobbles of the square, receding in the dawn like the tide. He almost had it, but the image dissolved and floated away with the passage of a draft, as Canidius stepped into the tent. He did not look up, did not need to see; only Canidius had the authority to enter without a word.

"Yes?" he asked. Canidius dropped the tent-flap, stepped over and squatted down close to him. He spoke very softly.

"Dominē, the men are afraid."

Quirinius dropped his hands and peered at Canidius. "Afraid? They were all enthusiasm a few hours ago. I had to upbraid them just to stop here and rest for tomorrow, So, now what? Afraid?" He began to rise, but Canidius, with unexpected boldness, put his hand on Quirinius' arm and kept him in his place. Surprised, he looked into Canidius' face for a long moment, and then frowned. "Why, you're afraid too. Why?" Unlike that of others, Canidius' fear was something to consider.

"It's the Stone Ring, Dominē."

"What about it? The place is harmless—it's just the tired wreck of something from the time when the world was new."

"There is a light there, at the Ring. It's the light that's frightening the men."

"Light? What sort of light? Why should a light frighten them?"

"Because it's in the Ring, Dominē, that's why. It's small, like a pinprick in the dark. Nonnius saw it first."

"Nonnius? He's an ass! It took him half a year to learn the drill properly! Who is idiot enough to worry about what Nonnius sees?"

"He called down from the bank where he was standing watch, and now everyone has seen it."

"And so?"

"The men judge it to be a bad omen."

"So, a score of yokels tremble at a rushlight, and now we'd all best beware—even you and I. Should we go home now and leave this country to the Saxons? Perhaps they find firelight less disconcerting than we do."

He glared, and the other man looked down. Quirinius rose. "All right. Let's go look at this marvel." He swept out of the tent and clambered up the bank, where he found a dozen soldiers peering down at the Ring across the plain. They moved aside to make room.

The waning moon stood above them, lighting the plain with a soft grey that brightened where it struck the great standing stones so that they stood out distinct and silver like the bleached ribs of an old shipwreck. The stones suggested to Quirinius some ancient structure floated out from the dim past and washed up, like an ark, stranded in a new world. The Ring did strike him as uncanny, but he showed the men nothing of its effect on him. Instead, he watched intently and soon saw a tiny yellow light among the stones. He watched patiently for a while and noted that, while it winked, it never shifted place.

"Do you see it, Dominē?"

"Yes, I do," he replied loud enough for all to hear. "This light has piqued my interest, yes indeed." He waited until all of the soldiers had turned to face him. "I'm going down there myself to see what sort of man cooks his supper among ruins."

He stepped down the bank, calling for his sword and horse.

* * *

With Canidius at his side and a half-dozen troopers trailing behind, Quirinius rode across the darkened plain. The men were with him not only to provide the usual dignity, but to learn from him not to fear whatever was going on ahead. They were to disseminate their new-found confidence to the other soldiers back at the ring-fort, after Quirinius had settled everyone's fears. They rode across a landscape limned in black and silver by the sharp, clear waxing moon, which struck a line of jagged shadows from the riders that surged and flowed across the plain beside them.

The stones ahead wavered and shifted ever so slightly in what was clearly the light of a small fire in the center of the ring, whose flames painted the far stones with a faint, yellow luminescence while outlining the rough edges of the nearer stones that stood before it. The moon, by contrast, dropped a weak silver light across the tops of the stones. This play of darkness and light, and the illusion it produced that the great stones moved, was disconcerting, but more disconcerting to Quirinius was the effect it had on the men. They grew entirely silent as they approached the ring. The dance of the looming stones was only a trick—there was nothing to it, really, but the men's fear was real enough and had to be dispelled.

Quirinius' chance came as they closed on the ring and found a litter of stony rubble about the perimeter, making it dangerous to ride the horses further in the dark. He dismounted and waved Canidius to follow him on foot. He strode in negligently, neither looking back at the men nor drawing his sword.

As he stepped into the inner ring, he found what he had expected, a traveller seated on a tumbled stone with the small, bright fire of twigs before him. The lively yellow flames cast the man's shadow, huge, fantastic, and constantly changing, across the rough face of the great standing stone that loomed behind him. Nor was the man himself insignificant. His legs were long—as he sat, his knees jutted up, and he rested his long arms across his long thighs. He was very tall and very gaunt. In fact, Quirinius was struck by the man's thinness, which was evident even through his heavy grey travelling cloak. His thinness was clear, too, from the shadows that trembled in the lines of his narrow face. A broad travelling hat, a staff and a satchel lay on the ground beside him. The man was only a wanderer, likely a vagabond of some sort. He watched Quirinius with great calm, as though to assess him.

"Your fire is very alarming, Old Man," Quirinius said without preamble. The traveller smiled wryly.

"To the contrary, Dominē. It is attractive."

"Oh, yes?" Quirinius crossed his arms to show Canidius and the soldiers that there was no need to rest his hand on his sword hilt and, at the same time, to seem truculent towards this stranger who, though he could plainly see that he was dealing with a magnate, had not risen.

"Quite simply, I have caught a bear."

Quirinius stiffened and glanced quickly over the openings between the standing stones behind the man. Canidius drew his sword and took a step forward, looking into the darkness behind the traveller. The old man shook his head. "I am alone. Quite, quite alone." After a few moments he dropped the point of his sword but did not sheathe it. Rather, he rested the point gently on the toe of his boot, and the length of it flashed yellow-orange and straight as a yardstick in the firelight. He raised his left hand, shouted, "Search!" and drew a quick circle in the air with his finger. Quirinius heard the steps of a half-dozen men as they dispersed and circled the stone ring. The old man ignored them.

"You know, then, who I am."

"Oh, yes. Yes, indeed. You are Dominus Flavius Quirinius Claudianus Ursinus, Count of the Britains. And Senator of course. Whatever that means these days."

"No insolence, old man," Canidius said, looking over his head, watching his men circle and weave among the shadowed stones.

"None intended," the old man said affably. "In fact, I came this way to see you."

"Who are you?"

"I am Durotorix." It was an old-fashioned name; the ending of it right out of the days before Rome ruled the island. Apart from that, however, the name suggested nothing to Quirinius. The man's bearing and diction were excellent, really, even though he had only spoken British. Perhaps the man might turn out to be some fugitive backwoods noble or perhaps the half-educated brother of a semi-civilized chief. Perhaps, perhaps.

"If you wished to see me, then why did you not come up to the camp? Do you have some information for me? What is your business?"

"I needn't come to you. I build a little fire and you come to me in fine estate with a grand entourage of soldiers." He warmed his long hands carelessly at the fire. Canidius took a step forward at the man's insolence, but Quirinius signaled him to stay where he was. There was something arresting in the man's comportment, something suggesting a subtle power.

"True enough, I suppose. I concede the point. I am here. What business have you that is so important that you," and here Quirinius hesitated for an instant to command the attention of Canidius and the troopers before he went on in an ironic tone. "What business do you have so important that you summon me?"

The old man cocked his head and looked at him, as though still assessing him. "I'm a sort of traveller. Of course, you see that for yourself." He waved his left hand vaguely at the hat, staff and satchel lying beside him.

"Don't waste my time."

"I'm a sort of traveller," he continued, indifferent to the injunction. "Where I come from—what province, what country—is not so very important. It was in the west, if you must know, though I have lived everywhere, it seems, from Glyvising to Pictland. But I am near the end of my time. I know such things; it is my business. And I mean to do a little more before I join Father Dis in the next world. I mean to tell you some truths, hard truths, but I must tell them all the same, must discharge that duty. And I must confess that I wished to see both Aelle and you before this fight that you will have."

Quirinius had been startled and irritated by Durotorix's pagan allusion; at the same time he was curious about these alleged truths and the old man's desire to speak with the Saxon king. But he addressed only the last point.

"How do you propose to meet up with Aelle? And survive if you do? That would indeed be playing with fire." He glanced at Canidius, but the captain was too uneasy at the turn in the conversation to show any reaction.

"I have already seen him," Durotorix said. Quirinius straightened, startled. The old man waved his hand. "That is not important. What I had to tell him, I told him. What I must tell you, I shall tell you. And then I will go west, perhaps to Hibernia, and prepare to meet Father Dis."

"Dis," Canidius echoed uneasily. "You are a druid."

"No, Canidius. He is only trying to gull us. The druids are long, long gone."

"I told you that I was alone. Quite alone."

Canidius stared wide-eyed at Durotorix. He took a step back.

"Gone. Two or three centuries gone," Quirinius said.

"Many things linger. All things, really, in some way. The world changes slowly as the past melts into the present and informs the future. Look around you." He swept his arms out. "Tell me that we do not live rubbing shoulders with the past. You, of all men, should understand. You fight both the Saxons and your fellows to maintain a world that is melting before your gaze."

"Fight my fellows? You're quite wrong about that, you old fool. I am their greatest ally, their greatest friend."

"I stand back; I see things clearly." He waved a hand casually, as though the point were unimportant. "It's that you fight for an idea that impresses me—not for whom you fight. And that you fight so late in the day."

"Late in the day?"

"You are a relic, Dominē, like this ruin. A thing of another time. A thing to be remembered, surely, yet understood only dimly." There was a silence between the two men during which the troopers who had circled the stones slipped quietly back into the Ring. Durotorix continued. "Like me."

"Late in the day?" Canidius echoed quietly.

"It is dawn for a man like Aelle, Count Quirinius, if not dawn for Aelle himself."

"Be clear, old man. No paradoxes!"

"*Veritas in paradoce revelata non minimis est veritas* 'truth revealed in paradox is no less truth.'" Durotorix continued before Quirinius could interrupt. "Look at this place," he said, hands out, palms up. "Who built it?"

"You, Druid," Canidius said. "Or your kind, anyway."

"No." The old man shook his head. "Some forgotten people whom we Britons shoved aside long ago. And yet, many of them, no doubt, are our ancestors. Yes, ours—yours too, for we are part of you, Bear. But they are strangers to us now, we who stand a thousand years away. But even so, we Britons are not what we would have been had we not come to live in this haunted island. We have been changed, even if we cannot say how. And then came the Romans, first the Divine Julius and then, with real intent, Claudius and all the rest." He paused. "And then Hengist and Horsa and Aelle and those who follow them." He looked into the fire for a few instants and then back to Quirinius. "My day is done—has been done for a long, long time. Oh, we've changed you island Romans in a hundred ways. We must settle for that—there is nothing else for us. No point in complaining, eh? Epictetus tells us that."

"Who?" Canidius asked.

"A Greek," Quirinius said.

"We all change. You see, my boy?" He grinned at the puzzled captain. "Yes, even Romans like you."

Quirinius said, "My people came from Liguria. We have had citizenship for four hundred years."

"Splendid. And the Quirinii have lived in Britain for what, three hundred?"

"Close enough."

"How are we not cousins, you and I? My compliments, by the way, on your British. Corinium diction, I would say."

Quirinius scowled. "A noble may speak with the greatest refinement to his fellows, but still he knows to whistle for a dog."

The old man laughed. "You are indeed prickly, just as they say."

"If I understand the burden of your half-wit philosophy, I must guess that you've come here to tell me that the Saxon will beat us when we run him down—you've come here to dispirit us and gloat." He pointed casually at Canidius, who raised the point of his sword from the toe of his boot. "It was a stupid thing to do." The druid ignored the trooper and bent forward and stirred the fire with a stick.

"Oh, no. I have not come for that at all. In fact, it is not you, but Aelle who will die in this next battle."

There was a stir among the men, a sudden whispering among themselves. Canidius dropped his sword point and looked questioningly at Quirinius. His master nodded and shook his head slightly to the right to make him step away.

"For the first time you interest me," Quirinius said. He was suspicious of predictions, but happy for any that might inspirit the men before battle, even if it came from some rural pagan.

"We are known for our inspiration, men such as I." Durotorix leaned back from the fire and closed his eyes for several moments before intoning

Contra Ursum cadebit Aelle in proelio
Et in terram iacibitur,

Sed nomen eius longe noscibitur.
Ursus triumphans dux et senator,
Tamen nomen eius vanescit,
Sed in inclitum regem mutibitur.

The druid blinked and looked about, as though awakening from a doze. Quirinius stood silent, thinking, disturbed by the last lines of the prophecy, but unwilling to contend with the old man in front of the credulous soldiers. It was better to take the prediction as it was—on balance it was very favorable and, besides, why should he think it true in all of its particulars? He looked around but could see that his men had not followed it well—the druid's Latin was, somehow, too classical, and therefore too ancient for them. So, he retailed the point of it for the men. "The old spook says we'll win and that Aelle will die. Right, Old Man?"

"Indeed, Dominē." And then, underlining the prophecy, he appealed to the solders. "I know my business, men," he looked at each of them in turn to gain their close attention. "And here's a proof." A sly glint in his eyes, he made several passes in the air with his hands, rubbed them together slowly, and then opened them palms up. In the left palm stood an egg, and in the right burned a small flame. The men gasped and Quirinius saw them take a step back. The druid laughed, clapped his hands together and, in that instant, both egg and flame were gone.

"Enough tricks! What can you tell me about Aelle? What is his strength, his disposition? Where is he?"

The druid stood up, slender, tall, and ungainly as a heron. He gathered his things with slow deliberation and put on his wide hat. "Isn't it enough to know the outcome, Flavius Quirinius Claudianus, Ursus et Senator? That Aelle will die?" He swept his great grey cloak about him with a magnificent gesture and turned and stepped through the gap behind him. And he disappeared in that instant—he faded into the darkness just as any man might do, but much more quickly than he should. The weirdness of it struck Quirinius, but more so Canidius, who sprang to the gap, but then stopped, puzzled. Quirinius watched the trooper look frantically from side to side.

"Come away from there," he called. And then to men generally he said, "Let the old man go. We are heading back to the camp. You have all heard the good news. Now spread it."

Twenty-One: The Monastery, October 491 AD

The five men sit around the table, Quirinius at the head and Valerianus at the foot. Moderatus and Pennomorix sit side by side to Quirinius' left, while Ambiorus sits across from the new arrivals and watches them like a dog. The old Bear puts his hands palms down on the table and leans back into the tall chair. It creaks at his weight. He turns slowly to Moderatus and says, "Let's get the background. How many Saxons are there, do you think?"

"A good two hundred. They've come up from near Vectis, according to report and from the markings on their shields."

"So, you've seen them?"

Moderatus nods and looks to Pennomorix, who says nothing. He looks back to Quirinius and adds, "A pair of scouts on foot, peeping out of a wood."

"Yellow and black shields," Pennomorix says.

"You couldn't catch them, of course."

Pennomorix is done speaking; he just stares stone-faced. Moderatus answers for him. "It would have been foolish to traipse into a wood after them. There might have been an ambush."

"Quite right. Commendable decision." Quirinius crosses his arms and looks up at the beams under the ceiling. "I'm sure there was no real need to learn whatever it was they knew of their raid. I'm sure we're all good guessers here." He glances over at Ambiorus, who shakes his head at them like a disappointed schoolmaster.

"And we agree on this as well," he says, the derision slipping from his voice. "That you've got the numbers about right. We also reckon them at two hundred, more or less." He looks at Ambiorus, who nods. "Now, two questions. Where, exactly, are they? And how do we bring them to battle?"

"The latter may not be so difficult," Bishop Valerianus says.

"Really? And the reason for your assurance?" He watches the Bishop redden. This surprises him.

"They're here for a fight."

"Are they?"

"Saxons love to fight."

"So, it's a matter of character."

"They are about three miles to the east of here," Moderatus says. "Stewing in a mucky wood just west of the road up to Deva Victrix. The place is uneven, full of wet swales."

Quirinius turns to Ambiorus questioningly, and the captain says, "It's likely, Dominē. They were close upon that place a day ago."

"You know it?"

"Yes. Enough to know that we don't want to go in and wallow with them there. It's almost a quaking bog."

"I can't recall the place just now." Quirinius closes his eyes. "Or perhaps I've never seen it." He rubs his face with his great hands and says, "I'm old. I'm tired. I doubt I'd recall it if I had seen it." He shakes his head to clear it, and then smiles with a sadness that Ambiorus is surprised to find touching. He wants to acknowledge this emotion, but can only say, "No matter, Dominē. They won't stay there. Wet ground makes bad sleeping." Quirinius nods and then signals to the little abbot, who has been standing behind the bishop's right shoulder. "Bring us a sheet of parchment—a big one—and something to write with."

The bishop says quietly, "A rough piece will do."

Quirinius drums his fingers on the table as he waits for the parchment. "Well, let us count our forces. I have fifty men, all mounted. Bishop Valerianus has as many, though only ten are mounted. His foot soldiers are not well trained, but they have good equipment and can, I am assured, move into the field without bowling each other over and, once there, draw themselves into a block and stand steady. If they can do that for an hour, that should be enough." He looks to Moderatus. "What have you two brought?" There is a brief interruption as the abbot lays a sheet of parchment on the table before the old Bear and sets a charcoal pencil beside it. Quirinius picks up the pencil, grinning. "Such economy! You mean to scrape the sheet clean after the battle is done!"

"To copy a book, Dominē," the abbot says quietly.

"Quite right! Always think of the future. I applaud your confidence." Quirinius waves the little cleric back to his place and hands the pencil to Ambiorus, saying, "Draw us up a plan of their position."

Ambiorus takes up the pencil gingerly, as though afraid of it.

"Go ahead! I'm not asking you to write! Just show us where we are, where the Saxons are, and what the country is like around here." The captain nods, and then begins to sketch out the neighborhood, the monastery on its island, the road leading south to Rutupiae, the marshy wood and the position of the Saxons in it. Quirinius stands up, leaning on his fists to stare down at the map. He swings his head toward Moderatus and Pennomorix and asks, "Do you agree?"

Moderatus nods. "It seems right. The trick will be drawing the Saxons out onto a meadow—perhaps this one," he points. "A place where the horsemen can really get at them."

"Our bishop seems certain that the Saxons will cooperate in some way." Quirinius smiles at Valerianus, who refuses to meet his eyes, but only looks at the table before him, as though now uninterested in the talk. "Bishop Valerianus, you saw nothing of the Saxons—their numbers or dispositions, on the way here?"

"I did not approach by way of that area."

"So, no, then?"

"They are cunning," he says, evading the question.

"They are not alone in it." Quirinius turns back to the others. "How many men do you have? Enough?"

"Yes, enough," Moderatus says, speaking for the two of them. "I have eighty men—thirty of them mounted."

"The old Cohors Equitata Dalmatorum."

Moderatus nods. "And my foot soldiers are drilled, as you know."

"You've brought more than I expected."

Moderatus shrugs. "I'm careful." He glances at the bishop, and then nods at his companion. "Pennomorix has brought sixty men. All footmen."

"Of course."

"But bold."

"If irregular and without discipline. We can put them in the center if need be. No mounted men?"

"My guard," Pennomorix says in his dead voice.

"What? Ten horsemen? And, of course, we could hardly attach them to another troop; they have their primary duty." Quirinius sits down and shifts about to loosen his stiff back. "Now, let's do our sums. Fifty and fifty makes one hundred. We add to that your eighty and Pennomorix's sixty and we have two hundred and forty. Quite a respectable number in this day and age. They might have made up half an Imperial cohort a hundred years ago. Enough to keep watch over a camp at night. Still..." He shrugs. "We do what we can with what we have, and it appears that we can match these Saxons pretty well."

"The numbers are about half of those at Badon, years ago. That came off very well," Bishop Valerianus says.

* * *

Mount Badon, July 483 AD

That was true—it had gone extremely well, in the broad scheme of things. All the same, when Quirinius thinks of Badon, he reflects less on the fight than on its aftermath and the numbers of the Saxons and their allies: about five hundred—perhaps a little more—about as many as the men under his command.

As he crossed the plain, he passed through hamlets, questioned the peasants and listened to their reports. What they told was really the same story—a few minor details were changed as though for emphasis or effect, but the thrust never varied. A strapping Saxon— he must be a king...of course, he's rude compared to yourself, Dominē, but it's clear his men esteem him, and his armor is quite fine. Ring armor and a gilded helmet. This king, he passed through here not long ago on a very fine horse. How long ago, Dominē? Yesterday in the morning. And twenty nobles. They are called *thegns*, Dominē. Quirinius nods in impatience, or perhaps dismay that they know the term. The nobles followed on twenty fine horses, some with mail shirts, and, last of all, followed many, many warriors on foot. Hardy men who move at a dog-trot for a half a day, shields on their backs and spears on their shoulders. Helmets? Some, yes. Some have helmets. And some of the footmen have swords too, but all of them carried the long Saxon knife, almost a sword. The seax. They did not take anything, and they carried little plunder from elsewhere. Oh, yes, a few of the common warriors rode farm horses they must have lifted—they were clumsy about it. The Saxons asked if we had a master and where he lived. We had to answer—everyone knows where the nobles and *clarissimi* keep their houses anyway--on the southern slopes of the hills. They are not hidden. And then they moved on to the north and west.

That was the story. After the third or fourth rendition, what interested Quirinius was how long it had been since the Saxons had passed. By the fifth day the answer was, "Yesterday in the afternoon," and, finally, "midday." He proceeded in the general direction of the reports and, finally, in the direction of a wide, grey column of smoke from a fire he judged was burning three or four miles away. He ordered the horsemen forward at a fast walk so that the footmen could follow at a jog, and, within an hour, came upon some Saxon handiwork: a small villa was in the last stages of a fire. A mile away from it was a village, apparently untouched; a few of the villagers stood at its outskirts and stared at the villa. Others drifted out of their huts as Quirinius and his troop approached the burning villa.

The wall about the villa was low. If it were undefended, a man could clamber over it easily, and this is what must have happened, for the gate stood open with no sign of forcing. Or perhaps the bailiff had opened it for the raiders because he could not defend it. Quirinius dismounted and walked to the gate to observe the situation. The villa itself was small, and, although the roof had fallen in after the joists had burned, the walls still stood, the doorway and the windows gaping, their lintels and the wall above each painted black with soot. The sharp smell of burning abraded his nostrils.

Quirinius turned to find Canidius at his elbow. "No bodies, Dominē."

"No. The place was abandoned or surrendered. This must be Laurentius Vetus' western villa. He's sitting in Deva with his soldiers. I'll remember that." He surveyed the smoking villa for a few moments. "He won't rebuild this place. That's the shame of it."

"Does it matter so much? This was not a great villa. Surely Vetus has another estate."

"He had three and this was by far the least of them, but they all matter. All of them. Remember Aelle aims to ruin, not loot." He leaned against the gate and crossed his arms in frustration. "Strip the country of its masters, and it will welcome new masters. Understand this, Canidius, the world will have masters. What matters is who they are."

He remounted and led the troop down toward the village to learn what the villagers knew. As he approached the half-circle of those who awaited him, it opened and an old man, better dressed than a rustic, shuffled forward. He was obviously the bailiff, but he seemed lost as he looked past Quirinius and over to the smoking villa.

"I could do nothing, Dominē."

"Answer me two things. When did this happen, and in which direction did the Saxons go?"

"You see, I would have done something," he continued as though he hadn't heard. "I lived and worked in that villa thirty years. No place was ever dearer to me. No. And my wife, she has been dead a good ten years. She is buried up there by the house." He pointed. "I meant to die there. It was a good place. And so, you, see, I would have done something if there had been something to do."

"Stop maundering, old man, and tell Dominus Quirinius what he asks," Canidius said, leaning down from the saddle. "Your home is gone. Now tell us which way they went."

"Dominus Laurentius used to keep five soldiers here, but he took them away a month ago. Who knows why?" The old man began to weep. "They could not have helped, though. Not really. I'm glad they're gone—they are good boys and would only have died."

"When did the Saxons leave, and which way did they take?" Quirinius' voice revealed his impatience, but, in his distraction, the old man could not hear.

"I saw them coming. Two miles away, I saw it. I rushed down and closed the gate. Barred it. I got a hayfork. We all eight got something—hayforks, shovels. A flail. I heard them come up to the gate and pound on it. We stood on the other side. We didn't know what to do. We just listened to them pound and shout at us, but we couldn't understand them. No Latin, no British. And then, suddenly, twenty of them were behind us—they'd climbed the wall on the other side of the house. They laughed at us and opened the gate. Shoved us out onto the wagon-track and fired the house. We were afraid for the women, but they didn't touch them."

There came a crashing in the distance as the second floor of the villa fell to the ground and a mass of dust and soot rose from the shell. The old man put his hands up and cringed. Canidius looked over his shoulder at the villa and then dismounted. He went over the old man and dispassionately slapped him across the face. The bailiff staggered a step or two. "Answer the Count Quirinius." The old man goggled at him a moment and shook his head like a drunkard. He took a deep breath and said, "They left here at about noon. They followed that track." He pointed. "It heads north and a little west."

Canidius laughed, then and patted the old man gently on the back. "That's a fine answer, grandfather. Now go and have a rest. Dominus Quirinius will take care of things."

* * *

It proved easy to hunt up the barbarians, though they would be difficult to get at. Eager to reach them, Quirinius had led his column off at a trot; the footsoldiers were to catch up when they could. It was gamble, but a small one, as too few of the Saxons were mounted to engage him, and Quirinius knew he could keep away from the footmen and, besides, he had thrown scouts to range ahead of him as a further precaution. This worked against him though, for the Saxons saw them, and Aelle, who was canny, found a place to retire to until he could assess his situation. By the time Quirinius had caught up with him, he had led them up the steeps of a very large hill and disposed his men over its crown while he waited to see who was in pursuit.

Quirinius regarded the hill for some moments in silence and then said, "I take them to be close to five hundred, though it is difficult to judge when they're jumbled up that way." He turned in the saddle and looked back the way he had come, pleased to see the footsoldiers approaching in the distance. He turned back. "Now, how do you suppose they led their horses up there?"

"I'll send some of the boys to scout about and find how they did it. There must be some sort of track."

"Do that. That will be the way they'll come down too. The nobles will want their horses and the common ruck will want their nobles.

Canidius nodded, squinting up at the hilltop to see more clearly. "Some of the men, Dominē, they aren't Saxons."

"No?"

"Their shields are oval, like ours. Not round. And not blazoned like the Saxons."

"So, some bandits or outlaw peasants have joined them. So much the worse for them." He looked up at the sun. "The afternoon is almost past. We'll keep them perched on the hill for the night." They could not successfully attack up the hill against an enemy unless they outnumbered them heavily, say, three or four to one; thus Aelle had realized his immediate goal to avoid a fight that day. All the same, he would have to come down soon--it was that simple.

Even if there was a spring on the hill somewhere, which was not certain, there was nothing for the Saxons to eat. They must come down in a day, at most two. "They will come down as they went up, if only to spare the horses."

"Icenius has found the track they took," Canidius said.

"You have checked?"

"I have. The hoof-marks are clear. And there's another way down they might take, but it's steeper."

"We'll watch both. We'll make camp back there near the stream, but we'll put pickets around the hill. Use some of your men until Rusticus' and Emporianus' foot soldiers catch up—they have discipline and will take orders. All the same, have an officer check the pickets to keep them awake and tell them to whistle or shout or beat their shields if they see any sign, however doubtful, that the Saxons are descending."

Canidius nodded.

"Send five of Antonianus' horsemen as messengers to Marc and Vortiporix. They should be in camp twelve miles west of here. I want their men here tomorrow by noon." Quirinius turned his mount and rode slowly to the spot where the camp was to be established. He already had the glimmer of an idea.

Aelle would descend, of course—it was only a matter of time, but he might do so before Marc's and Vortiporix's men arrived, and, without them, Quirinius could not apply the tactic he favored; he needed those footmen to anchor his line. Towards evening, though, the foot-soldiers of Rusticus and Emporianus, whom he'd left behind in his pursuit of the Saxons, joined him, and that was inspiriting, but he needed more men yet. He let most of the new arrivals rest, but he set a score of them on watches around the hill. All he had to do was keep Aelle penned on the hill for about a day, and the thing should go well, druid foretelling or no druid foretelling.

Aelle had made a mistake by forsaking the forests and coming out onto the plain. He could move quickly with his band of lightly-equipped warriors, but not so quickly as Quirinius' mounted troopers, and so he could not refuse to fight if Quirinius wished. All Quirinius needed were a hundred more men, and the battle would be his.

And they came trudging up to the camp at the end of the next morning, led by their kings and the five bucellarii of Honorius Antonianus. Quirinius sighed when he saw them, unaware that he had been so anxious. Relieved, he slept heavily that night until Canidius shook him awake in the chill, grey dawn. "They are coming down, Dominē."

Quirinius sat up slowly, shaking his head, still tired. He rubbed his eyes. "Aelle is bold—I'll give him that. Of course, he wants light to see by during his descent, but he's trying to give himself a whole day after the fight to get away. Not a wise move. No, it would be better to fight in the late afternoon and hope to slip away in the night when the horses couldn't follow easily. Perhaps he's certain of victory."

"He shouldn't be so certain, Dominē."

"No, indeed." He stood up and took his sword and belt down from the tent-pole. "Leave the pickets where they are and muster everyone else." By the time he had buckled on his sword, Canidius was out bawling and whistling to round up the men.

* * *

An hour later the Saxons and the Romans stood ready for the battle. As Quirinius had foreseen, the Saxons had threaded their way down the hill by the way they had earlier gone up and, when the barbarians had reached the foot of the hill, Quirinius had disposed his troops. In the center were the warriors of the reguli Marc and Vortiporix. It was the place of greatest glory, as Quirinius had told them the day before. In any case, someone had to hold the center, at least for a little while. They were two hundred savage west-country hill men in a loose phalanx (to put it charitably) with two dozen Roman foot soldiers on either flank to align them, steady them, and close the flanks. They were not quite fifty yards across the front. Behind each flank was a troop of horsemen. On the right, Quirinius was at the head of a hundred men, eighty of his Thracian Lancers and a score

345

of bucellarii from other magnates; on the left, Canidius was at the head of another hundred, the Bucellarii Quiriniani and another forty horsemen levied from the magnates.

The barbarians and their bandit confederates came down the hill path in twos and threes and ranged themselves to right and left in a mass of about eighty men across and six deep. The king and his thegns sat their horses here and there amid the men to encourage them, though their animals shifted uneasily and sent waves through the formation. Quirinius smiled at this inept use of twenty mounted men who, properly positioned, might have done some good.

The two sides stood facing each other, fifty yards apart for the better part of an hour, nothing more than shouts and taunts passing between the Saxons and the west country hillmen. Quirinius and the Romans sat quietly on their horses waiting for the battle to start. The morning brightened as the men faced each other, and just as the light grew, so did the excitement or tension. Quirinius could feel it and wondered when the Saxons would advance—for he judged that, of the two forces, they would be the least able to contain themselves. He hoped so, in any case. Marc's and Vortiporix's men were hardly more than barbarians themselves and might break into a charge or a flight if the wait grew much longer. If the latter, he doubted he could salvage the situation.

Vortiporix sensed it too—he rode over to Quirinius and, leaning over, said, "Let us get on with it. Let's rush them now." He settled his helmet on his head—a barbaric leather thing reinforced with iron straps. Quirinius, turned his gaze back toward the enemy and shook his head. "The battle plan is agreed. To improvise now would be stupid."

Vortiporix scowled. "Now is the time. A fool can sense it."

"Indeed, a fool would think so." Quirinius turned to him a moment and smiled. Vortiporix looked truculently about at the troopers around them. They looked away, all except the signifer with the dragon-headed standard, a young man named Ambiorus, who regarded the Briton kinglet closely, but without expression.

Vortiporix glared, sullen, at Quirinius, who said, "We have agreed to my plan and to my command. Only a fool would needlessly change battle-plans in the face of the enemy, most particularly when there is no chance to communicate those changes to anyone."

He leaned forward in his saddle until his lips almost brushed Quirinius' helmet, and he whispered harshly, "So, then, I am a fool?"

"We'll all be judged after the battle. Why not be judged a hero? And, better yet, a victor?"

"My men and those of Marc are ready. And they will never be more eager."

"Eager? Uneasy, certainly. Possibly even afraid, and so they crave action." Quirinius turned to regard Vortiporix closely for a few moments, his dark eyes little more than glints in the shadow beneath the brow-band of his helmet and behind its nosepiece. "Perhaps they are not alone."

Vortiporix's lips tightened and disappeared into his grey beard. The men watched each other closely for few moments. "I will remember this."

"Do so. But remember too what we have agreed. That you meet Aelle when he advances and hold him. The rest will take care of itself. When you've become a hero, you won't have any use for rancor." And he turned away to observe the Saxons, who stood stolid, behind a bulwark of yellow- and black-overlapping shields. In the very center were their bandit allies, hemmed in where they must fight, like it or not. "Go on," he said sharply. Vortiporix spat to show his anger but turned away and rode off to sit his horse beside Guledig Marc among the rear ranks of the Britons.

Quirinius put the old chief out of his mind for, only moments later, the Saxons began to shout and then advance. In response, Quirinius gave his orders, the dragon standards dipped several times, and the Briton and Roman foot soldiers took up the military shout and began their advance. As they had been instructed, they advanced more deliberately than the Saxons, and that was good. The different groups of men were not used to fighting with each other, and it was most important that the line not lose cohesion. Were it to loosen, the Saxons might cleave it into sections and hack apart the fleeing fragments before Quirinius could retrieve the situation.

As Quirinius expected, the advancing line did not hold entirely straight. Marc's men on the left of the formation held back a bit, perhaps unconsciously, and Quirinius was dismayed to see a gap of thirty feet open between Marc's and Vortiporix's men. The Saxons, by contrast, kept together as they trotted forward, but they slowed and then halted as they approached the Britons, and then drew themselves back into their shield wall. The captain of Antonianus' foot soldiers noticed the gap and, while Vortiporix's men halted to dress their line before contact, the captain urged them forward and obliquely to the right, thus driving some of Marc's men ahead of them to close the gap. Marc's men stumbled as they drifted right, and Quirinius could see the disorder pass all along the line to the end of the flank, but there was no harm done because it took the Saxons some time to realign themselves and, when they had done it, the Britons were standing steady.

Quirinius waved at the signifer, and he waved the dragon standard. Its silver head flashed, its silk tail describing scarlet half-circles. Canidius' standard bearer, watching from some fifty yards away, replied. The two squadrons of horsemen then advanced at a walk toward the rear of the infantry line, and then each drifted off to wait behind a flank. When the horsemen had completed the maneuver, the lines of footmen were only some fifty feet apart. Both sides had leveled their spears and, after a few moments, in response to the shouts of their captains and kings, the two lines met at a walk, each man glancing briefly at his neighbors to be sure of his position and support. The lines met, and spears struck shields with dull thuds and, sometimes, passed through gaps with a sinister silence.

Quirinius watched as the footmen engaged briefly with each other and then pulled back spasmodically as half a dozen combats erupted here and there along the line and then died away as men tired, lost heart, or, occasionally, fell. Now and again, he heard the crack of a breaking spear, and now and again saw flashes as swords were swung by Britons or Saxons who hoped, somehow, to bring an edge past a shield. After a while, a few had managed, and a man would reel back, perhaps with an inaudible shriek or a groan, for Quirinius could hear nothing over the general shouting of the hundreds of excited men.

Quirinius continued to wait. His idea was simple. Let the Saxons engage as long as possible so that, when he struck the flanks, they would be both fully occupied and half exhausted. That meant he must wait until the block of British footmen was on the verge of dissolving. He knew they would melt at some point. Most of the footmen were west-country mountaineers and hardy, but they were as much serfs as warriors and not so desperate as the Saxons. True, they might prevail, but that certainly did not come into Quirinius' calculations. No, they had only to engage for some substantial period before dissolving. But how long?

Not long. After less than a quarter of an hour the two lines recoiled from each other as though by tacit agreement. Quirinius watched as the Saxons took the opportunity to open their ranks a bit and replace many of the men in the front with fresher fighters. The west country Britons could not do this. The days were long gone when the Roman drill taught how to replace soldiers in the front line, even during a fight. This was was no great matter in what Quirinius hoped would be a short, sharp contest, but during this pause he could see the Britons in the last rank looking about and drifting, almost imperceptibly, back. It was a subtle thing, but he knew what it meant. The infantry line, already shallow, was at the point of dissolving. It would begin when the last rank fled. Quirinius had the signifer signal with the dragon again, and then he swept from behind the left flank of the infantry until he was confident that he had drawn all of the hundred troopers out of the shadow of the footmen.

Once clear on the field, Quirinius led his men past the Saxons' right flank and to their rear. The barbarians were already shifting in his direction. Good. That meant that their line was recoiling from Canidius' squadron on their left. The Saxons moved not only to their right, but forward—the British line was disintegrating, but this did not matter, for it had done its work. Now it parted to leave a wide channel through the middle, and the Saxons poured through it in what became a disordered column. Exhausted by the fight, however, they could not move quickly at all, let alone quickly enough to outrun horsemen. There were copses and hills, but they were far from the battlefield, and they took time to reach, time that the troopers used to lope after Saxon warriors and lance them as they scattered across the field.

And so, the battle dissolved. Most of the Saxons fled, spreading across the field, flinging aside their shields, leaving the green of the field scattered with yellow and black disks, like giant cloak brooches. The Britons on foot could not pursue and, in any case, were largely disordered themselves and had drawn back from the fleeing enemy into a pair of pullulating defensive masses, one surrounding Vortiporix, the other Marc. Between these formations, if they could be so called, were Aelle, his thegns on horseback, and his picked footmen. These hard, practiced men might have fought their way off the field had they so chosen, but instead they turned about on all sides to challenge Quirinius and the kings and to delay the pursuit of their fellows. They were, in that way, at least, rather a marvel.

Before the Saxons could draw themselves together tightly enough to prevent it, Quirinius gave the command and led his troop at a trot and then a canter through the Saxons, horse and foot. The horses of both sides, as herd animals, knew what do and shifted beneath their riders to allow the troopers a clear passage. In moments Quirinius and his men were through the Saxons and wheeling about for another pass. He himself had not managed to strike anyone, although one of the thegns had struck him a glancing sword blow on the helmet, and a spearhead had bitten into his shield--the notch showed clean and white in the bright blue rim.

Canidius' troop had joined him, but Quirinius was puzzled not to see the captain beside him. Well, the armored troops looked much the same; still, Canidius did have a silvered helmet like his own. Where was it? He looked right and then left, his horse turning in place as he sensed his rider's movements. Then he noticed Ambiorus pointing back to the Saxons through whom they had just passed. Although now reduced in number by a handful, they had closed themselves up. Though their center boiled, fighting continued, and in an instant a riderless horse broke out of the formation and galloped away.

The trooper whose mount had bolted was not to be seen. Surrounded by the barbarians, if he were yet alive, he would not be for long. "Again!" Quirinius shouted and spurred his mount toward the Saxons and toward Aelle in their center. Ambiorus dipped the standard, and then raised it, and the troops advanced. Suddenly, Canidius rode beside him with his lance leveled, ready for any likely opponent. Quirinius, as commander, had foregone a lance, though he did the same, sword in hand, hoping that the shock of a second passage would disperse these Saxons and make them easy targets.

This time, however, Aelle and his thegns, now only four or five, had managed to integrate the huscarls into a block before them, and Quirinius' troopers either flowed around them as their horses refused to approach the immoveable footmen, or else found themselves drawing up sharply a dozen feet away from the enemy. Their horses stopped and then branked and pranced at their dilemma—urged on by their riders, but menaced by the close-packed spearmen. But no matter, the rest of the horsemen sweeping behind them should rattle them, cause them to dissolve—they were warriors, after all, not soldiers. But, because they were warriors and not soldiers, they were impetuous and, seeing the troopers at the halt ahead of them, the footmen surged forward with a great shout. Almost at once two of the troopers found their horses transfixed by spears and themselves on the ground facing the Saxons on their natural element.

Quirinius dug his heels into his mount and urged it forward through the now open order of footmen, hoping to spare his animal and maintain his advantages as a cavalryman--speed and intimidation. Both Canidius and Ambiorus followed him and, in a moment, the three of them found themselves in front of Aelle, a huge man in a flashing gilded helmet. Aelle drove his horse up against Quirinius, who had wanted to approach him from his right, but his mount, jostled, turned away and circled. When he had mastered his horse, he found Aelle in a hot fight with Canidius, the latter taking the brunt of it as the Saxon king, a man as big as Quirinius himself, leaned from his saddle and delivered hard sword strokes, steady and fast. Quirinius called on Canidius to pull back, but the captain could not hear or, perhaps, attend to anything else as he took the sword-strokes one after the other on his shield. He cast aside his lance--he was too close to use it--drew his sword, and wove a bit behind his shield, as he looked for an opening.

Quirinius noted that most of the Saxon footmen had dispersed or lay wounded or dead, but the bodies of the fallen troubled his horse, which constantly turned and shifted sideways, fastidiously stepping where he could sense solid ground. This impeded Quirinius' advance on the Saxon and delayed him in helping the captain. At least Aelle's sword-work was primitive--he continued to just strike and slash wildly at Canidius' shield, depending on the speed and force of his blows to stun his opponent and trusting his sword not to shiver into flying shards.

Canidius took the blows handily, but he could not recover quickly enough to find an opening before the Saxon was dropping another blow. Eventually, when the Saxon tired, he would no doubt find an opening through which to slip his blade or deliver a calculated cut, but, in the meantime, Aelle, with remarkable strength and almost unnatural speed, struck the captain's shield repeatedly and kept him huddled behind it.

Quirinius gradually got his mount to approach the fight, but it was difficult to achieve the right position. Although while Canidius and

Aelle stayed in relatively the same position with regard to each other, their horses were turning about. Quirinius had almost positioned himself where he might reach Aelle with his sword, but in that instant Aelle landed a blow that split Canidius' shield with a jarring, whip-like crack. The boards flew apart down to the boss and, for a moment, Aelle's sword was wedged in the cleft. With an effort, he drew it back and Canidius seemed to ease back in his saddle. He dropped his sword, and his horse, sensing he was no longer mastered, pulled away, carrying Canidius from the fight, his cloven shield appended to his dangling arm.

Aelle turned about to take his bearings and noted Quirinius' approach from the left and, though the two men's horses turned, as though on a pivot, again the fighters stayed in a position to engage each other. Quirinius tilted and swung his elliptical shield over his horse's neck to cover his body as he faced to the right. He knew what Aelle would do, and he himself did what Canidius had done. He held his sword out while looking for a chance to thrust or to cut with the tip. He pulled his horse back, however, and kept a very little more distance from Aelle than the captain had done.

Aelle, flushed with his success in hammering at Canidius, leaned out to do the same again. He was a poor horseman, however, and couldn't or didn't know to urge his mount against Quirinius'; thus he delivered his strokes at the limit of his reach, a little too far away to achieve much with his now-blunted sword. Although Quirinius could feel the shock of the strokes, Aelle's sword slipped across the shield without effect. Quirinius rode on his turning horse, waiting for his chance, indifferent under the litter of blows, and he could gradually feel the contest turning in his favor—Aelle was growing tired. His blows fell more seldom and with less force than at first, and certainly with less force than he had mustered to cleave Canidius' shield. Quirinius waited, took another half-dozen strokes on his shield, and then edged in close and, finding his chance, leaned in and thrust solidly at Aelle's chest. He could feel the contact, could feel Aelle driven back half a foot, and heard him gasp, but the rings of the king's mail shirt held fast, and, in the end, turned away the point. Quirinius straightened up and pulled back, watching for his next opportunity. It came in that instant. Aelle instinctively drew his round shield up high to better cover his trunk, and, as he did so, Quirinius drew his sword up by his left shoulder and slashed back-handed and down at Aelle's unprotected leg, just below the knee, at the same time spurring his horse so that it sprang away before Aelle could give an answering blow.

There wasn't an answering blow. Quirinius pulled his horse up and turned to face Aelle about thirty feet away, and he knew then that the fight had ended. He had not severed the king's leg, but the wound was very deep, the bleeding prodigious, and, in a very few moments, the Saxon king must faint from the loss of blood. Indeed, Aelle shouted something incomprehensible at him, kicked his mount forward into a trot with his good leg, and then fell out of the saddle in a swoon. His riderless horse passed Quirinius on the shield-side, and one of his troopers cantered up, as though out of nowhere, and transfixed the Saxon king with his lance.

* * *

The Principal Estate of the Quirinii, July 483
Quirinius forewent the celebratory feast insisted upon by Marc and Vortiporix. Instead, he hurried his force south-south-east across the plain as quickly as he could. Though he posted horsemen at the head and tail of the column and outriders on the flanks, there could hardly be any threat now. A few dozen Saxon prisoners walked in the rear with the British footmen, and, in the middle, rolled a two-wheeled farm cart drawn by a mule on which Canidius' body rested. It was rigid in death and rolled from side to side like a log with every bump and jar for the two days it took to reach Villa Quiriniana. During all of this time Quirinius said nothing apart from the most necessary orders. He felt a surprising and profound loneliness at the loss of his captain, and he wanted above all things, to see Caelia. The shield across his back recalled her to him. With her he would not be lonely. The Saxons would not trouble anyone any further and so

now there would be time to work out something that would satisfy them both.

Caelia was not in the crowd along the road to the estate, nor was she in the courtyard of the villa, even though Quirinius had sent a rider ahead to announce his arrival. He told himself that he had done it to be assured that the men would be taken care of immediately upon their return but, in his heart, he knew that he wanted Caelia to turn out for him. He was chagrined and ashamed of his weakness when he did not see her shaggy, reddish head among the crowd of villagers, tenants and servants.

Ah, well, he told himself, she must be up in our room airing it. He could imagine her leaning out of the window to set the shutters open, he could see her from behind, as he'd seen her do it a hundred times, leaning forward, her shift tightening over her rump and slipping up to show her strong white calves. Yes, she'll be doing that and sweeping the floor too, setting out a bowl of summer flowers, or plumping up the quilt.

He dismounted in the courtyard where Albinia, the bailiff, and the estate's priest stood waiting for him. He nodded at Albinia, politely, automatically, and without emotion. She, contrary to her usual practice, allowed herself an expression, tilting her head ever so slightly to the side and regarding him with some curiosity, as though she anticipated something from him. But what? He turned to the old priest Remigius and allowed him to bless his return. The dodderer got the Latin right, but he seemed a bit vague about the nature of the occasion. Good thing Caelia looked after the old man. Sequanius greeted him, "Congratulations, Dominē. The good news has preceded you. You have won a victory such as we have not had in two hundred years."

"Let's not exaggerate." All the same he felt an unexpected, almost paternal affection for the man.

"The report is that the Saxon king is dead."

"And so is Canidius." He gestured to the cart as it rolled in, a servant leading the mule with a hand on its halter. "I want a funeral for him tomorrow. See that he gets a proper headstone, even if you have to send to Corinium for it."

"Yes, Dominē."

Quirinius waved him along as he entered the house. He said to the bailiff, "Send Caelia up to me in an hour." Oddly, perhaps, the bailiff said nothing, merely inclined his head to show that he had understood and faded away into a side room.

An hour later, as Quirinius, exhausted, sat dozing in his chair, a rap at the door awoke him. Odd—Caelia had no need to knock. The room was now as much hers as his; he could see one of her combs lying on the little table by his elbow. He picked it up absently and went to the door. When he opened it, he found Sequanius silent and anxious.

"Well?" Quirinius asked.

Without speaking the bailiff handed him a folded little scrap of parchment—a tag of palimpsest saved for making notes—and he stepped away without asking leave. Caelia had learned to write as an adult, and so, although her script was legible, she had never developed a good hand. It was distinct, however, and Quirinius recognized it at once from the single word, his name, on the outside of it, Urso. He felt very uneasy—she had written lists, but she had never written him a note. He closed the door and leaned back against it. The note was in the common Latin that she spoke.

urse, nonc scis, eo son andata. tornai ad clostrum. tentai esplicare ad te, sed tu no voluisti comprender. eo comprendo id sera difficil per te et etiamsi per me perque te amo. autem eo obligationum habo quomodo cum toti mondi. te amero semper. sta bene. caelia

There it was. She was gone.

Twenty-Two: The Principal Estate of the Quirinii, July 483

He had fought for three days at Mons Badonicus and three hundred Saxons had died and he alone, Quirinius had slain them, leading in his wake the kings of Britain. That was the substance of the songs the British sang. A greater truth, perhaps, than the very truth—years had passed, and no Saxons had raided past the frontiers. But the grandeur of the whole affair quite escaped Quirinius at the time.

The next morning, he awoke and, finding himself alone and recalling why, swung his legs out of bed and, for just a moment, thought of ordering Canidius to have his horse saddled and half a dozen men mustered to attend him while he rode to the abbey to take Caelia back. But, of course, Canidius was dead—no doubt already lying in the coffin the carpenters had turned out the evening before. He'd been distracted from his brooding in the study by the shrieking saws and murmuring planes as they cut and smoothed the boards.

Quirinius sat for some time on the edge of the high Roman bed, his feet dangling like those of a little boy too small for his chair, his head sunk on his chest. At length he roused himself to go and open the shutters of the little room—formerly Caelia's task—and then gazed up at the pewter sky and down upon the cold, formal garden below with its grey pebble paths. Rain was on the way. Although it was still summer, the air was cool, and a gust swept in and touched Caelia's note where it lay on the little table by the chair. The stiff parchment quivered and rattled as though for a moment alive, quickened by the draft. Quirinius looked at it dully for a few moments and then took it up, folded it gently with his big hands and put it into a small, wooden box bright with marquetry that rested on a shelf along the wall. Then he left the room, calling out for Sequanius. Let him get the soldiers assembled after the funeral.

The Abbey, July 483 AD

He should have waited until the following day to head out to the abbey. It would be evening when he reached it and, if he returned forthwith as he planned, he would not reach the estate until the middle of the night. Well, let things take care of themselves—he did not wish to wait.

And so it was late in the afternoon when he led the little cavalcade over the rough wooden bridge spanning the stream at the foot of the rise on which the abbey sat. Quirinius looked down from the saddle over the bridge's parapet to where, years ago, he had seen Caelia standing, her firm white legs glistening in the stream, her red head burning in the sun. Her hair was not so bright now; it didn't matter in the least.

Once over the bridge, the little troop found itself very soon at the abbey gate. Ambiorus, now captain, called to a trooper to pound on the door set into the gate but, before anyone could act, Quirinius said "no" and, disregarding his dignity, dismounted and swung the black, iron knocker three times, slowly and deliberately. Soon a little peephole slid open, and he looked into a pair of eyes. They were bright blue, not Caelia's. This unreasonable disappointment brought to him how much he wished to see her.

"I'm here to see Caelia. Let me see her now."

The eyes shifted left and right, taking in the soldiers, there was a moment's hesitation and then the peephole shot closed. He stood for some moments listening to the indistinct sound of two women speaking quietly behind the thick, low door. This was followed by the slap of a woman's footsteps as she ran, and meanwhile the door swung open. Quirinius unbuckled his sword and handed it to Ambiorus. Then he stooped, passed inside and turned to his men about to follow. He signaled them to wait, and the nun who had regarded him through the peephole swung and barred the little door behind him. She turned her light eyes back on him, and he was startled to see that she was not the girl her clear eyes had suggested, but rather a woman of about sixty. Could she be the new abbess? Old Pulcheria had finally died, he recalled, just as he was in the thick of a campaign. Which one? The fight near Linuis? No matter. But, no, of course not—this nun could not be the abbess. Whoever the new abbess was, she wouldn't concern herself with menial tasks. No, there were other occupations, bookkeeping, planning, hectoring the local nobles—all the things Pulcheria had done so well. The nun bobbed her head deferentially, but she found it difficult to address him.

"Well?" Quirinius asked.

She ducked her head again and then signaled him to follow. The way led up from the gate because the abbey was what had been a modest villa built, as was typical, halfway up the southern slope of a hill. Its entrance, hidden in a deep porch, faced the south. The building was really very little changed from the time when the Decii—or was it the Centenarii?—still held it. Not far from the little villa was the small chapel of wattle and timber that had once been the granary; beside it stood the wooden belfry, rickety as a scarecrow.

"Wait here," the nun said when they had reached the porch of the house, and she disappeared into the shadows beyond the open doorway. Quirinius stood and looked out at the leaden sky and watched the first drops of rain spatter the courtyard. He turned at a sound behind him and watched four nuns carry out a pair of heavy chairs, set them in the shelter of the porch, and retire indoors. Quirinius frowned, musing on what this might mean.

"Hello, Bear."

He looked up from the chairs at the sound of Caelia's voice. Once again in the plain unbleached shift of a nun, and once again with her hair bound up in a cloth, she stood watching him from the doorway. "Sit down, Bear. You must be tired." She sat down herself and smiled at him, but sadly. He did as he was asked, wondering at her calm authority.

They sat a few moments in silence, looking at each other, and then she spoke. "Let me say first that I cannot return with you. Do you understand that?"

"It wasn't so difficult to obtain your release from old Pulcheria. Who is the abbess now?"

Caelia smiled, but with that melancholy cast of face of one giving difficult, but unavoidable, news. "I am, Bear. I am the abbess."

He stared at her for several moments and then stood up and laughed softly. "The sisters think I'm so easily manipulated?"

"Sit down, Bear." She leaned forward and patted his chair. When he had complied, she went on. "You think the sisters acted rather cannily, don't you?"

"Not half so cannily as they think."

"I understand how you see it, but I can see that they need a protectress, and I am she."

"So, you're conniving with them."

"If you like. But, perhaps, to serve God we must, at times, connive."

Quirinius looked away and shook his head. "I would never have thought it. In your way, you're as cunning as a bishop."

"Everyone—or most of us—who must discharge responsibilities must use a bit of cunning."

"Oh, yes?" He turned back to her.

"Even you. Oh, you're direct enough. More than most. More, I think, than is good for you, and so you don't see the shifting and cunning in others. You don't even see it in yourself. But ask yourself, wasn't every action of any significance that you have taken tinged with some second subtle purpose?"

"What are you talking about?"

"Serving the Idea, perhaps?"

"When I came for you eighteen years ago and took you from this place... Well, that was a... That was an untinged action."

"You acted from a pure motive."

He smiled against his will. "At the time, perhaps, I did not act with a pure heart, but my motive, my desire was unalloyed. You may believe that. And that is just as true now. I love you." He blushed as he said it.

"I know it." And she too reddened as she looked down. He turned away, to watch the rain that pelted the courtyard. He didn't wish to see her face as he said, "And you love me. I'm sure of it."

"Yes, I do." He turned back to regard her closely, his pulse quickening in hope, but she only sat there, as before, her head bowed. "I do, and that is why it is so very hard to leave you." His heart sank.

"Look here." Suddenly crafty, he glanced about, leaned over and said very quietly, "I've got a troop of men at the gate. If I call, they'll have it open straight away and I can snatch you and take you back."

Caelia looked up at him and shook her head, smiling. "In other words, you ask me to connive with you in overcoming my scruples. You are uncommonly subtle today, Bear. Quite out of character yourself."

"Tell me what you want, Caelia. Just tell me. I'll put Albinia aside—I'll send her to Moderatus' estate."

"You have practically put her aside. No, I don't blame you. But I wouldn't have you dispossess her of her rights on my account. I lived with you eighteen years, and now I have left you."

"But why? Why now?"

"Everyone must do what he must. How can I say what I mean so that it's clear? I have no education and can't express things well. So, let me just try to illustrate. You are quite assured, quite bold. I would even say that you are comfortable in the world."

"But not happy."

"But, you see, that is a different thing. Should we expect happiness here? Perhaps you can cultivate contentment someday. But what is it that anchors you in this life?"

Quirinius shook his head, staring at her.

"It's the Idea, isn't it? Everything you do is focused on it—saving scraps..." Quirinius flinched at the word. She went on softly. "Saving the scraps of this Roman world as it fades into the twilight. The estates, the provincial council, the old Roman families. Can this be done? Can even you do it? Everyone says you've just come from a great victory over the Saxons, but what of the magnates? And the little British kings?"

"What of them? Do you think I trust them too far?"

"I think perhaps you do, but, in a way, what does it matter? Still the country is sliding away from us, isn't it? Your army is stronger than that of any chief, granted, but as time goes on, how much Latin will the common folk speak?"

"You think I'm a fool, then, to struggle to save this corner of the Empire? It was only fifty years ago that a count at the head of an imperial army held these provinces."

"You've told me what happened, that he took himself back to the continent."

"They may come again. We must be ready."

"Oh, there hasn't been an emperor in years."

"So then, what's your point? That I've always been a fool? And my father and Maximianus and all the rest? Just fools?" He felt his pulse race, whether in anger at her words, or in distraction from her purpose, he couldn't tell.

"Oh, no, Bear. No. My question is just this; what would you do without the Idea? Could you live without it?"

Quirinius said nothing.

"And I don't mean only that you would have trouble justifying your actions."

"What actions must I justify?"

"Oh, flogging priests, for one."

"I've only ever flogged one. To encourage others."

"Stories grow among the people."

"Encouraged by other priests."

Caelia shrugged to show it didn't matter. "Flogging a priest, then. Bulllying senators, threatening the little kings, making yourself Count of the Britains, taxing the churches."

Quirinius laughed at the catalogue. "That's just government."

She smiled. "You say that without cynicism, you old innocent. Well, then, how about when you took me from the abbey years ago? There was no reason of state behind that, was there? No—don't answer! Yes, I know I was willing, but that's beside the point. That is my burden. My point is to tell you how you justified it. Yes, of course you told yourself what was true enough, that I desired it too. A fair point. But God judges. And yet he forgives. And so, the action seemed only a peccadillo in the middle of your busy life—one little sin balanced by all of the good you were doing. Or would do. Am I right?"

"Let's not visit all of this. It's cavilling."

"But are we cavilling?" Caelia looked out at the rain. "Your men must be sodden. I should let them wait in the stable."

"Forget them. Don't let us drift from the subject."

"Don't you see? You can be so insensitive."

"Really? And so why am I here? And why pleading?"

"You can be. And I worry for you."

He snorted.

"Yes, really."

"Well, don't. The nobles are in my hand—they do as I wish. The little kings too. The Saxons have been so hard drubbed that they'll keep to their lands—for our lifetime, anyway."

"Doesn't it seem, however, that your Idea, Romanitas, is raveling about the edges like the hem of an old cloak?"

"What do you mean?"

"The threads of the world, yours and mine, are coming undone and yet are knitting themselves back into something new. Perhaps whole patches are saved and worked into this new world, who knows?"

"A transmogrification, then."

She smiled at the pompous word. "Yes."

He shrugged. "Perhaps, but I still must do what I must do"

She nodded. "Yes. So must you, and so must I." She waved an arm. "And this is part of the world that must be saved. And perhaps I may help save it. I must certainly try."

"A patch in the new fabric incorporated whole?"

"Yes. Something like that."

They sat in silence a while, both looking out at the rain. Finally, Quirinius shifted and said, "I can find another abbess." He nodded at the doorway. "I can find one who'll do nicely, and I can do it before suppertime."

"Oh, can't you see? I'm speaking of myself. I must do it. And that is why we are done. The time has come for something new, something different."

He stood, bent down and kissed her. And then, without a word, he strode out into the evening rain and to the little doorway in the gate. He pulled the bolt back with a sharp report and stepped out to see his men huddled grim, hoods drawn up, in the rain. He mounted his horse without a word and led the troop off into the gloom fast drawing itself into night.

Twenty-Three: The Monastery, October 491 AD

In the first light of dawn, as the morning gathered itself into an impasto of light, birdsong, and the soughing of wind, a stout knock sounded at the door of the meeting house. The council of war sat in glum silence; even Quirinius was all out of talk. He rubbed his sticky eyes and watched as the little abbot hurried to the door and opened it to a trooper whom Quirinius did not recognize. The soldier brusquely brushed aside the abbot and strode in, his helmet dangling from his hand by the chin strap.

Quirinius turned questioningly to Moderatus, who said, "One of mine." He looked back at the man. "Well?"

The soldier bowed his head to Moderatus and, ignoring Quirinius, said, "When I left the outpost, the Saxons were gathering and preparing to leave their bivouac. Their scouts had started this way, and I judge they'll move out to a meadow about four miles east of here."

"So, you judge, do you?" Quirinius asked the man. "You must be very astute." The man turned to him and glared, but he said nothing. Moderatus broke the thread. "Find a fresh horse and lead us there." The man nodded and was gone before Quirinius could put any questions to him. Ah, well, even if the Saxons numbered two hundred, he could handle them with his allies. Probably even with his men alone. Odd, though, that they had come in such numbers: almost, but not quite enough, to fight a set battle.

* * *

Quirinius' plan was simple: a slow advance in order to spare the men and horses and, upon arrival, no paltering over dispositions or battle-plan. In contrast to the fight at Badon, Quirinius and his men would take the right flank. But, just as at Badon, the two cavalry troops would sweep the Saxon flanks after the bishop's and Pennomorix's footmen had joined the battle. Moderatus would lead his horsemen around the Saxon right; Quirinius would lead his around the left.

Despite the ease with which Quirinius had gotten the agreement of his allies, he was plagued with a sense of unreality. It was as though he labored in a dream smoothly, but with no clear purpose. Yes, of course, he was to meet the Saxons again but, really, why? Why were the Saxons back just now, and just here? Their presence was the sort of odd, brute fact encountered in a dream, unlikely, but there, just there. Anyone might note their presence, their numbers, the direction of their travel, and from this draw some conclusion, but would the conclusion be likely, still less correct?

At midmorning they reached a rise over the field onto which, just as the scout had said, the Saxons had advanced and were awaiting them. Quirinius squinted at their shields, trying to make out their blazons, but his eyes weren't what they had been. He asked Ambiorus.

"Quartered, Dominē. Madder and cream."

Quirinius grunted. "Cantii, then."

Ambiorus nodded, dropped his helmet on his head and tied the strap. Taking their cue from their captain, the rest of the troop did the same and, last of all, so did Quirinius who, for once in his life, seemed to feel the weight of the helmet. *I'm growing too old for this, Another few years and I'll be sitting at home watching the sky and hoping for the best.* The thought that there was no one to take his place flickered through his mind, but he turned resolutely from the thought. He shrugged to settle his armor more comfortably. It seemed unaccountably heavy. He looked up for a few moments at the drear sky, a grey not far removed from that of the scales of his armor and, in its way, as heavy.

He turned to Moderatus, Pennomorix, and to the captain of Bishop Valerianus' men, a certain Decianus, unknown to him. The bishop, as befitted a man of his calling, was at the monastery awaiting the outcome of the fight.

"They see us and are forming up. See them closing up on their right, up there? It's a shield wall; they may break up into a boars' head. We outnumber them a bit, and there is no reason to change the plan we agreed to last night. The footmen advance in a block to provoke the engagement. After the fight is joined, then, Moderatus, you sweep to the left while I lead my troop to the right and we'll get at their flanks, and that way they'll dissolve. After that we'll strike them individually at will."

There was really nothing much to the battle-plan from a tactical viewpoint, although Quirinius would have called it Alexandrian from what he had read of history. But lack of novelty was unimportant—the superior numbers of the British and the drill and discipline of his horseman would decide everything even if the Saxons guessed how the blows would come.

Pennomorix backed his horse from the conference, glanced at Moderatus, who seemed to ostentatiously ignore him, and then, with the help of Decianus, shouted the orders to arrange the footmen into a proper unit. He used more words to do this than Quirinius had heard him speak during the entire night.

Once the footmen were formed up, Quirinius gave the signal to begin the advance. The footmen started down the slope at a slow, steady walk, careful to keep their order and not open any breaches. After an advance of some fifty yards, Quirinius and Moderatus drew apart, and each led his troop behind the agreed flank.

The Saxons stolidly awaited the advance. They waited so long, in fact, that Quirinius was surprised. They seemed resolved to stand entirely on the defensive and merely receive the attack. He watched, scowling and puzzled, as he led his troop at a slow walk behind the right flank. Such Saxon immobility was not unknown—they would stand defensive this way when trapped, but Quirinius found it odd, even unsettling, that they would advance this far into the province, and what was more, come out of the protection of the woods as though to engage, and yet lack the spirit to advance.

At length, when the lines were within twenty yards, the Saxons rolled slowly forward, but sluggishly. Even their accustomed shouts faded by half, carried off on the wind as the lines came near meeting, but, oddly, without the dull clacking of shield meeting shield. Still, the joining of the lines was the signal for the cavalry sweep, and the fight must progress as planned or else fall apart.

"To the right. Sweep!" Quirinius shouted to Ambiorus, who, nodding, signaled to the standard-bearer. The gleaming silver dragon head dipped, drawing the silken tail into a scarlet arch against the cool grey sky, and, in response, the troop moved off to the right from behind the British flank and then came forward, first at a walk and then at a trot and finally at a canter as it pressed on to achieve the envelopment. Quirinius drew his sword while the troopers around him lowered their lances and, unconsciously, closed about and in front of him, keeping their commander out of the first line. *Good boys,* he thought, and felt a certain warmth for them.

It took only a few moments for the troop to pull out from its position behind the British footmen and to flow beside the Saxons' flank and veer to the left behind them. Surrounded though he was by his own men, Quirinius could still see that the Saxons now stood fixed, immobile and facing out on all sides—even their rear presented an unbroken wall of round red-and-tan shields, spears thrust out above the joins where they overlapped.

In a cooler moment, Quirinius might have wondered when they had acquired the unaccustomed discipline to respond to a flanking attack so well and so fast. It was as though they had known how the attack would come, as though they received it with an unnatural prescience. The tactic, though purely defensive, was effective; although a handful of the troopers cast their lances like javelins into the Saxon line, the horses veered away from the shield wall, giving the rest of the troopers little or no chance to use their lances effectively. Quirinius tried to think quickly what tactic to use next, as the Saxon line had not dissolved. He had not found their flanks weak or provoked their dissolution; he would need to draw his men back across the field and try some other maneuver when the clash of the footmen resulted, as it must at some point, in a disordering of the Saxons, whether they won or lost that part of the fight.

But even as these thoughts flashed across his mind, he was startled to see the troopers ahead of him rock forward and back in the saddle, and their horses' heads swing from side to side as the troop was brought sharply to a halt. His animal, blocked by the suddenly static mass of horsemen ahead, stopped as did the balance of the troop behind him, their horses, herd animals, instinctively grasping the actions of the lead horses. A halt? But why? His own animal backed suddenly and turned in a circle, driving other troopers away. And then he saw why. As he viciously turned his mount's head to bring him around to the front, he saw Moderatus' troop charging—Moderatus' men passing through his own horsemen with lances levelled or swords swinging. Unable to grasp what was happening, several of his men were struck or unhorsed and the remaining troopers were at a standstill and utterly vulnerable.

Quirinius, exhausted from the long night and too shocked by Moderatus' action to understand it, looked about here and there, unsure for the moment what to do. He received a second shock, for the Saxon rear, now having the advantage over the stalled cavalry, advanced in a tight block against them, and Quirinius found himself buffeted from the left by troopers attacked at the standstill by Saxons who speared horses and men at will. As both went down, the remains of Quirinius' troop grew suddenly disordered and then dissolved. The men who could rode or fled afoot from their fallen mounts and away from the Saxons.

It was in that instant that he grasped the true battle-plan, the one that he had not made, the one engineered weeks, even months, before he had been called on campaign. Moderatus, the bishop, Pennomorix, Romans and Britons now allied with these Saxons, had been ranged against him, had acted in cunning and deadly concert.

He burned as with fever in the instant that he grasped the betrayal and its extent, but he could decide on nothing besides killing

Moderatus. He dug his spurs brutally into his horse's ribs and, when it hesitated at the crowded field ahead of it, he struck its flanks with the flat of his sword, driving it through the disorder of men and horses toward Moderatus' standard, where he guessed he would find him, obvious in his splendidly gilded helmet.

Quirinius kept his shield as much before him as he could, presenting his protected, left side to Moderatus' passing horsemen until he saw Moderatus himself, his helmet gleaming in the grey autumn light. Moderatus had seen him too. He hesitated, uncertain whether to move forward with his men and risk engagement, or whether to drift aside and avoid Quirinius. But in the instant of his indecision, he lost the choice, for Quirinius was on him. Moderatus lowered his lance and, leaning forward, struck Quirinius' shield, but without much force because he had been compelled to act before he was ready. The lance point did not seat in the shield but slid upward and, passing above the shield rim and below the left cheek-plate of Quirinius' helmet, opened a large gash in his neck. Quirinius leaned out to the left, almost dangerously, and, before his opponent could recover from his lance-thrust, swung his sword down where Moderatus' neck met his left shoulder.

Although Moderatus flinched at the blow, Quirinius' blade struck where he had aimed, just below the helmet and above the neck of the mail shirt. Quirinius, still powerful at his age—and in a fury— found that he had cleft Moderatus' neck so deeply that his sword stuck fast for a moment and was nearly wrenched from his hand as their mounts passed each other in the encounter. Quirinius could hear Moderatus' groan, even amid the shouts of other men and the screaming of horses. As he circled back for another pass, he saw that the wound he had dealt was terrible, indeed would shortly be fatal. All the same, in his anger he could not turn away to join the fleeing remnant of his men. Instead, he raised his red sword as he came alongside Moderatus, who turned to him, but Quirinius could see that his eyes were blank—that he was seeing nothing at all. Quirinius delivered a final backhand slash across Moderatus' face. The sword jarred and vibrated in his hand from the blow, which shattered the nosepiece of Moderatus' helmet and tumbled the man, dead, from his saddle.

Quirinius felt suddenly tired, filled with an odd, atypical lassitude, and he noted, almost as in a dream, that his shield arm was wet and oddly darkened. He looked down at his arm and knew that he had been struck, that he was bleeding and faint. He looked about him and saw a handful of Moderatus' troopers sitting in a grey mail-clad half-ring ahead of him. He looked about further and saw that, somehow, he had drifted to the edge of the fight. He lifted his sword, now oddly heavy, and advanced on Moderatus' men, but they were awed by the Old Bear, and, as he advanced, he saw them, as, in a dream, veer away from him, unwilling to close. He passed through them and out further onto the field.

Once away from the battle, he sheathed his sword. It was difficult because he had suddenly grown clumsy. He rode off to the east, his shield dangling on his arm. Who knew where his men were? But east was home. The horse went at an easy trot across the meadow, following the scent of the mounts of the surviving troopers until it reached a road where Ambiorus and a dozen troopers stood, resting their horses and trying to decide what to do.

"Ambiorus," Quirinius said.

"Yes, Dominē." He looked up, exhausted, slightly ridiculous, his helmet under his arm and his wet hair standing up around his head. He dropped the helmet without a thought and reached up to Quirinius.

"Ambiorus," Quirinius said again and then frowned, confused, unable to think of anything to command or even to say. Ambiorus signaled the men, and they took Quirinius from the saddle and laid him softly upon a cloak on the ground.

Twenty-Four: Near the Abbey, October 491 AD

A weathered skiff was drawn up on the edge of a silver-grey mere, and in the bottom of it lay Quirinius, white-faced and, despite three cloaks, shivering with fever. The wound on his neck, though staunched the day of the battle, had gone very bad, and Ambiorus had, therefore, sent to Caelia to tell her the Old Bear was dying. They stood together at the edge of the mere.

"Thank you, Ambiorus. We will see to him." She glanced over her shoulder at Quirinius as he lay in the bottom of the boat. A raw-boned young nun sat in the stern with a punt-pole balanced across her knees. She stared stolidly over the water.

Ambiorus nodded but didn't speak.

"And you?" she asked.

"I spoke with Albinia as I passed the estate. It was very hard. She wasn't leagued with her brother and the others against Quirinius, but she is indifferent. Bishop Valerianus has told her everything, and she accepts it all as though it were some natural event and not to be judged. She is mad, I think. Romans, British chiefs, all against Quirinius. She told me plainly. And they used those Saxons as their allies against him. She says that they told her Quirinius wasn't a realist, that he didn't understand the times, that after Badon, he was a danger to everyone. And, of course, they must give some estates to their Saxon allies. A new order against his Idea."

"But you?" Caelia said.

"Albinia will take the survivors of the troop back, but I can't stomach her. My country is fading away. Perhaps I'll go to Armorica or Aquitania." He walked slowly over to the skiff and stood looking down a few moments at Quirinius. He spoke then, without looking back at the abbess. "I am glad that he can't understand this. Things won't dissolve tomorrow. But soon, I think. Our world will be faint as the memory of a dream at noon." He turned back to Caelia. "Albinia won't trouble you. She doesn't want Quirinius buried at the estate, but otherwise she asks nothing of you."

The two looked at each other silently for a few moments, and then Caelia turned to the skiff, pulled up her shift and stepped into the boat. Ambiorus stooped at its stern and shoved the boat out onto the mere. Once the skiff was afloat, the young sister rose in the stern and poled the boat away from the shore. Ambiorus stood watching for a few moments, and then turned, mounted his horse, and rode away.

The young nun polled the skiff slowly across the shallow mere, keeping her eyes steadily ahead of her, fixed on the rise on the opposite shore upon which stood the nunnery. Caelia sat in the bottom of the skiff, one hand on Quirinius'chest, the other stroking his hair. He looked up at her face and frowned as though trying to work something out. She guessed the cause of his distress and reached up, undid her headdress, and shook her shaggy red-grey head. She smiled down at him, and they watched each other in silence for a while.

"Where are we, Caelia?" He asked the question with a placidity that was uncommon for him, and he spoke in British as he used to do with her only when most affectionate.

"We are in a boat, Bear."

He nodded slowly at the answer, not questioning it.

"I'm cold."

"I know, but it will pass."

"It isn't winter."

"No."

"Of course not. A boat."

"The cold will pass."

"I remember so well when your hair was red. There was a time I couldn't think of anything else. Not anything. So red."

She stroked his head. "I know. It was very red then." She wiped tears from her eyes with the back of her other hand. Some quiet moments passed when he seemed to sleep, and then he opened his eyes and looked into hers.

"How are the children?"

"They are fine."

"All three?"

"All three."

"Are we old now?"

"We are pretty old, Bear. Yes."

"I always tried so hard at whatever I took up. And now I'm tired."

"Yes, I know."

"I suspect that I'm near my end, though I can't quite think why. These last few days, I can't seem to recall them."

"Don't worry. I'm here."

"I know it, Caelia. Let me tell you something important. The best thing I ever did, of all that I ever did, was to marry you."

"Oh, Bear."

"I'm going to sleep now, Caelia."

"Yes." And she bent down and kissed him.

And then he was gone as the skiff moved over the cool, gray water.

AFTERWORD

Quirinius is a novel in which I attempt to tell a story of the twilight of Roman culture in a Britain at first severed from the Empire and then persisting, in a tenuous form, after its collapse in the west. A glance at the map at the start of the book should give an idea of the isolation of the Romanized remnant of fifth-century Britain. In telling this story, I have tried to show readers some aspects of late Roman life and culture which many may not be familiar with, and which distinguish the late from the early empire: landed aristocrats in control of the countryside, an incipient feudalism, private armies, the death of towns and cities, the ceding of territory to less Romanized provincials, the resurgence of native identities, the constant threat of invasion, the diminished size of forces defending the country.

Close readers may have noticed echoes of the old Arthurian legends and, yes, they are there. Quirinius' story is modelled broadly on them as well as on the writings of Gildas, the entries in the Welsh Easter Annals, and Nennius' *Historia Brittonum*, which latter two support, without much detail, the existence of Arthur as an (admittedly vague) historical figure. Thus, a number of characters from the earliest historical records appear: Uortigern (Vortigern, as a title), Moderatus (Modred), Ambrosius Aurelianus, Vitolinus, and the Saxon Aelle. Contemporary Romans appear or are mentioned as well: Aetius, Syagrius, and Zeno. Other characters are fictional, such as Albinia, whose name is meant to evoke, in Latin, that of Ganufara (Guinevere).

No Arthur is mentioned by name, but Flavius Quirinius is often known by his nickname, The Bear, which, in Latin, would be Ursus. In Old Welsh "bear" was *art-*. There is apparently a Welsh philological argument against the development of *art-* into the Welsh *Arthur* (some argue that the name should derive from the Roman cognomen

Artorius), but as this is a work of fiction, I have chosen to equate **art-** with **Arthur**. I can't judge the philological question, but the identification of the two names was formerly accepted and is, frankly, hard to resist. Arthur is named in Nennius and in the Welsh Easter Annals compiled not long after the time in which *Quirinius* is set. Quite obviously the idea in this novel is that Quirinius, a Roman provincial aristocrat, is mis-remembered in legend as a king whose name is a mere Celtic translation of his Latin nickname. Thus, at bottom, King Arthur is a Roman and not a Dark Age Celtic warlord.

Some of Quirinius' battles are patterned after those listed in Nennius, and the Battle of Badon (Mons Badonicus) is given the earliest defensible date and so is about thirty years earlier than some readers may expect.

A word about the Latin may be necessary for readers who have studied it but are dubious about certain passages. Some are in a "classical" style—they follow the generally accepted rules of Latin grammar—and some are not. The latter are in what I guess to have been the vernacular speech of the province at that time. There are no surviving examples of British vernacular Latin apart from a few inscriptions, so there is no alternative to guesswork. Mine is based on examples of late Latin from other places and upon the theories of Latinists who have written about the shift of late Latin into the Romance languages. Therefore, the passages intended as vernacular have features from both late Latin and Romance.

Any questions about these or other topics are welcome at my website.

erikhildinger.com

Printed in the USA
CPSIA information can be obtained
at www.ICGtesting.com
LVHW042049270823
756387LV00016B/550